Ploro
10
Park 1

DADDY'S GIRL

Margie Orford is an author, photographer, film
director and award-winning journalist. She was
born in London, grew up in Namibia, and attended
university in Cape Town. While there, she was
detained for student activism under the newly
declared State of Emergency, and ended up writing
final exams in a maximum security prison. Since
then, she has moved back to Namibia, studied in
New York on a Fulbright scholarship, and eventually
led in Cape Town, where she now lives with her
huband and three daughters.

—

For Bella

Margie
Orford
DADDY'S GIRL

CORVUS

First published in South Africa in 2009
by Jonathan Ball

This paperback edition first published in the UK in 2012
by Corvus, an imprint of Atlantic Books Ltd.

9 8 7 6 5 4 3 2 1

A CIP catalogue record for this book is available from
the British Library.

Paperback ISBN: 978-1-84354-947-5
E-book ISBN: 978-0-85789-267-6

Printed in Italy by Grafica veneta s.p.a.

Corvus
An imprint of Atlantic Books Ltd
Ormond House
26-27 Boswell Street
London WC1N 3JZ

www.corvus-books.co.uk

August the eighth
THURSDAY

Peterborough City Council	
60000 0000 65486	
Askews & Holts	Jun-2012
THR	£7.99

one

A grey heron waited in the reeds, beak poised above the pool. When the prison gates opened for the man, the bird flew off. The fish dived, a flash in the tea-brown water.

Five-thirty. Nearly weekend.

The guards impatient to get home at the end of a long shift.

The man's parole papers filed under a name not his own.

His fingers curled around the hundred rand note from the Prisoners' Friend Society. He'd already discarded the address of the Christian halfway house expecting his arrival.

The man crossed the deserted road.

He wore borrowed trousers, a jacket that exposed his bony wrists, a white shirt. The smell of another man's day in court, the sweat that came with the clock-stopping moment of sentence.

He waited, the last rays of the weak August sun warm on his back.

The guards packed up, listening as the radio spat out Cape Town's news.

In the distance, the rattle of a minibus taxi.

It crested the rise, and he flattened his blade-thin body into a ditch next to the road.

The driver stopped. The guards glanced up: the new shift arriving. Nothing much to mention. Thursday would be a quiet night. They handed over, boarded the taxi, sped home.

Darkness descended.

The prisoner dusted off his clothes, eyes focused fifty metres ahead. The length of an exercise yard.

Ex-prisoner.

He cut through farmland, a shadow slipping down the serried vines.

The runty dogs lying between the workers' cottages yapped.

A woman making her way home, stopped. She listened, but the dogs fell silent, and she walked on. Uncertain.

The man watched her, at ease. Prison erases a man's smell, teaches him the art of absence.

Above him, the stars wheeled, freed from the barred square that had contained his nights for so many years.

On the stoep of a gabled farmhouse, dogs lifted their heads. Then settled again. Inside by the fire, the owners sipped brandy as they glanced at the day's headlines.

He did not slow down as he scythed through the night.

At the crossroads, he orientated himself and headed for Cape Town.

No one would be waiting for him.

No one had, not since his mother's funeral. His twenty-seven-year-old mother, shot five times by her pimp.

Twice in the face, twice in the heart, once in the cunt.

He had hoped, then, that someone would claim him. No one had, after the funeral. Except the pimp who'd pinned him down for an old man to sample, both of them laughing at the blood, the tears.

Payment for the bullets used to kill his insolent mother.

He had melted into the cold Cape drizzle, sharpened a bicycle spoke, and gone to the shebeen where his mother's killer sat. A beer in one hand and a girl in yellow hotpants in the other.

He had inserted the spoke into the pimp's back, pressing upwards until the tip pierced his heart. Then he'd disappeared into the night.

Sorry Mom.

He'd had that inked on the skin above his heart.

Vrou is gif.

That above the other nipple, for the whore in the yellow shorts who'd pointed at him in the courtroom.

Woman is poison.

A taxi pulled over with its cargo of late-shift workers. He settled next to a window and watched the new housing developments whip past. Villas hiding behind security booms; an empty soccer stadium where armed guards with leashed Alsatians patrolled the encircling razor wire; a shopping mall offering discounts.

He'd been gone for years.

Things had changed for the rich.

The roads became clogged arteries. Factory shift workers hurried home in the dark. Young men swaggered on street corners.

He got out where the land was flat and the southeaster howled around huddled houses that stretched as far as the curve of False Bay. Government-built boxes for the people.

Nothing had changed for the poor.

He breathed in the smells of the place that had been his home. Car fumes, a dead dog, the tang of salt from the distant sea.

The outside.

A forgotten dream that he had buried when he'd first gone to prison and been absorbed by the Number, the brutal prison brotherhoods. A killer at ten, the 27s had embraced him, the gang giving him rank and purpose and a sense of family more powerful than anything a mother outside ever presided over.

On the corner was the Nice-Time Bar, a corrugated iron lean-to attached to a brick house. White plastic chairs clustered around red Coke crates; five men sat drinking.

Inside the bar, a television flickered.

He ordered a beer from the barmaid, and stared at the woman on the screen who was unbuttoning her shirt.

The girl gave him his drink.

'*Pop Idols*,' she said, flicking through the channels. 'It's the final tonight.'

'Go back to it,' he ordered.

'It's *mos* a rerun of *Missing*, that Doctor Hart's gang-cherrie programme.' The barmaid rolled her eyes. 'Just some Number gangster's daughter showing off her scars. An excuse to show off her tits on TV. Hoping the *Voice of the Cape* will pay her for her story.'

'Go back. Turn up the sound.'

She knew enough to do what she was told.

'All the same when they come out,' she muttered, lighting a cigarette. 'An inch of skin, and the brain's dead.'

He ignored her, listening to the rasp of the woman's voice.

Pearl, she called herself.

Stupid name.

The barmaid finished her cigarette, going off to serve another customer.

The programme ended, the man drained his beer, and left.

He stood in the alley behind the shebeen, running through the plans he'd made with the other 27s, the generals who'd crouched in a circle.

The custodians of the unwritten law of the Number gangs had decided who should die, and when.

Any slight, any unearned claim to rank, any secret revealed, was a betrayal that had to be paid for in blood.

That was the law of the 27s.

He did not have much time.

He did not have enough information.

But he knew where to start.

He took the hand-fashioned knife from the sole of his shoe, slipped it into his pocket.

An expert at prising open secrets.

August the ninth
FRIDAY

two

Green.

Clare Hart nosed across the Friday morning traffic, the taxis and bakkies surging towards the city.

Red.

Three Indian crows feeding on a dog's carcass hopped back and forth at the lights, black eyes fixed on the traffic, their timing impeccable. A huddle of boys rolling dice, betting with bottle tops, stared at Clare. Chained dogs barked in the litter-strewn yards. She was looking for a street with no name – its sign long since torn down and sold for scrap metal.

Clare looked up at the pockmarked buildings; three-storeyed walk-ups that baked in summer and froze in winter. The Flats. The buildings were named after battles fought long ago by people who'd lived far away. Waterloo, Hastings, Agincourt, Trafalgar, Tobruk.

The people who lived in this place called it Baghdad.

Coke adds life.

A hand-painted slogan in red and white on the wall of a corner café, its small dispensing window covered with hand grenade mesh. On the opposite corner the primary school, rubbish swagged against rusting barbed wire. The playground was filled with children in white shirts. The girls wearing bottle-green skirts; the boys in grey pants. In a corner, a little girl stood alone under a bullet-riddled sign.

Your Neighbourhood Watch watches out for you.

The child was clutching a lunch box. Her eyes, large and dark, were on Clare as she drove past. A group of older boys appeared out of nowhere, swarming around the little girl, knocking her sandwiches from her hands, jerking her between them. The child did nothing to protect herself. One boy pushed a rough, probing hand up her skirt. The child's tears tumbled down her drawn cheeks. Clare pressed her hooter and the boys – ten, eleven years old – turned to stare. She was on one side of the fence; they were on the other. They gave the girl a final shove and were off in a pack, joining a game of soccer on the dusty field.

The girl picked herself up and left, straightening her skirt as she ran, tucking in her white shirt, absorbing the casual violation, abandoning her trampled lunch.

The lights changed and Clare drove on. The *hoekstaanders* eyed her, the smallest of them disappearing down an alley as she passed. News of her presence was travelling ahead of her. She checked the car's central locking.

Orange.

Clare slowed. The shabby buildings were pitted. In a fortnight, five children had been killed in a surge of gang warfare. Small white coffins were brandished at funerals by grim-faced uncles and brothers promising revenge; in tow were the resigned mothers, who sobbed when they went home to wait for the next convulsion of violence, the next lot of casualties. It had not come. Not yet.

El Alamein.

Bleached to a trace, the letters indicated the block Clare was looking for. A freshly painted hammer and sickle claimed the territory for the Afghans.

She stopped.

A boy detached himself from a wall, sauntered over, jeans slung low. Clare was in his territory and he knew it; knew that she knew it. Smiled. Her pulse quickened as she keyed in the text she'd been instructed to send. Another youth, mongrel-thin, materialised at the corner. Two more peeled themselves off the wall, joining the others. Grouped together, their bodies coalesced into a multi-limbed creature.

She checked the screen of her phone.

No response yet.

She looked up at the council block's windows. All of them closed. On the third floor, a curtain fell back into place. Ahead of her, movement. The boys on the corner slouched towards her.

The youth at her window had both hands on the glass. He bent down, his eyes a startling shade of green. Clare wound down the window. Behind her, the hiss of a match was followed by the sharp tang of tobacco.

'You don't smoke?'

He had seen her nostrils flare.

'No.'

'You're the doctor my mother called, then.'

Clare nodded. Not the time to explain the difference between a medical doctor and a PhD in rape and serial femicide.

'Put it out.'

His pitch of his voice changed slightly – all the authority that was needed. The smell disappeared.

'She's waiting for you.'

A taxi, the bass vibrating through the tar and up her spine, thudded its way up the street. Clare slung her camera bag over her shoulder and got out of the car.

'You can relax. You're with Lemmetjie.' Thin as the blade that had given him the scar on his neck and his nickname, Lemmetjie raised both arms in a circular motion, possessing her, the street. 'No one will touch you.'

He fell into step beside her as she walked to the building. The graffiti-covered door opened before Clare could knock. The woman standing in front of her was tiny. She looked fifty, was probably thirty-five. She took Clare's hand.

'Dr Hart?'

'Clare.'

'I'm Mrs Adams,' she said. 'Come inside.'

Clare followed her into the living room, where the kitchen had been curtained off from the sofas crowded around the television. Above the screen was a studio photograph of a little girl. Her white dress spotless, the halo of curls tamed for the photographer, green eyes fixed on Clare.

'That's her, Doctor.' She lit a cigarette.

The ghost of that perfect face still hovered in the woman's own hollow features, despite their being scripted with the story of the place where she lived. The scar on her lip was the signature of a husband's fists. Her eyes were fierce, green. The same colour as Lemmetjie's, as those of her missing daughter.

'Where is she?'

'I want you to film this,' she said. 'So you'll have the truth down.'

Clare took out her camera and panned from the photograph of the little girl to the woman by her side. 'Gone. Yesterday.'

'You saw her yesterday?' Clare probed. 'She was here?'

The woman dropped her head into her hands. 'I thought she was at my mother's.'

'She's not?'

'My mother sent her for cigarettes. She didn't come home. They thought the child had come back home, here. Lemmetjie and his *tjommies* went to look for her, but she was gone.'

The weight of it closed in on Clare. 'You've looked everywhere?' she asked Lemmetjie.

'All her friends, my aunties,' said Lemmetjie. 'My other *ouma*.'

'And no one has her?'

'Nobody.'

'You checked at the shop?' asked Clare. 'She arrived?'

'Ja. The woman there gave her the cigarettes.'

'No one saw her with anybody?'

Lemmetjie shook his head.

'What else?' asked Clare.

'Sê vir haar,' said Mrs Adams.

'There was a car in the street. Tinted windows,' said Lemmetjie. 'Someone else says an uncle was talking to her.'

'I saw you on the TV last night. *Missing*, your programme about that gangster's daughter, Pearl. The *Cape Sun* had an article about you, too. They said you've found some of the missing girls,' said Mrs Adams. 'She's *mos* missing, a – what did you call them? – a Persephone, taken down into hell. You said that's what you did with your project. Looking for missing girls, bringing them back to their mothers.'

'I track what happens to them,' said Clare, taking her eye from the camera. The girls I found' – no way to say it gently – 'they were already dead.'

Mrs Adams folded her arms around her hollow belly. 'If she's dead, then I want her body. Find me something to bury at least.'

Mrs Adams shook another cigarette from the pack on the table, wormed her way to the window through the narrow space between the wall and the couch, and lifted the curtain. She sucked on her cigarette as if it were a lifeline.

'Harry Oppenheimer has gold mines. Voëltjie Ahrend and his gangsters have this.' She waved her hand at the warren of match-box houses and backyard shacks. 'A gold mine too. They own the police. If I go to the police then my baby is dead, for sure. They're not going to watch so much power get sold out from under them.'

'Who's buying?' asked Clare.

'Buying, selling. Gangsters, police, politicians.' Mrs Adams turned her green eyes on Clare. 'For us that lives here, it's all the same. We're the ones who pay in the beginning and in the end.'

'Your son's in the Neighbourhood Watch,' said Clare. 'He told me on the phone. You have to call the police,' said Clare. 'They'll mobilise the Neighbourhood Watch, get everyone looking. I can't do that.'

'Neighbourhood Watch *se moer*. Lemmetjie knows nothing about nothing. Twenty years old and never even been to jail. I told him that. What does it help to hold a vigil outside a gangster's drug house?'

'The Number's taking over here, Ma,' said Lemmetjie. 'Voëltjie Ahrend and his 27s.'

'Voëltjie Ahrend knows *fokkol* about the Number, in jail for a year. Out again because his lawyer bought a judge. Now he's claiming territory he never fought for. The cops are owned by those gangsters – and it's us,' she stabbed her finger into her chest, 'the women, our little girls, who pay the men's price. That's why I called you, Doctor. If you make your film then they will look for her. Otherwise they just say, wait twenty-four hours and then report her missing.'

'I told you, Ma, you're wrong.' Lemmetjie didn't look her in the eye. 'What I do is for Chanel. To make it safe for my baby sister to play outside.'

'Who you *are* hurts your sister,' spat his mother.

A retort in the distance: a gunshot, a car backfiring? Mrs Adams didn't move from the window.

'Chanel,' said Mrs Adams. 'It's a warning. To me. To him. To stay out of the way.'

'Ma,' said Lemmetjie. 'We've got to fight back. I'm going to call the cops.'

'Tell me, Doctor.' Mrs Adams faced Clare's camera. 'What does one more little girl mean, in a war?'

Clare turned the question over in her mind as she drove back. As she got closer to town, the pavements became less cracked, then they sprouted trees, and the houses were set further and further back from the road. There were walls instead of wire fences, and soon she was back in the oak-lined avenues of the suburbs that sheltered in the grey skirts of Table Mountain. She stopped at the dry cleaners and picked up her evening dress, buying a pair of high-heeled sandals on her way back to her car. She put them in the boot, then went to the studio to approve the final sound mix for that night's broadcast of *Missing*. She requested two minor changes, and sent the programme off to her producer.

Taking her copies of *Missing* with her, she drove home. She unlocked her front door and went upstairs to her quiet white sanctuary. Clare opened the sliding doors that led onto the balcony overlooking the Sea Point Promenade, her cat twisting between her ankles, purring its welcome. She picked Fritz up. The sea beyond sparkled in the afternoon sunlight. On the lawn near Clare's house, a young woman was pushing her daughter in a yellow swing.

'Higher, Mummy, higher!' the child was calling, her hair flying in the wind. 'I'm flying! Look at me, like a bird.'

three

The afternoon sun broke though the cloud, splashing small hands on the barre and pooling on the floor; the girls' serious faces looked straight ahead. From the piano, a simple minuet. One, two, three. One, two, three. Slow enough for everyone in the class to keep up, their tummies tight drums in new pink leotards.

'First position. Heels together. Feet out. Hands held correctly, chins up, *plié*. And smile and turn. And smile. And turn. And hold. Hands in front and second. Curtsey.'

The ballet teacher marched down the line of little girls, adjusting a hand, a foot, tapping at protruding bottoms, bellies. She paused next to the dark-haired girl at the front of the line, touching her long nails to the girl's cheek.

'Smile, Yasmin. This isn't a funeral.'

The child smiled obediently. Her slender limbs were correctly positioned; she knew this from her ballet teacher's approving frown. Madame Merle moved on.

'Hands graceful, girls. First position and music, Mister Henry. And smile. And smile. And curtsey.'

Clapping her hands, she dismissed the class and accepted a cigarette from the pianist. Mister Henry lit it for her.

'What, Yasmin?' Madame Merle became aware of the lingering child.

'Isn't it too early, Madame?' Madame Merle blew a smoke ring, round and perfect, over the child's head.

'Darling, it's the gala tonight.'

'*Persephone*. The ballet about the girl who disappears,' Mister Henry explained. 'At Artscape.'

'Oh.' Still, Yasmin lingered.

'Run along.' Madame Merle turned away. The class was over. The beam of her attention switched off.

Yasmin felt Mister Henry's eyes on her as she negotiated the stream of six-year-olds rushing to the cars idling outside. Ever since her older friend Calvaleen had stopped dancing, hers was the only dark bun among the blondes.

The change-room door burst open and the older girls billowed out, all tulle and chatter. Yasmin pressed herself against the wall, and then went to her locker. She had a proper ballet dancer's crossover cardigan, which Amma had knitted for her as an early birthday present. She tied the bow. Thinking about her birthday gave her a knot in her stomach. It was her birthday that had started all the trouble. Last year, when she turned six. In three sleeps she would be seven. She hoped it would be better this year.

Yasmin reached into her bag for her takkies. Her mother always threw a fit if she went outside in her satin pumps. She pulled out her old shoes, dislodging a piece of green paper as she did so. She unfolded it, her heart beating faster. Zero-to-panic. That was Amma's nickname for Daddy. That's how she felt now. Zero-to-panic. She realised that it was another thing she'd forgotten. Madame Merle had handed out the notices with strict instructions that they get them signed and return them to her.

'So I can be absolutely sure that your mummies and daddies know to fetch you early, darlings,' is what Madame Merle had said in her posh voice.

Another thing that would make her mother strip her *moer*. Two things! She'd forgotten to give her mom the paper. And the picking-up time had changed. Yasmin felt shame wash over her. She tried so hard to do everything right, to make her mother happy, to make

23

her smile like she used to. But everything she did just seemed to make her mother angrier. Ever since her daddy had kept her for the weekend and that Aunty Ndlovu had come with the police papers that said her father was bad like the gangsters he was meant to catch, things had been even worse.

Yasmin smoothed open the notice that Madame Merle had handed out. The notices were only mailed if you missed a class. 'Saving money, darlings!' said Madame Merle. 'Do you think a person can eat from teaching ballet?'

Her mother wouldn't know that the school was closing early today because of the performance of *Persephone*. Calvaleen was meant to be the star, Persephone. But she'd have got the notice in the post because she had stopped going to the older girls' class a long time ago. Yasmin missed her. She crumpled the paper. She didn't like to think about girls who disappeared. She didn't like to think that her mother was on shift and that she would shout at Yasmin if she phoned her. No one would come to fetch her for a long time.

She was going to be in trouble again. She knew it.

She could hear Madame Merle's voice.

'One, two, three.' Madame Merle's voice cut across the music. It was the end of the dance: swan-like in their white skirts, the girls would be skimming across the room, their necks elongated, trailing their arms behind them.

'Like air, girls. You're ballerinas, not bricklayers. Jeté, jeté, jeté.'

The tight burn in Yasmin's throat told her tears were coming. She took a deep breath and made herself think. She was a big girl. She could make a plan. She unzipped her emergency money pouch and looked at the coins in her palm. Two fifty cent pieces. She repeated the cellphone number she needed to dial and stood on tiptoe in front of the call box in the passage. She slotted in the first coin, then the second.

'Oh Eight Two,' she whispered. 'Five Four Two Two Oh Oh Seven.'

The coins clicked down the gullet of the call box. Yasmin's tummy unclenched when the phone began to purr.

'Faizal.'

'Daddy.' A lilt in her voice.

'Leave a message.'

Her father's voice for other people.

The call box swallowed the last coin, cutting the connection before she could leave a message. She replaced the receiver. The piano had stopped. Mister Henry would be closing the lid, gathering his score. His eyes were always watery behind his glasses. He smelt funny. Calvaleen had told her. Yasmin didn't want to have to wait with him. She hoisted her pink rucksack, then slipped past the security guard and through the gate to wait until her mom came.

The afternoon sunlight slanted between the Roman pines lining the steep street. Yasmin did not like to look at them. They were like the trees in the dark Russian fairytale forests in her book. Forests where cannibal crones like Baby Yaga Bony Legs lurked, waiting for young girls. The street was empty; only one car near the park. Dog walkers. Yasmin could hear barking. She told herself that an hour was not so long, not while it was still light.

She listened to Madame Merle herding the older girls into the parking lot. When the security gate opened, unleashing the mini-bus with its cargo of sylphs, Yasmin pressed herself deep into the bougainvillea hedge. She put her hand to her mouth, sucking the bright bead of blood where a thorn had pierced her skin.

The saltiness reminded her how hungry she was. She had nothing in her bag but a peanut butter sandwich from yesterday. The bread was dry and the peanut butter stuck to the roof of her mouth, but she took another bite as she watched two *bergies* make their way up the steep hill. The woman stopped to rummage in a dustbin over the road, giving Yasmin a toothless smile. Yasmin did not smile back, but she did wave. The hand with the sandwich she hid behind her back, ashamed to eat in front of people looking for food in a bin. The homeless couple drifted up the road towards the mountain and she ate again.

She looked up when she heard the car, swallowed, a smile starting as she stepped towards the opening door.

The arm snaked around her body, squeezing the narrow cage of her ribs until she felt the bones would snap. She bit down hard when the hand clamped over her mouth, pushing her scream back down her throat. The hand fisted into her upturned face. Another slammed into her belly, winding her. Yasmin crumpled forwards into the pizza boxes and Coke bottles littering the floor of the car. The driver slid down the hill, and Yasmin rolled sideways as he turned. He cut the engine, but neither he nor his passengers moved as the afternoon faded into night.

The beginning of forever.

She lay still, her mouth full of blood. The tooth that had wobbled for days on its last thread lay on the cradle of her tongue.

four

Captain Riedwaan Faizal scanned the building. Nothing moved in the shadowed stairwells. On the top floor, the corner of a curtain twitched against the cinder blocks. He figured out the number of the flat. There weren't that many people around here who had jobs. Whoever was behind the grimy lace would have been watching all day. That was not where the call had come from.

A concrete wall ran along the length of the street, separating the pavement from the derelict sports field wedged against the freeway. It was freshly graffitied with chubby, rainbow-hued numbers: 27s. The gang tag stretched its tentacles from the Cape Flats, claiming Coronation Street and its surroundings for the Afghans. Just another franchise establishing its brand. That's what a sociologist in Jesus sandals had told Riedwaan Faizal. Like McDonald's handing out happy meals. Riedwaan snorted. More like dogs marking their territory. Dogs with new masters, hoping that a bit of piss and a lot of terror would hand this territory to them.

The girls had sprinted across the sports field that day, dropping their satchels and scattering schoolbooks along the way. Their shoes and grey skirts were streaked with mud. The younger girl's bobby socks had slipped below the plaster on her left shin. They had known what was coming. The older girl's arms were wrapped around the younger one. The bullets that ripped through her back had exploded through the smaller one's slender body, just below the badge on her maroon school jersey. Puberty had just settled, light as a butterfly, on the child's body – glossing and thickening her hair, swelling the exposed nipple.

Riedwaan had brushed her cooling cheek, the coin that was balanced on her open eye sliding into his palm. Heads. It was still warm.

Sergeant Rita Mkhize was tracking the girls' path from the pavement. Short hair twisted into dreads, just over a metre and a half tall, forty-five kilograms: too small to hold a machine gun properly. Which might have been a good thing: she got the *moer* in quickly, and she was a lethal shot. She had been his partner for a couple of months now. She kept an eye on him, but she knew how to watch his back. He was getting used to her.

She held up a bloodstained algebra paper.

'The Maitland School for Girls.' Then she read out the names on their school bags. 'Sisters. Grade nine. Grade four, the little one.' Rita stood up, zipping her hoodie and stamping her feet, 'Can't be more than ten. A baby.'

'My baby's seven on Tuesday,' said Riedwaan.

'You signed the Canada papers yet?' Rita asked.

'Van Rensburg would never have asked me a personal question like that,' said Riedwaan's.

'He's not your partner any more,' shrugged Rita. 'So, did you?'

The arrival of the ballistics van saved Riedwaan from having to answer. Shorty de Lange was alone, the way he liked it.

'Keep that lot away from me,' De Lange greeted them. The five o'clock crowd, on its way home from work, was pressing against the crime scene tape. The woman who ran the corner café was telling everyone who'd listen what she had seen; it was not much. She had heard the shots. She had waited for a bit. She had heard a car – it sounded like an expensive one – going fast, doing a wheelie. Then she had gone outside to look. Nothing in the street, just the two girls in the field, dead. Riedwaan had written this down in his little black book. Statements walked, in cases like this.

'I'm going to mark my territory and then I'm going to start working. If one of your friends here crosses the line, Faizal, I'm out of here.'

'Nice to see you too, Shorty.' Riedwaan moved towards the tape. He was not a big man, but there was a tautness to his shoulders that made the murmuring onlookers take a step back.

'A gang hit?' De Lange scanned the ground. There were a couple of casings on the pavement, one near the bodies. He bagged and tagged them.

'Some slime with a lot to prove climbing the ranks, looks like,' said Riedwaan. 'Really proves you're a man, shooting a girl in the head from close range.'

'Makes a change from cops taking out their own families,' said De Lange.

'Been bad?' asked Riedwaan.

'Worse than Christmas. One this month and three in July. Where've you been?'

'Busy,' said Riedwaan.

'I heard,' said De Lange. All the time he was talking, he was working too. Close-ups of things that people from ballistics find interesting. Twists of metal. Angles. Grooves in a piece of wood. Holes in things. Casings. Where they were lying. Why they were lying there. 'This special operation of yours. Got some stupid name, hasn't it?'

'Operation Hope.'

'More stupid than I thought.' De Lange retreated behind his camera, bending his lanky frame over the girls for close-ups of the bullets' entry and exit points. 'Whose idea was that?'

'Communications said we should project a more positive image to the community,' Riedwaan said. 'Not stereotype the disadvantaged young men who might have wished to make alternative life choices. That's how they put it.'

'How would you put it?'

'Not like that,' said Riedwaan.

'You know these girls?'

'Not yet,' said Riedwaan. 'Although I imagine they had an alternative life choice in mind when they got up in the morning.'

'Pathologist here yet?'

On cue, the black 1972 Jag nosed its way through the crowd. Same vintage as Riedwaan, though better cared for than himself during the past year or so.

'Doc,' said Riedwaan.

'Faizal, you fucker.' Piet Mouton heaved his considerable bulk out of the car. He was in black tie, his professorial wisps of hair tamed for the occasion. 'What've you interrupted me for this time?'

'Skipping meals will do you good,' said Riedwaan.

'This wasn't dinner, Faizal. My wife has ballet tickets. She's going to kill me for this.' Mouton pulled his bag out of the boot. 'Not a good sign that you're here, Shorty. High e.tv factor?'

'Couldn't be higher. Schoolgirls who live in a proper house. By the looks of their uniforms, Mom and Dad have jobs. The Minister's balls on toast for this one.' De Lange stepped out of the way.

'Shit.' Mouton paled at the bloody love knot of limbs tangled on the path. 'When did this happen?'

'Anonymous call to the gang hotline half an hour ago,' said Riedwaan.

'You got a trace yet?'

'We're working on it,' said Riedwaan. 'This area, though, the only eyewitnesses you get are blind or dead.'

Mouton knelt down beside the bodies. He uncurled the fourteen-year-old's fingers, first the right hand, then the left. There was no staining on the thumbs or the index fingers.

'Makes a change,' said Mouton. 'She's not been smoking tik, this one.' He lifted the older girl's skirt and pulled away her panties to reveal pale, unblemished skin. 'No tattoos. Not gang cherries, these.'

'Captain Faizal?' Riedwaan turned, facing straight into a lens. 'Good to see your suspension's over.' Stringy hair, not much chin, zoom lens a third arm – the photographer flashed his camera.

'You.' Riedwaan put his hand up to avoid being flashed again. 'How do you vultures get here so fast?'

'I got my contacts, Captain. Like you.'

'Faizal.' Next to him a journalist. Similar-looking, with even less chin. Between the two of them, they had the Flats covered. '*Voice of the Cape*,' he announced, jerking a thumb backwards in the direction of the dead girls. 'Names?'

'Next-of-fucking-kin first.'

The photographer zoomed in on the bags, intending to decipher the names later from the jumble of pixels.

'This linked to your one-man crusade against gangsters, Captain Faizal?' The journalist flipped open his notebook, pen poised.

'I'm a Muslim,' said Riedwaan. 'Crusades are not my thing.'

'You giving up?' Camera shutter firing.

'We're following procedure.' The words unfamiliar. A month ago he had told a journalist how many shootings there had been in Cape Town, how many dockets had walked, and which gangsters had hosted cocktail parties for which city officials. This had pleased the public, but it made the politicians look bad. Politicians were not people Riedwaan lost sleep over, but the threat of permanent assignment to the evidence store had persuaded him to give them and their euphemisms some consideration.

'What does that mean, Captain?' The journalist again. 'In practice – when you've got two girls executed on the way home from school? It's got Voëltjie Ahrend's signature all over it. Voëltjie Ahrend and his new best friends, the Afghans.' The journalist held up two yellowed fingers. 'The horsemen of the apocalypse, Captain. You know who they are. You know what they drive. You know where they live. What the fuck kind of procedure do you need?'

31

'I suggest you phone the SAPS Director of Communications and ask her.' Riedwaan put his hand in his pocket. The coin was there, in a bag. The third in three weeks. 'She should be able to explain – if she can get her nose out of a communications manual long enough to pick up the phone.'

'I've heard you're being moved out of the Gang Unit.' The reporter flipped through his notebook, found his notes, and read from them. 'A Director Ndlovu has been critical of you. No place for your attitudes, your methods, in a force that focuses on community policing, she says. Any comment?'

'Our communications department will tell you that the human resource deployment strategies of the SAPS are confidential. Shall I explain what that means?' Riedwaan had him by his shoulder. His mouth was close to his ear. 'It's government for fuck off.'

Riedwaan let the journalist go and wiped his hand on his jeans. 'Persuade this lot that the show is over,' he said to a uniformed officer.

'Rita, will you finish here?' said Riedwaan. 'I have a strategy meeting with Phiri.'

'You want me to bring you something to eat later?' she asked.

'The way to a man's heart.' Riedwaan had to bang the Mazda's door twice before it would shut. 'What you getting?'

'Nando's.'

'I can live with chicken,' said Riedwaan. 'If it's peri-peri.'

Riedwaan's phone vibrated against his chest. He pulled it out to check the calls he'd missed. At five-thirty-two, a missed call from a number he didn't recognise.

He called it back.

Somewhere, a phone began to ring into the silence.

After twenty rings, the network cut him off.

five

Clare Hart stood in her bathroom, her nipples darkening as the late afternoon chill came in through the open window. She snapped it shut and turned on the shower, lifting her face to the water and washing away the day. It was a while before she turned off the taps.

Clare dried her hair, twisting it before pinning it on top of her head as she faced her reflection. Dark rings under the sharp blue eyes. Too much coffee, too little sleep. She erased the rings with concealer, and put colour back in her cheeks with a brush. Her public face.

She was famished. In the fridge was a punnet of strawberries, a jar of mayonnaise, whiskey. And cat food that she tipped into a bowl for Fritz. Clare settled for the strawberries, looking out of the window as she ate, the moon a pale crescent above Lion's Head. The muezzin's call to prayer, beckoning above the melancholy sound of the late-afternoon traffic, insinuated itself into the cold air coming off the Atlantic. She finished the strawberries. The whiskey was tempting, but it did not seem a good idea on such an empty stomach, not tonight.

Shower. Hair. Face. Food.

Clothes.

That's what she needed next.

In the spare room Clare searched her underwear drawer, finding a pair of black panties but no stockings. Shaking out her dress, she slid it over her head, the black silk settling against her skin. She slipped on her new shoes and turned in front of the mirror, swirling her dress against her bare legs, a child for a second, playing dress-up in her mother's finery.

Her handbag was on the floor in her bedroom. She rifled through it.

Phone.

Comb.

Driver's licence.

Lipstick.

Speech.

Keys.

Gun.

Taking it out of the bag, she held it a while, the metal warming in her hand. Neither of her sisters liked guns and she'd be seeing them both later. She put it away in the drawer next to her bed. She had an hour or so yet, so she made herself a cup of tea and took it through to her study.

Clare had designed this eyrie for solitude, the furnishings pared down to the minimum. Shelves. Desk. Chair. The shelves were filled with files, books, and her investigative documentaries. Recording equipment was stacked on the floor next to the desk Clare had inherited from her doctor father, her laptop looking out of place on its worn oak surface. One wall was a pinning board crammed with notes, press cuttings, photographs, invitations. An aerial map covered two more walls. The fourth wall was glass, giving her an ever-changing view of the sea. On her desk were the final cuts for her television series *Missing*. Each one twenty-seven minutes long, cut to fill television's prime-time slot. Each programme bore a girl's name; each was the portrait of a girl who had gone missing. The quick and the dead, survivors and victims. Not always easy to tell them apart.

Clare rummaged through a box under her desk. She had already packed her tapes away, the bits she'd culled that could still be used for another half-hour programme. She pulled out the one she wanted to see again. The one that haunted her, the one Mrs Adams's question had recalled.

Pearl.

The camera had been locked onto her. She faced it, head and shoulders framed by the light filtering through the square of window. Her hair short, spiky; her neck drawn into shoulders that had at an early age discovered the advantage of brute strength, and worked hard to achieve it. Even so, her stance, her man's shirt, the baggy khakis, the boots – all of this failed to conceal the small bones, the narrowness of wrist and ankle.

'Tell me who you are.' Clare's own voice, off-screen, startled her.

The silhouetted girl did not respond at once; yet watching her now, once again, Clare could see her draw herself up. She reached for the Coke in front of her and sipped it, preparing for her confession as she faced the eye of the camera.

'You can call me Pearl.' Her voice harsh from many years of smoking. 'My last name I'll keep for myself. I'm twenty-two years old and I grew up there.' She pointed behind the camera towards the cinder block flats bedecked with washing and adorned with graffiti; stone-eyed men were draped against the entrances.

'It's not a place for a woman.'

Clare had zoomed in on Pearl's twisting fingers, the nails gnawed down to the pink half-moons.

'And it's not a place for little girls. If I tell you my story, you'll know why.'

No one else in the room, just the two of them, with the comforting whirr of the camera. Pearl's eyes were a yellow-brown – tiger's eyes – though the left one drooped; a scar ran through her eyebrow, across the lid, disappearing onto the high, wide plane of her cheekbone.

'Are you sure about this?' Clare's voice interjecting off-camera.

'How must I tell my secret if I stay hidden?' Pearl's hands turned outwards, asking a question she had already answered.

'My name is Pearl and this is my story,' she repeated, not to Clare this time, but to some imaginary audience.

'My mother didn't stop it. My grandmother didn't stop it, even though they could have so easily by just telling me who they were, who my father was. If they'd let me carry their secrets in my heart, they'd have become my weapons. I could've protected myself.'

Pearl leaned forward, her face filling the screen.

'They could have protected me.'

No tears in her eyes: much too late for that.

'Go on then, Pearl.' Clare felt it again, the weight of confession, of being the person who asked the question, who appeared to ease the load because her camera recorded the story, the secrets, the hurt. 'Start at the beginning.'

'I always thought I would know where to begin. I would be able to go back there and restart things another way.' Pearl slowly shook her head sideways. 'The beginning is lost, but where I can start is at the end. Because the end is always a new beginning.'

Voices in the distance, shouting, a woman singing. Clare had got up and closed the door, entombing them both in silence as they sat on either side of the bare wooden table.

'Okay,' Clare had said. 'I'm rolling again.'

Pearl had looked down at her hands as if they were not part of her body. She'd undone her top button. Then the next, and the next, until she could shrug off her shirt like a skin she no longer needed.

She moved her fingertips across her clavicle. Smooth on the right, the left jagged where the cracked bone had knitted beneath her skin. She put her hands over her breasts, full against the ribs ridging her skin. Around the left breast a circle of round scars. Bite marks.

'This is where my story is written,' she said. 'On my body. Maybe I should start here. It's not the beginning but it is all part of the same book. My name is Pearl. Pearl de Wet. My father is a general in the 27s. Those are the two most important things you need to know about me.'

She peeled back her clothes, revealing the script that bore witness to her secret. Tattoos, scars, cut marks – the slender white lines on her thighs – until she stood naked in front of the camera. Clare froze the image. A daughter of violence, made lean and sinewy by her refusal to die. This silent witnessing had not made the final cut. Too raw, too shocking for people eating dinner in front of their TV sets.

Clare's tea had grown cold while she watched. She pushed her cup away and looked out over the choppy ocean. The programme, *Pearl*, had run again last night, moved to prime time on the eve of Women's Day.

Giles Reid, her producer for the series, had loved the Pearl episode, was thrilled with a second sale, the publicity it had given the gala performance tonight of the ballet, *Persephone*. He had left her two messages to tell her this – and one to ask about her speech before the gala, reminding her that it would be a live broadcast. She had not replied, unable to think of what she might say, knowing what he wanted from her.

Clare switched her camera on. It hummed as that afternoon's footage digitised, the images flickering on her screen. She checked through the tape, jumping through the rough footage until Mrs Adams's face filled the screen as she pleaded for her daughter. Clare had panned to the child's portrait in the display cabinet: the kernel around which she would wrap her next film.

The search for the child had begun in earnest after the local police were called. The last part of her interview was done outside: the head of the Neighbourhood Watch street committee and some uniformed cops, behind them a rubbish-filled culvert, the metal grille propped open to reveal an ambiguous heap under a sack in the shadowed tunnel. The credits would run over the image of a missing green-eyed child, framed and sealed behind glass – before the screen went black. 'What does one more little girl mean, in a war?' The mother's anguished question floating in the dark.

The phone was ringing. Clare scrabbled for it, finding it under the *Cape Times*.

'Hello.'

'Dr Hart?' The voice knotted her stomach.

'Yes.'

'I've got another one for you.'

'Who found her?'

'Kids. Playing. She's Muslim, so I'm doing her now. Bring a pair of socks.'

The kitchen clock chimed six.

Clare put on her coat, pulling the belt tight over her hollow belly. She set the burglar alarm, locked the front door and hurried to her car. No one about, except the Congolese car guard who was her self-appointed protector. She waved at him as she joined the stream of cars heading into town. She pushed in a CD, turning up the volume. Moby. The music so loud it drowned her thoughts. She would have just enough time for her detour if the lights were on her side.

She put her foot down and took the first set on orange.

six

'What size are you?' Dr Ruth Lyndall's dark hair was cropped short. If the pathologist had put on make-up that morning, it had long since worn off.

'Five,' said Clare. 'Why?'

'I thought I might as well set you to work right away. Try these, then.' She selected a pair of gumboots from the communal heap. 'They're our new director's. She's the same size. As stubborn as you, too, convinced that if enough people know what's happening to our little girls, it will stop. And Senior Superintendent Edgar Phiri signed the approval for your research this afternoon.'

'Head of the Gang Unit?'

'That's your man,' said Ruth.

'What's he like?' asked Clare.

'Reminded me of those early pictures of Mandela. Tall and honourable and saintly-looking, but looks like he knows how to fight his way out of a corner.'

'He must stand out in the police force.'

'Phiri's unit gets things done, and that has pissed off some senior people. Don't be too hard on the cops. Phiri's approved your research.'

'All of it?'

'All of it,' said the pathologist. 'That's why you're trying on the new boots. You're going to be attending more autopsies than you can imagine.'

Clare took off her heels and pulled on some socks. She pushed her feet into the white boots and pulled a green hospital gown over her evening dress.

'Let me help you.'

Ruth Lyndall took the belt, looping it twice. She rested her hands on Clare's narrow waist, her face next to Clare's in the mirror. Forty-three. Ten years older than Clare. Ten years wiser.

'You're running on empty, Clare.'

'I'm just running.'

'It won't fix things.'

'It might fix me.' She took a mask and unclipped the perspex eye shield, throwing it into the bin.

'You won't be needing that?'

'I won't be staying for the blood splatter,' said Clare.

'I didn't think so, dressed like that,' she smiled. 'A date?'

'The gala ballet I'm hosting.'

'*Persephone*. Of course. Your fundraising thing.'

'Finding missing girls, helping them heal, returning them to their mothers.'

'It's not going to help the little one on the slab. She's with Hades for good.'

'Does she have a name?' asked Clare.

'A *weggooi kind* like this?' Ruth's voice was bitter. 'Even a throwaway child has a name. Look in the docket there. She's one of yours.'

Clare opened the folder. 'Noor Khan. No address.'

'Her mother lives in that squatter camp in the Maitland Cemetery. Tik addict, according to the cops. They're trying to sober her up now.'

'Where was she found?'

'Kids found her in a field, that empty land between the docks and Cape Town station. The cops said they were playing. I would've said scavenging.'

'When did she go missing?' asked Clare.

'She didn't, not according to anybody who should've noticed.'

'No one reported it?'

'The cops who brought her here spoke to the mother. She said she hadn't seen the child since yesterday. Maybe the day before. Said she didn't think about it because she often ran away.'

'How'd they identify her?' asked Clare.

'One of the boys knew her. Her cousin, I think. The mother came here. Confirmed it. Looked tearful for the tabloids that some enterprising uncle had thought to call.'

'It says here that someone's been arrested,' said Clare.

'A man who lived nearby,' Ruth explained. 'He had blood on his clothes and the mother owed him money. A bit of DNA will tie up that loose end.'

Clare put her mask on, tying it tightly in place. It wouldn't help with the smell, but it was a barrier of sorts. She followed the pathologist into the section of the mortuary where no living members of the public were admitted.

'No investigating officer?' asked Clare.

'She couldn't be here now. She'll come by later, if she can,' answered Dr Lyndall. 'Friday night rush. Two girls dead in Maitland.'

'When did they go missing?'

'They didn't,' said Ruth. 'Shot on their way home from school. Gang crossfire, if you're feeling charitable. An execution so that someone could move up the ranks of the 27s, if you're not. Makes no difference to them now.'

'Were you at the scene?'

'Piet Mouton went,' said the pathologist, unlocking her office. 'But they're coming here, so I said I'd see to them. I just have to get something to eat first.'

Dr Lyndall greeted the two orderlies smoking outside. '*Sal julle*

41

die kind inbring?' Discussing that night's soccer match, the orderlies sauntered off to fetch the child's body.

Clare waited in the draughty passage. To the left of the room facing her, the day's carnage had been cleared away. Twelve clean metal trays were lined up, six on either side of the room: ready for the first batch who weren't going to make it through the weekend. To the right, hidden from her view, were the fridges. The orderlies returned, deftly manoeuvring the trolley, and parked it in an empty space in the cutting room.

'You ready, Clare?'

'I'm ready.'

She wasn't. The gurney was too big. And the body on the steel tray too small, as the pathologist pulled back the sheet. The child's bloodless lips curved in a parody of the grin slashed into the slender column of her neck. Clare squeezed the palms of her hands together, the pain of the ring biting into her fingers a distraction.

'You're pale, Clare.'

'I'm fine.' Clare swallowed. 'You carry on.'

Dr Lyndall eased the child out of her clothes: pink pants with yellow daisies stitched on the knees, and a shirt, with its bib of dried blood. PEP Stores panties, one red thread unravelling from the thigh, the static lifting it against the pathologist's sleeve as she set to work.

Dark lashes fanned out against the child's cheeks. Ruth Lyndall smoothed the dark curls, the instinctive gesture of a mother. She worked carefully over the body, photographing, cataloguing, the pattern of injuries, old and new. A yellowing bruise on the back – last week's. A ridging in the left clavicle. An old break. There was a healed tear in the thin skin folded between her legs. Ambiguous. Abrasions on the knees and palms. Ambiguous. The injuries of childhood play, perhaps. Swings, slides, seesaws. Not necessarily a little girl running hell for leather to escape, falling, not getting

42

away. Scraps of pink nail varnish clung to her torn fingernails. Dr Lyndall scraped under them, hoping there might be some scratched skin amidst the dirt. On her upper arm was a series of round prints. An adult's hand – a man's, judging by the spacing of the marks – had held her tight. Then the throat. A knife lifted high in his free hand, plunging down.

'This girl walked across some rough ground,' said Clare, a finger hovering over the girl's instep.

Ruth Lyndall cupped the child's feet in her narrow hands. There was a fading henna tattoo on the sides of her grubby feet. A white shoe clung to the left foot.

'Let's have a look inside her.'

Clare helped the pathologist position the trolley under the low dose X-ray machine, relieved to move her eyes away from the naked child. She looked at her ghostly double. The spectral image on the computer screen, surrounded by start-up, documents, trash icons, was bearable. The original was not.

'What I was looking for.' The pathologist moved the mouse arrow along the pale lattice of rib bones on the screen. On each rib was a bead of white bone. 'This little girl's only jewellery.'

'What is that telling you?'

'That this child has been abused for a long time,' Dr Lyndall explained. 'You only get those in kids who've been badly shaken as babies or toddlers. The bones crack and then heal in this formation. It's called a string of pearls fracture.'

'You going to open her up?' asked Clare.

'I have to. This – the old vaginal injures – the fact that her disappearance wasn't reported, make this look like a family affair.'

She switched off the machine, enveloping them in silence.

'I'd better go if I'm going to make my speech, then,' said Clare, pulling off her mask. 'Did you get a chance to dig out those reports I asked you for?'

'On my desk,' said Ruth. 'There's an envelope with your name on it. The raw data. Five years' worth of violent deaths. I pulled out the female victims, then separated the children for you.'

'You see a pattern?'

'I've been here since five this morning. I got my morning coffee at three this afternoon. The only patterns I've seen were those from the start of a migraine.'

'I'll start going through this tomorrow, do the mapping too,' said Clare, 'then I'll call you.'

'Monday. Call me Monday. My family's in town.'

Ruth Lyndall's husband and only daughter grew olives in the Karoo. She saw them at weekends. Her way of doing marriage. Her way of keeping her daughter alive. It seemed to be working. She opened the leather case next to her. The blades flashed under the neon.

'Monday, then.'

The pathologist watched Clare disappear into the change-room, then she selected a knife. Lifted it out. Measured. Cut.

seven

The wind whipped the car door from Riedwaan Faizal's hand. He had parked opposite Caledon Square. The forbidding stone plinth was punctuated with small barred windows. The holding cells. Above these, the Victorian brickwork contained a warren of offices. It was quiet, except for some muffled shouts from the cells and tuneless Friday night singing from the bar on the first floor.

Climbing a flight of stairs, Riedwaan turned where the sign said Organised Crime and Drug Unit in bright orange letters. The younger cops doing correspondence courses in criminal psychology called them the OCDs. Thought their joke was hilarious. Fuck them. Though only an obsessive compulsive would stick with gangsters long enough to bust them. The work was dirty and dangerous and it had broken up his family. They were probably right, he thought grudgingly, as he knocked on the secretary's door. Sticking with this unit had to be a kind of disorder.

'You're late, Captain Faizal,' said Senior Superintendent Edgar Phiri's secretary.

'A double murder,' said Riedwaan. 'Two girls. So sorry, Louise.'

'Senior Superintendent Phiri and Captain Delport are waiting for you.' Louise's expression did not soften, but she held out her hand. 'You'll need copies of your report?'

'It's sorted.' he said. Riedwaan's report existed – just not on paper. What he had to write down was in a notebook he carried in his breast pocket. The important stuff he kept in his head.

Louise tossed her greying blonde hair and returned to her keyboard, dismissing him and his lie.

Edgar Phiri, lean and fit, with just a sprinkle of iron-grey at the temples, turned from his vigil at the window when Riedwaan opened the door.

'Faizal.'

Phiri's promotion was recent, but authority sat comfortably on his shoulders. He had earned it, and he did not think coming from Jo'burg was a handicap. His competence had not harmed his reputation, but it was not making him many friends either.

'Sit, please.'

A folder was placed in front of Phiri's empty chair, Operation Hope stencilled on it in orange.

'Delport.' Riedwaan acknowledged the other man in the room.

'How was the loony bin?' Delport was doodling crosshairs on his folder, turning the 'o' in Hope into a target. 'A month on a Karoo funny farm cure you of your anger management issues?'

Riedwaan sat down, pulling out his cigarettes. One raised eyebrow from Phiri told him he was not going to be smoking, but he left them on the table in front of him.

'Good to see you're still concerned about my welfare, Delport.'

Tertius Delport, seconded from Narcotics to Phiri's Gang Unit. The burst capillaries on his face a map of the bars he had made himself at home in. He had reason to drink. Before '94, he'd kept human rights lawyers busy; the suspects he questioned sometimes took a bit of time to walk unaided again. He hadn't changed his methods, but these days the suspects were gangsters and addicts and dealers, and nobody worried much about his methods of winnowing them out.

Riedwaan switched off his phone. Phiri did not tolerate calls during his meetings.

'Van Rensburg will join us soon.' Phiri sat down, opened the orange file, took off his Rolex, and aligned it with his paperwork. 'Shall we begin?'

Delport hid his six o'clock tremor by keeping his hands under the table.

'Faizal.' Phiri sat with his back to the door. 'I got your apologies from Rita Mkhize.'

'Another shooting,' said Riedwaan. 'In Maitland, this time.'

'Gangsters,' said Delport. 'I like it when they do our job for us.'

'Two schoolgirls,' Riedwaan cut in. 'No gang links in the family, according to the database.'

'You're linking it with the Unit's current joint operation?' asked Phiri.

'A territory claim, is my guess.' Riedwaan put his hand into his pocket and took out the coin labelled as evidence at the crime scene. He put it on the desk. 'The signature.'

'Soviet kopek.' Phiri picked it up. '1989 mint. Same as the last time.'

'The coin was on the victim's face, the little girl. Means the killer got out of the car and put it there. Whoever does that is sure that no one's going to remember seeing them – or live long enough to say anything, if they do.'

'Drugs,' said Delport. 'Someone they know owed money.'

Riedwaan shook his head. 'This is some Number gangster proving his manhood, moving himself up the ranks. There's talk of the 27s everywhere. Dogs marking new territory, those two girls in the wrong place at the wrong time.'

'Bullshit,' snorted Delport. 'The Number does that inside prison. What's it going to help anyone on the outside?'

'If I knew the answer to that, Delport, maybe those little girls would be eating lamb curry right now.' The pain behind his eyes again. Riedwaan rubbed his temples, thought about having a drink.

Phiri pulled out a dog-eared, hand-written page. 'Yours is an unusual interpretation of the facts, Faizal.'

'Makes a change that he's got any facts to interpret,' muttered Delport.

'We'll hear him first, Delport, and then comment on it. You'll get your opportunity to raise objections and offer alternative viewpoints. Faizal?'

Delport folded his arms and watched as Riedwaan took a street map out of his pocket. He swivelled it round to Phiri.

'The area from Sea Point,' he swept his pen across the Promenade and the strip of beach north of the harbour, 'to Maitland, up to Milnerton. All this behind it,' he indicated the swathes of security estates and new suburbs that had mushroomed on the wetlands and abandoned industrial areas inland, 'is up for sale.'

'Pam Golding doing the transfer?' Delport asked.

Ignoring him, Phiri uncapped his pen and opened his notebook. 'For sale to whom? And for what period?'

'My bet is that Voëltjie Ahrend is in on this land deal,' said Riedwaan. 'But there's also international interest. The Russian mafia. The big boys hope to end the turf war. The 27s are the foot soldiers, very effective, very brutal. They'll see to it that all the other gangs – the 28s, the 26s, the Americans, The Firm, the Mongrels, or whoever else – obey the Keep Out sign. It's a red ink deal: sealed in blood. Blood brothers, rather than partners in crime, you could say.'

'What about the Italians, the Colombians?'

'The Italians wrapped things up years ago. Bought the politicians they needed,' said Riedwaan. 'The South Americans like it here – shipping lines are good.'

Riedwaan pocketed the bagged coin.

'You're not convinced?'

'I've been trying to fix on what's bothered me,' said Riedwaan. 'It's the type of violence. This is something new. A warning.'

'These Russians.' Phiri, expert in reading the small calibrations of falsehood and truth in a man's face, kept his eyes on Riedwaan. 'Tell me more.'

'My sources aren't sure who they've given it to, but I heard a three-year lease.'

'Your sources,' Delport stabbed a thick finger at Riedwaan's map. 'Ex-gangsters and prostitutes. No names. No dates. On the basis of that and a couple of small drug busts, you want frozen assets, blanket search-and-seizure orders, and six arrest warrants.'

Riedwaan counted the items off on his fingers. 'That's about it,' he said. 'Plus full witness protection for my informants.'

'Who you don't name.' Delport pushed his bull neck forward. 'There was a truce – no killings, no collaterals like your two dead schoolgirls – until you started stirring things up.'

'Captain Faizal,' Phiri headed off Riedwaan's response. 'Perhaps you could build your case a little more before we decide on what action to take?'

'This spate of murders.' Riedwaan swallowed the antagonism he felt towards Delport and spoke directly to Phiri. 'Here, here and here: the negotiation. Drugs, talk of heroin, pure and cheap. You had any of that, Delport?'

'Couple of busts,' said Delport. 'Nothing that looks like it's going to flood the market. Seems like the tik merchants have got that wrapped.'

'Adult entertainment, upmarket strip clubs, protection. Something called Gorky Investments came up a couple of times. Seems quite legitimate, but they're skating on the edge of legality. And that edge, in South Africa, has been pushed even further away from honest, thanks to our esteemed leaders.'

'You've got something on them?' Delport cracked his knuckles.

'They've got friends.'

'Who?'

'I don't know yet.'

'So, all speculation again, Faizal?' said Delport. 'You think they might be behind JFK's assassination too?'

'There's a gap in the market here. Space for a small outfit. Niche marketing. Boutique services, is what you'd call it if you were running a hotel. Voëltjie Ahrend's the muscle,' said Riedwaan. 'Small outfit. Young. Didn't spend much time in prison, but was in with Graveyard de Wet. Learnt his tricks from the master. Now he's using the branding of the 27s like a franchise.'

Riedwaan waited as the sirens outside went past. 'All you need is a way of managing it. Violence is easy. You teach one person a lesson once, and everyone gets it. These people don't decide things by committee.'

Leaning forward, Delport cut in, 'Don't tell me you've bought this bullshit about the 27s moving out of the prisons and onto the street? One or two body-building clubs, a bit of extortion, a few strippers. Anything more organised than that is a figment of the media's imagination. It's throwing money away, going after them.'

'The capital.' Phiri kept his eyes on Riedwaan.

'One kopek is hardly capital,' Delport sneered.

'Let me hear this,' said Phiri. 'I'll decide. Who's backing Ahrend, Faizal?'

'I'm trying to pin it down. Hard to find an individual. Shell companies behind shell companies in the property that's been selling. Management outsourced, the muscle, too. Whoever it is gets others to take the risk, guarantees a flow of merchandise, skims their fees off the top. Low risk. High reward.'

There were muffled voices at the door. Seconds later it opened, and a statuesque woman filled the doorway. The charcoal skirt and jacket were so tailored that she may as well have worn her uniform. Behind her were two men in Special Directorate uniforms.

'Special Director Ndlovu. I didn't expect to see you in Cape Town.'

'Phiri.' The woman nodded.

'Captain Faizal,' said Director Ndlovu. Riedwaan was on his feet. The woman held a folder with his name on it. They had crossed paths before. 'What have you done with your daughter this time?'

'I don't have her.' The pen in Riedwaan's hand snapped. 'Where is she? What's happened?'

'Your wife went to collect her from her ballet class, Captain. She's gone.'

'She's gone home with one of the other girls, surely?' Riedwaan's chair toppled as he stepped towards the door.

Ndlovu blocked him.

'Shazia checked that. She checked with Yasmin's teachers too.' The expression in her eyes was arctic. 'You knew she'd be there, and now she's gone.'

Delport, Phiri, Louise standing in the doorway behind the uniforms, Ndlovu – all had their eyes on him. 'Just the week before your wife was going to take the child to Canada. The family court ordered that you return the papers on Monday. Have you signed?'

'No,' said Riedwaan, shoving his cigarettes into his pocket, feeling for his keys. 'I have not signed.'

Salome Ndlovu turned to Phiri. 'Then …'

'Don't you fuck with me, Special Director Ndlovu.' He had his hand on her arm, the grey silk of her jacket slippery under his palm.

'Is that another threat, Captain Faizal?' She didn't flinch.

Ndlovu's men stepped into Riedwaan's body space.

'No.' Riedwaan's hand dropped to his side. 'But I don't have her. And the longer you believe I do, the harder it's going to be for me to find her.'

'Given your own history, the police's history for family violence, this restraining order—'

'What I'm telling you is a fact, Director. Something that your years in the Soviet Union may have taught you to overlook.'

'Director Ndlovu,' said Phiri. 'Captain Faizal's been working all day. I will deal with this. The explanations are simple, I'm sure.'

'Shazia Faizal is moving to Canada, she is taking the child with her. The father's reaction to this has been violent.' Ndlovu held up an official-looking document. 'For men with Captain Faizal's record, there are protocols that must be followed. In the interest of the safety of the child and the mother.'

'For fuck's sake.' Riedwaan snatched the interdict from her. 'I'm going to look for her.'

'Your protocols will be followed,' Phiri said, a restraining hand on Riedwaan's arm. 'I will vouch for Captain Faizal.'

'To the letter. Your unorthodox approach to discipline has been noted.'

'You've brought this to my attention before,' said Phiri. 'But in these matters my loyalty is with my men and with my unit. The Party does not employ me. Nor, I should point out, does it employ you.'

'It will be your head on a plate if Faizal is out of line.'

'Moscow was a long time ago, Special Director,' said Phiri. 'Is that what you are still after, Salome?'

'Don't make this personal, Phiri. My concern is for the well-being of the child. Yours is too, I trust.'

'That you can be sure of,' Phiri replied, but Salome Ndlovu was already halfway down the passage, her entourage at her heels.

'I'm going to speak to Rita and Van Rensburg to organise a proper search,' said Riedwaan, his face ashen, 'to find out what the fuck is happening.'

'The end of our meeting,' observed Delport.

'For now,' said Phiri. 'Did you have anything to report?'

'It can wait,' said Delport. 'What happened in Moscow?'

'Old history,' said Phiri. 'Should have been buried years ago.'

'You trained with Salome?' asked Delport.

'We knew each other. We all did back then,' said Phiri. 'But on her return from exile she slipped back into what she knew best. The Soviet Union was home to her. It might be called Russia now, but with so many of the faces the same, solidarity has transformed smoothly into business.'

'So, what's with her and Faizal?' asked Delport.

'Captain Faizal thinks for himself, acts alone, doesn't take to authority, doesn't take to being told what to do by her. A bit like I was,' said Phiri, gathering up his papers. 'We'll meet tomorrow, Delport, with Van Rensburg. Eight sharp. I must see to this business with Faizal.'

'Needle in a haystack,' Delport muttered to Phiri's secretary as he left, papers under his arm, 'finding a little girl out there.'

eight

'What've you been doing, Faizal?' Superintendent Clinton van Rensburg had the broad body of a rugby lock. He'd played for the police team for years, and sat on the bench during a Springbok Test, once. He hadn't been called to play, but the South Africans had won anyway.

'Trying to speak to Shazia,' said Riedwaan. 'She took one call, said I must bring Yasmin back. Now she won't take my calls.'

'Where have you been this afternoon?'

'Where do you think I've been?' demanded Riedwaan. 'I was at the crime scene in Maitland. Two little girls not much bigger than my daughter shot to shit.'

'Don't give me shit.' Van Rensburg stood up. He wasn't as big since being shot in the spine during a routine drug bust. Two operations later, he was out of his wheelchair – but on the streets he was no use, except as target practice. 'Where are you hiding her, Faizal?'

'I don't have her.' Riedwaan leaned on Van Rensburg's desk, knocking over a framed photograph. 'You've known me for fifteen years. We founded this fucking unit together.'

'Put your wife out of her misery.' Van Rensburg may have lost the full use of his legs, but he had not lost his contacts, or his knowledge of the men he worked with. And the man whose service file he had on his desk, he'd made it his job to know better than most. 'She's taking your child to Canada,' said Van Rensburg. 'Last time she tried, you did take Yasmin.'

54

'I know,' said Riedwaan. 'I know. It was a mistake. I was desperate, but I would never harm either of them.'

'The stress has got to you, Faizal. Look at you. You're fucked up. Can't think. Can't sleep, can't eat. Can't face what happened to your dream,' said Van Rensburg, righting the portrait of him and his family. It had been taken when they were whole and happy, before he'd had to use a crutch. 'You tell me where she is. I fetch her. This whole thing goes away, and you get work in private security. No trouble.'

'You've got a daughter …'

'Listen to your wife, Faizal.'

Clinton van Rensburg pressed play on the digital recorder, filling the room with Shazia's voice.

'Yasmin, Yasmin.'

'Calm down, lady.' A woman's bored call-centre voice. 'What's your name? What's the address? What's happening?'

'Yasmin Faizal, my daughter,' Shazia alternating between panic and rage. 'She's not here. I'm here to fetch her and she's not here. This has happened before! My husband. He was here and now she's gone …'

'Who is your husband?' Alert now. New training. New questions. New interest. The computer had flagged the cellphone number on the screen.

'Captain Riedwaan Faizal. Gang Unit. He's taken her again.'

'Let me process this, madam.'

Van Rensburg switched off the sound.

'What have you done this time, Faizal?'

'This is a mistake.'

'Here's the restraining order your wife got against you two months ago, Faizal. Her call automatically activated it,' said Van Rensburg. 'You know how it works now: making the law work for women. Damage control, I'd call it.'

'This is a set-up, Clinton.' Riedwaan's hands were shaking as he pulled a cigarette from his pack. 'That's what I'm praying for. Because if it's not, then the longer we spend with this bullshit the less chance I have of finding her.'

'Then take me through your movements late this afternoon, Faizal.'

'The crime scene in Maitland.'

'And then?'

'Then I came here to meet with Phiri and Delport.'

'It took you a while to get here. Where were you?'

'The mother,' said Riedwaan. 'To break the news.'

'And before?'

'I went for a drive.'

'A drive?' Phiri looked Riedwaan in the eye. 'A drive to where?'

'I went past the ballet school.' Riedwaan took a cigarette from the pack, turned it in his fingers. 'I was going to see two dead girls. I needed to see her.'

'And how was she?'

'She was fine. I spoke to her in the car, then she ran inside to go to her class.'

'Faizal, the last time this happened she was found with you.' Van Rensburg rifled through the file, found the notes the family court magistrate had made, and read them. 'Yasmin Faizal. Age six. Incarcerated in a fishing shack for two days by her father. Reluctant to hand child over.' He put the notes aside. 'I won't read the rest. You know what happened.'

'She wasn't incarcerated.' Riedwaan paced. 'Bullshit American word. She wasn't even locked in. The southeaster was blowing so we had the door closed.'

'And you threatened to throw the family court representative into the Atlantic, if I remember.' He turned the page. 'The time before that, she was found with you in a shopping mall.'

'She's my child. I picked her up from school. We went ice-skating. She loved it.'

'Not what this affidavit says.' Van Rensburg's voice was quiet, measured. 'Here it says you went into her classroom and removed her against the express wishes of her teacher. And her headmistress and her mother. That's abduction, Faizal.'

'You've been to my house? You've been to the fishing shack?' Riedwaan leaned over Van Rensburg. 'So, where is she then?'

'That's what we want to know.' Van Rensburg did not flinch.

'I don't have her,' said Riedwaan. 'I've been working. Two night shifts and a day – in a row. You're a detective, Van Rensburg. Look at those two cases. Both times, I was off. I picked up my daughter, my only daughter, so that I could spend time with her. So why'd you pull me down here as if I'm a criminal?'

'This is why.' Van Rensburg handed over a document.

'I've never seen this.' Riedwaan skimmed the document, paling as he did so.

'Confidential. The Family Unit's Police Psychological Review,' said Van Rensburg. 'All officers have been assessed. You rang every warning bell they have.'

'Who wrote this nonsense?'

'The psychometric tests identified insomnia, aggression, hyper-reaction to stress, incapacity for teamwork and compromise, inability or refusal to express your feelings, and an exaggerated sense of possessiveness about your family.'

'Tell me one cop working on the Gang Unit who doesn't have that feeling,' Riedwaan demanded. 'Tell me you don't have it.'

'Not the point, Faizal.'

'Tell me you don't have that feeling about Latisha, about Calvaleen?'

At the mention of his only daughter's name, the lines around Clinton's mouth deepened. His gaze drifted towards the portrait of

57

her on the desk. It had been taken a year earlier. A graceful girl in white, slender arms poised above her head, in the shape of a lily.

'Don't go there, Faizal.'

'I'm sorry, man. Sorry for what happened. To you, to her, to all of us.' Riedwaan pushed his hands through his hair. 'But you're a father. You know. You'd kill for Calvaleen. But you'd die before you'd hurt her.'

'Haven't I?'

'What happened wasn't your fault.' Riedwaan lit a cigarette.

'No,' said Van Rensburg. 'You're right there. It wasn't my fault. But look how much use I am to her now, a cripple on crutches who can't even shoot straight any more.' He jabbed his finger at the shooting medals and marksman trophies on the wall.

Van Rensburg straightened the perfectly aligned pages of the report.

'This report, peer reviewed and approved, states that you are high risk.'

'High risk what?' Riedwaan's anger shifted from red to white.

'For assault. For family violence. For spousal abuse.' Van Rensburg trailed his thick finger down the list. 'For binge drinking. For suicide. For murder. For family murder and suicide.'

'You think I'm going to take my family out?'

'That's what Director Ndlovu thinks, and it seems she got the magistrate to agree with her.'

'For fuck's sake, Clinton.'

'She also noted a "dismissive attitude to gender transformation and the new community cooperation policy". Also mentioned is your attitude towards gender-sensitive policing.'

'I arrest people,' said Riedwaan. 'I'm not some armed fucking social worker there to offer counselling as well. I put how many gangsters behind bars in the last two years? You did it with me. Explain to me how that is not a good thing for women.'

Riedwaan took a deep breath.

'What's being done to find her?'

'Shazia went to fetch her but she was gone, the ballet school was shut. Early closing because of some charity performance. Security guard says everyone left. He says Yasmin was waiting. He saw that fucked-up blue Mazda of yours and then he didn't see her again. He says she must have gone with you.'

'This is a set-up, Van Rensburg. For what, I don't know – but it's not good for finding Yasmin.'

'There's a technicality with this arrest warrant, so I suggest you leave now and that you don't cause any shit about handing in your weapon. Otherwise you'll be in the cells until the magistrates get themselves out of bed on Monday. There's also a warrant—'

'To search my house and my car. Get that done. She's not there. Once you prove what I'm telling you, after you've wasted that time, maybe we can start looking for her properly,' said Riedwaan. 'When did she disappear? An hour ago?'

Van Rensburg looked away.

'Two?' asked Riedwaan. 'That means we've got twenty-two hours left to find her alive.'

nine

The mortuary parking lot had emptied, the admin staff long gone. Two orderlies sat outside listening to a soccer game, watching Clare in her car.

The nausea was always worse once she'd left the morgue. She closed her eyes, but that was no good because then she saw the dead girl again. When her phone rang, she grabbed it as if it were a lifeline.

'Darling.' Her other life. Giles Reid again, impatience clipping the producer's BBC vowels. 'It'll be a monumental cock-up if you're late. Are you dressed? Do you have your face on? The cameras are ready to go. It's a live feed. There's no time to be African with.'

'I'll be there in ten minutes.' Clare started the car.

Silence at the other end.

'Okay, five.'

'I'm waiting with your punctual sister and your nieces at the bar.' She could hear Beatrice wheedling for a packet of Whispers, Imogen for a glass of champagne, just this once. Julia saying that every time they went out it was just this once, so no.

'Clare …' Giles's voice gentler. Intimate. 'I …'

'I'm on my way.' Cutting him short.

Clare joined the flow of cars, speeding down the taxi lane towards the city centre, then parking outside the theatre and slipping in through a side entrance. She stepped into the whirl of people finishing their champagne, moving towards their seats.

Her youngest niece, Beatrice, spotted her first.

'You look beautiful, Auntie Clare,' hooking sticky fingers into flame-coloured hair.

'She can't help it, darling,' smiled her mother as she kissed her younger sister.

'I know,' said Beatrice. 'I was just telling her.'

'Hi Julia, sorry I'm a bit rushed.'

Clare drew the little girl into the circle of her arms.

'Here's a flower for you.' Beatrice handed her an arum lily, its white sheath furled around the deep yellow stamen. 'I picked it.'

'Come on, darling, save it for later.' Giles Reid took charge. 'You're on in a few minutes.'

He swept her ahead of him, one hand in the small of her back, greeting those who mattered and ignoring those who didn't, until he had her at the stage entrance.

'Dr Hart,' he announced to the relief of the production manager. 'Mike her up.'

A technician threaded the wire up the inside of her dress and clipped the microphone to the neckline. The cameramen lounged next to their idle cameras, checked batteries, adjusted their head-phones.

'Good luck, darling.' Giles Reid kissed her cheek. 'We'll do dinner afterwards.'

Clare stepped onto the stage, away from his hand that had slid uninvited to her bottom.

She stood without notes, or a lectern to shield her, the familiar whirr of the cameras a comfort. The audience, fingering programmes and sweet wrappers, settled. The rustle was like rain on leaves.

'What does it feel like to come back from the dead?'

Clare let the question hang over her audience, invisible in the velvet darkness around her.

'That is the question which Persephone, goddess of the spring, must surely have been asked when she returned to the world of the living. *Persephone*, the ballet you've come to see tonight, tells Persephone's story, and also that of her mother, the goddess Demeter, who avenges Persephone's abduction by Hades, King of the Underworld. Demeter lays waste the earth, her wintry grief freezing the land until Hades agrees to let Persephone return, bringing the spring with her.'

The orchestra shifted in the pit, and was still again.

'So, what does it feel like to return?' Clare's eyes were adjusting to the dark. She could make out the shapes of the seats, of heads in the darkness.

'What does it feel like to return but to be unable to live, unable to love?'

Darkness, except for a single spot trained on her, its light bleaching her skin; the lily she held was stark against her black dress.

Clare clicked the remote in her hand. A series of faces appeared on the screen behind her, some culled from Christmas and holiday snaps. Many had the stilted innocence of school portraits. A single professional portrait of a redhead. Each one with her name, her date of birth, the date she disappeared and, if she'd been found, that date too. Only two did not have crosses next to their names. Two found alive. Just.

'Ours is a nation of missing girls.' In the wings the dancers checking their shoes, tucking away tendrils of hair.

'But tonight we are here to celebrate all the Persephones. Those we managed to find, and bring back from the dark grip of Hades. Like Demeter, who did find her lovely lost daughter.'

The lights went off, plunging the theatre into darkness. Clare left the stage, slipping into her seat as the applause faded away.

The conductor took his bow and the orchestra began to play, the sombre cellos haunted by a single violin. The dancers stirred, their tulle skirts fluttering, like moths drawn by the light. Then the slide of pointe shoes as they took up their positions.

The curtain opened to reveal the chorus poised around the dark-haired principal, her tutu silvered, like water catching the light of the dawn. Then the music started, a chorus of morning birdsong, and the dancer began to move.

Beatrice put out her hand and caught the tear sliding down Clare's cheek, then she leaned against her aunt and soon fell asleep, her small body a comfort.

The ballerinas glided onto the stage for the first act, the pale greens and yellows and blues the colours of spring. Persephone drifted like a white butterfly into the centre of the stage. Beneath the dancers was a vertiginous drop. Hades and his henchmen stirring below them in the depths, awakened by their dance, beginning the climb out of hell.

'You were wonderful.' Giles Reid's breath was warm in Clare's ear as he settled his hand on her knee. She crossed her legs away from him, annoyed with herself that she'd slept with him.

ten

Rita Mkhize's office ended up as the unofficial search and rescue centre for the Yasmin Faizal case. The room was taller than it was wide. It had been a storeroom before Rita commandeered it, tossing out a heap of Remington typewriters that had last seen action in the 1970s. Her dockets stacked, pens in a jam jar, pot plant watered – Rita had learnt long ago to order the small things. For there wasn't much one could do about the big things.

Because the single sash window opened onto the street, it had been nailed shut; its lower pane was painted the yellow-green found in hospitals and reformatories. Mental asylum green is what Rita called it. The room smelt of damp, and stale cigarette smoke. There were two chairs, one desk, one phone, one laptop. Rita had found an aerial map of Cape Town and put it on the wall. Someone had pinned a pink ribbon onto the place where Yasmin had gone missing.

Rita crumpled her Nando's bag and lobbed it into the dustbin. It joined the remnants of Clinton van Rensburg's Steers burger. He was on the phone to his wife. Rita was listening with half an ear. He was heading home, no, they hadn't found the child, no Faizal wasn't under arrest yet, yes it was a good idea that she go and see Shazia. Tomorrow, not tonight, there was someone with her, yes, they would find Yasmin. Alive, yes, of course alive. His voice soothing but strained, as it had been since his shooting, their own troubles with Calvaleen.

'Still the netball queen, Mkhize?' Delport leaned against the door frame, gnawing at a rib. He eyed Rita's pert backside.

'Takes one to know one, I suppose,' Rita shot back.

'What?' Delport licked the tangy sauce from his fingers.

'One queen,' said Rita, 'to know another one.'

Delport threw his takeaway packaging after hers. Missed. 'Fuck you.'

'You wish.' Rita took the tacks out of her pocket and pinned up the printout she had brought with her.

'Delport,' said Clinton van Rensburg. 'Go home.'

'What about this weekend's operation?'

'Nothing's happening tonight.'

'How convenient,' Delport sneered.

'We'll meet tomorrow. Reassess.'

'I'll see you then.' Delport sauntered out; the noise of the bar on the first floor was loud, enticing.

'There's him, home but not dry for the night,' Rita said. She examined her printout. Timelines. Places. People. The when-where-who of an investigation. Just a few sparse facts on the vast savannah of their ignorance. Opposite, she pinned up two headings. Method. Motive. The how, the why. Journalists' questions. No press yet, but they were sniffing.

She went through the list of numbers that the ballet school security guard had given her, the same numbers Shazia had called, hysteria rising, as the guards had hunted for her child. All of them sure she was somewhere, asleep with her head on her school bag. Riedwaan had called Madame Merle, the ballet teacher. She had seen Yasmin in class, that was it. The piano man said the same. Mister Henry, the kids called him. Surname Harries. On the surface, nothing.

She tried Yasmin's best friend, but she hadn't seen Yasmin either.

She tried Calvaleen van Rensburg, but she didn't pick up.

'Was your daughter not at dancing this afternoon?' she asked Van Rensburg.

'No,' he said. 'She's not dancing much. I've got to go too. Latisha … She's nervous.' Van Rensburg's euphemism for his wife's unravelling; his inability to reach her.

'And this?' Rita gestured at the phones, the map, her scraps of information.

'He'll bring her back,' said Van Rensburg, gathering his things, awkward with his crutch.

'Captain Faizal doesn't have her,' said Rita, anger rising in her chest. 'Why are we doing this?'

'Special Director Ndlovu's orders,' said Van Rensburg. 'She's taking this domestic violence in the police seriously. Her career's on the line if another officer takes out his family.'

'She wants an operation to be in charge of,' said Rita. 'She's a civilian who was parachuted in on the back of some dodgy degree from a country that doesn't exist any more. She's using him, she's made this happen so she looks good for her political bosses before the minister's budget speech next month.'

'Rita,' he said. 'You have a blind spot for your partner. Try to see him as he is, not as you wish he was. He'll bring his daughter back.'

'Say he doesn't have Yasmin, Captain van Rensburg.' Her voice was a dart in his back as he made his awkward way down the passage. 'Then what?'

'He'll take out whoever's got her.'

From down another passage came the sound of raised voices.

'Your service pistol, Faizal.'

'"Captain" to you, Sergeant.' Riedwaan's face was inches from the junior officer's. He did not flinch.

'Your gun, Captain Faizal.' He pushed a piece of paper across the desk towards Riedwaan. 'Hand it in. An order signed personally by Special Director Ndlovu.'

Riedwaan tore it in half. 'You tell Special Director Ndlovu to take this and put it in a special place ...'

'Not the best idea I've heard, Captain Faizal.' Rita Mkhize put her hand on Riedwaan's arm. It was small, her hand, but that she meant business was clear. She picked up the pieces of paper.

'In the drawer, Sergeant.' She gave him a practised bat of her eyelashes. 'The Sellotape's always there, on the left.'

He felt in the drawer, pulled out the tape.

'Two pieces, please.'

He tore them off and passed them to her. The paper was whole again. She smoothed it out.

'Your weapon, Captain?' Her grip on his arm tightened. She reached around with the other hand and unclipped his gun.

'I've got it, Sergeant,' she said sweetly, and sauntered down the passage.

She did not loosen her grip as she walked Riedwaan down the corridor.

'Ndlovu wants you arrested,' she said, her voice low. 'Don't make it easy for her.'

'I haven't got her,' said Riedwaan.

'I know,' said Rita. She unlocked her office, shoving the door open with her hip.

'I'm not going to ask what you were doing there,' she said, 'just take my motorbike and get out of here. Go find her. Don't go home. Don't go to Shazia's. Don't go to your mother's. If you've left, you don't know about it.'

She handed him the keys to her Yamaha.

Riedwaan hesitated.

'Go!' she said. 'You're going to be in the cells for the weekend unless you get out of here.'

'I'm going to need help finding her,' said Riedwaan.

'I'm doing what I can.' She handed him a sheaf of papers.

'You're something, Rita.' Riedwaan looked at the time codes, preliminary interviews, contact numbers. 'You'll get fired,' he said.

His phone flashed.

'Things don't look good, Faizal,' said Edgar Phiri. 'And there's only so much I can do for you if you don't cooperate.'

'I am cooperating.'

'Not answering your phone is not cooperating.'

'I was looking for her,' said Riedwaan. 'We need a proper door-to-door, not Ndlovu and her muscle-men asking if someone saw me kidnap my child.'

'If Rita Mkhize organises, will you accept that?' asked Phiri.

'Do I have a choice?' asked Riedwaan.

'No,' said Phiri, 'and the more trouble you cause, the more Ndlovu can nail you. She wants you in the cells.'

'This is my daughter we're talking about,' said Riedwaan.

'I know that, Faizal,' said Phiri. 'And believe me, I want you to find her. So work with me on this.'

Phiri disconnected.

'I'm sharp,' said Rita. 'But you're going to need more help. Call Dr Clare Hart.' She wrote down a number, handed it to him. 'Remember her? She gave that lecture on profiling rapists in that series Supe Phiri organised: "Extending the Police Skills Base".'

'You must be joking. She's like Jodie Foster in *Silence of the Lambs*, but without the sense of humour. I'll be right up there on her top ten feminist favourites: cop with restraining order against his wife and a kidnap charge against his daughter.'

'You asked her a stupid question that day. What's new?' Rita lifted an eyebrow. 'Call her, say you're sorry you pissed her off. Grovel. Do whatever. She'll help you. She won't care about you, but she'll care about your daughter and she'll know how to find her. '

'Profilers. Journalists. I might as well go to a fortune teller.'

'You might as well get over yourself, Riedwaan. She knows how to investigate. She's got connections you don't have. She has brains,' said Rita. 'And she's not trying to arrest you. That Persephone Project of hers – Clare's been tracking missing girls. Sometimes she finds them.'

'Dead, usually,' said Riedwaan.

'Not always.' Rita Mkhize stood closer to him, her seen-it-all eyes on his face. 'Maybe she can find Yasmin.'

'I'll call her.'

Rita's phone was ringing. She checked the caller ID. 'It's Director Ndlovu. Now go, so I'm not lying when I tell her I don't know where you are.'

'She'll kill you.'

'I've handled worse.'

'Sergeant Mkhize—'

Rita closed the door on Riedwaan, trying to remember when she'd had to handle worse, but an occasion didn't leap to mind.

'No, ma'am,' she said. 'Captain Faizal's not with me.'

Outside, the roar of the bike. Riedwaan Faizal doing a U-turn, jumping the red lights, as he headed up towards Devil's Peak.

eleven

The ballet school was shuttered and dark. Riedwaan cut the engine where his daughter had last been seen. Returning – like a textbook suspect – to the scene of a crime. Except that there was nothing, no crime-scene tape, no blood, no curious onlookers, to mark this as the place where a few hours earlier Yasmin Faizal had left her ballet class and stepped out of her life.

His little girl. Yasmin. Just two and a half kilograms at birth.

He had taken her into his arms and she had quieted, dark eyes searching his face, imprinting her features on his heart – instinctively staking her life on that. As he cupped her tender skull in his hand, her butterfly breath settled on his skin, staying with him. He and Shazia had looked at each other over the infant's dark, downy head, measuring the distance between them.

Riedwaan phoned the place that had been his home. He imagined the phone ringing less than a kilometre away in the flat where Yasmin should at this hour be curled under her quilt.

'It's Riedwaan.'

'What do you want from me?'

'To come home,' he said. 'To find her.'

'You had your chance,' she said.

'Shazia, our daughter is missing. If we work together—'

'It's too late for sorry, Riedwaan. If that's what you are.'

'If we're going to find her,' he tried again, 'then we need to talk to each other.'

'Bring her back, sign the papers, and then we can talk.'

'Shazia, try to hear me. I loved you. I love her. I don't have her. I would never harm her. She's gone, yes, but not with me. Not this time.'

'Bring her back to me, Riedwaan,' she hissed. 'You were there. The security saw you there.'

'Try and listen. I went past the ballet school. I saw her. I left her there to finish her class.' Riedwaan felt for a way to get round her anger. 'Listen to what I'm saying. I don't know where she is. The longer you shift the blame onto me, the less chance I have of finding her. For Ndlovu, Yasmin is a pawn in some other game.'

'You're always full of conspiracies, Riedwaan. They're games you've been happy to play.'

'I'm not playing anything, Shazia.'

'You're going to sign those papers so we can go to Canada?'

'I'll sign anything you ask me to if it brings her back,' said Riedwaan.

'So why didn't you sign before? Why did you push it so far? Why must you always do this? You made this happen. You and your work; you and your pride; you and your walking out on us instead of facing what you created.'

'Let me come home,' pleaded Riedwaan. 'Let's do this together.'

'Not until you bring me my daughter.'

Disconnection.

Riedwaan lit a cigarette, the smoke burning the back of his throat and blurring the city spread beneath him, a carpet of lights and secrets. His daughter hidden there, somewhere. His phone still in his hand, Riedwaan scrolled through his helter-skelter day again, finding the missed call from a number he didn't recognise.

Five-thirty-two. He dialled the number again. Inside the ballet school, the phone rang into the night.

He dialled for a message, found it. No words; nothing. Just silence.

Riedwaan rode along the back road behind the windswept tree

line and the blocks of flats. Disa Towers was ahead of him, its three cylindrical tower blocks dwarfed by Devil's Peak. The lights in 512 were a beacon. Where Yasmin should be asleep under her duvet. The place that used to be his home. He turned his back on the light, flushing out a nightjar as he made his way through the park that ringed the three bleak blocks.

Less than ten minutes later, he had the door open to the block he used to live in. He'd found the key to the basement in its usual place under the rock near the pine tree. Yasmin had hidden in the basement before, slipping out of the flat while her mother raged and her father refused to talk. The first time, it had taken him half an hour to realise that she was gone. He'd hunted for her for hours, eventually finding her down here, asleep on a shelf. Riedwaan felt along the shelf where she'd hidden the first time. Nothing but last summer's beach bats and a faded picnic rug.

He pulled himself onto the shelf. Above him were silky black hairs, snagged on a splinter in the wood. Carefully, he unhooked his daughter's hair and spread it on the blanket, three black strands on the pale wool.

So this is what it felt like to have your heart break.

twelve

'Join us, darling.' Giles Reid had his hand on Clare's elbow. He had been drinking too much again. The champagne was finished and the after-party was breaking up. They began heading up Long Street: the younger dancers to catch the Friday night clubs; the critics, older dancers and single men for a late dinner.

'I've had a week from hell,' said Clare. 'I need to get home.'

'It's been your night.' He gripped her arm. 'People will want to talk to you, congratulate. They want their pound of flesh, remember, for all the money they've donated to your cause.'

'Let go of me, Giles,' Clare lowered her voice. 'You're hurting me.'

'It really would be worth your while.' He leaned closer.

'The final cut for tomorrow's programme's been approved,' she said. 'And I need to start on the next one early tomorrow. You'll excuse me.'

She fetched her coat, one eye on Giles Reid bearing down on the prettiest dancer. So English, so charming – until you crossed him. She leaned her head on the steering wheel for a second, letting the silence wash over her. Her ears were buzzing with music, people, talk. She drove home, longing for her crisp white sheets.

It was late, and Beach Road was empty. She saw Fritz silhouetted at her bedroom window, watching. A ragged mist was rolling in, the foghorn wailing its plaintive warning. Clare parked on the street, too tired to get out and open her garage.

It was only when she was already out of the car that the man appeared from the shadows of the half-constructed wall nearby. His hands were deep in his pockets, his jacket pulled close around his lean body. He had been waiting for her for a while; at his feet were several cigarette butts.

She clenched her fist around her keys, the longest one protruding between her second and third fingers, a weapon.

He was in front of her, taller than she was – but at five foot four, most people were. There was nobody else on the Promenade.

'Dr Hart?'

Play for time.

'Yes.'

'I didn't mean to frighten you.'

He was reading her wariness, trying to put her at ease. His hands were at his side, empty, but he had blocked her path.

'What do you want?'

He handed her an ID. Captain Riedwaan Faizal. It felt warm from being against his body. Something familiar in the photo of his face, black hair growing straight up, full mouth, lines that said there'd been laughter in his eyes. She glanced up at him. There was none now.

'I remember you.' She handed it back to him. 'My lecture. Profiling sexual predators.' The man at the back of the classroom, his head at an angle. Sceptical. Asking questions that had disconcerted her, seeing past the surface of what she was saying. Past her suit, the white shirt, the mask of a professional woman in a man's domain. She handed his badge back.

'I … yes. Last year.' His voice caught in his throat. 'You might have heard the news. The little girl …'

On her way home last night, the newsreader's voice. 'Missing. Six. Dark hair tied in a ballet bun.' That's when Clare had muted the radio, not wanting to think about Chanel Adams, pinned like a butterfly to the board in her study – just like the others.

'My daughter.'

'What do you want from me?' Her guard down.

'You're going to help me find her.' His hand around her wrist.

'I can't.' She gripped the key tightly between her fingers. 'All you'll do is make things worse. The cops will find her. You're one of their own.'

Clare had her back to the wall. His fingers were around her wrist. His other hand was against the wall next to her face, his feet were planted on either side of hers, trapping her knees between his. She could feel the heat of his body, his arm close to her face. Her alternatives: knee him quick and fast, or jab a key into his eye.

'Why don't you let me go?' There was sometimes a third way. 'And can we talk about it.'

He released her. 'I'm sorry.'

'Why me?' Clare didn't relax her grip on the keys. 'In the middle of the night?'

'Rita Mkhize gave me your number.'

'Doesn't answer my question. Why aren't the cops looking for her, you with them?'

'They think I have her.'

'Do you?'

'Would I be here if I did?'

'You might well,' said Clare.

'Won't you help me?' he asked. 'Please.'

Clare's refusal died in her throat. And with it, her better judgement.

'What's her name?' asked Clare.

'Yasmin,' he said. 'Yasmin Faizal.'

'You want to tell me what happened?' asked Clare. 'Roma by Night is open.'

Riedwaan was already walking. The motion helped quell his fear, which felt like a pit bull in his gut, about to eat him alive.

thirteen

Clare took the booth furthest from the entrance. Riedwaan slid a photograph out of his breast pocket, placing it on the table. It lay between them, its corners rumpled, curved in the middle where it had moulded to the shape of his chest. A little girl in a pink leotard, her black hair in a ponytail. Gold hoops in her earlobes, her dark eyes glittering with laughter. Clare glanced up at Riedwaan. The same full, perfectly formed mouth.

'This is her?' asked Clare. The question unnecessary, a rope tossed over the gulf of loss. Riedwaan looked at the coloured lights looped along the Promenade. Many of the bulbs gone.

'That's her,' he said. 'Will you find her for me?'

'This is a first,' said Clare, 'a cop asking me for help.'

'I've seen your work.' Riedwaan took out a cigarette, and bounced it on the table. No Smoking signs everywhere. 'You've got connections I don't have. The cases I've been working on … I need someone who can get under the skin of these gangsters, and find her.'

'You think she's …'

'Alive?' Riedwaan said it for her. 'If she wasn't, I'd know. The people I deal with use bodies instead of email. More direct way of getting the message across, harder to trace.'

'Explain to me why you're a suspect,' said Clare.

'*The* suspect.'

'Okay, the suspect. Why aren't the cops looking for her? They have that new child-track system. Why not this time?'

'New unit. New policy. Still trying to straighten us old-school cops out,' Riedwaan took his lighter out of his pocket, lit his cigarette. 'Run by a Special Director Ndlovu. A PhD in *rondvok* from Leningrad University or some fact-free place like that. She got hold of me and my psychological profile. When that happens and you've got a profile like mine, you're fucked.'

'Why's she on your case?'

'Hard to tell if she's on my case or on Phiri's case via me. There's some exile history there. Phiri doesn't do the reciprocal altruism that the struggle has spawned.'

'Reciprocal altruism?' asked Clare.

'I did you a favour twenty years ago. Now it's payback time. Contracts, blind eyes, backhanders. Phiri is as straight as they come. Ruffled some senior feathers by expecting them to be the same.'

The waitress brought their coffee, ignored Riedwaan's cigarette, sauntered off and lit her own.

'Convince me that you haven't got her.' Clare stirred in the milk.

'My wife reported Yasmin missing to the police hotline. There's a new policy that's meant to stop the SAPS from shooting our wives and girlfriends on rugby weekends. Because there was a complaint against me with the Family Unit, an interdict was activated.'

'An interdict?' asked Clare.

'I hadn't seen Yasmin for weeks. It was my weekend to see her. Her mother refused. I …' he stopped.

'You what?'

'I took her anyway.'

'So you hire me and you look innocent.'

'It's not as simple as that.'

'Captain Faizal,' said Clare. 'Things are usually simple. We long for complex motives, but you know what? Most of the time, it's nothing. Just an impulse.'

'You think I don't know that?' asked Riedwaan. 'Sometimes I'd have a gun in my hand and I see two limp, bloody bodies at my feet and the gun is in my mouth, cold and clean and sweet as a Coke on a hot afternoon. Then I'd wake up.' He focused on her, as if seeing her face for the first time. 'And they would be breathing, Shazia and Yasmin, in their beds. Alive. Director Ndlovu's idea of sorting out my head was to send me to a government-issue shrink. She asked me questions about my family, my fantasies, my thoughts about love, about death.'

'What did you tell her?'

'I asked her how you told love and death apart. She made me another appointment. I didn't pitch, so that flagged me in some Swedish computer programme that measures mental health, gender attitudes and compliance with authority. I was marked as a man to watch, a man with secrets. A man made dangerous by love, according to the report. Or was it by death? I can't remember now.'

'And if I find her for you?' asked Clare. 'Then what?'

'I didn't say I wanted to kill them,' said Riedwaan. 'I'm telling you what gets into my head if I sleep. I'm telling you what I saw when we were called to a house in Goodwood. A whole street of policemen. A crescent. That house at the end. A guy I knew who was in the riot squad. He came home one day and shot his family. Then he called us and waited – with his service pistol in his mouth. He pulled the trigger when we opened the door – we went through and found them all. Wife. Two sons. Baby daughter. Bullet in the forehead. Each of them. I'm telling you why I moved out.'

Riedwaan stopped speaking.

'Okay.' Clare held up her hands. 'I'll accept what you're saying for the moment. You've looked at all the places she might have gone to? Granny, cousins, friends, hiding at school somewhere?'

'What do you think I've been doing while you've been watching ballet? She's nowhere.' Riedwaan pulled out his cellphone and pushed it across the table.

'Check that. Not one message, not one missed call. Except ...'

'Except what?' asked Clare.

'A missed call while I was at a crime scene. It was the call box at her ballet school.'

'What time was that?'

'Five-thirty-two. Her class should have finished at six-thirty. I didn't know and neither did Shazia, but they finished early today.'

'Who knew?'

'I checked with her teacher. Everybody, it seems.' Riedwaan lit another cigarette. 'Except me and Shazia, because she won't …' He stopped himself. 'Because we are unable to speak to each other, we seem to have missed that crucial little detail.'

He looked out of the window. Clare watched his reflection, wishing she still smoked.

'It's as if she vanished. No sign, no demands, no …' He couldn't say body, but both of them thought it, saw it. Saw her in the cold, eyes open, seeing nothing.

'Help me look for her.' He faced her again. 'View the CCTV footage at least. Cyclops Centre tomorrow morning. On the Foreshore.'

A siren blared in the distance. Riedwaan flicked his cigarette into his coffee cup.

'It's midnight.' The waitress had her coat on. 'We're closed. That's twenty rand.'

Clare and Riedwaan crossed the road together and stopped outside at her door.

'A deal?'

Clare put her hands on his arms, held him for a moment, her face against his. She hadn't meant to, but he looked so stricken.

'I'll see what the cameras have to say.'

She pulled her door closed behind her, leaned against it, listened to his footsteps recede. The smell of him lay on her skin. Fear, loneliness, cardamom.

fourteen

The light on Clare's desk was a golden splash in the darkness. The Promenade was empty; even the homeless were tucked away in doorways and bus shelters, out of the wind. A taxi stopped opposite the mini-golf course, which was closed for the winter. A single passenger alighted, a thin man wearing a mismatched suit jacket and pants. He walked towards the copse of trees that surrounded the overgrown labyrinth. Plenty of place to sleep there, but unpleasant in the cold. He turned once and looked back, seeming to stare straight up at Clare's window before disappearing into the darkness. Clare, chilled, took the white shawl from the back of her chair and wrapped it around her shoulders.

Her Apple laptop bleeped, signalling that the pages she wanted had been downloaded. She turned her attention to the internet search she'd done on Captain Riedwaan Faizal, the reports that had made it into the press, and a few others from websites she knew how to get into.

He had joined the police in 1990, the year of Nelson Mandela's release. In 1994 he'd been awarded a degree and transferred to the Detective Services. He had quite a reputation. A series of high-profile arrests. An apparent obsession with bringing in the hard men who stalked the Cape Flats. The senior gang members. The few cases against Riedwaan – one for assault and a couple for searches without a warrant, had melted away in court. His Gang Unit successful, so far. Most of the cases he'd brought, stuck. Even more unusually, his witnesses survived. An award for bravery for rescuing a fellow officer. Both of them wounded. What they were doing in the alley behind a crackhouse not well explained. The list of people who'd want him out of the way would probably fill a filing cabinet. A straight cop with a temper, who the tabloids loved?

The tip of an iceberg of trouble.

And his daughter? Maybe Yasmin had gone to visit an auntie or granny in a household where no one wondered at the presence of another six-year-old. She had simply been fed then ignored, and left to fall asleep with a heap of cousins. One more child, unnoticed. There was a chance – always prayed for, though seldom the case.

Not really.

Clare got up to look at the map on the wall. The wind had dropped, the quiet tightening a knot of anxiety in her throat. She opened the window to hear the waves slapping against the sea wall. Then she looked again at the portrait that Riedwaan had given her. A delicate oval face balanced on a slender neck. In her ballet pink, what she'd be wearing when they found her.

If they found her.

Clare pulled out her notes, skimming through what Riedwaan Faizal had told her. Winnowing the kernels of fact from the chaff of emotion.

1 Yasmin Faizal. Gifted dancer. Scholarship to expensive ballet school, six years old, seven on Tuesday. Weight 20 kilograms. Height 115 centimetres. Shoes: child size 12. Eyes dark brown. Hair: black, curly, waist-length when loose. Ears: pierced. Two gold hoops. Body: small birthmark on left hip; scar on right elbow from falling off a merry-go-round.

2 Shazia (mother, estranged wife) comes to collect Yasmin at ± 18:30. The ballet school is closed. No Yasmin. Shazia calls husband. No answer. Calls friends/relatives. No sign of her.

3 Shazia Faizal reports Yasmin missing. Police hotline. Call is logged.

4 Special Director Ndlovu is notified. Activates interdict against Faizal. Ndlovu declares him chief suspect. Ambiguity: Suspension? Arrest?

5 Yasmin has run away from home twice before. Once she went to her grandmother's.

6 Another time she refused to say where she had been, but showed no signs of physical harm. Both events happened after her parents had argued.

7 Riedwaan Faizal (father) misses call at 17:32 from the call box at the ballet school. No message.

8 Neither parent aware that that the school is closing early on Friday. Yasmin forgets to give them the note? Pianist Henry Harries (Mister Henry) closes up and leaves later. He said he had not seen her.

9 Yasmin's father went to the school at 16:00. Before her lesson.

10 Barred from case. Main suspect.

Clare ran her hand over the map, her fingers catching on the red pins she'd pushed into it. Open fields, dumpsites, subways, nightclub toilets, homes, an office, a churchyard. Each with a girl's name and a date attached to it. Her Persephone charts. Little girls, their truncated lives reduced to a single red flag on a map, to notes in the brown folder on her desk.

She opened it. Name, date of birth, date of death pencilled on the sheets. Her notes a summary of the evidence, if there was any, statements from witnesses, if there were any. A blurry snap of a smiling child at her last birthday party before she disappeared. That was usually all that remained: the photograph and a mother trudging daily to work, her grief clutched in her heart.

Noor Khan, who had been post-mortemed that evening, was slaughtered like a goat by a man her mother rented a room from.

Chanel Adams had gone to the shop and vanished. Bernadette Jaantjies, seven, was last seen by her friends walking hand-in-hand with an 'uncle' wearing jeans and a blue shirt.

Two little girls she'd tracked with the help of Pearl de Wet to a shebeen in Maitland. Sent by their gangster stepfather to pay off a drug debt. Yvette and Yvonne, six and nine. Cleaning toilets in the morning, their skinny bodies rented out at night. Too little evidence to jail the fat Austrian who'd been caught with them, and who claimed that girls in hot climates matured younger. He had thrown money at the case. In the end, the frustrated judge made him commit to the New Beginnings Clinic's sexual rehabilitation programme. The man complied and then flew home.

Then there was Tiffany Cloete, three, playing in the yard one minute, a bullet lodged in her back the next. Whether it was intentional or a stray from a gang fight, remained unresolved. Lindiwe September, six, seen getting into a taxi with a man nobody on her street recognised. The driver who dropped them in town said the child was crying, and the man told him he was taking her to the doctor. Body found in a drain near the harbour a week later.

Too many of them, the detail blurring with their faces. And now this new one. The one who didn't fit.

Yasmin Faizal.

Clare had to presume she was alive; had to bury the image of the child's body discarded like a used tissue. This work is what her life had become. Work she was good at, maybe the only thing she was good at. She didn't seem to be good at life.

The twinge of a headache. She switched off her light and put on the Beethoven piano concerto, as familiar to her as her own breathing. Closed her eyes, willing the music to ease the slow crescendo of the headache, the chords of her secret music.

One-thirty.

Clare closed her folder, the night's silence whispering around her. She walked down the passage, pulling her evening dress over her head, the black silk clammy as seaweed on her body. Then she wrapped herself in her gown and stepped onto the balcony off her bedroom. A fine spray drifted over the sea wall. In the pools of darkness between the lights along the Promenade, the shadows shifted.

The policeman's daughter, her photograph lying on the desk, another girl alone in the night. Another one. By now, Clare's headache was a vice.

fifteen

The pressure of her heart beating against her ribs.

Cold.

Dark.

So cold, so dark.

She tries to remember. The food. The takeaways. She'd tried to run but they were too fast for her.

The smell of oil burns Yasmin's throat. She feels a stickiness against her cheek. She moves the tip of her tongue. One, two teeth, then a gap. The bleeding has stopped but it still feels raw. Her tongue continues to probe. Another tooth, the pointed canine. Another gap, this one familiar. The tooth mouse had brought her ten rand for it.

She wants her mother.

The burn of not crying turns into a fire. A sob squeezes past her throat, and tears sting where the man's ring split the skin on her cheek.

She wants her father.

He will find her, save her from the darkness she's so afraid of.

He promised.

She breathes in, like her daddy said he does when he's afraid. The thud of blood in her ears fades, and she can listen.

Silence.

Absolute.

No washing up.

No television.

No mother murmuring into the phone.

She'd got used to her daddy's voice not being there in the night any more. But this didn't mean that she did not miss the steady deep note of his voice below the angry fizz of her mother's.

The pain in her face is real.

The cold is real.

The hunger twisting in her belly is real.

The piece of metal pressing into her is real.

She tries to lift her right hand but it will not move. Neither will the left. The attempt hurts, as the plastic tie cuts tighter into her wrists. She keeps still. That saves you if you are in danger. Keeping still, thinking. Her daddy says so, but making her mind work is not easy. Her thoughts are like birds caught against a window. The more you try to help them, the harder they fly into the glass, until, stunned, they fall to the floor, bleeding.

In her mind's eye she puts out her hands, picks up her thoughts, helps them to the open doorway. Tries to feel where she is.

If she knows where she is, her Daddy will be able to find her.

Her hands cannot move, but her legs can. Both together. There is a tie biting into her ankles. She swings her feet up, her knees hitting metal. She rolls her knees over to the right.

Metal again.

Back up and to the left. Nothing there. Except for hard rubber against her shins. A tyre. Metal presses into her back. A jack. Maybe a spanner. She breathes again. The smell of oil. She is in the boot of the car.

So cold, so dark.

Better than being dead.

A rectangle, where the dark is less dense. She twists her neck towards it. Glass by her head, a chink to the outside. Yasmin lies still, listening to the layers of silence beyond the broken tail light. The muffled sound of a dog barking. Then other dogs. And far, far away, the muezzin, calling her. Tears slide down into her ears. How will he find her when she can tell him so little? Diesel oil, a broken light, a dog, a faraway muezzin.

Footsteps.

A new voice.

The boot opens and hands reach in.

Her bladder, filled to bursting, overflows. She cries at the shame of wetting herself, not for the blow that it earns her.

August the tenth
SATURDAY

sixteen

The Saturday papers avalanched through Clare's front door, waking her from a restless sleep. She fetched them on her way to feed Fritz – as taciturn as Clare was until she'd had her morning coffee. She spread the papers out on the kitchen table. MISSING: TOP COP'S GIRL. Yasmin Faizal smiled up at her, hair netted, leotard encircled at the waist with a narrow band of elastic, skinny knees holding a plié. A photograph of Shazia Faizal, prim in her nurse's uniform. A picture of Riedwaan next to the two crumpled bodies of the girls shot dead in Maitland.

The story was spare on facts; generous on speculation. There was an undigested statement from Director Ndlovu on the need to stamp out domestic violence. An admission from her that searches of Captain Faizal's residence, that of his family, and other places where the child might be held, had been fruitless.

Unnamed sources talked about Riedwaan's service record, his heroism in rescuing his partner, his mandatory leave of absence, the stresses of work in the Gang Unit, the shooting of his previous partner Van Rensburg, the increasingly public feud between Phiri and Salome Ndlovu.

A police spokeswoman said that a search of the area – house-to-house questioning, dogs, specially trained officers, had revealed no evidence of the missing child. A homeless couple said they'd seen her waiting when they searched the dustbins across the road, that she had been eating something. But the caves nearby had been searched, and the gullies around the river combed for signs. There was no evidence of the child or her possessions.

Clare turned to page three and was startled to see a picture of herself, taken at last night's performance of *Persephone*. The ambiguously worded caption said that the child had disappeared during the performance, and there was speculation that Dr Clare Hart, who had been researching the recent murders of young girls, was involved in the case. Publicity. That was all she needed. She looked over the notes she had made last night. Very little pointed away from Yasmin's father.

Riedwaan Faizal had been seen there.

He had taken the child on previous occasions.

He had a motive. What would a father do if someone was planning to take his only child to Canada?

What would she do in that case?

Clare opened the kitchen window and put her crusts out for the sparrow waiting on the ledge. A bright-eyed urban survivor, the bird pecked hungrily.

The child's vanishing, going unnoticed in a quiet, policed suburb, indicated someone close. Someone intimate, someone inconspicuous. And yet something told her no.

Clare had believed him. It was that simple. That bothered her, though. She shoved her pepper spray into her pocket. Her phone, notebook, camera and recording equipment went into her leather backpack.

It was cold out; and too early to see Rita Mkhize. The sky was silvering above the distant Hottentots Holland Mountains as Clare drove across town and climbed up Buitenkant Street to the crags at the base of Devil's Peak. Gorge Road was narrow, and it fell steeply towards the city. A century earlier it had been a winding footpath, and before that a game track where animals ran, single file, to escape sharp-eyed hunters. At six-thirty it was deserted. Just sprays of glass from smashed car windows. Cape Town's confetti. The old-aged home opposite the school lay asleep, waiting for the morning staff to arrive and start the day – except for one square of light on the top floor, five flats along. And in the wooden hut nearby, a nightwatchman sat hunched over a crackling radio.

If Yasmin had walked off, it would have been with someone she knew. It'd be hard to pull a six-year-old down a long street, unseen. Clare walked towards the overgrown entrance to the ballet school. Next to it was a recess in the foliage, offering respite from the wind. As she hunkered down into it, Clare saw the bright pink, a snagged strand of wool. She eased it off the bougainvillea thorn. Yasmin's ballet cardigan. The child must have waited in this spot, in the gathering dark. Clare photographed every angle, picturing a man in a car, hidden among the pines.

A stalker would have waited right there, tucked out of sight behind the scrub, watching for his prey: Yasmin's vulnerability logged, her abduction precisely planned – and then executed. Or if it was chance, Yasmin being in the wrong place at the wrong time, the abductor would have seized the opportunity that is a solitary child. Either way, the hunter would have tensed, leaned forward, his breathing becoming shallow the second the child stepped into view.

A car slipped down the road towards Clare. With barely a glance, the driver swept past her.

She walked up the hill, past open bins with their evidence of too many meals eaten alone, single servings of ready-prepared food, chocolate wrappers, the sad pleasures of the lonely and the old. Three men – SOLID WASTE emblazoned on their yellow shirts – were tossing the bins up onto the back of a truck. Clare walked to the driver's door.

'Yes, lady?' He leaned out of his window.

'This your route?' asked Clare.

The driver took a drag of his cigarette.

'Friday evening, Saturday morning. Why?'

'I'm looking for a girl,' said Clare.

'So was I.' The man's mouth curled into a thin smile. 'Looks like I found her.'

'A six-year-old,' said Clare. 'She went missing yesterday afternoon. Were you here yesterday?'

'We came this way about six. Half-past, maybe. Did the houses. Today's *mos* institutions. The school, the old *toppies*. The council outsourced us. Made us free enterprises. Means we work seven days a week for the same money we got working for the council for five. What's she look like?'

Clare showed him the picture.

'Ag, shame. Such a small girlie. I didn't see her.' He gave a loud whistle. The men loading were around Clare in a second. 'Ask them,' he said.

'Did any of you see this little girl yesterday?' asked Clare. 'About the time you came through here. After five, before six.'

The men wiped their hands on the sides of their pants and passed the photograph round.

'No.' One after the other.

'Anything you saw here yesterday that was different?' she asked.

'Like what?' A skinny man, putting his gloves on again.

'Something different from what you usually see,' said Clare. 'A smell, some sounds, someone you don't usually see here. A car in an odd place. Could seem like nothing.'

The men passed the photograph of Yasmin around again. Shook their heads.

'Sorry, lady.' The driver handed the photograph back to Clare. 'I hope you find her.'

Clare was doing her seatbelt up when the man appeared at the passenger window. He was out of breath from running. The rubbish truck was back, idling in the empty street.

'Sorry, sorry for the fright.' He was studying Clare's face, hands clamped onto the car window. 'I've seen you before. I told them. Aren't you on TV?'

'Sometimes,' said Clare

'I told them.' Triumphant. '*Survivor*?'

Clare shook her head.

'*Idols*?' Sceptical.

'No,' said Clare. '*Missing*. About the missing girls.'

'Pearl,' he said to her. 'I remember her. Pearl, was that her name? Thursday night, *mos*. For Women's Day. She said her father's a general in the 27s. He did things to her. That everyone thinks he's this strong man, but he's a coward because he picks on young girls.' The man's voice rose in indignation. 'His own daughter, *nogal*.'

'That's the one.' Clare started her car.

'It's her.' Pointing at Clare, grinning gummily at his companions. 'The one who went after the gangsters, told their secrets on TV.'

'You should watch yourself, *nooi*.' He turned back to Clare, his hand on her window again. 'The 27s kill people who tell their secrets. You didn't show the girl's face, but they can find you easy.'

He sprinted up the road, swinging himself up onto the truck. The driver hit the sound system and the bass juddered.

seventeen

The only car parked outside the ballet school was an old yellow Beetle. The piano music, a waltz by Liszt or Schubert, stopped when Clare knocked.

'Dr Hart.' Madame Merle was taken aback as she opened the door. 'Are you here about last night's performance?'

'It was a great success.' Clare stepped past Madame Merle into the cold room. 'But that's not why I'm here. I've come about one of your little scholarship girls, Yasmin Faizal.'

'I have a class in fifteen minutes.' Madame Merle tapped her wrist. 'How have you become ensnared with the Faizal family?'

'I look for little girls who go missing.' Clare followed Madame Merle into her studio. 'Yasmin went missing from here.'

A man stood by the window, his figure dark against the morning light.

'You've not met my piano man.' Madame Merle followed Clare's gaze. 'Henry Harries, officially. Everyone here calls him Mister Henry.'

'Hello.' Clare put out her hand, and the man's pallid fingers lay limp in hers.

'We went over this with Captain Faizal last night. With the mother, too.' Madame Merle fitted her cigarette into the long filter, flared her lighter, and leaned against the broad windowsill. 'I had a call from the mother first. Told her that if Yasmin wasn't at the school, it was probably the same as last time.'

'And Captain Faizal?'

94

'Told him that if Yasmin wasn't with him this time, then she probably went home with one of the other girls.'

'But she didn't,' said Clare.

Madame Merle blew smoke rings in the air.

'This has happened before, Dr Hart. Last time there was all this song and dance and it turned out that the child had run away from her mother. A difficult woman. Volatile. The child wanted to go and live with her father. She was found unharmed. The next time, it was the father who took her. Picked her up early from school and kept her for the weekend in some beach shack.'

'If I'm to find her,' said Clare, 'I need to know who she is and what she does.'

Madame Merle sighed. 'Yasmin comes here straight after school every day. I assume her taxi dropped her as usual yesterday. She joined her class and danced perfectly. Class was dismissed. She gave me a hug and left. I didn't see her again. I have a class straight after – the senior girls. You saw them last night. The chorus in *Persephone*.'

'Where did she go after she said goodbye?'

'That way.' Madame Merle waved a manicured hand towards the passage. 'The change-rooms are that way. Big girls on the right, behind that door. Little ones on the left.'

'Who keeps an eye on them?' asked Clare.

'Nobody. We're a ballet school, not a crèche.'

'Yasmin spent long hours here.'

'An exception,' said Madame Merle. 'A police officer and a nurse can't afford an au pair. Yasmin has a scholarship, so she has to dance every day. As I said, she comes here after school, then does her homework while waiting for her class. Her mother always fetches her after her shift ends. Six, sometimes half-past.'

'So who waited with her?'

'Calvaleen used to—' Henry began.

'I teach till seven,' interrupted Madame Merle. 'She was never fetched later than that.'

'Calvaleen?' asked Clare, turning to Henry

The ballet mistress pivoted on an elegant ankle.

'One of our older dancers. Dropped out. Yasmin looked up to her – they came from the same background – but she hasn't been here for some time.'

'There was no one else that Yasmin was close to?'

'I've no idea. She was so much better than the other girls. Is. Is so much better ...' Her voice trailed off; silence hung in the cold air. 'I'm sorry. It's just that ... we've been so busy recently.'

'You finished early on Friday,' said Clare. 'How were the parents informed?'

'The children were given notes to bring back signed,' said Madame Merle. 'I'm not very good with email yet.'

'Yasmin brought hers back?'

'She must have done.'

'Who collects the notes?'

'Henry does.'

'Can I see?' asked Clare.

'Get the folder, will you?' Madame Merle turned to Henry. 'It's in my desk, top drawer.'

'The change-rooms,' said Clare.

'Of course. This way.' Clare followed Madame Merle down the dimly lit corridor.

'There are few who can tolerate the discipline of ballet,' said Madame Merle. 'Though not a meek child, Yasmin was one of them.'

The 'was' again. Clare let it ride.

'Tell me about her,' said Clare.

'She's a self-sufficient little girl. Tougher than the pampered Constantia princesses I teach. And she had something. An attunement to music. It was as if she absorbed its sound through her skin, and the music then moved her. That's what dancing should be, a physical manifestation of music. And another thing: Yasmin had a resilience beyond her years.'

'You said she wasn't easy.'

'How could she be?' was the response. 'Look at her father. A law unto himself.'

'How was she on Friday?'

Madame Merle closed her hooded eyes, thoughtful. 'Maybe she was anxious. Maybe not. Maybe she just wanted a hug. She's a lonely little girl. She loves me; all my pupils do. Love and fear: it's what makes them dance.'

Yasmin's locker was empty, except for a half-eaten banana. Madame Merle took it out and dropped it in a bin.

Henry stood at the end of the passage, an envelope in his hand.

'You find it?' asked Madame Merle.

'No signed form from Yasmin's family. An oversight.'

Madame Merle flicked through the contents, twice. Dug for another cigarette.

'You get one from Calvaleen?' asked Clare.

Henry rummaged through the sheaf of papers. 'Ja. Here it is. Looks like her father signed it.'

A car crunched on the gravel outside. A door slammed shut and two sets of feet pattered up the path. Two little girls burst into the door, skidding to a stop when they saw the three silent adults standing there.

'Good morning Madame Merle and Mister Henry and Miss ... Lady.' The two girls stood staring at Clare. Madame Merle clapped her hands.

'Off with you, girls. Change and go and warm up on the barre.'

They slalomed off to the change-rooms.

'Can I keep those forms?' asked Clare. 'And your class lists.

We'll need to contact these parents. See if any of them saw anything, do some background checks.'

'You'll be discreet? This is my livelihood.'

'Of course,' said Clare.

Mister Henry gave Clare the envelope.

'Anything else?' asked Madame Merle.

'A word with Mister Henry.'

'He's never with the girls unsupervised,' said Madame Merle. 'The rules are so strict these days, especially after there was an incident at the school – with that chess teacher, wasn't it, Henry? Nothing to do with us. Anyway, class begins in ten minutes.' Madame Merle turned around and disappeared into the studio.

'You're here every day?' asked Clare.

'Every afternoon. Monday, Wednesday, Friday evenings. Saturdays. On Tuesdays and Thursdays I do some voluntary work.'

'Oh, what kind?'

'Music therapy,' said Mister Henry. 'At an addiction clinic.'

'Do you manage to make a living from your music?'

'Well, I don't really need much.'

Mister Henry walked outside with Clare.

'So, Yasmin's here every day?' she asked.

'Pretty much,' he said. Her dancing's been the one thing that hasn't changed in her life.'

The parking lot was clogged with cars. Pink-clad girls spilled out, chattering as they swirled up the path, shoes in one hand. A piece of elastic circled their little bodies where their waists should be.

'Tell me about Yasmin.' Clare leaned against her car, making no move to open the door. 'What she was like when class finished early?'

'She seemed upset. She asked Madame Merle about it.'

'And what did she say?'

'She sent her packing.' Mister Henry pulled at a piece of skin on his thumb. 'She only sees the children when they are dancing.'

'And you?'

'I see the dancer.' Mister Henry looked at the stragglers dawdling up the path. 'And I see their pain.'

'Shazia Faizal tells me you saw a blue Mazda here in the afternoon.'

Henry nodded.

'Captain Faizal's car?'

He nodded again.

'You know the car?' asked Clare.

'I know it,' said Henry.

'He was driving?'

'He was here in the middle of the afternoon. That's what I told Mrs Faizal.'

'You didn't tell him the school was closing early?'

'I didn't think about it,' said Mister Henry. 'Everybody knew.'

'She's missing, Mister Henry.' Clare stepped closer to him. 'What else did you see?'

He stepped away from her, and a gust of wind off the mountain snatched the words from his mouth.

'What did you say?' asked Clare.

'I saw her here.' He bit the loose skin next to his fingernail. 'After the class.' He pointed to the overgrown gate. 'I'd come out for a smoke. I saw her.'

'You saw nobody else?' she asked.

'Not a soul. This is a wealthy area. Once the maids go home there's no one about.'

'What was she doing?'

'Standing there near the gate. I called her and she looked at me. That's when I saw the tears.'

'Did you ask her why she was crying?'

'Madame Merle called me right then, so I went inside. I was going to ask her afterwards, but by then she was gone.' The sun came out. It was behind Henry, and Clare couldn't see what was in his eyes.

Madame Merle leaned out of a window.

'Mister Henry,' she called, 'warm up.'

'I must go.' He hurried away.

A few seconds later, Mister Henry appeared at the window. He held Clare's gaze for a moment before banging it shut.

eighteen

Riedwaan's hands were scratched and his shoes wet from working his way up the ravine that separated Devil's Peak from Table Mountain. After leaving Clare the night before, he'd ridden directly to the mountain. There, he'd repeated the search organised by Rita Mkhize that Friday evening. He had zigzagged his way up territory familiar from his childhood, when, with his friends, he'd slid down the smooth granite cliffs of the waterfall.

Like the police dogs, Riedwaan had found no trace of Yasmin. By four, the tablecloth of cloud forced him, cold and exhausted, to take shelter under an overhang. He'd slept fitfully for a couple of hours. At dawn he had worked his way down again, past the ballet school with the Beetle parked outside. Next to it was a green Mini. Clare's car.

Riedwaan headed towards his house in the Bo-Kaap. Unlocking it, he paused briefly at the second bedroom.

'Yasmin's Palace' – the sign hung askew on her door.

Feeling his knees give way, he dropped into an armchair. The only chair in the room. He looked at the scattered bits of bunk bed he'd promised Yasmin he'd assemble, the tools still lying there from his first and only attempt. The Jack Daniel's beckoned him. His glass next to the bottle on the table. Riedwaan got up and put it away in a cupboard, ignoring the voice that said one whiskey wouldn't hurt.

One wouldn't. It'd be the second that would cause the trouble. And the third and the rest of the bottle. He took the glass to the kitchen and filled it without rinsing it, swallowed the water. Traces of whiskey under the dust. He filled the kettle, put on the gas, splashed his face above the dirty dishes in the sink. The kitchen air smelt stale, so he opened the door onto the courtyard. When the kettle boiled, he spooned some Nescafé into the least dirty mug.

Riedwaan Faizal's phone was out of his pocket before the second ring. 'Private number' flashed on the screen.

'Faizal.'

'De Lange.'

Shorty de Lange from ballistics, the lab buried in trees and scrub forty kilometres east of Cape Town.

'I heard about your daughter,' said De Lange. 'You find—'

Riedwaan cut him off. 'Not yet.'

'I'm sorry, man.' Riedwaan waited; Shorty de Lange was not a man you hurried. 'I didn't like that crime scene, those two little girls. Something new, that – two girls with no known connection to any gangsters, shot like dogs.'

'Ja.' The kitchen door blew shut. 'Fuck it.'

The two warm bodies heaped together in that open field in Maitland seemed like a lifetime ago.

'Come over to the lab,' said Shorty. 'I think you should see what I've got.'

Riedwaan left the mug on the counter with last week's bread, and shut the front door behind him.

Half an hour later, he swerved onto the off-ramp to the lab, daring the road to claim him. It didn't, and he slowed down at the security entrance. The guards waved him through.

De Lange was waiting for him.

'Rita Mkhize called me.' He held Riedwaan's eye. 'Said you'd been suspended.'

'What else?'

'Said I should keep you in the loop. That she'd answer for it.'

'She's a good girl,' said Riedwaan.

'Tough, that lady.'

They were walking down the unlit corridor. It was empty except for the posters of gunshot wounds tacked onto the walls.

'What you got here?' Riedwaan's voice was working, but only just.

'A feeling.'

'Since when did you get feelings, Shorty? Unless it's winter or your wife forgot to pack your lunch. Cold. Hungry. Those are your feelings.'

De Lange's office was decorated with the colours of the Free State rugby team. The walls were lined with pictures of the players. Two were autographed by a lock whose parents had been shot on their farm. Shorty had found the cartridges, tracked the guns, matched them. The killers were both fifteen years old. Third offence. They got thirty years each.

De Lange picked up a brown folder and several small, clear packets. All except one contained cartridges. The other held two crumpled bullets.

'From the younger girl,' explained De Lange. 'The pathologist got them for me. Looks like they went straight through her older sister's body. She didn't weigh much, according to the post-mortem report – but still, her fifty-two kilos was enough to slow them down. They lodged in the little sister she was trying to protect.'

Riedwaan picked them up. So small in his hand. No dark family secrets to reveal, just bullets crashing through young lungs, stopping young hearts.

'I'll show you.' De Lange unlocked the computer room. Inside, the air conditioning hummed, cooling the four large computers standing on a scuffed square of linoleum. De Lange tapped a keyboard.

'Here.' He pointed to the close-ups of cartridges, the six grooves distinct where the bullet had spun down the barrel. 'Six perfect matches. Same gun fired all these shots. Ibis went into orbit over these.' He'd called up the International Ballistics Information System on his computer.

'So, what were those?'

'That gun's been out of action for a while, but it has been used before. Five cases came up on the database.'

'Let me see them,' said Riedwaan.

De Lange downloaded the files. No arrests, but a record of all the bullets that were found at the murder scenes. De Lange kept track of them all, trying to find patterns in the shootings that terrified people living on the Flats.

'Gang violence?' asked Riedwaan.

De Lange nodded. 'Turf war.' He opened a map of the Cape Peninsula. 'A dealer in Heideveld, a couple of gangsters, a mother going to church in Mitchell's Plain – she was a witness to the first shooting, apparently. And a kid reading a story in bed to his little sister caught a bullet in the head.'

'Where?' asked Riedwaan.

'Edge of Maitland.'

'Okay, but that's four,' said Riedwaan. 'You said five.'

'The fifth case is this one.' De Lange opened the last file. The same detailed close-ups of the bullets found in the bodies, and the casings sprayed across the crime scenes. 'That triple murder near Paarl. Mother, grandmother, a little girl. The women were farmworkers. The little girl just happened to be there.'

'Graveyard de Wet,' said Riedwaan.

The name cooled the room as effectively as any air conditioning.

'A general in the 27s, last time he was inside,' De Lange said. 'It was one of the cases I gave expert testimony in. You sent him down. No weapon ever found, but the judge didn't care. Life without parole. This gun was only ever used where Graveyard de Wet was involved. This is his gun.'

'I know, Shorty, I know. You said so at the time,' said Riedwaan. 'But what have those two schoolgirls got to do with a long-dead turf war?'

'Nothing, that I know of,' said Shorty. 'But this gun knows.'

'Guns and gang wars,' Riedwaan was thinking out loud. 'The last time I looked, that lowlife de Wet was in jail.'

'You've checked?' asked Shorty. 'There was the president's prisoner amnesty so that he could free all his buddies who are in jail for corruption. He let out a few other lowlifes to make it less obvious.'

'No one got amnesty if a weapon was involved. Members of parliament, fraudsters, shoplifters, embezzlers, yes. But no gangsters, no rapists, no killers.'

'You sure?'

'I saw the list,' said Riedwaan. 'New legislation. They have to.'

'You know who those girls were?' asked De Lange.

'Identified at the scene. Father, brothers, uncles all clean. They were in the wrong place at the wrong time. Some gangster moving himself up the ladder.'

'You should check it out yourself, Faizal. I'm suspicious. It's my job. It's been a long time since that gun was used. And now it's back.' De Lange paused. 'The same day your daughter goes missing. The day you get suspended.'

'I'll check it out.' Riedwaan scrolled through his phone for his contact in Correctional Services. He gave him the name – Graveyard de Wet.

Five minutes, and he called back.

'And?' Shorty asked.

'Graveyard de Wet's not been using that gun,' Riedwaan said. 'He's dead. No relatives want his body, so there's a pauper's funeral on Friday.'

'That's good news, then.'

Riedwaan took out a coin. He tossed it: heads. He flipped it again: tails.

'I suppose it is.'

Shorty walked with Riedwaan to his motorbike. He rested his broad hand on Riedwaan's shoulder for a moment. A bontebok grazing nearby bolted, her calf at her heels, when Riedwaan kicked his bike to life.

nineteen

An invisible eye on Clare's face, the oculus in the door darkened for a moment. Then the deadbolt unlocked and Shazia Faizal stood framed in the doorway.

'Yes?' A wedding photo hung on the wall behind her. Shazia in white satin, her swelling belly only partially hidden by the bouquet. Riedwaan next to her, handsome in a dark suit, his eyes focused on a spot beyond the photographer. Clare felt as if he were watching her.

'Dr Hart. They said you'd be coming.' A thin woman, her black hair cropped short, appeared behind Shazia. The hand she extended to Clare was papery to the touch. 'Latisha van Rensburg. My husband is Inspector Clinton van Rensburg. Come through.'

In the sitting room, the television chattered to itself. Latisha van Rensburg led Shazia to the sofa.

'Please sit, Dr Hart.'

The two women were silhouetted against the view of Table Bay wallpapered across the window. Clare sat opposite them.

'Special Director Ndlovu assured Shazia that she must just wait,' said Latisha. 'That Captain Faizal was profiled as risky but not homicidal, and that he wouldn't bluff it much longer.'

'He knows where she is,' whispered Shazia. 'He must.'

'We'll find her again.' Latisha put an arm around her. 'You did before.'

'Why is he doing this to me?' asked Shazia, all authority relinquished to the older woman at her side.

107

'What happened the last time?' asked Clare.

'Riedwaan took her, he kept her for the weekend,' said Shazia. 'That's when I got the interdict against him.'

'Did you think Riedwaan would harm Yasmin?' asked Clare. 'Or you?'

'Not that time.'

'Has he ever hurt you?'

'No, but he's never here, is he? Always at work, always with his unit.'

'So, why the interdict?' asked Clare.

Shazia's eyes flashed, the slow burn of marital anger flaring beneath her anxiety.

'They told us after the family violence workshop. You might have heard, the police captain who shot his wife and his three children. Director Ndlovu didn't want us to take any risks. Riedwaan wouldn't sign the papers for Canada. We're going in a week, and Riedwaan has to sign if I'm going to get there in time to start my new job.'

That explained the pale patches on the walls where pictures had been removed. The uncurtained windows, the boxes stacked behind the furniture.

'Your husband's not going to follow you?'

'He was offered a job there, but he won't. I said he had to choose, and he chose his work. Chasing those gangsters is all he cares about. He said he'd sign, but when I went to fetch Yasmin and she wasn't there and he didn't answer my calls, I knew it was just another one of his lies. He's got her, and this time he's not going to let her go. So I phoned the hotline.' Shazia twisted her hands together. 'Director Ndlovu said we were to phone directly. The call centre routes any calls to her so that she can see that something's done before ... before ...'

'Before any violence,' said Latisha. 'It was to prevent any more family murders.'

108

'Director Ndlovu is a psychiatrist,' said Shazia. 'She assessed him and she says that he's a risk.'

There was doubt in her eyes. Because she was wrong about her husband? Or the doubt that gets you killed, that lulls you into giving the man who sleeps in your bed, the father of your children, one more chance. The gap he needs to kill you. Clare rubbed her temples, feeling the familiar dull beat behind her eyes.

'What do you need from us?' Latisha asked.

'Photographs,' said Clare. 'Pictures of Yasmin. There's a chance that if she was taken, there may be an image of her somewhere on one of the cameras in the city.'

'Shazia?' Latisha put both her hands on Shazia's face. 'Look at me. Listen to her. Yasmin's your baby. You must keep the possibility in mind that … that she's somewhere else.'

Shazia shook her head.

'Can Dr Hart have the photographs?' asked Latisha. 'She'll return them soon.'

'In the cabinet in the sitting room there's an album.'

Latisha fetched it, handed it to Clare. On the first page, a shock-haired infant – a hospital tag still on her wrist – lying in the crook of a muscular arm.

Then Yasmin's first portrait, both parents leaning over her, their dark heads touching, eyes on the sleeping baby between them. On the swings in the park, feeding the squirrels in the Gardens, on Riedwaan's shoulders on the top of Lion's Head. In a ruffled *Eid* dress at the end of Ramadan. First day in Grade One. And this year, her wild hair plaited, Yasmin as Bo Peep. A graceful child in a tulle skirt, surrounded by blonde sheep. White leotards, black shoes, little black ears pinned onto their buns. A photograph taken at a picnic, before Clinton van Rensburg had needed a crutch.

One of Yasmin holding hands with a girl in lemon tulle and pointe shoes.

'Calvaleen auditioning for *Persephone*.' Latisha trailed her fingers over the image. The mother's angled cheekbones, her closed expression, were echoed in the girl's face. 'My daughter.'

'I'd like to talk to her. See what she can tell me about Yasmin.'

'It's been a while since we've seen her,' said Latisha. 'You know, she's always been so kind to little Yasmin – it's not easy for these girls, having a policeman as a father. And Calvaleen's not dancing much any more, either.'

'That's a pity,' said Clare, admiring Calvaleen's graceful limbs in the photo.

'She's only seventeen, but she's been making a living from it with the Russian ballet,' said Latisha. 'She was lucky to get into the Winter Palace, considering.'

'Considering what?'

'She's had a tough time since her father was shot, *mos*,' Shazia said. Latisha put her hand on Shazia's arm, and she fell silent again.

After a few moments, Latisha looked up at Clare again. 'Competition, you know, from overseas, it's always tough.'

'Dancing is tough,' said Clare. 'She must be in her last year of school if she's seventeen.'

'She manages the dancing okay,' said Latisha, folding her hands in her lap. 'She's become – well, independent, in the last few months.'

'Can I have her number? It wasn't on the list I got for Rita.' Notebook out, pen poised as Latisha recited the cellphone number to her.

Clare turned to the next page in the photo album. Nothing. The blank pages waiting for Yasmin's life to unfold. Silence in the stuffy room, and outside, the sound of the southeaster moaning around the building. She put the album in her bag.

'Shazia, can you tell me what happened yesterday, in detail, starting in the morning,' Clare asked. 'Everything, doesn't matter how small. To find Yasmin, we need information.'

110

'Okay,' said Shazia. 'I'll try.'

'Who wakes up first – you or Yasmin?'

'Me,' said Shazia. 'I wake up and go through to her room.'

'Then let's start there.'

Yasmin's bed was unmade. A discarded pair of *broekies* lay on the floor.

'We were late,' said Shazia, walking towards the kitchen. 'Again. I had coffee; she had breakfast.' On the counter, an open box of Coco Pops, a plastic bowl and spoon. The fridge was festooned with Yasmin's drawings.

'I took her to school and I kissed her goodbye. I went to work, to the hospital. I was working overtime, so I said I'd pick her up at six. I didn't know they were finishing early.' Shazia shook her head. 'Riedwaan must have known. Must have used it.'

Clare looked through the notices on the fridge, half of them out of date. Homework, ballet schedule, a cake sale at school. Another possibility: a distressed little girl had forgotten to give the notice to her harried mother, wanting to avoid more conflict, more shouting, trying to solve a problem she had created by falling into the chasm between her parents. Had she hidden? Waited? Told herself her mother would come? That nothing would happen if she kept still as a mouse?

'So, you went to work,' said Clare. 'And then you went to fetch her. When?'

'Six, maybe just after.'

'Try and remember exactly.'

'Director Ndlovu didn't ask me all these questions,' said Shazia. 'Only Riedwaan asks me questions like these.'

'It'll help,' said Clare. 'Everything you can remember.'

'Maybe six-thirty.'

'What did you find?'

'It was dark; all shut up. She wasn't there.' Shazia covered her face with her hands. 'Mister Henry said he'd seen Riedwaan's car. That's when I called the emergency number Director Ndlovu gave me. I had to. He's not going to stop me from taking her to Canada.'

'Did Mister Henry say he'd seen Yasmin?' asked Clare.

'How would he?' asked Shazia. 'Her head doesn't show over the back seat.'

'Let's bear in mind the possibility that her father did not take Yasmin,' said Clare. 'He has asked me to help find her.'

'That will just make people think that he doesn't have her,' Shazia interrupted.

'But if he hasn't got her, ' said Clare, 'we need to find her now.'

Shazia's arms folded around her empty lap.

'I'll let you out,' said Latisha.

Clare took the stairs, expelling the flat's stale air from her lungs.

twenty

'It's still Friday night in here, this early on a Saturday morning,' said Rita Mhize.

She led Clare through the charge office where a bemused reservist was trying to persuade a woman not to strip. 'D'you always have this effect on the ladies, Brown?'

'She refuses to be released.' In the second that the Sergeant's attention was distracted, the woman had her top off and was bolting back towards the cells, singing the national anthem.

'A regular,' said Rita. 'She takes her clothes off when she's arrested and she takes them off again when she's released. The poor guys never know where to put their hands.'

They turned down a dimly-lit passage, its walls cutting off the hubbub of the charge office.

'Captain Faizal said you've agreed to help him ...'

'Not exactly,' said Clare. 'I said I'd look at the CCTV footage.'

'You've been talking to his wife, though.'

'Hedging my bets,' said Clare.

'I haven't had breakfast yet,' said Rita, stopping at the vending machine. 'You want a Coke?'

'I'd love one.' Clare rooted in her bag for change.

'Don't worry about it.' Rita slotted in a few coins and jabbed a button. Two Cokes plummeted down. 'This machine always gives two.' She handed one to Clare. 'And can you believe this? A building full of cops, and it's never been reported.'

'Shocking.' Clare cracked open the can.

A door opened, spilling light into the passageway.

'Morning, ladies.'

'Superintendent van Rensburg. You gave me a fright. This is Dr Clare Hart,' said Rita. The man with the crutch nodded towards Clare.

'My wife says she met you. Latisha. She's with Shazia,' said Van Rensburg, stepping aside. 'This is Delport.'

'Faizal's lady friend?' Delport looked Clare over.

'News travels fast,' she observed.

'Unusual choice for him, you.' Delport slotted in coins then shook the machine for a Fanta.

'You here to work?' asked Rita. 'Or you just here to clash with the décor?'

'Things to do,' said Delport, following Van Rensburg into his immaculate office.

'Who're they?' asked Clare as they went downstairs.

'Gang Unit. Van Rensburg and Captain Faizal go back a long way,' said Rita. 'His mentor once; his buffer when he joined pre-'94. I don't think it was so easy then. Delport was with narcotics, seconded into the Gang Unit when Van Rensburg was disabled.'

'You don't like him?'

'I don't like men who try and grope me while I'm on duty,' said Rita.

Clare followed her into the cramped room. A single photograph of Yasmin had been stuck to the wall, next to the charts of completed searches.

'Your show now?' asked Clare.

'There's no way Special Director Ndlovu's letting this one go. She's decided that Captain Faizal's bluffing and that she's going to call it.'

'She'll sacrifice Yasmin for that?'

'She's got some political agenda of her own that she's following. For herself or for someone high up.' Rita closed the door. 'The gravy train's a struggle. You have to fight to catch it, it's slippery once you're on, but if you hang in there, you're made for life. What's one little girl in that equation?'

Rita banged open a window, the air a welcome relief.

'She adores her father, that little girl,' said Rita. 'Things have been tough for Riedwaan and she hasn't been able to spend time with him.'

'Troubled kids go missing,' said Clare. 'Tell me about her father and mother.'

'Shazia says Captain Faizal's a bad husband. Ndlovu agrees.'

'Is he?' asked Clare.

'Wives and cops,' said Rita. 'Not a winning combination. She's so angry with Riedwaan that she takes it out on Yasmin sometimes.'

'Poor little thing,' said Clare.

'She's her daddy's girl. She's tough like him. Stubborn. Smart, wants to know why all the time. Can see no fault in her father. Drives her mother crazy.'

'What are his faults?' asked Clare.

'Good faults,' said Rita. 'Cop faults. It's the job. Works three weekends out of four overtime. Follows through on his cases. Earns nothing. Not much he can do about it.'

'So, what's the problem?' asked Clare.

'Shazia wants the world to be predictable. She picked the wrong man for that.'

Rita had been sifting through witness statements from the shooting of the two girls in Maitland. She moved them out of the way to clear space on her desk.

'Find anything?' asked Clare.

'Nothing,' said Rita. 'Two girls shot in broad daylight, and no-body hears or sees anything. And you?'

Clare handed Rita the list of parents that Madame Merle had given her.

'The parents who would have been fetching last night. Maybe

the might of the law that you have behind you will trigger their memories.'

'I doubt it,' said Rita, scanning through the list. 'What about the staff?'

'Madame Merle and the piano player.' Clare checked her notes. 'Henry Harries.'

'Anyone else?' asked Rita.

'Check out all the fathers too. You never know, maybe one of them went back to the school.'

'You have a low opinion of men,' Rita commented.

'Hasn't paid, in my experience, to give them the benefit of the doubt,' said Clare. 'Nothing on the dedicated line?'

'A few of our usual *malletjies*, but otherwise, nothing.'

'Can you do one more thing for me?' Clare asked.

'I'm all yours, for now.'

'Henry Harries – everyone calls him Mister Henry – plays the piano at the ballet school.'

'Any particular reason you want me to check him out?' asked Rita.

'Proximity. Opportunity. He seemed on edge.'

'Clare, you could put anyone on edge,' said Rita.

'You've spoken to her teachers?' asked Clare. 'Everyone at the school?'

'All the numbers I have are in your folder.' Rita looked away. 'There've been some issues.'

'You must tell me,' said Clare.

'The security says Captain Faizal was there that afternoon. At the ballet school,' said Rita. 'Before he came to Maitland, where those girls were shot. He tell you that?'

'Yes. And Henry Harries told me too. Riedwaan said he just wanted to see her,' said Clare. 'That he drove away and left her there.'

'You believed him?' Rita searched Clare's face for the answer she wanted.

'I didn't believe or not believe,' said Clare.

'You're working for him, though.'

'I want to find that little girl,' said Clare. 'If he took her, I'll work it out.'

'I need to believe in my team,' said Rita, shaking her head. 'I need to know I've got back-up.'

'That's why you joined the force?' asked Clare. 'To have a team?'

'The long answer or the short answer?'

'The long answer's good.'

'When I was eleven, my father was shot twice in the head for his gardener's pay packet. A hundred bucks, after the taxi fare from Rondebosch to Crossroads,' said Rita. 'I knew the boys who did it. They were *skollies* who lived at the end of our street. Where we lived, there were no street names, no numbers on the houses. Hard to get the cops to come there for one more body in a ditch by the N2. I went with my mother to confront them, but they just laughed. Later that night, someone wedged our door shut and torched our shack. I was skinny, so I could wriggle between the corrugated iron wall and the sand floor.'

Rita tossed a piece of paper at the bin, scoring a direct hit.

'My mother didn't make it. I stood there, watching my house burn. I didn't even have a body to bury. Mother, mattress, mielie pap, school books. All turned to ash, all mixed up together. I stood there until this old cop put his hand on my shoulder and asked me if I had somewhere to go. I said no. I told him we were new from the Eastern Cape. Just me, my mother, my father. Not a proper Xhosa family.'

'And then? What happened?' asked Clare.

'He asked me if I wanted to come home with him, said his wife would give me something to eat, and they'd get me sorted out with social welfare on the Monday.'

'You went?' asked Clare.

'I went. What else was I going to do? She was kind, his wife.

I was there a long time before anyone from welfare came to fill out my forms. Welfare said I'd fallen through the cracks, but the social workers never came back. In the end, they kept me, the old cop in Goodwood and his wife.'

'You find them yet, those boys?'

'Many like them,' said Rita. 'There's more people willing to burn a woman in her bed than you think.'

'Has it helped,' asked Clare. 'Being a cop?'

'You know,' said Rita, 'there's forms and procedures and shit, but sometimes you can help. You don't think about it, you don't get permission, you just do it.'

'Riedwaan does that?' asked Clare

'May not always be legal. May not be procedure. But if it's right, you do it and deal with the consequences later.'

'D'you know why he became a cop?' asked Clare.

'You'd have to ask him that. He never said.' Rita's cellphone rang. 'Excuse me, Clare. Sir?'

She listened, nodded, said 'sir' again.

'The boss.' Rita's eyes were wide. 'He wants to see you.'

'You told him I was coming in?'

'Senior Supe Phiri was in intelligence for a long time. There's not much that he misses.'

'Where does Phiri stand on Faizal's record?'

'He prevented Director Ndlovu from having Riedwaan arrested last night. Really pissed her off. He picks his men carefully – and Riedwaan he picked against most recommendations,' said Rita. 'Understands the way his mind works, I think.'

'How does it work?' asked Clare.

'Riedwaan's mind?' Rita thought about it. 'I think Phiri saw right away that Riedwaan doesn't break the rules just because he doesn't like them.'

'Why does he break them then?' Clare was framed in the doorway.

'I don't think he's realised they're there.'

Rita had one hand on the phone, and the index finger of her other hand on the first number on the list. A for Appleby. The phone was answered almost as soon as she'd dialled. Yes, they knew the child. No, they hadn't seen anything.

'You'll find Phiri's office easily.' Rita waved, dialled the next number. 'Up the stairs, at the end of the corridor. Just knock. He's waiting for you.'

The door opened, revealing a handsome man with wide cheekbones and iron grey hair, his uniform tailored to fit his lean body.

'Commander Phiri?' The hand she extended disappeared in his.

'No commanders any more, Dr Hart. I am a Senior Superintendent.' He stood aside so that she could enter. Phiri's wood-panelled corner office, high above the squalor of the street, was filled with light. The books in the glass-paned shelves caught Clare's eye: Sol Plaatje, Chinua Achebe, Ngugi wa Thiong'o, Wole Soyinka. The grandfathers of African literature, moral lodestars ignored in the headlong rush for money and power.

'You've read them?' Phiri saw her looking, and pulled out his dog-eared copy of *Things Fall Apart*.

'I have,' said Clare.

'My only friends when I was in exile,' he said. 'I read them during the long Moscow winters, when it was too cold outside for a civilised man to breathe. These writers brought me the sun.' He gestured towards a chair. 'Please sit.'

Clare waited for him to continue.

'Dr Hart.' Phiri sat opposite her, the tabletop polished to a sheen, clear except for a chessboard with a game in progress. 'Captain Faizal has asked for your assistance in this unfortunate business, am I correct?'

'He has,' said Clare. 'Did he tell you?'

'I spoke to him late last night. He said he'd seen you,' said Phiri. 'This is procedurally unprecedented.'

'Captain Faizal asked me to help him. I've been tracking some missing girls. You might have seen the programme? A mixture of reality television and documentary.'

'I know your film work,' said Phiri. 'I've also read your doctoral thesis. I'm familiar with your research, too; I just signed off on your research with Dr Lyndall, so you have a quasi-official status with the SAPS now.'

'Thank you,' said Clare. 'She told me yesterday.'

'But this case,' said Phiri. 'You know her father is the chief suspect?'

'He told me,' said Clare.

'What do you know about Captain Faizal?'

'Not much,' said Clare. 'He came to the lecture I gave; I spoke to him last night; I've read what's on the internet about him.'

Phiri steepled his fingers. 'He has an unusual reputation.'

'As does your Gang Unit, Superintendent.'

'We've been effective. We have the trust of the public, but we aren't that popular with politicians and those who play their politics for them.'

'So, you don't wish me to work on this case?'

'Captain Faizal is a very valuable member of my unit. He does not endear himself to his superiors, however.' Phiri pulled the chess set towards him. 'But he gets things done.'

'Do you think he abducted his own daughter?' asked Clare.

'Dr Hart, I've known men who have shot their wives in front of their children; I've had men who have shot their own children in their beds. I've had too many men who've put a service pistol into their own mouths and pulled the trigger. Do I think that Captain Faizal has done anything to his own child? No. Do I think that the work he has been involved in has put her in harm's way? Yes.'

'Then call off the investigation, get rid of Ndlovu, and do a proper search for Yasmin.'

'I can't,' Phiri picked up the white queen. 'Not yet. Even if I did, I'm not sure it would help us find the child at this stage. Does Faizal seem like a man who would harm his daughter?'

'So hard to say,' said Clare. 'Probably why so many women get themselves killed.'

'But you're working with him.' Phiri's dark eyes on her, as he put the queen back.

'Move that bishop and you'll block the check,' said Clare.

'Do you play, Dr Hart?' His eyes on the board, assessing the move she suggested.

'I do,' said Clare.

'Who taught you?'

'My father.'

'I never knew my father,' said Phiri. 'I learnt in exile. There were many hours to fill. I was taught by an old man in Gorky Park. He taught Salome Ndlovu too – she turned out to be a formidable opponent.'

Phiri took a card out of his pocket and handed it to Clare. 'My private number. Call me when you need me. I don't sleep much, so any time.'

He moved the bishop, as Clare had suggested. His queen was now securely defended. 'Win or lose, chess is the best way to learn about your opponent.'

'Am I an opponent, Superintendent Phiri?'

'That remains to be seen, Dr Hart.'

twenty-one

The Cyclops Centre was housed in a building on the Foreshore so anonymous that it took Clare a few minutes to find it. Riedwaan Faizal was waiting for her next to his motorbike. A security guard escorted them to the lifts, keyed in a PIN code and sent them to the top floor.

'Morning, Pretorius,' said Riedwaan.

'Faizal.' Arno Pretorius's pale eyes rested on Riedwaan's face for a second longer than necessary. This was more sympathy than he showed most people.

'Arno Pretorius, Clare Hart,' said Riedwaan, introducing them. Pretorius nodded.

'Good to meet you,' said Clare.

But Pretorius was already at the door. Down the passage, he ushered them into the command centre. Consoles of CCTV screens were banked up from eye level to ceiling, a giant insect's eye seeing everything within range.

'What the 2010 World Cup has given us,' said Arno. 'A way of watching all our citizens all at once.'

'You use face recognition software?' asked Clare, staring back at the compound eye surrounding them, showing images of cars, quiet streets, two men walking too close to a woman, her nervous backward glance, then into her car, gone, the men exchanging looks, continuing to walk.

'We do,' said Pretorius, 'but we've only managed to scan in a thousand of our most wanted criminals, and English soccer hooligans so ugly, not even their mothers could love them.'

'So, no way of tracking Yasmin?' asked Clare.

'Not from this.'

Pretorius walked on and opened the door to his inner sanctum. Here, the panoramic view of Table Bay was blocked out by black velvet, and the morning sun defeated by the relentless glimmer of television screens. A pile of DVDs lay on the desks.

'For you, Faizal,' he said. 'Five-fifteen to six-fifteen. All exits.'

'Anybody else request these?' asked Riedwaan.

'You're the only one looking,' said Pretorius. 'I pulled them last night. Whole city. Every entrance, every exit. All the speed-ing cars,' said Pretorius, pointing to a sheaf of papers stacked on his desk. 'You want to run through those? You can check back with the time codes. A few coming into town, then leaving later.'

Pretorius was already logging onto a computer.

'Gallows Hill Traffic.' Grudgingly, the database loaded. He turned the screen for Riedwaan. 'Use my access codes. See who was speeding, jumping red lights. Check them out.'

'You see anything?' Riedwaan took a seat in front of the com-puter screen, hand awkward on the mouse.

'Nothing jumped out, but run through the registered owners, see what you find. She's your daughter,' said Pretorius. 'You'll know better what to look for.'

Like looking for a needle in a haystack. Both men thought it, neither man said it.

'I called in a couple of favours and got you the private stuff,' said Pretorius instead. 'Garages, fast food outlets, home systems. It's all here, too.'

He pushed another box towards Riedwaan.

'You have Gorge Road in here?' Riedwaan was rifling through the DVDs. Pretorius had noted down place, date and time in his precise handwriting.

'It's one of the blinds,' said Pretorius. 'I did get what footage the school had.'

'Show it to me.'

'She's standing inside the screen and then she just steps,' said Pretorius. 'Doesn't come back.'

'Show it to me.' An edge to Riedwaan's voice.

'Faizal, you don't want to see this, man. There's nothing. She's there. Then she's not.'

'I said show me,' Riedwaan insisted. 'I want to see her.'

Arno Pretorius pressed two buttons, and a screen that had been blank flickered to black-and-white life, the time code five minutes after Riedwaan had missed Yasmin's call from the payphone. The gates of the ballet school, the tangled bougainvillea, the road plunging towards the city. The time code jumped ten seconds. A little girl was pressed into the shelter of the hedge. Yasmin, holding something, putting her hand behind her back. Another ten seconds, and she was eating her sandwich. Then she lifted her head, looking directly at the camera, smiling, her hand still behind her back. A ten-second jump on the time code, then Yasmin was stepping out of the frame.

Another ten seconds, and the screen was empty.

Trees, hedge, gates, street.

No vehicle.

No pedestrians.

No child.

'Why did she smile?' Riedwaan was ashen. 'Who was she smiling at?'

'The logs?' asked Clare. 'You have them here?'

'Copies in there,' said Arno. 'Ours and theirs.'

Riedwaan picked up the boxes.

'You owe me, Faizal,' said Pretorius. 'We'll be even when you find her.'

Alive.

They were all thinking that, but no one was going to say it. Not yet.

The wind buffeted Clare and Riedwaan as they stepped out of the shelter of the building.

'You want to put those in my car?' Clare opened the boot.

'What're you going to do with them?'

'I've got a friend who does face recognition stuff. He did the software for this. Maybe he can find something.'

Riedwaan was pulling out his phone. 'You got something, Pretorius?'

'I ran the number plate checks on speeding cars.'

'I know,' said Riedwaan. 'You just gave them to us.'

'I thought I'd check for cars going at the speed limit, stopping at the red lights. Those are the drivers to be suspicious of in this country.'

'What'd you find?' Riedwaan's body was taut with concentration.

'A lot of law-abiding citizens and a Maserati,' said Pretorius. 'Midnight blue, going at sixty all the way from the Winter Palace to the end of the cameras on the N2. Beautiful vehicle if you're not fussy about the origins of the cash that paid for it.'

'Voëltjie Ahrend?' asked Riedwaan.

'Your man,' said Pretorius. 'I ran some number checks.'

'And?' said Riedwaan.

'He came into town at five. Against the traffic, clear as day on the last camera on De Waal Drive.'

'Did he turn towards the mountain there?'

'He turned.'

'Voëltjie Ahrend.' Riedwaan snapped his phone shut, turning to Clare. 'You heard of him?'

'I've come across him,' she replied. 'I've interviewed some of the women who've survived his ministrations.'

'He's been off the radar for months. Went to ground. Now he's in town just before Yasmin disappeared.' Riedwaan lit a cigarette, one hand against the other to contain the tremor. 'I've been on his case.' He looked away. 'This operation – the one before Yasmin. He's involved.'

'You didn't think to mention it?' asked Clare.

'Whole thing's not his style,' said Riedwaan. 'He likes attention, likes to be seen. More like that shooting in Maitland. That would've been his style, except—'

'Except what?' asked Clare.

'Shorty de Lange. You know him? Ballistics?' Clare nodded. 'He ran some tests on the bullets in those girls. Nothing to do with any of the guns we know Ahrend controls.'

'Who, then?' asked Clare.

'Graveyard de Wet.'

'The 27s general?'

Riedwaan nodded. 'He's in jail. Life – no parole.'

'You sure?'

'I checked with the prison. But De Wet died on Thursday. In his sleep. Natural causes, apparently.'

'You think that's true?'

'The natural causes?' asked Riedwaan. 'There's no one who'd care. As long as he's dead, no one's going to ask too many questions. Especially not Voëltjie Ahrend. He's taken the 27s brand, even though he only spent less than a year inside. He and De Wet were in Pollsmoor Prison together, and they took quite a shine to each other. Ahrend sat at the feet of the master and learnt to *sabela* – to speak the language of the Number gangs. De Wet was being a father to the son he never had. Men of Blood, the soldiers of the Number. It's useful to Ahrend: total loyalty, unquestioning brutality. Works for him and his plans for Cape Town.'

'So, a conversation would be useful?' asked Clare.

'You coming?'

'I need to get these tapes started,' said Clare, finding Charlie Wang's number. 'Where will Ahrend be?'

'I've never known him move before two in the afternoon. I'll check if he's at home.'

'Where's home?' asked Clare.

'These days, a penthouse apartment at the Waterfront.'

'Sounds very grand.'

'How else you going to sell a two-bedroom flat by the docks for a couple of million,' said Riedwaan, 'unless you call it a penthouse? If he's not at home, there's a couple of bars he goes to. A restaurant in Sea Point. His new thing, the Winter Palace. We've had him under surveillance for a while. Bought-and-paid-for relationships,' said Riedwaan. 'There's a lot to be said for them. I'll find him, talk to him.'

'You've certainly got his routine worked out,' observed Clare.

'Been watching him for the past year,' said Riedwaan. 'I've seen his face more times than I've seen my own in the mirror.'

'Nothing to bring him in, yet?'

'These days you need a judge's order to be in the same street as a gangster,' said Riedwaan.

'So it's true what the newspapers say?'

'What's that?'

'That your gang unit plays by its own rules.'

'Hard to do anything else, when our opponents have no rules at all.'

'I'll meet you later,' said Clare.

'This afternoon,' said Riedwaan.

'Where will I find you?'

'You know the Bo-Kaap? Signal Street, number 17. I'll call you. Meet you there later.'

'Okay. And the sooner I get this stuff started, the better. It's going to take time to build Yasmin's profile with the photographs I got from Shazia.'

'How's she doing?' asked Riedwaan.

'She's okay, I think. Latisha van Rensburg's with her. But she swings from rage to terror. She's convinced you've got Yasmin, Riedwaan.'

'If you were her, wouldn't you be?' Riedwaan pulled on his helmet. 'Considering the alternatives?'

twenty-two

Voëltjie Ahrend had been true to his name. The little bird who'd become an eagle, flying so high he'd bought the penthouse in a plush Waterfront block. Riedwaan turned at the block hunkered down near the harbour. A concierge stared through the glass-fronted entrance doors as Riedwaan rode past and turned into a narrow service alley. It was lined with dustbins, all overflowing except for the one marked Number One. The Penthouse. He flicked it open. Empty.

He checked the garage, half-full with over-priced cars. The blue Maserati was nowhere to be seen.

Riedwaan knocked on the janitor's door.

'Sir?' A dapper man in a navy-blue uniform appeared, a two-way radio crackling at his belt.

'Goodman,' said Riedwaan. 'How's your family doing in Harare?'

'Captain, thank you, living here now, sir. Children at school.'

'Papers done?'

'You pay a lot for them in Zimbabwe, sir. And even more in South Africa. It helped that you knew who I should speak to.'

'You're doing well here, though.' Riedwaan eyed the man's snow-white Pumas. 'I'm sure you wouldn't want to take a message from me to Mugabe any time soon?'

'No, sir.'

'Then you won't mind if I look at your logs, will you, Goodman.'

'No, sir,' the man replied, his face expressionless. 'I cannot mind.'

The janitor ducked back into his office. Detailed computer

logs, a bank of CCTV cameras showing all the entrances. A screen image of Riedwaan's bike in the alley.

'What do you need, sir?'

'The penthouse,' said Riedwaan.

'No one in there now, sir.' Goodman pointed: an empty lift, a closed front door, the balcony empty, all the windows and doors shuttered.

'When last was anyone there?' asked Riedwaan.

Goodman typed in the plate number Riedwaan gave him. Shook his head. 'Not for a week,' he said. 'He came in last night, was here for a few hours, then he left.'

'He was alone?' asked Riedwaan.

'He's never alone,' said Goodman. 'He had his men with him, five of them. They came in a BMW, they went up, then they all left.'

'No one's been back since?'

'No one,' said Goodman. He typed a query into his computer. 'See, sir? No one has gone in. Each time the door is opened, front or back, it triggers the cameras and there's a record. This is the last one.' He called up the images. Voëltjie Ahrend in his white suit, behind him three of his foot soldiers, pants low, not even bothering to hide the bulges their weapons made.

'Nothing else?' asked Riedwaan. 'You can't enter from the roof?'

'You go past me, or you must have a helicopter,' said Goodman.

'If you're lying, Goodman ...'

'What are you looking for?'

'My daughter,' said Riedwaan. 'She's missing.'

'How old is she?'

'Six.'

'Same age as mine,' said Goodman. 'You think I'd risk having her deported?'

'No,' Riedwaan looked at him. 'You wouldn't.'

'You want to check?' asked Goodman. 'Okay, you've got three

minutes for the alarm – I'll turn the power off. And I'll give you fifteen minutes without cameras.'

An expensive friendship. But a rewarding one, nonetheless.

Riedwaan knew the layout of the building well enough. He'd been on Ahrend's tail for months, combing through every transaction they could track, watching the buildings where he did business, getting to know the maids and drivers – better than any phone tap and never needing a warrant. Riedwaan didn't bother with the entrance lobby, using the service entrance instead. Here, in the domain of cleaners and delivery men and undercover cops, the steps were raw concrete. He took the fire escape steps two at a time, holding an illegal master key in one gloved hand.

The kitchen was chrome and steel and black slate. He moved through the rest of the apartment. It was as bland as a hotel. In the guest bedroom, a bed that still had plastic on the mattress.

The master bedroom showed signs of occupancy. The bed was unmade and the television remote lay on the duvet. Voëltjie Ahrend had spent his last night here, alone. Riedwaan switched on the television. The Money channel. He tried the DVD. Porn. Asian girls, so skinny they looked like boys, servicing a huge man in battle fatigues. Riedwaan ejected the disk. Its cover showed a girl in dark glasses sucking a red lollipop. Foreign-made, distributed by Lolita, a city address, a perfectly legitimate pornographer, as far as these things went. He tried a few more. The rest of the Ahrend collection seemed to be much the same. Bored-looking young women, pig-tailed and skinny; no children, though. 'Barely legal' was the by-line of all the titles – but legal, nonetheless.

Nine minutes had passed, and Riedwaan moved on to the bathroom. Damp towels on the floor, a line of scum on the bath, the mirrored cupboard empty except for a packet of Viagra.

In the living room, a couple of glasses and a bottle of vodka. On the desk was a top-of-the-range Apple Mac in its box, the packaging untouched. Riedwaan didn't bother with it. If you grew up as Ahrend had, then rule number one was not to hide anything that might incriminate you on your body or where you slept. And Voëltjie Ahrend could barely read, let alone type. Nothing in the drawers either, apart from a few cigarette boxes and a boarding pass stub. First class. London – Moscow. Two months ago, issued in the name of Jan Niemand. A sure bet that the picture on Jan Niemand's passport would be Ahrend's handsome, scarred face.

Riedwaan opened the door to the balcony.

Four minutes left, and he still had nothing.

A flock of gulls wheeled above the yachts rocking on the water of Table Bay. Behind Riedwaan was Table Mountain. Ahrend's new territory. Sealed with the blood of the two girls in Maitland, the apex of the triangle of territory that stretched from Sea Point in the south-west to Milnerton in the north-east. Somewhere in that windswept concrete sprawl, Yasmin was waiting for her father to find her. Someone had the key, Riedwaan knew, but it sure as fuck wasn't him.

Two minutes.

Riedwaan eased the glass doors closed again, but the heavy glass stuck, just short of the latch.

A minute till the cameras would be activated again. Riedwaan swore under his breath and pushed the heavy glass back again, feeling along the runners – dislodging the obstruction.

A small pink hair clasp, an iridescent butterfly attached at one end. It lay in the centre of his palm, the icy focus of his despair. He closed the kitchen door behind him once more. Ten seconds to spare.

twenty-three

'Hey, Doc.' Charlie Wang, blinking like a mole exposed to sunlight, had torn himself from his computer screen. 'Are you okay?'

'Fine,' said Clare. 'You been up all night?'

'I guess so, if it's morning now.' He took off the security chain, opening the door wide for her. 'Come inside, come inside. It's dirty, I know. I'm sorry.'

The curtains were closed, like the windows. The large room where Charlie Wang worked, ate and slept smelt of old takeaways, coffee and sweat. He shoved a couple of pizza boxes under a couch and tugged at a curtain. The whole thing slipped off.

'I give up, I give up.' Charlie peered up at the pelmet. 'Sorry for you. And sorry for the mess, Dr Hart.'

'I'd be at home if I wanted to be in a tidy place,' smiled Clare.

'I hate to imagine, Doc. I bet you already went running today, ate fruit for breakfast and did five hundred tummy crunches.' He patted the bulge of his belly. 'I look like a geek, I smell like a geek, so you'll spurn me forever.'

'Your body, maybe,' said Clare. 'But not your mind.'

'You're looking so like Angelina in all that black, but you're not here to play Tomb Raider with me, are you?'

'Not today,' said Clare.

'You want more stuff for your murder maps?' asked Charlie Wang. 'The psycho-geographies of your missing girls? That's why you're here today?' Charlie Wang had been plotting maps for Clare since she'd started her research, fixing onto the bland record of streets and subways and houses the coordinates of where girls went missing and where they were found dead.

'I've got another one,' said Clare, tipping the album she'd got from Shazia onto the table, and stacking the digitised CCTV footage next to it. 'Not dead yet.'

Charlie Wang rifled through the photographs. He whistled. 'Too pretty.'

'Disappeared last night,' said Clare. 'So far, no trace.'

'I've tried before for your other little Persephones. It hasn't worked. Maybe it just doesn't work.'

'They've all disappeared from out on the Cape Flats,' said Clare. 'That's outside the camera's eye, so they weren't going to register anywhere, were they? This little girl vanished from a wealthy, watched suburb below Table Mountain. She'll be there. Somewhere on a camera. She has to be.'

'Clare,' Charlie shook his head, 'we've tried this before.'

'She's six years old.' Clare held up a picture of Yasmin on the beach. Blue sea, red swimming costume, yellow bucket and spade.

'Okay,' Charlie sighed. 'Who is she?'

'Yasmin Faizal,' said Clare.

'Captain Faizal? That gang cop's daughter?'

'That's her.'

'Are you mad?' Charlie tossed her the *Weekend Argus*. 'Look at this. The paper says he took her.'

'Her father hired me to find her,' said Clare.

'It'll be unusual if it isn't the father,' said Charlie. 'You know that. This country of yours, it almost always is. Father, stepfather, uncle, brother, cousin. A kind of family free-for-all, most of the time.'

'This time, I think not,' said Clare.

'Well, great alternatives then,' said Charlie Wang. 'If it's not him, then one of those gangsters he's been arresting is after him. Let's take our pick about how we want to die. A drive-by? Throats slit by a psychopath with a handmade blade? A hand grenade from that new lot, the Afghans, with a kopek or two placed on our eyelids for good measure?'

'Might not be them, Charlie,' said Clare. 'It might have been a man with some cable ties, a scalpel and a thing for little girls.'

Charlie Wang straightened the photographs.

'I suppose running her through my programme won't hurt.' He scooted his stool back to the screen. 'Tell me where.'

'Gorge Road.'

'You got anything on it?' he asked.

'This DVD here – this is from the camera at the end of the street. There are none in the place where she was. Quiet residential street, so most of the cameras are blind.'

Charlie Wang found the coordinates and fed them into his computer. The machine whirred, sifting through the compressed information. A three-dimensional map appeared on the screen, showing the street, the school, the kramat.

'Hand me those photos, will you?'

He was scanning in the photographs of Yasmin, cropping to eliminate everything but her face. Laughing, serious, smiling, asleep, her head resting on a shoulder, leaning against close-cropped black hair.

'The father?' asked Charlie.

'That's him.'

'Nice-looking,' Charlie looked at Clare from behind his thick glasses. 'Looks kind of like you.'

'You think so?'

'Lean, and like he worries a lot.'

'Not my type.'

'So there is hope. Knowing you have a type means I've got a chance of a date. I just have to work on myself a little,' he smiled.

'This is going to be a while, Doc. This face recognition stuff uses algorithms. Got to get it set up. I'll run all these in and compare it to all this CCTV footage you've brought. You got something to do, someone to see in the meantime?'

'I've got someone to see,' said Clare. 'Someone who knows how much it takes to survive.'

'Good, then,' said Charlie, talking more to himself than to Clare. 'I'll call you as soon as I've got something. Right now, I'm going to get some more pictures.'

His attention was on the screen. Using the elegant algorithms of the programme he'd invented, Charlie had already begun building up a composite of Yasmin's face. A web of mathematical information was culled from Yasmin's plump cheeks, her winged eyebrows, the pink bow of her mouth. He teased out the hidden architecture beneath the surface distraction of honey skin and expressive features.

'Come on,' he muttered, manipulating Yasmin's smiling face into usable information. 'Uncle Charlie will find you, baby.'

Clare let herself out. On the landing she made a call.

'Pearl?'

'Yes.'

'Another little girl is missing. I need your help. Can we meet?'

'Who is she?' asked Pearl.

'Yasmin Faizal,' said Clare. 'Captain Faizal's daughter.'

'Gang Unit?'

'That's the one.'

Clare was already at the bottom of the stairs before Pearl made her decision.

'The Arderne Gardens,' said Pearl. 'I'm on tea in half an hour. The children's park. The benches on the other side of the labyrinth.'

Clare did a U-turn in front of a minibus taxi, accelerating away from it as the driver yelled abuse at her. She turned up Roodebloem Road, hoping that the Eastern Boulevard would be quicker than clogged-up Main Road. A children's park. Not quite the place where she'd have expected Pearl to spend her breaks.

twenty-four

Riedwaan parked in front of La Perla on the Promenade, where Voëltjie Ahrend often enjoyed his breakfast at two in the afternoon. The manager hadn't seen Ahrend since Wednesday. The next stop was the McDonald's drive-thru near the Waterfront. Voëltjie's favourite eating establishment. Riedwaan ordered himself a burger and chips and ate them while he flicked through the CCTV. Not a sign of him.

On to the Winter Palace in Maitland. The place advertised itself as a gentlemen's revue bar, but at noon it was just a strip club on the dingy urban fringe of Cape Town. The girls sleeping off the night before told him Voëltjie would be in later. They hadn't seen him there for a couple of days, he'd been coming in less often now, ever since he'd appointed a night manager. He seemed to be onto better things. Bigger things. They lit cigarettes and watched Riedwaan leave.

Just one place left to look. Riedwaan took the dogleg off the highway, dropping into the no-man's-land beyond Cape Town International. The signposts had long since been stolen for scrap metal, but Riedwaan was riding back into a past he thought he'd buried. Smoke swayed over the shanties, where men slumped against cracked walls, enervated from waiting all day at the side of the road for piece work that never came.

This was where Voëltjie Ahrend had grown up; every pair of ears, every pair of eyes his, bought and paid for. No questions asked by the hard-eyed little boys running down the sandy paths between the three-storeyed blocks of flats. The bleak walk-ups were gang-tagged, the territory claimed for the 27s.

On Midnight Street, a few tattered posters hung from broken fences and lamp posts. MISSING, written in red ink, gashed the face of a little girl. The first poster brought Riedwaan to a halt. The small face with its halo of black curls, so like Yasmin. The green almond eyes stared back at him. Chanel Adams, from this street, missing since Thursday. Last seen walking alone.

He turned again and rode on through the narrowing streets. But first he had to find Yasmin. The houses were crowded against barbed-wire fences, windows closed, curtains drawn tight against the silent street. The only thing shiny and new was the razor wire looped across every window and door of a freshly-painted house. There was no number behind the razor wire. But Riedwaan didn't need the number to know it was the right house. The Maserati filling the front yard set it apart. Riedwaan parked his bike on the pavement littered with broken bricks and debris. He kicked over a placard lying against the fence.

SAY NO. The rest of the slogan had been burnt off.

'Say no to drugs.' A heavy-set woman leaned over her wall. 'It's what the poster says. Some people had a vigil here last night. Against those gangsters selling tik. It's not safe here for adults. How must it be for the children?'

'I'm looking for a little girl,' said Riedwaan.

'I thought you looked like police.' The woman looked Riedwaan up and down. 'There were people protesting about that little Chanel Adams who disappeared. Her brother's *mos* in the Neighbourhood Watch too.'

'What do gangsters want with such little girls?' asked Riedwaan.

'They smoke *tik*, they sell it to people. It turns them into animals. Then they see a little girl by herself, they don't think she's only seven. They just feel *jas*, so they *sommer* take them, rape them, kill them afterwards. For the most, it's not that lot.' She gestured at the house with the razor wire. 'It's the people they sell to.'

'And Chanel Adams?'

'Her brother's Lemmetjie Adams. He thought maybe because of what we've been doing in the Watch, they went for his little sister to warn him.'

'They inside now?' Riedwaan gestured towards the fortified house.

'They'll be waking up about now. Nobody moves in there till late afternoon.'

'Was the Maserati here last night?' asked Riedwaan.

'*Ma se wat?*' asked the woman, straightening her *doek*.

'That car, there.' Riedwaan pointed.

'It wasn't there last night when the Neighbourhood Watch had the vigil. Nobody would try anything with Voëltjie Ahrend in the house.'

Riedwaan ran his hand over the car's cool flank. It had been freshly polished.

'It woke me up at four this morning,' said the woman. 'That *ma se* car over there. The engine growls, like his dogs. And they were cleaning it too. With a hoover. They've got no respect, those gangsters. For them day is night and night is day. You know Voëltjie?'

'You could say that.' Riedwaan pushed open the gate. Inside the house a dog bayed – a Boerbul, judging by the huge muzzle pushing through the bars.

'I'll watch for you,' said the woman. 'See if you come out.'

'Thanks, Aunty.'

Riedwaan knocked. The door opened a crack. A boy of about fourteen stood in the gap, his body lean beneath his baggy shirt, his eyes flat and hard.

'*Waar's Voëltjie?*' asked Riedwaan.

The boy pointed down the narrow pathway along the side of

the house, revealing the 27 tattooed on his wrist as he did so. Voëltjie Ahrend's new branding, one that had been bought, not earned in the old way through jail time. Riedwaan pushed open the back door. The smell of onions and cumin frying. Supper. The woman at the stove put her spoon down when she saw Riedwaan, a lopsided smile working through the lines criss-crossing her face.

'Riedwaan Faizal.'

'Auntie Ruby,' Riedwaan responded.

'You swore you'd never *kuier* here again.' Ruby Ahrend snapped her fingers at the supine girls on the couch. One of them slid off, taking her snivelling infant with her.

'Never is a long time,' said Riedwaan. 'Where's your son?'

'What do you want with Voëltjie?'

'Go and call him, Auntie Ruby. I want to speak to him now.'

Her black eyes flicked past Riedwaan's shoulder.

'You up early today, Ahrend.' Riedwaan didn't look around. He could see Voëltjie's reflection in the stainless steel pot. Ruby Ahrend was not a woman you turned your back on, not in a kitchen full of knives.

'Voëltjie's always up for business.' He knotted his dressing gown cord. 'But it's not that often that Voëltjie gets house calls these days. *Kom sit by jou Voëltjie, Ma.*' Ruby Ahrend sat next to her son, resplendent on a red velvet settee.

'What do you need from Voëltjie, Captain Faizal? A golf membership? An invitation to the J&B Met?' He studied his nails. 'Money? Drugs? Women?'

Riedwaan put a small pink hair clasp on the coffee table.

'Where is she?' he demanded.

Voëltjie Ahrend picked up the clasp, turned it over in his hand, discarded it.

'A little girl. Of course. Voëltjie heard the news. That pretty little

TV doctor with a thing for gangsters, she hasn't worked it out for you yet?'

'Fuck you, Ahrend.'

'Information's *mos* Voëltjie's speciality. If you can afford it.' His eyes, black and hard as his mother's, glittered.

'I was wondering how long it would take you to come to Voëltjie, Faizal.' Ahrend extended a hand, and a girl on a settee opposite handed him a lit cigarette. 'Thinking that if something goes wrong with your kak life it must be because of Voëltjie.'

'What do you want for her?'

'What could Voëltjie want that you could give Voëltjie?' He looked Riedwaan over. 'Everything Voëltjie wants, Voëltjie *maar* takes.'

'Where's my daughter?' Riedwaan kept his voice even. 'Your car's on CCTV leaving town at the time she disappeared. And I found that in your apartment.'

'Did you, now? Voëltjie would like to see your warrant some time. But Voëltjie won't get technical, will he? Rather tell Voëltjie this: Why would Voëltjie take her? How would all this attention work for Voëltjie? Voëltjie's a busy man. Deals here, deals there. Voëltjie doesn't need your attention. Voëltjie doesn't want your attention. If your work with your little unit bothers me, I speak to people who understand how business works.'

'Then why were you cleaning your car at four in the morning?'

Ahrend unwrapped a Sweetie Pie. 'Voëltjie knows how you feel.' He licked the chocolate fragments off his palm. 'You see, it hurt Voëltjie, losing that boy you shot. He was like a son to Voëltjie.'

'You set up that ambush, Ahrend,' said Riedwaan. 'You set it up so he could prove himself.'

'So eager to please.' Ahrend shook his head. 'So much promise. Van Rensburg's walking again?'

'It took two operations and three months.'

'Really?' Ahrend sneered. 'His daughter? Pretty little thing, as I remember. Yours too.'

'I'll trade,' said Riedwaan.

'What could you have that Voëltjie could want?'

'We tracked the gun you used on those girls in Maitland.' Riedwaan watched Ahrend's face. Expressionless, except for the dilation of his pupils. 'If the price is right, an eyewitness won't take that long to find.'

'*Nog altyd die slim kind in die klas.*' Ahrend leaned back in his chair. 'Such a waste, when you think what you could have made of yourself.'

'Graveyard de Wet's gun. Interesting,' observed Riedwaan, 'using it the day after he died.'

'Graveyard's not dead.'

'Nobody inside tell you?' asked Riedwaan. 'You, laying claim to the 27 as if you somehow deserved to be called General? Not the old general making way for the new? Or was it just to impress your new masters?'

'Fuck off, Faizal,' said Voëltjie, standing up.

'*Hoor wat hy will sê.*' The mother put her hand on her son's arm and drew him down again.

'If those girls were supposed to seal the deal by guaranteeing the 27s territory, Ahrend, then you're going to be nothing but a boy again. A boy at the beck and call of your new masters. A little Voëltjie again. Rich, yes, but a Russian's servant. If my daughter's part of that, then you'll lose it all, you'll be history. You give her back to me and we can work something out.'

'If that little girl of yours comes back – and it's a big if, from what I know about little girls – then her life won't be worth living unless you stay out of Voëltjie's way.'

'Where is she?' repeated Riedwaan.

'Voëltjie doesn't want to kill you, Faizal. Voëltjie just wants to make you understand something.'

'What would that be?' Riedwaan braced himself, calculating the odds.

'That Voëltjie is a businessman now, and that you, Faizal, won't be giving me shit for very much longer.' Voëltjie Ahrend snapped his fingers. 'You saw what happened to your friend Van Rensburg. Don't you think that's worse than being dead?'

Six at the door. And the three women inside – the kind you counted when calculating the odds in a fight.

Riedwaan caught the biggest of Ahrend's men under the chin, the man's head jerking backwards with a satisfying snap. He fell, knocking the TV to the floor. Riedwaan pushed over the display cabinet, the figurines and photographs shattering on the tiles. He landed two more good punches before his arm was twisted behind him.

'Voëltjie spoke nicely to you.' He lit a cigarette. '*Maak oop.*' The boy who had let Riedwaan into the house pulled his shirt open, the buttons skittering across the floor. Voëltjie Ahrend held the cigarette, glowing orange in the dim room, against the smooth skin on Riedwaan's chest.

'It seems like you're a slower learner than I thought,' said Ahrend. '*Vat hom buite.* Teach him a lesson, *een wat hy sal onthou.*'

Three of the men frogmarched Riedwaan out of the house. A gun rammed into his back. In the yard a dog lifted its head and growled. The boy's kick was dead on target. The animal howled, snapping to the end of its chain.

The yard opened onto a littered stretch of wasteland crisscrossed with paths. Car wrecks listed into the sand, tattered plastic bags snagged against their broken-down bodies. Five hundred metres away, in the gathering dark, the dense Port Jackson scrub was a dark smear against the white sand.

Riedwaan twisted towards the man with gun, dropping to his knees. Not much of a start, but at least the gun was no longer jammed into his kidneys and his arm was at his side again, his hand balling around a rock in the sand. Riedwaan swung up and back, dropping the youngest. This was going to hurt, of that he would make sure. In the open: this was the place to fight.

The butt of the gun cracked across his jaw, the man's fist in his face. They weren't shooting yet – a good sign. But if they got him to the scrub beyond the dunes, Riedwaan knew that in a couple of days a pathologist would be standing over him, cradling blowfly maggots to estimate the time of death.

twenty-five

At three-fifteen Clare paid the entrance fee to the Arderne Gardens. The traffic on Main Road was muffled by the shrubs planted along the palisade. She turned up an avenue of trees towards the shadowed centre of the garden, the path disappearing into a maze of trees and cool undergrowth. The oaks seemed to be taller, denser, but she hadn't been back for fifteen years. She walked on into the emptying park, holding the past at bay. As she navigated her way past the scent garden she crushed a leaf of lemon verbena between her fingers, but the fragrance failed to mask the rankness of the undergrowth.

The labyrinth lay to her right. A golden orb spider had spun her web across the pathway to the maze. A trapped insect struggled, suspended on a deadly silk trapeze. Clare ducked under it. Feeling uneasy, she spun round. But all she saw was shadows in the late afternoon light, insubstantial and shifting, along the avenue of trees. She checked Pearl's instructions again and hurried on, the rustling foliage closing over her head.

She hurried towards the lawn on the other side, relieved to be back in the sunlight.

'Dr Hart?'

'Pearl?' Clare turned. She hadn't noticed the slight figure in the deep shade of an oak tree.

'You're so *bleek*, Doc. You look like you seen a ghost.' Pearl lit a cigarette.

'I get claustrophobic in that labyrinth.'

'You know the place?' asked Pearl.

'Yes. I used to go to school over there,' Clare said, pointing.

'That fancy school?' asked Pearl, cocking an eyebrow at the tiled roof visible above the trees.

'That's the one. You can see it from the children's playground.'

'I know,' said Pearl. 'Let's go sit there.'

'You come here often?'

'Lunch and tea break,' said Pearl. 'It's peaceful there. I can keep an eye out.'

'For what?' asked Clare.

'Things,' said Pearl. 'Kids playing. Little girls need someone to watch out for them. Used to be a gang initiation place, these gardens, after everyone who lived around here got dumped on the Flats in the seventies. They'd come back here, make themselves into men by sharing some girl's body.'

'I know,' said Clare. 'Happened once when I was at school.'

'Your twin that no one ever sees?'

Clare nodded.

'I'm working now, thanks to you.' Pearl tapped a cigarette from a packet. 'I can spare you a smoke.'

'I'll manage without,' said Clare.

'Of course you'll manage.' Pearl flashed her a rare smile. 'But you'll feel better if you have one.'

Clare took one, lit it, the smell masking the stench of decay that was turning her stomach.

'Follow me,' said Pearl. 'I don't like it here either. Too many ghosts.'

Just five metres, and Clare had left the reeds behind and the path was sunlit. Another five metres and there was the fenced-off children's park, with its newly built red slide, yellow swings, orange roundabout.

The two women sat on a bench nearby.

'Pearl, I need you to help me find Yasmin Faizal.'

'*Fok*, what is it with these gang cops and their daughters? There was another one. Her mother brought her for counselling. Calvaleen. I gave her my cell number. She phoned a few times.'

'She knows Yasmin,' said Clare. 'But I can't get hold of her to talk to her.'

'She's not easy,' said Pearl. 'Self-medicates, as they say in the magazines. See that little girl on the swing? She looks about the same age as the one you're looking for. Captain Faizal's daughter.' A dark-haired woman was pushing the child on the swing. As she plunged forward, she shut her eyes against the rush of air, then dipped her head to her chin as she swung back again to her mother's waiting hands.

Pearl pulled a copy of *Die Son* out of her bag. 'Look at this case he has.' Pictures of the two dead girls in the field in Maitland.

'There's a connection?' Clare had worked with Pearl before, and again, it was like coaxing a wounded animal out of its hiding place.

'Riedwaan Faizal's the one who caught my father, put him away for life. Life three times for that family he killed.' Pearl chewed at a nail. 'I've been hearing things, that Captain Faizal's been opening up the space for new people.'

'Which new people?'

'People who know how to do business. These new people taking over. New drugs. Heroin, girls from Russia, taking over the old businesses, living soft. Claiming the Number without earning their tattoos. The old Number gangsters, the ones who paid the hard way for their chappies in jail, aren't happy with what's happening.'

'But who would've taken Yasmin Faizal? There's been no ransom, nothing.'

Pearl yanked out a daisy that had fought its way through the grass.

'I haven't heard anything except rumours. Some say it's free-lance. Others say it's Voëltjie Ahrend because he wants to clear space for the 27s to make an alliance with the Afghans. I also heard it could be other *boere*.'

'The police?'

'Some cops'll do anything for money. They'll make a docket walk, so why not a child?' asked Pearl. 'Especially if it gets the Gang Unit out of Voëltjie Ahrend's face while he does his deal with his overseas friends.'

'Who are they?'

'They say Russians,' said Pearl. 'But people think if you've got black hair and a thick gold chain and you're not a Portuguese running a corner café, you're a Russian. Let me check it out a bit. If we're not careful, it'll get that kid killed. You too, Doc. You must take more care.'

'Why are you telling me that?'

'People smoke, then they talk shit,' said Pearl. 'What you've been doing isn't making you popular. You've disrupted some operations. Interfered with income. Drawn attention to things that were working smoothly. Working with Captain Faizal won't help you.'

'Who are you talking about, Pearl?'

'Watch your back, is all I know,' she warned. 'I'll talk to you again when I've got something concrete. Something you can use. Something that won't come back to me. Or,' Pearl looked towards the play park, 'back to her.'

Clare followed the direction of Pearl's gaze. The child on the swing.

'Who is she?'

'Look at her. Look at her face,' ordered Pearl. 'Now look at mine.'

The high, wide cheekbones, the slanted eyes, the dark hair. So like Pearl, and yet so different. There was an openness in the child's expression – and the joy in the mother's face contrasted with the yearning in Pearl's.

'My daughter. The reason I help you. Her name is Hope. When I gave her away, I told them the only thing I wanted her to keep was the name I'd given her. That's all she has of me.'

Pearl listened as her daughter's laughter rang out.

'Now her name is Hope Pennington. Her mother's a lawyer who lives with another woman in a nice, smart flat. Two mommies. Completely safe. Hope goes to that school there, the one you went to, the one that only has girls.'

Behind the razor wire and the electric fence, the high white walls of the school were visible. A modern-day cloister that kept the world at bay and provided a few lucky girls with a temporary shelter.

'Is that why you took the job close by?' Clare asked. 'So you can watch your daughter play?'

Pearl nodded. 'Sometimes it helps. Other days ...' her voice drifted off. 'Other days I can't bear that everything precious was taken from me. That's when I used to go to my dealer – but that's over now. The drugs gave me up, and these days when I want to die I get under my blankets and sleep for a day or two until I can get up again and start over.'

The woman helped her adopted daughter off the swing, and hand-in-hand they set off towards a large white car. Pearl lit another cigarette. Inhaled, blew a smoke ring. Inhaled again.

'Does she know you?'

'I made her promise that she'd tell Hope I'm dead, that I had no family,' said Pearl. Her knuckles were white on her knees as she watched the woman buckle the complaining child into her car seat.

'I never want her to look for me, to find out whose daughter she is.'

'She'd be proud of you if she knew,' said Clare.

'It's not me,' said Pearl, pulling up her shirt, exposing the faint white marks on her soft belly. Clare put her hand out and touched the evidence of Pearls' pregnancy.

'Her father?'

The sun was beginning to dip behind the cloud tumbling over the mountain.

'It's a wise child who doesn't ask that question.' Pearl tucked in her shirt. 'Especially with a father like mine.'

Pearl and Clare walked back to the entrance. They skirted the lawns where the last of the Saturday brides clustered with their bridesmaids, awaiting their turn with the photographer.

A flower girl hurtled across the grass, colliding with Pearl.

'What's the matter?' she asked, wanting to know what had catapulted the child into her legs.

'My mommy said I must look for my big sister.' The child's breath was ragged with fury and fear. 'And I got a fright because she was hiding. I saw her and I called her but she ran away. She didn't wait for me. Then I saw that man who was walking behind you.' She looked at Clare.

'Which man?'

'How must I know?' asked the child. 'He was behind you when you went in there.' She pointed at the reeds. 'And then he was sitting behind the trees when you talked to the aunty.' Clare looked about. There was no one. 'He was sitting behind you. I thought you knew him and then he looked at me and I ran away and I fell and now my ma is going to *klap* me.' She put her hands over the mud stain on her skirt.

'Let's see if we can clean it off.' Clare brushed at the stiff pink tulle. The girl grinned at both of them, her teeth white against her pink gums. Six, she must be. Seven. The same age as Yasmin.

'There's my mommy.' She darted off, weaving between the

wedding parties on the lawn, where she flung her arms around her mother's sturdy legs. Her panic kissed away, she pointed towards Clare and Pearl, and waved.

'Should always go like that, nê?' said Pearl, climbing into a minibus taxi on Main Road. 'A kiss and everything's fixed.'

Clare noticed the obscenity when she checked her rear-view mirror. The word POES, scrawled across the back window. Her windscreen wiper erased the word, but not her unease. Riedwaan not answering his phone compounded Clare's anxiety.

twenty-six

Yasmin lifts her face from her knees. A shaft of sunlight has found its way through the murky air, a splash of yellow against the wall. She tries to count the motes of dust, then takes the seed out of her pocket and holds it to her nose.

Cardamom.

The smell of her father.

She pulls the blanket closer around her shoulders and stares at the dust sparkling in the air. Tears begin to well as the ray of light dims.

She thinks of her daddy, the times he took her walking up Lion's Head, when she'd pretend it was just the two of them in the whole world. She wished he didn't go away for days and days and then come back with ghosts in his eyes.

Yasmin sees the ghosts even when he smiles. She can feel them, cold feathery things, when he hugs her carefully so that she doesn't bump her face on the gun under his shirt.

Her sunbeam fades and disappears. Hunger claws out of her belly and into her throat. The wind whines as it whips through the broken panes. The steel rafters are skeletal fingers against the sky. A bird flies in, and disappears into a ragged nest.

On the edge of the nest is a movement, a chick seeking its mother.

Yasmin holds up her hands as the tiny body tumbles through the air, then lowers them again to cushion its fall. When she cups her hands over the fledgling, she can feel the fast flutter of its heart against her fingers. It pecks at the fan of skin between her thumb and forefinger.

Footsteps echo in the empty space, and Yasmin slides down the wall onto her haunches. She closes her hands around the bird, shutting her mind against what is coming.

twenty-seven

The District Surgeon turned in at the prison gates, startling the heron hovering over a pool of water in the vineyards next door. Kobus Hoffman would rather have been in bed watching the Saturday cartoons with his daughters, but he needed the overtime pay. His Land Rover was a familiar sight, so the guards waved him through and he parked in his usual bay outside the admin block. He lingered for a moment in the cocoon of the heated car, listening to the news. The bulletin warned of an approaching storm, but natural disasters were so much more tolerable than gang slayings like the recent one in Maitland. It turned his stomach to think of it. And yet here he was, about to hand out painkillers to the very men who committed such acts – usually with as much thought as one would give to swatting a fly.

Hoffman clutched a satchel containing folders from the morgue, X-rays, reference letters and a stethoscope.

'You can't get enough of us, Doc,' quipped the warden on duty.

'Governor wants every man, sick or dead, accounted for before the ceremony tomorrow,' said Hoffman. 'A group of ex-political-prisoners-turned-Jo'burg-empowerment-billionaires will be unveiling the statue of some struggle hero who was careless enough to die before he got rich. So, no sick people allowed.'

The warden laughed, unlocking the gate that led to the separate hospital wing. 'Paradise, that's what they'll find here tomorrow.'

The benches lining the corridor were filled with men, their legs sprawled across the narrow passage. Hoffman felt their eyes on him as he opened the consultation room. The doctor arranged his folders, checked his stethoscope, and poured himself a glass of water. He took out his wallet, passing his thumb over the faces of his wife, his daughters, and then slipped the photograph into his breast pocket. His talisman, close to his heart. A nurse handed him the patients' cards and Hoffman flicked through them.

He was ready when the first knock came.

'*Binne.*'

The first one. Behind him stretched an orange ribbon of tough, hard men. Throughout that day, Hoffman looked into throats and ears. He listened to chests that rattled with TB, examined the skin lesions that come with AIDS. There were no ARVs to dispense and the local hospital wouldn't accept prisoners from maximum, so he gave them cheap painkillers and sent them back to the cells.

The nurse brought Hoffman a cup of lukewarm tea. A brown film floated on the top but he gulped it down anyway. As he completed the notes for his previous patient, he sensed a man standing in front of his desk.

'*Naam?*'

'Khan.'

The voice was quiet, authoritative. Kobus Hoffman looked up at the patient standing nonchalantly in front of him. The tall man with the bulky torso looked strangely familiar.

Dr Hoffman found his card. Rafiek Khan – the last in the queue. Complaint: Chest pains. Cough.

'*Hoes?*' Hoffman asked.

'Ja, coughing,' the prisoner confirmed as he unbuttoned his shirt, revealing the 27 tattooed on his neck.

Hoffman put the stethoscope to his ears.

'You married, Doc?'

Hoffman was listening to the chest rattle typical of TB, and the question caught him unawares.

'Ja,' he said.

The prisoner's lips parted. 'Your wife is a *lekker vet boeremeisie.*' His slim hips snapped forwards. And back again. A practised gesture of domination.

'You'll die in here, Khan.' Trying to conceal his unease, Hoffman wiped his stethoscope and folded it away.

'Inside, outside. It's the same to me.' As the gangster spoke, his lips curled and the 27 above his jugular pulsed.

'Then why are you here?'

'To make sure that my work gets done, Doc. To make sure you're giving me what I need.'

'You have your pills,' said Hoffman.

'You'll know, Doc.' Khan's orange shirt was back on. 'You'd better know. For the sake of your loved ones.'

'You, general or not, mean fuck-all outside of these walls,' said Hoffman as the man turned his back. 'You Number gangsters, you're losing the war.'

'I don't need the war, Doc, I just need the battles.' The prisoner turned around and held up a photograph, waving it at Hoffman. The doctor's hand went instinctively to his empty pocket.

'*Gee dit vir my, jou vuil hond.*' His voice was hoarse as he snatched at the image of his family imprisoned between the gangster's tattooed fingers.

Khan laughed. 'I took this out of your pocket with you standing right next to me, watching me. You didn't know a thing. Would have been as easy for me, a 27, to slip a knife between your ribs, like what happens all the time to the little *franse.* A quick lesson at 32 Flamingo Crescent?'

'How do you know where I live?' whispered Hoffman.

Khan ran his tongue lightly over his lips. 'Your wife's there now? Katinka and Ciara, your daughters? Who do you think decides how long your wife lives, those unripe little girls. What are they? Four? Five? Tight as little green figs.' He rubbed the photograph. 'Who decides how they live before they die?'

Hoffman lunged at him, but the prisoner flicked the photo away. The doctor picked it up, the image of his wife holding his happy daughters on her comfortable lap. Hoffman slammed the door on Khan's laughter. He pulled out the pile of folders sent by the morgue – a heap of perfunctory autopsy reports he needed to sign. For an hour or more he worked his way through the forms, the routine calming him. The last file recorded the most recent prison death.

The form had been filled in correctly, the body documented, and the cause of death noted by an intern whose name was indecipherable. Heart attack caused by overdose. Natural. As natural as anything could be, in this place. Except for the tiny tears on the inside of the mouth, and the marks on the lids that looked like miniature galaxies. A pillow over the head, held down until the man had stopped struggling – if he had ever started. Hoffman pulled out the pictures, checking to see whether the man's thinness was the result of addiction rather than just a spare diet and fear.

Hoffman checked the name again. Graveyard de Wet. He noticed the dead man's skin. No tattoos. A *frans,* given a gangster's name in death.

He remembered, now, where he'd seen Rafiek Khan before. He'd had to examine him and Graveyard de Wet – it was just before they'd begun serving their triple life sentences. For the disembowelling of a nine-year-old, her mother and her grandmother. Hoffman uncapped his pen. Rafiek Khan had made it clear what the consequences would be if he didn't sign the form.

Hoffman looked at the blank space waiting for his signature, the routine mark that would bury this forever. The room was silent, but beyond was a cacophony of clanging, shouts, and the dull roar of three thousand men behind bars.

He signed.

Then he headed for his car. If he drove at top speed he'd be home in forty-five minutes. He was halfway there, when he thought of a person who should know that Graveyard de Wet was out. He'd come looking for her. The woman whose testimony had put him and Khan away.

He should tell her. He would tell her.

But later.

He had to get home first. Had to make sure they were there, safe and happy. So that he could hold them again, their bodies warm against his. The needle hit a hundred and sixty. Still, he put his foot flat.

twenty-eight

'Faizal. Leave a message.'

His bloody voicemail again.

Clare called Rita. 'Has Riedwaan phoned?' she asked, negotiating a corner with the phone clamped to her ear.

'Nothing,' said Rita. 'I called him a couple of times. Just said out of range. Where was he going?'

'He said he wanted to find Voëltjie Ahrend,' said Clare. 'See what he knew.'

'Daniel into the lion's den.'

'So, what now?'

'Give it a while,' said Rita. 'He knows what he's doing. Most of the time, anyway. He may have switched it off so the signal can't be tracked.'

'He's being followed?'

'It's best to presume so,' said Rita. 'With Special Director Ndlovu on his case.'

'Okay,' said Clare. 'There's something I have to check.'

Clare tossed her phone back into her bag, her unease turning into dread. Driving along the wide avenue that skirts Cape Town, she turned up one of the steep streets of the old Malay Quarter, the Bo-Kaap, with its jewel-bright houses stacked around Signal Hill. She took two wrong turns before she found Signal Street, its cobbled surface perilously steep.

Clare knocked. The sound ricocheted in the silence behind Riedwaan's front door.

She pushed open the letter box and listened. A footfall, perhaps an old house settling at the end of the day. It was so faint it was almost inaudible.

She rang the landline, cutting the call when she heard the answering machine. She tried his cell. Silence inside the house. She stabbed at the red button, cutting off his voicemail in her ear.

Again, she pushed the flap open and listened. The sound again. 'Riedwaan?' she said.

In the periphery of her vision, a shadow.

'Yasmin?'

No movement.

No sound.

Clare stood back, surveying the shuttered cottage. To the left of the front door was a garage door, slightly askew. She ran her hand over the runners, finding the place where it was sticking. She rifled through the tools in her boot, pulling out a screwdriver and wedging it between the door and the runners.

Nothing.

It took two whacks with a brick to pop the door off its runner. She pulled it up. A metre or so, enough for her to wriggle under.

She found herself in an enclosed courtyard.

'Hello?'

Nothing, just her breathing.

Opposite her was a door. The kitchen. Going inside, she noticed a painting stuck to the fridge: a girl in a tutu, flying above the earth, with stars daubed in yellow across the blue sky. Five dirty cups in the sink. Clare put her hand on the kettle. Cold. A full cup of coffee on the counter. Cold. On a shelf above the counter were unopened treats for a child. Coco Pops, hot chocolate, chips.

In the living room there was a single armchair with an empty glass next to it, and a pizza box on a table. On the mantelpiece, a portrait of a little boy standing between a beetle-browed woman and a handsome man. The boy's shock of black hair was distinctive, still, in the man she had recently met.

A telephone stood on a table in the hall, the red eye of the answering machine steadily winking.

There were two doors off the living room. One was open, revealing a bare mattress and the kit for a bunk bed strewn on the floor. There was a thin film of dust over everything. Clare opened the music box on the bedside table. A little dancer popped up and twirled on her rotating base. Clare lifted out the photograph folded into the tray. Yasmin aged about four, arms around her parents' necks, pulling them in to kiss her round cheeks, her eyes sparkling at the photographer.

Clare tried the other door. A double bed, the duvet pushed back. A bedside light, a pen, a dog-eared thriller. Elmore Leonard. She stepped back when she opened the cupboard, the smell of Riedwaan's clothes too intimate. Jeans, shoes, shirts, a formal suit. That was it. She closed the doors again.

The bathroom was in a small annexe off the kitchen. Razor and soap on the bathroom sink, an unopened pack of sleeping tablets on the shelf next to it. A large white geyser at eye-level. Below it, a large suitcase.

Space enough for a little girl to hide. Or be hidden. She pulled at the heavy case and it fell over, nearly toppling her. She popped it open, relief making her smile when she saw what it contained. A full set of the *Encyclopaedia Britannica*, the 1976 edition. She opened the first volume. The inscription: To Riedwaan, from your father on your seventh birthday. June 16th 1976. The year Clare was born.

She closed the book when she heard the phone ring, and stepped back into the living room.

'Faizal.' His voice startled her. 'Leave a message.'

Clare listened. Nothing. She stepped back into the living room. She flicked back through the messages. Her own, from outside on the street. A marketing call from a timeshare company. Still the machine winked its mechanical eye at her. She rewound it to the beginning, and the child's voice tumbled into the room.

'Yasmin,' Riedwaan's daughter whispered. 'It's me, Yasmin. Daddy, please, please find me, Daddy. I'm so cold, Daddy, so cold. The man says you must find me, Daddy.'

The child's voice again, flat with terror.

'I heard him. He said you know what they want. He said you know what to do. That if you lose me it's because you don't love—'. The child's sobs, dammed by fear, give way.

'Where are you, Daddy? It's very dark …' A crash, a whimper. Then silence.

Clare played the message again, listening for something in the hollow silence that might reveal where the child was.

She called Riedwaan again. Voicemail. She rewound the cassette and listened once more to the child's disembodied voice, her sobs. The crashing sound, and her frightened cry.

Rita picked up her phone after a single ring.

'Where are you?' she asked.

'At Riedwaan's.'

'You looking for traces of Yasmin there?'

'I came here to look for him because he wasn't answering his phone. I heard something in the house.'

Rita was silent.

'I found nothing,' said Clare.

'Of course not. I told you.'

'A call came through to him, on the answering machine,' said Clare. 'From Yasmin.'

'She's alive!'

'She was when she made the call. Can you get me a trace on the number?'

'I'm on it,' said Rita. 'I'll call you as soon as I have something.'

'Still nothing from him?'

'You're the first person he's going to call, *sisi*,' said Rita.

'The other places,' Clare tested. 'The fishing shack near Slang-kop where he took Yasmin the last time she disappeared. The other places Ndlovu had on her list, where Riedwaan might go to ground. You know them?'

'I've checked them,' said Rita.

'Yourself?'

'Of course,' said Rita. 'You going home now?'

'I'll go crazy just waiting.' Clare saw her face reflected in the dead television screen and turned away.

The answering machine's red eye was steady in the dark. She ejected the tape and put it in her pocket. Then she took an extra tape from a jar filled with koki pens, and slotted it into the machine.

The front door had a Yale lock, so Clare let herself out that way. The street was empty. The only sign of life was the blue television flickers visible between the gaps in the curtains.

A vehicle was angled across the narrow street, blocking Clare's way. The passenger window opened.

'You're connected with Riedwaan Faizal?' The woman's voice matched her perfectly tailored jacket.

'You could put it like that. I'm Clare Hart.'

'I'm Special Director Salome Ndlovu,' said the woman. 'Dr Hart, you should be more careful about who you associate with, a civilian like you.'

'I'm very selective,' replied Clare. 'Is there a reason why you're wedging me against the wall?'

The driver stared straight ahead.

'We have some things to discuss with Captain Faizal,' said Salome Ndlovu. 'I suggest that you inform me of his whereabouts.'

'I have no idea where he is.'

Salome Ndlovu opened the folder on her lap. She flipped through the transcripts, the surveillance reports, and the intercepted phone calls. The ones they had managed to trace. 'You're adept at making yourself invisible, Dr Hart,' she said. 'Rather like Captain Faizal.'

'Shall I tell him you're looking for him, if I do see him?' Clare asked.

'No need, my dear. We'll have him soon. And when we find him we'll return the child to the mother.'

'You're that sure that he has her?'

'Motive leads you to your suspect,' she replied.

'What motive would that be, Special Director?'

'Revenge on the mother for asserting her independence. It's always the same. With your expertise, you should know that, Doctor. Even if the man in question is as attractive as Captain Faizal.' She reached out an elegant hand and the window glided up again, reflecting Clare's face back at her for a disconcerting moment before the black BMW purred down the hill.

twenty-nine

Clare nosed her way into the thickening traffic heading towards town. Long Street was busy. It was too early for the clubbers, but the area was packed with tourists looking for dinner, and drug dealers looking for tourists. There was still parking on Flower Street, though. Clare pressed the buzzer, slipping in as soon as the door unlatched. The studio was quiet and dark, and the only sound was the distant thump of Long Street waking up for a Saturday night.

'Up here.'

Light spilling onto the mezzanine landing; Danny Roman standing in the doorway. Faded black T-shirt, black jeans, spiked hair greying – his was a nocturnal face. 'Look at you. So sleek and professional.'

'Thanks,' said Clare, kissing his cheek. '*If* that was a compliment.'

'If you need a compliment, then take it as such,' he smiled. 'It's good to see you. I only ever see you on TV these days.' Danny closed the studio door, shrouding them in silence. 'I'm guessing you want something more than my company?'

'I want you to help me find somebody.'

'Try an on-line dating service,' said Danny. 'It works for me.'

'Very funny,' said Clare. 'I'm looking for someone in particular and the only trace I have of her is her voice.'

'You think she wants to be found?'

'Play this.' Clare handed him a cassette. Danny pressed play, filling the room with Yasmin's voice.

'Yasmin. It's me, Yasmin. Daddy, please, please find me, Daddy. I'm so cold, Daddy, so cold. The man says you must find me, Daddy. I heard him. He said you know what they want. He said you know what to do. That if you lose me it's because you don't love—'

Sobbing.

'Where are you, Daddy? It's very dark ...' A crashing sound, a whimper.

Then silence.

'Who is she?' Danny swivelled round in his chair so that he could look at Clare.

'A little girl who's missing. Her name is Yasmin. I was at her father's house when the message came through.'

'Have the cops got this?'

'He is a cop, the father,' Clare explained. 'He asked me to find her.'

'Why would a cop ask you to help find her?'

'Long story,' she grimaced. 'For another time.'

'So what do you want me to do with this?'

'Find out where it was recorded,' said Clare. 'I thought if you could work that out, I'd have some idea of where to start looking. You know you can do anything with sound.'

'I make music,' said Danny. 'I put sound together.'

'So, this is the same. Just in reverse. All you have to do is take the sound apart,' she said. 'If anyone's able to find something in that cassette, you are.'

'Clare, Clare, why so obsessed?' Danny searched her face. 'Where did she go, the laughing girl I once knew?'

'Hey, no personal questions.' Clare handed him the tape. 'Just do my tape for me. Please.'

Danny fiddled with some machines and cables and dials. Behind him, Clare paced up and down.

'You're making me nervous,' said Danny. 'I can't do anything until its digitised, and I can't think with you striding about like a tiger. Go and make some tea or something.'

Clare went through to the kitchen and put the kettle on. She looked in the fridge for some milk, and found a slice of pizza. She wolfed it down. The kettle boiled and she poured water over the teabags.

Putting Danny's tea next to him, she pulled a stool over to sit on.

The computer gurgled.

'There,' he said. 'It's done.'

He fingered his keyboard and the screens jumped to life.

'Okay, it's digitised now. I'll put it onto my hard drive and then I have a lovely little plugin called Smack.'

'What do you think you'll find?'

'Be patient, Clare,' said Danny. 'I have no idea. I've never done this before.'

'Okay, then, tell me what you're trying.'

'There's a compressor in the mike of a cellphone,' said Danny. 'To cut out background sound. You'd still hear stuff in the gaps, though. Smack knocks out the background sound when you speak, and allows it back in during the gaps.'

'So, what are you doing?' asked Clare.

'If you have a strong compressor like this one, then you can go in between voice sound, right in between words. See? This is a graphic rendering of the sound.'

On the screen was what looked like an ECG graph, turning the spikes of sound into vital signs.

'It smacks the peaks down and you can hear more of the background sound if you push up the volume. Usually, I know what the elements are that I put together to make sound. This is something else, this is doing the whole process in reverse.' He ran his cursor over the peaked lines on the screen.

'Here, this is your little girl speaking ...'

'Yasmin,' said Clare. 'Call her by her name.'

'Okay, Yasmin. This is her speaking. It's a voice print. A person's voice is like their fingerprints. Almost impossible to disguise.'

Clare listened carefully to the ambient sound that Danny was unpacking for her as he scrolled through the recording. Wherever it was indistinct, he replayed the section again, trying to identify the fragments. She closed her eyes, immersing herself in the sounds of the space that Yasmin occupied when she spoke. Filtering out her own self, her agitation.

A scrap of melody.

A church bell, perhaps.

An Imam's call?

The hubbub of taxis.

The whine of a car.

Dogs baying.

A low thud, a deep sonic boom.

Beneath it all, a low rhythmic rasp. What you heard when you lay with your head on someone's chest.

'Is that her?' asked Clare.

Danny adjusted some more dials, breaking down the sound into more spikes. The disembodied breathing filled the studio.

'That's not Yasmin breathing. Listen. It's coming in between the spikes of her voice.' Danny massaged the corners of his eyes. 'That's someone standing close by.'

'Wait a minute,' said Clare. 'What do you mean, he's standing there?'

'Someone was with her,' said Danny. 'Or near her, when she phoned.'

'Someone who wanted this message to come through,' Clare said to herself.

'I'd be careful if I were you. These don't sound like people you should mess with. You told her father?'

'I can't get hold of him,' said Clare. 'Not since this afternoon.'

'You're not worried?'

'Yes, I'm worried.' Clare put her tea aside. 'But there's not much I can do.'

'Well, this is as much as I can do,' said Danny. 'I'll print it for you.'

Clare spread out the sheets covered in black spikes and asked, 'What is this?'

'Your aural map. A bell, an Imam calling people to mosque, flower sellers, children's voices, a deep boom, dogs. A door slamming or something heavy dropping.'

'You think it happened inside?'

'In some kind of covered space. A big one, there's a lot of echo,' said Danny. 'But that's a guess.'

'An educated one?'

'An educated one, yes. There's a lot of echo on everything. Doesn't sound like a house to me, but that's not something that'll get you anywhere in court.'

'I'm not in a court, not yet.'

'Take this disk. Play it in your car, play it at home. Maybe it'll speak to you, like music used to. I copied the Smack plugin too. If you're cutting your documentaries on your laptop, you'll be able to use it if you need it.' Danny took a stray lock of Clare's hair and tucked it behind her ear. 'Then maybe you'll find her. Your lost girl.'

At the door, he rested his fingers in the hollow of her throat for a moment.

'I still feel sometimes that I'm going to find mine.'

'Yasmin,' said Clare. 'Her name is Yasmin.'

thirty

'I'm sorry, Doc.' Charlie Wang let Clare in and darted back to his stool.

She saw three monitors, each filled with Yasmin's face fragmented into cheeks, forehead, jaw, neckline, eyes. A fourth was running CCTV footage. The fifth monitor was screening a slideshow taken from Yasmin's photograph album: with her mother and father, dancing with Calvaleen van Rensburg, holding a gold certificate at an Eistedfodd, running into the sea at Camps Bay.

'This stuff just takes time. You've just got to pray there's something to find.'

'If there is, you'll find it, Charlie.' Clare unbuttoned her coat.

'You got more pictures for me?'

'Sound, this time.'

Charlie took the CD from her and slotted it in. Yasmin's voice filled the room.

'Skip ahead,' said Clare. 'It's too eerie, with those pictures of her everywhere.'

Charlie jumped the sound.

'There. Stop. Danny Roman isolated the sounds that he could identify.'

Charlie Wang listened, his head to one side.

'You want me to locate those?' he asked, keying the information in. 'There you go, Doc.' The satellite map of Cape Town appeared on his screen.

'You see this?' He pointed to an area highlighted in green.

'These are the areas where you'll find these combinations of sounds – if they're identified correctly, of course.'

'Go through them,' said Clare.

'The Bo-Kaap, Sea Point, Green Point, the Waterfront, Maitland, Milnerton, Muizenberg, Kalk Bay. Pretty much all the urban areas along the seafront, and anywhere you've got mosques and churches next to each other.'

'That really narrows it down, doesn't it?'

'I'll email it to you. At least you'll know where not to look,' said Charlie. 'I wish I could help you more.'

'You can,' said Clare, her eyes fixed on the pictures of Yasmin. 'You can help me see someone. Get your jacket.'

At the Salt River circle, Clare took the road to Maitland. Alongside it, shipping containers were piled high, destined for the trucks that thundered northwards on the highway to Johannesburg. Beyond the scrapyards and container lots was Coronation Road. Bedraggled houses on one side, derelict sports fields on the other.

'This is over and above the call of duty, Doc,' said Charlie.

A blonde girl wearing a fur bikini and white boots stood outside the Winter Palace, just visible at the end of the discreet drive. The entrance had been planted with firs and other conifers. These softened the bleak surroundings; they also offered privacy for the customers. Clare drove on and parked close to a clump of stunted trees some distance from the entrance.

'Do you think we should park so far away, though?'

'I don't want my car noticed,' said Clare.

'What do you want me to do?'

'All I need is cover, Charlie. Don't take this personally. I go in on my own and I stand out. I go in with you and no one pays me any attention.'

Clare undid the top buttons of her blouse, shook out her ponytail and fluffed her hair around her face. She found a red lipstick in the cubbyhole and applied it.

'Wow, you look … different.' Charlie stared at her. 'Is that all it takes?'

'Looking pretty isn't rocket science,' said Clare. 'So, we go in, you come with me. We sit for a bit. I go to the bathroom. You take a taxi home. Okay?'

'Okay.' Charlie was straightening his jacket over his T-shirt.

'You nervous?'

'I don't go out much, Doc,' said Charlie.

'One double whiskey, and you'll be fine.' Clare shoved a wad of R100 notes into his pocket. 'You pay the door fee, otherwise it'll look weird.'

'It's already weird,' said Charlie.

A couple of BMWs were parked under the watchful eye of the bouncers. Further away there were other cars, with tinted windows and mag wheels. And also a few family cars – teachers, doctors, getting rid of the family blues.

'A gold mine, married men,' Clare muttered as the burly bouncer took their money and handed them their gold tickets. Covered in Cyrillic script, these offered a complimentary White Russian cocktail.

The lighting was low, absorbed by the red and purple plush on the walls, gleaming on the white couches arranged around small gold tables. Music thumped, and above the stage a sign flashed information about the next show – something to do with two bad girls and a riding crop. Some men were seated at tables arranged around the elevated stage.

'Could we sit in the corner?' Clare requested of an usher.

'This way, please,' he said, leading them to a table on the other side of the bar.

'Your drinks,' said a girl, putting them on the low table.

A man wearing a white suit sat at a table near theirs. He snapped his fingers at the barman.

'Two for the ladies.'

The barman poured two vodka shots and pushed them across the bar towards two young women. They tipped pale cleavages in the direction of the man. Crooking a finger, the man unwrapped a Sweetie Pie, and the two girls got up. Long pale legs on high heels, breasts pushing against sheer tops, hair bleached and bouffant. They sat down and smiled, eyes blank.

'Tatiana.' He leaned forward, cupping the woman's breast in his hand as if he were weighing fresh meat at a butcher. Then he dropped his fist lightly into her lap. Tatiana did not move.

'This is like a movie,' breathed Charlie Wang, draining his glass. 'Who are these people?'

'Not people you want to get to know, Charlie.' She hadn't touched her drink. 'I'll be leaving now, and won't be back for a while. You watch the show, then go outside and go home.'

'What're you going to do?'

'I want to talk to one of the girls who works here.'

'Is that safe?'

'Of course it's safe. I just want to do it in private.' She kissed him on the cheek. 'Thanks for doing this.'

Charlie watched Clare make her way between the tables. The man in the white suit was watching her too. She went into the bathroom and washed her hands, waiting a few minutes before she came out. Charlie at the table, watching the show. No bouncers nearby. Nobody looking at her as she walked towards the exit. She pushed open the curtains and stepped into another world.

Overhead strip lighting. Scraps of clothing, sequins, dressing gowns and shoes heaped onto white plastic chairs and on the floor. A girl wrapped in a grubby pink dressing gown sat with a Russian-English dictionary in one hand, a cigarette dangled in the other.

Against a nearby wall, six mirrors were lit with unforgiving neon. In front of two of them sat girls applying make-up, their blonde hair pulled tightly back, exposing dark roots. The riding-crop girls, judging by their jodhpurs.

'Is backstage here, not audience,' said the girl closest to her in heavily-accented English. She had one false eyelash in place, and was holding the other in her hand.

'I'm looking for Calvaleen,' said Clare.

The stripper stuck on the other eyelash.

'Local girl,' said Clare. 'Ballet dancer.'

'We all begin as ballet dancers. Me from St Petersburg, her from Moscow.' The girl screwed open a brush and painted her lips scarlet. 'Name again?'

'Calvaleen,' said Clare. 'Calvaleen van Rensburg.'

'What name is that?' asked the other girl, loosening her candy-floss hair. 'Not good for working.'

'We have one local girl here. She leave.' The girl in the pink gown put down her dictionary and rummaged in a heap of make-up at the mirror next to her. 'Here, is photo from party.'

She handed it to Clare. Ten young women wearing T-shirts and short skirts. All of them bottle blondes.

'Maybe this one?' She pointed to a girl in the corner. It was hard to tell, the picture was small but there was a familiar grace to her limbs.

'Her name wasn't Calvaleen?' asked Clare.

'She say her name was Marlena,' shrugged the girl.

'She's not dancing any more?'

'She take too many drugs, give Valentin too much trouble.'

'What happened?'

'She owe money. Valentin beat her,' the girl shrugged. 'She talk back. Says she don't need club pimp to beat her, take her money for her. She say she can get beaten for free on the street.'

A bell rang and the two girls in jodhpurs turned towards their mirrors again.

'You must go now or there is trouble,' said the other girl, who had changed into a ringmaster's outfit. She held a rhino-hide whip under one slender arm.

'You know where she went?' asked Clare.

'Home, maybe?' The girl's eyes were hooded. 'Why you asking so many questions?'

'I need to speak to her,' said Clare. 'A little girl she knows is missing. I need her help.'

'What's your name.'

'Clare Hart. Tell her.'

'If I see her.'

A sharp knock on the door.

'Quickly,' she said, opening the back door. 'You go out the back. We all get fined if Valentin hears you are in here.' .

Clare picked her way past the overflowing dustbins. The parking lot was filling up, and bouncers were opening the doors of the flashier cars. Clare cut across the lot, keeping behind the tree line. Stupid, she knew. But she didn't have a choice.

She walked faster, stopping once to listen. But the music that seeped out of the club made it difficult to discern the subtle night sounds around her.

She quickened her pace. After two hundred metres she broke into a run, but it was too late. She came down with the full force of his body weight on her, the sack slipping over her head, the noose tightening around her neck. The hessian made it hard to breathe, hard to hear anything but the drumming of her blood in her ears.

His hand under her top, clawing her bra out of the way, twisting her breasts. His face inches from hers, invisible on the other side of the hessian. Clare locked her ankles together, keeping her knees tight. He smashed his fist into her pubic bone.

At the sound of a car pulling up, she twisted away from the man and screamed. But he tightened the noose around her neck and punched her again – this time in the belly. He dragged her further into the trees, bumping her over the rough ground.

Something jagged ripped her skirt and Clare grabbed onto a tree stump, holding on tightly.

'Jou vokken tief.' Hard words, a silky voice.

He kicked her in the kidneys.

Fire shot through her body, but she ignored the instinct to clutch her back. Still gripping the tree stump with one hand, her other curled around the hard cylinder in her pocket.

He pulled the noose tighter around her neck.

The rasp of her breath was the only sound she could hear.

Breathe, breathe, she told herself.

The suffocating weight of his body on hers.

Something cold and sharp against her neck.

'Keep still.' His hands scuttled over her body, his grip loosening a fraction.

She pressed the nozzle hard, spraying the pepper directly onto his face, his eyes.

The weight of him off her.

Scrambling to her feet, pulling the sack off her face.

Hearing him behind her as he struggled up.

Running towards the lights penetrating the murky darkness.

Breathing hard. Faster and faster.

Her hands shaking as she reached her car.

Car doors slamming.

'Dr Hart,' a hand on her shoulder. She struck backwards, hard, her elbow connecting with a body. She spun round.

'Dr Hart.' The Special Director. Next to her the driver. 'What happened?'

'A mistake,' said Clare, her voice hoarse.

'I warned you about the company you keep.' Ndlovu folded her cellphone.

Clare coughed. 'Do you have some water?'

'Sorry,' said Ndlovu. 'Only this.' She popped open a Coke Zero for Clare.

'You want to call the police?'

'I thought you were the police.' Clare tucked in her shirt, her back and breasts sore.

'For counselling,' said Ndlvou. 'You of all people know how necessary it is to debrief after an attack.'

There was no movement in the trees, no sound. Just the growl of the highway a kilometre away.

'Did you see who it was?' Clare was beginning to shake.

'We saw nobody.' She turned to the man standing next to her. He shook his head.

'You should be more careful, Dr Hart, walking alone in terrain like this,' said Ndlovu. 'You'll be fine getting home?'

'I'm fine.' Clare steadied her breathing. 'I'll be fine. Thank you.'

'Still no sign of Captain Faizal?' Ndlovu touched a bruise on Clare's arm.

'No.' Clare moved her arm away. 'None.'

'Have a hot bath,' said Ndlovu. 'Stay home.'

Clare got into her car and rested her head on the steering wheel, her heart rate slowing slowly and the smell of the hessian fading as she tried to recall the attack. She cast about for signals she'd missed. She put her hands to her face and breathed in deeply. No trace of the man who'd tried to rape and kill her. No smell at all. It was as if he didn't exist.

Opening the cubbyhole, she found two aspirin. Found half a valium, took that too. Brushed off the dirt and wiped her face. There. Fixed. She checked herself in the rear-view mirror. Not that much worse for wear.

thirty-one

The car guard sheltered from the black southeaster in the lee of the empty block of holiday flats. A short-skirted girl, takeaway coffee in hand, hair spruced, lipstick on, joined him. A Pajero slowed down – a single occupant. The girl shoved her coffee into the car guard's hand and leaned in at the window, her bottom tilted up, breasts on display. Deal done. Down the alley.

The car guard sipped at the coffee. Three sugars, nice and sweet. She wouldn't be long, he'd keep half for her.

The flat on Beach Road was in darkness, the doctor not home yet. Jean-Luc watched out for Dr Hart; she had visited Goma, his blood-bathed home in the eastern Congo. She understood why he'd had to come to this freezing peninsula that tried to pass itself off as Africa. And when his shack was torched by teenaged boys with machetes in their hands and hate in their hearts, she had found him a safe place to stay.

It was only when Clare's car slowed that he noticed the solitary man leaning into the bus shelter. Motionless. The Congolese refugee had spent enough time watching soldiers in the bush to be able to read the angle of the man's body. Pain, he guessed.

The guard eased himself out of his shelter and moved towards Clare.

'*Bon soir*, Jean-Luc,' she said, locking her car, '*ça va?*'

'*Bon soir, Madame.*' An eye on the man approaching her. '*Bien, merci.*'

'Clare.'

She turned to the man that Jean-Luc was blocking.

'Riedwaan.'

'You know him, Madame?' asked Jean-Luc.

'I know him,' said Clare. 'Your face, Riedwaan. What happened?'

Riedwaan put his hand up and touched his cheek.

'I ran into some people,' he explained, 'who decided my face needed rearranging.'

'Don't give me stupid answers,' she said. 'Why didn't you reply to any of my messages? I've looked for you everywhere. I found Director Ndlovu looking for you too, outside your house.'

'I know.' Riedwaan coughed, bending forward to ease the pain in his ribs. 'That's why I'm here. Can we go inside?' he asked when he got his breath back. 'I need to sit down.'

'If you can make it up the stairs.' Clare turned towards Jean-Luc. 'It's fine. He's a policeman.' The sceptical look on Jean-Luc's face told her that a cop on his own, covered in blood, in the middle of the night, meant trouble. But just then the driver of one of the cars he'd been watching appeared, and Jean-Luc went to claim his tip.

Hearing the churn of an expensive engine and the squeal of tyres, Clare and Riedwaan both turned round.

'You rushed off last night, darling. Bad form.' Giles Reid, one or two drinks too many, was out of the car and loping towards her, dinner jacket open, hair flopping boyishly in the wind.

'Have you only just noticed, Giles?' Clare asked. 'I did everything that was required of me; then, as I'd told you, I went home. Alone. I'm presuming you didn't, if it's taken you twenty-four hours to notice?'

'I just thought I'd check on you. And a good thing, too, it seems. Is this man bothering you, darling?' Giles looked at Riedwaan for the first time.

'We're discussing business.' Clare glared at Giles.

'This late?' Giles looked Riedwaan over, seeing only the biker's jacket, the faded Levi's, the chain-store shirt – and the blood on it.

'Take me upstairs, Clare,' said Giles, a proprietary hand on her elbow again. 'I brought some champagne to celebrate your ballet.'

Riedwaan decided that if he'd been Giles, he'd have stepped out of range about now.

'The work's done. We're done, Giles. I'm busy. Goodbye.'

Reid's hand clamped onto Clare's shoulder.

'That's not how it works with me, darling.'

She could smell the alcohol on his breath.

'You feel this in your back?'

Riedwaan Faizal's left arm was locked around Giles Reid's neck, his keys bunched in his right hand, hard against the other man's kidneys.

'That's not because I'm pleased to see you, pretty boy that you are. Believe it or not, but I'm a police captain, and this is my pistol. Next to it is a set of handcuffs. I'm going to give you a simple instruction. Are you concentrating?'

Giles gurgled.

'You let the lady go now.'

Giles complied.

'Now I have a question,' said Riedwaan. 'Do you want to hear it?'

He tightened his grip and Giles Reid nodded.

'You would? Okay, it's a simple question. Requires a simple answer. Even you could work the answer out fast. Would you like me to arrest you and put you in a crowded cell for the weekend or would you like to fuck off?'

Giles gurgled again, his face purple with rage and lack of oxygen.

'You'd like to fuck off?' said Riedwaan. 'In that case, be my guest.'

Riedwaan released his hold.

'I'm going to lodge a complaint,' he spluttered.

'Complaints Department, Caledon Square,' said Riedwaan. 'Ask for Special Director Ndlovu. She doesn't like me either.'

Giles Reid considered his options and made the obvious decision. He got back in his car, flung the word 'cunt' as he closed the door, then revved, turned, and was out of sight.

'I could have handled that,' Clare said.

'I'm sure you could, but I couldn't.' Riedwaan swayed slightly on his feet. 'I spoke to Rita. She said you had something.'

'A message on your landline,' said Clare. 'From Yasmin.'

Riedwaan smashed his fist into the wall, blood welling on his knuckles as he drew it back again. Clare slipped her body between him and the wall. Catching his fist in both palms, she slowed the punch, and deflected it onto her breastbone. Riedwaan held his hand against her chest, his blood staining her white shirt. Feeling the rage in him, she pulled him closer until his forehead rested against hers.

He collapsed against her, a hand at the back of her head, holding her face so close to his that she felt his breath.

'Don't fight,' she whispered.

'I'm sorry,' said Riedwaan.

'I'm not,' said Clare. 'Not yet.'

He cupped her face in his hands.

'But you will be.'

thirty-two

Fritz disappeared into the dark when she saw Riedwaan coming inside.

'She has a low opinion of men,' said Clare.

'An intelligent cat.' Riedwaan followed Clare into her study.

Clare played Yasmin's message for him, the child's anguish unbearable in the stillness of the night. Riedwaan pressed the play button again.

He searched Yasmin's words for a hidden message, a clue. Nothing there, besides her terror. In the background, the sounds that Charlie had teased out. Taxis, imams, church bells, dogs, trains, the ocean. The sounds of his city. They had surrounded him his whole life.

Clare printed out the aural map that Charlie Wang had emailed to her. She put that and the sound analysis in front of Riedwaan.

'These are the places where you'd get these combinations of sound.'

Riedwaan looked at the swathe of territory.

'Is this what we have?' Riedwaan asked. 'One missed call, a frame of CCTV footage, and this?'

'And a message from Rita,' said Clare. 'Call her to see if she got a trace on the number Yasmin called from.'

He dialled, pulling a pen and a notepad towards him.

Minutes later, Riedwaan turned to Clare. 'Between the eastern edge of the City Bowl and Milnerton, Woodstock and Maitland to the south and east.'

'That's hundreds of blocks, a jumble of warehouses and industrial buildings, thousands of houses and flats, acres of empty land,' said Clare.

'She managed to track it again. It was either in a moving train or a vehicle moving along the N1. Then the signal disappeared.'

'And the phone number?'

'From a SIM card bought on Thursday with R20 worth of airtime, from a stall near Cape Town station. This is the first time it's been used.'

'She found a way to use that phone, so there's no way anyone's going to use it again,' said Clare.

'Did your sound guy say if anyone was with her?'

'Yes. Because of the breathing. He thought it possible, yes. It's like a lure,' said Clare. 'Leading us in one direction, but pointing in the other.'

'What were you doing in my house?' Riedwaan asked. 'Looking for Yasmin?'

'Looking for you,' said Clare. 'I didn't find her, either."

'But you thought you needed to look?'

'You disappeared. What was I to think?' said Clare. 'Are you going to tell me where you were?' asked Clare. 'And what happened?'

'I went looking for Voëltjie Ahrend,' said Riedwaan.

'On your own?'

'On my own.'

'What a brilliant idea,' Clare said. 'And now you need to go to a hospital.'

'Not a chance. Ndlovu will have me in three seconds if I go to an emergency room looking like this.'

'She's been after me too. I saw her twice this evening – once outside your house,' said Clare.

'What do you mean, outside my house?'

'Come into the bathroom so I can clean you up a bit,' said Clare, ignoring his question.

Riedwaan followed her and asked, 'Do you know what you're doing?'

'I'm a doctor's daughter.'

Looking anything but reassured, he watched her open the medicine cabinet.

'Sit on the edge of the bath,' she ordered, 'and take your shirt off.'

Obeying her rather warily, he dropped the shirt on the floor.

Clare kept her eyes on his face and ran her fingertips over his cheekbone. Then, taking a pair of tweezers, she carefully worked a piece of gravel out of his forearm.

She slid her fingers over the black scorpion tattooed on his shoulder. The smooth brown skin was turning purple.

'Someone hit you with a gun butt?' she asked.

'Could be,' said Riedwaan. 'Felt more like a crowbar, though.'

'So, not too much common ground in the conversation?'

'We didn't see eye to eye, no.' He winced as she cleaned the torn skin on his temple. 'On certain issues. My daughter. The murder of those two girls in Maitland. Graveyard de Wet's gun.'

Clare stopped swabbing for a second. 'Graveyard de Wet, the 27s general?'

'You know him?'

'I saw his daughter today. Pearl.' Clare dipped a fresh swab of cotton wool in disinfectant. 'She told me she'd been hearing things about Yasmin. Rumours. She's trying to find out more.'

'Why's she doing this?'

'She's got a soft spot for little girls,' said Clare. 'No one ever had one for her. Pearl herself never stood a chance with a father who was a 27. He raped her mother when she was fifteen, that's how Pearl was conceived. She never knew him, but she bore the brunt of her mother's rage. He was released from prison when Pearl was twelve. She was desperate to meet this father-hero that everyone talked about, and begged her mother to let her go to him. He raped Pearl the night she met him. When her own little girl was born, she gave her away to keep her safe.'

'He's dead now,' he told Clare as she resumed her cleaning. 'When I found out about the gun, I checked. He died last week. Natural causes.'

'I hope that makes Pearl breathe easier,' said Clare. 'What she'd heard was rumours. Mainly about Voëltjie Ahrend, that he owes money, that things are being stirred up. She was planning to find out more.'

'Voëltjie Ahrend,' said Riedwaan. 'He's using Graveyard de Wet's reputation to advance himself. He's as ruthless as any 27, says he's a general, but hasn't spent the time in jail to earn the rank he's claiming.'

'If you went looking for this fight, how come you're alive?'

'A woman from the Neighbourhood Watch – I'd spoken to her before I went into the Ahrend's house – she saw me being dragged into the bush. She said she hadn't heard any gunshots so she waited until it was dark, and then she came to find me.' He held out his wrists, his ankles, showing Clare where the wire had bitten into his skin. 'She untied me, brought me round, took me to my bike. I managed to get back okay.'

'You'd be dead if that woman hadn't found you. Or else they wanted you to survive. In which case, why? What use are you to them alive?' Clare hooked a piece of gravel out of his cheek. It clattered into the sink.

'That was a rock,' observed Riedwaan.

'You look better without the blood, but only marginally.' Clare taped up the worst cuts. 'My reputation,' she said. 'It's going to be finished, working with you.'

'What do you mean?' asked Riedwaan.

'That was the other rumour. That some cops might be involved in Yasmin's disappearance. You know, making this case you're working on walk – the one involving Ahrend and the 27s. Happens to dockets all the time.'

'The cops, we're like America,' said Riedwaan. 'Everyone loves to hate us, but when they need help, they call, and then we can't get there quick enough for them. Everyone has an idea of how we are and how we should be – even our own bosses. And it changes every few weeks, depending on which way public opinion blows. It's right to be prejudiced against us, you just need different prejudices. The ones you have are the wrong ones.'

'Which ones are wrong?' Clare washed her hands.

'That we're all on the take. Or that half of us are so strung out that we'd shoot our families in a fucked-up moment of revenge. Or because of a misguided saviour complex – what the shrink I was sent to called it.'

'And you, have you—?'

'I've often thought about saving them,' said Riedwaan, 'from me.'

He caught her arm, pulled her close to him, so that her head was against his chest. She winced.

'What's the matter?' he asked.

'I'm fine.'

'No, you're not.' He held her at arm's length and rolled her shirt up; the bruises were already purple on her ribs and on her hip bones above her jeans.

'Who did this to you?' He turned her around, saw the mark next to her spine, the span of a man's foot.

'Forget it,' she said. 'I also have conversations that go wrong sometimes.'

'Where was this little conversation?'

'I went to find Calvaleen. I still haven't managed to talk to her,

186

though,' said Clare. 'Someone jumped me in the scrub outside the Winter Palace.'

'And how come you're alive?' he asked.

'Your friend, Special Director Ndlovu, has been looking for you. She obviously decided that I'd lead her to you. So she came along. Right place, right time.'

Riedwaan pulled her shirt straight.

'You were lucky too,' he said. 'Maybe.'

'I suppose so,' said Clare.

'Doesn't really add up, though. What was she doing at exactly that spot?'

'I didn't think to ask, I was too shaken,' said Clare, cleaning the last wound. 'Over to you, now. You can do the rest. Have a shower and we can get to work.'

She disappeared down the passage. Riedwaan could hear her moving about. The click of her answering machine. A woman's voice. Then a man's voice. Riedwaan froze. Cape Flats. Saying his name was Lemmetjie Adams. That his mother told him to phone. She wanted to know if Clare had anything for them. Chanel. The other little girl who had gone missing.

Riedwaan stepped under the hot shower and the water hurt every inch of his body – but silenced the desperate voice on the phone. He wished he could escape the torture of his thoughts as easily. The head-doctor had given him pills. She gave everybody pills. The pills were in his bathroom cupboard, each one snug in its flat foil bubble. Not much use to him here.

Coming out of the bathroom, he asked, 'You haven't maybe got any cigarettes?'

'Nothing,' she shook her head. 'You'll get some across the road.'

Riedwaan went to the garage down the road to pick up some Camels. On his way back, he saw Clare watching him from her balcony, a cup of tea in her hands.

Upstairs, he tapped out a cigarette. By some miracle, his lighter had survived his encounter with Voëltjie Ahrend. He turned it over in his hand, revealing the engraving of a scorpion's tail.

'Yasmin saved her pocket money to buy this for my birthday. A scorpion because I'm Scorpio,' said Riedwaan.

'That explains the tattoo, then,' said Clare.

Riedwaan nodded. But he didn't tell Clare how he'd pulled Yasmin onto his lap and she'd moulded her body to his, curling one arm around his neck.

'Her birthday's on Tuesday, isn't it?' Clare asked.

Riedwaan nodded. 'I asked her what she wanted. She said she wanted me to come and live with her and her mommy again.' Riedwaan lit his cigarette. 'It's like her heart's been balanced on a high-wire that stretches between me and her mother. No fucking safety net. All I could say to her is that we needed more time.'

'What adults always say, I suppose,' said Clare. 'When they can't tell the truth.'

'Yasmin wanted to know what we did with all that time, all by ourselves.'

He flicked his cigarette off the balcony. It glowed orange for a second, and then died.

'Let's get to work.'

Clare spread her map out on the table. Table Bay, the sweep of white beach, the jumble of the harbour, the contours of Table Mountain. She traced the arterial roads, the side streets, the empty spaces. Parks, fields, dumpsites, riverbanks that Clare had marked with black roses.

'You think it's the same man?' asked Riedwaan.

'There're similarities in all of them. Lonely, isolated children. Very young. They all went missing, but it wasn't noticed immediately.'

'Anything else?' he asked, with just an inch of professional distance between himself and what he was looking at.

'The injuries.' Clare took a deep breath. Professional was good, better than looking at this man in front of her and thinking that it was his only child they were talking about. 'Their feet,' she said. 'The soles of their feet were full of lacerations, fresh ones. As if they'd run over hard stony ground. Three of them were found with just one shoe on.

'A hunter. He makes them run, his quarry. Puts one shoe on the child, and then dumps her. Keeps the other shoe.'

'A *memento mori*,' said Riedwaan. 'Like a saint's relic.'

'A trophy, the technical term.' Then, almost whispering, 'They're so intimate, a person's shoes. Tell you everything – and nothing.'

Riedwaan fingered the single rose at the edge of Table Mountain.

'For Yasmin?'

Clare nodded.

He took his phone out of his pocket. 'Listen to this,' and he turned up the volume. The wind in the pines, the rush of water coming off the mountain, the swish of a car, the faint echo of piano music drifting – one, two, three, one, two three. As faint as a pulse.

'This is what it sounds like,' said Riedwaan when the recording finished playing. 'The place where she disappeared. You'd think there'd be more, wouldn't you?'

Clare was silent as she relived the sounds of that place.

'Tell me. What am I missing?' Riedwaan ran his fingers over the clusters of pins on Clare's map. 'Why can't I see her?'

He played Yasmin's message again, the sound of her voice an exquisite torture.

'Sound can be as intimate as touch,' Clare said.

'"The comfort zone",' Riedwaan read, peeling a Post-it off Clare's map. 'The East City, Salt River, Maitland. That's not what I'd call these parts of town.' He faced her. 'Does it mean anything? Has it got something to do with my daughter?'

'The comfort zone.' Clare looked away from his bruised face. 'It's where a killer feels safest, the area around his house, or whatever hole it is that he lives in.'

'The area where Rita tracked the call.' Riedwaan's voice cracked.

Clare could not think of anything to say, so she put her hand out, intending to soothe the muscles knotted into cables across his shoulder blades. But Riedwaan put his hands on Clare's hips, the sharp angle of the bone cradled in his palm. He pulled her towards him, his head against her heart, The warmth of his body penetrated the thin silk of her shirt.

'Some coffee,' said Clare. 'That would help.'

A heartbeat of silence. Then she disentangled herself and pulled away, closing the door behind her.

August the eleventh
SUNDAY

thirty-three

The plumber was an early riser, so he was dressed and finishing his second cup of coffee when the doorbell went.

'I'm sorry, Jimmy, so early.' The old widow from next door.

'Sunday, bloody Sunday, I don't do work, but I do climb Lion's Head. But why you up so early, Aunty?'

'I woke from the stink,' she said. 'I think my drain is blocked. I saw your light was on, and I thought maybe Jimmy'll check for me.'

'Right, I'll come over now.'

She spent most of her time keeping an eye on the neighbourhood. Nothing else to do, now that all her sons were working in Dubai. No one to look after her either, except Jimmy next door.

Jimmy locked the house as he left. He took her arm and guided the old lady home, settling her back into her seat in the spotless kitchen.

'Okay,' he said, 'so where's the problem? I don't smell anything.'

'It comes and goes, so it must be coming from outside. Must be the outside drain or the manhole,' she said. 'I could smell it from my bedroom.'

'You wait here,' he said. 'I'll take a look.'

'You're a good boy, Jimmy. Can I make you anything to eat?'

His heart sank. He'd be late, but she had no one else to cook for, and she'd go on at him until he ate something.

'Something small, Aunty, would be nice.'

Jimmy went into the neglected yard. The air carried the night chill, with just a hint of early-flowering jasmine. Underneath that, a hint of wet decay. He checked the outlet pipe from the kitchen, scooping out the leaves blown in by the wind, but found nothing blocking the drain. Following the old pipes, he moved along the perimeter of the house. Nothing at the bathroom either.

A trace of the smell caught the back of his throat. He followed the sewage pipes to the manhole set in concrete below the washing line. The smell was stronger here. Jimmy prised off the metal grille. The smell of a drain, not pleasant, but nothing a plumber wasn't used to. He put the cover back just as the wind gusted across the barren yard, blowing sand into his eyes.

A dead dog. Or maybe a cat that had given up its mangy ghost on the scrubby lot that stretched away behind the row of semis that ended at the old lady's house.

There was a gate in the corner of the hibiscus hedge that screened her yard from the open field. Jimmy cut through the wire and pushed it open. Nothing but heaps of litter, a couple of used condoms, weeds. He picked up a stick and poked at the heap of rubbish. Loose bags, a rolled up piece of carpet. He poked again. No cats. No dead dogs. Jimmy stood up, the sweet, rotting smell twisting his gut into a knot of anxiety. He stood up and tugged at the carpet, hoping not to find a smothered litter of kittens or puppies.

A bit of twine came loose at one end. He peered inside. A bloodied sole, five little toes as tender and round as peas curved along the ball of the foot. On the other foot, a white sandal buckled around an ankle. Some mangy dogs that had been hanging around nearby moved nearer. He picked up a rock and flung it at them, catching one on the flank. It howled and bolted, then sat down just out of range.

Opening the gate to the yard, Jimmy met the old lady as she came out of the kitchen, a steaming plate in her hand. Eggs, bread, two samoosas.

'Your breakfast, Jimmy.'

Scarlet tinged the clouds above the mountains, the morning carrying on, regardless.

'I'm calling the police,' said Jimmy. 'It's a little girl, Aunty.'

thirty-four

When the wind subsided, Clare pulled on a tracksuit; the bed-room window was her mirror as she twisted her hair up. The lights strung along the Promenade winked at her in the dull light of dawn. She ran to the pool at the end of the Promenade. The water was ink, and the lights glinted on its flat surface. Then she turned and headed home, the scudding clouds whipped pink as the sky lightened in the east.

Fritz sat, a cut-out at her bedroom window. The light was still on in her study, where Riedwaan Faizal had kept his night vigil, anxiety and anger shadowing his eyes. Thirty-six hours had ticked past since Yasmin's disappearance. And Clare had nothing for him. The plaintive cry of a pair of oystercatchers drew her attention to the beach. They dipped their orange beaks into crevices in the slick black rocks, hunting for scraps as the waves ebbed.

All she had was scraps, thought Clare, as she let herself in again. The scraps of information that she and Riedwaan had analysed end-lessly last night.

A note lay on the table.

Clare
Took your notes. Thanks.
Getting coffee. Checking some things with Rita.
R F

Clare took her coffee to her study, where Riedwaan had fallen asleep the night before, his face on Charlie's aural map. The place where Yasmin had last been seen was circled in red. She made a tag for Yasmin, pinned it to the map on the wall, and stood back. Still, it made no sense to her. She laid out the photographs she'd taken the previous morning while crouching down in the hedge where Yasmin had hidden.

The jarring sound of her phone at that moment was no help either.

'What?' Clare said, shuffling the pictures, imagining something there – like the shadows imagined on the periphery of one's vision.

'Clare?'

'Yes?'

'I think we might have found her,' said Rita Mkhize.

'Where?' Clare prayed silently to a god she did not believe existed. She wrote down the address.

'What about Riedwaan?' she asked.

'I thought maybe you would get hold of him.' Rita paused. 'I don't think I could tell him.'

Clare dialled his number, wishing that this time, just this once, he wouldn't answer.

'Riedwaan, Rita called. She said they …'

'Where?' he cut in. 'Give me the address.'

Clare drove straight to Maitland, the Monday morning placards announcing Yasmin's abduction flicking past her.

She found the street, where small front gardens were planted with daisies and marigolds, the easy, eager plants of the working poor. She didn't need the street number Rita Mkhize had given her. Several police vehicles were parked outside the last house in the row, their blue lights flashing. Neighbours pressed in, the news travelling fast, bringing the press and onlookers from further afield. Two people were getting out of an old red car. They nodded at Clare. Mrs Adams and Lemmetjie – the son's arm tight around his mother's hunched shoulders. Members of their Neighbourhood Watch crowded round them.

Clare didn't wait long for Riedwaan. When he arrived a greeting seemed pointless, and in silence they walked round to the back of the house. An old woman was sitting in her kitchen, a plate of food in front of her. She pointed towards the hedge. Jimmy April hovered nearby. Not his fault. Not his child. But that small foot had got to him, and he was waiting for her to be unrolled from the grey office carpeting.

Station cops, detectives, the press. Clinton van Rensburg arrived, his crutch digging into the damp sand. He greeted Clare and Riedwaan, then stood aside and waited calmly.

Riedwaan's hand shook as he lit a cigarette. The mortuary attendants arrived next and waited for forensics. Forensics arrived and waited for the area detectives. They arrived and waited for the police photographer. The police photographer arrived and waited for the pathologist. When Ruth Lyndall arrived, everyone set to work.

The pathologist unrolled the carpet.

A sandal on the left foot. The right one torn and gashed. The big toe, with its swirl of pink nail polish, was bloodied.

A torn scrap of skirt, the little triangle between her legs a bloody pulp.

A tumble of black hair. Plump earlobes pierced with gold rings.

Green eyes open in her battered face.

Riedwaan's intake of breath.

Not Yasmin.

Mrs Adams's knees buckled and she slipped through her son's arms, her high-pitched wail slicing open the new day. A woman in uniform helped her up and escorted her into the old lady's kitchen. Van Rensburg headed back to his vehicle.

Riedwaan let go of the breath that it seemed he had been holding forever.

His phone rang and he turned away, his conversation rapid and urgent.

'Riedwaan, I was …' Clare began.

'Can you give me an hour? Rita and I need to get back and strategise with Phiri,' he cut in. 'The press will be all over Phiri about this child. Nothing the tabloids love more than the hint of a serial killer.'

He was already on his phone, walking back to his car with Rita Mkhize. Clinton van Rensburg turned and drove away in the opposite direction.

'This is quite a way to start a Sunday, Clare.' Ruth Lyndall's lipstick left a red imprint on her takeaway coffee cup.

'Ruth – I didn't see you there.'

'Where's Rita Mkhize?'

'She and Captain Faizal have just gone back to Caledon Square,' Clare said.

'His daughter still missing?'

'A flash of CCTV footage from Friday night, a voice message, then nothing.'

Ruth Lyndall took in Clare's pallor, the shadows under her eyes as dark as bruises. 'You're sure about what you're doing?'

'This little girl went missing on the same day as Yasmin Faizal,' said Clare. 'When we found her, Riedwaan looked as if the world had come to an end. And then they unrolled her, and he could breathe again – because somebody else's world had come to an end.'

'The identity's confirmed?'

'Chanel Adams. She disappeared three days ago.'

'Her poor mother,' said the pathologist.

'Mother and brother,' said Clare. 'They've been hunting for her all weekend.'

The pathologist drained her coffee. 'What happened?'

'The family lives in a gang-infested area. 27s. The child's mother had sent her to her grandmother's after a couple of kids were killed in crossfire. She went to the shop to buy cigarettes for her ouma. Was last seen talking to an 'uncle' outside the shop. She never came back. They called me there last Friday morning to tell me she was gone. The mother wanted me to do something – put it on television. Mrs Adams was convinced that she'd be killed if they went to the police. But the son, Lemmetjie, reported it to the police – against his mother's will.'

Dr Lyndall nodded at the two mortuary assistants. They strapped the body to the gurney and bumped across the uneven ground.

'She's been dead three days. She'd have died of these injuries. Looks to me like this happened at exactly the time she went missing.' The doors of the mortuary van banged shut. 'So in the end, your knowing about it would probably have made no difference.'

'And the others?' asked Clare. 'That child you autopsied on Friday evening?'

'There is no pattern, Clare. But I know why you look for one. To give this some coherence, some sense of order.'

'Their feet,' insisted Clare. 'Missing shoes. The cuts on the soles.'

'Little girls trying to get away. Running on hard ground.'

thirty-five

The photographs of the place where Yasmin had waited lay where Clare had left them. They were far too dark; there hadn't been enough light when she'd taken them. At the time, what she'd been reaching for wasn't an idea yet, just a feeling, a ray of hope. Not at all scientific. Clare picked up her clothes, shoved them into the machine, washed the dishes in the sink, letting her thoughts follow their own path, undirected.

Yasmin Faizal had waited outside this gate.

She had called at five-thirty-two.

She had returned to wait in this leafy niche.

At five-forty she had stepped off the pavement, out of the CCTV image, and disappeared.

Yesterday morning there had been darkness everywhere.

Just one light gleamed.

The detail that had been nagging at Clare.

Fritz jumped off the window sill, flicking her tail from side to side.

The sound wrong for Sunday: the clack of the letterbox. Clare was downstairs in seconds. An envelope lay at the front door, her name on it in plump, unfamiliar letters.

Inside, a single sheet of paper torn from a school exercise book, with three bulleted numbers, one below the other. Clare's heart lurched when she took out the loop of worn elastic.

She scanned the boulevard. To the south, a woman roller-blading. To the north, a shadow moving along the buildings where the road curved out of sight. Clare took the bend at a sprint. She was gaining on the shadow, though it kept ahead of her, cutting across the lawn as it headed for the taxi coming down Beach Road. A hand out, slowing the taxi, a tattooed arm sliding the door shut. *Sorry mom, sorry dad.* The prison-gangster tattoo was blazoned on the back window of the taxi, pulling away.

Clare got into her car and went after it. She knew the route, but the taxi eluded her. No commuters, so no stops this early Sunday morning. When she arrived at the taxi rank above Cape Town Station, she pulled up next to the driver and asked him about his last passenger.

'Got on at Beach Road, *nê*?' He called his conductor, a skinny boy who'd had his front teeth pulled.

'Ja,' he said. 'Got on there. Gave me the right change. Sat in the back. Got out before we turned into the rank.'

'You seen him before?' asked Clare.

'You know how many people we drive, lady?' asked the driver.

'But it wasn't a he,' said the conductor. 'It was a girl.'

'Oh?' said Clare.

'Sat in the back. Said nothing, but you can always tell with the hands, *mos*. Women have small hands.'

'You see where she went?' asked Clare.

'Took off towards Woodstock. I *mos* told my friend someone would be after her,' said a stout woman, pointing towards the Victorian slums on the other side of the dilapidated Civic Centre. 'I was right, but you're not going to find anyone in there that doesn't want you to.'

Clare pulled out her phone. One ring, and Riedwaan answered. 'Just a moment.' Noise in the background and Phiri's deep tones. Hope flared in Riedwaan's voice. 'You got something?'

'An envelope,' said Clare. 'A sheet of paper with three numbers on it.'

202

'What's that got to do with Yasmin?'

'There was a piece of elastic, Riedwaan.' Clare had it, grubby and pink, in her hand. 'Tummy elastic. Young dancers wear them around their tummies. It's so they can imagine where their waists will be when they grow up.'

'Read me the numbers.'

Tension in his voice. The sound of a door closing behind him.

Clare reeled off the numbers and asked, 'They mean anything to you?'

'Docket numbers,' said Riedwaan. 'But I don't recognise any of them. Who did the drop?'

'I don't know,' said Clare. 'Jumped into a taxi on Beach Road, disappeared from the rank above Cape Town Station, then headed for Woodstock. Slim. Black hoodie. Jeans. Adidas takkies.'

'A girl?'

'That's what they said,' said Clare.

'Must've been Pearl,' said Riedwaan. 'She said she'd get something to you.'

'Yes, could have been,' said Clare. 'But Sea Point's way out of her comfort zone.'

'Who else?' asked Riedwaan.

'Someone who wants to make the link between these case numbers and Yasmin.'

'Fucking cryptic ransom note – if that's what it is,' said Riedwaan. 'I'll wrap up with Supe Phiri as soon as I can. Then I'm going to check on the numbers. You coming?'

'Well, I was busy on something—'

He disconnected before she'd finished. Clare felt strangely bereft.

thirty-six

The security guard opened the gate for her. He called up and spoke briefly, then he stood back and let Clare in, pointing to the entrance. Third floor, flat number five.

The polished floor gleamed. Clare walked up the stairs, then pushed open the swing door on the top floor. Under one of the doors, a dull strip of light.

A nameplate: 'Joan & Hymie Levy', with a wavering blue line through 'Hymie'. Clare knocked. A shuffle. The door opened. One beady black eye, a strip of wrinkled skin and a nimbus of white hair was revealed in the space allowed by the security chain. The door closed again before Clare could say anything – and then she heard the chain shift as it was unlocked.

'You don't look like a burglar.' Joan Levy stood aside. 'You may come in.'

'Thank you,' said Clare, and introduced herself. 'It's very early, I know, but I saw your light was on and I wondered if I might ask you some questions.'

'What about?' A trace of eastern Europe in her accent.

'A little girl disappeared on Friday evening,' Clare began, 'from outside the school over the road—'

'The ballet dancer?' interrupted Mrs Levy. 'I heard it on the news. What's she to you?'

'I'm working with the investigation.' That sounded broad enough, but Mrs Levy's eyes were sharp and clear, and they searched Clare's face.

'Is she yours?'

'No,' said Clare.

'Mm. I didn't think so. Too skinny to have a baby.'

'I saw your light on early Saturday morning,' said Clare. 'So I thought if you don't sleep—'

'Sleep!' Mrs Levy snorted. 'I'm eighty-nine. I'll be dead soon. For what should I sleep?' She shuffled across a sitting room jammed with large pieces of furniture, relics of a long-gone past. The glass-fronted dresser was filled with white crockery, ready for Shabbat suppers that probably no longer took place, Clare thought, noticing photographs of young parents and children taken against the back-drop of the Sydney Opera House.

'Come, my dear. Come and sit.' Mrs Levy perched on her chair by the window. Clare sat opposite her.

'Hymie's chair,' observed Mrs Levy.

'I'm sorry,' said Clare.

'Don't be,' said Mrs Levy. 'He had a long life. He was difficult, but I didn't kill him. I think I deserve a bit of peace before I meet up with him again. Now, what did you want to ask me?'

'I thought maybe you saw something unusual,' said Clare. 'Or heard something that struck you as out of the ordinary. You sit here most of the day?'

'I do,' said Mrs Levy. 'I sit and listen and watch. Once a week we are taken down to the shops. Once a month, to a movie. Once a year, to a play. I didn't see your little girl, the one the policeman lost,' she said. 'I thought about it when I heard the news. She disappeared when I was watching *Generations*.' The old woman pulled a crocheted rug over her knees. 'I thought of that last night too, that if I didn't watch TV, then maybe I'd have seen who took her.'

She held her head to one side, a little old sparrow. 'That's funny.'

The rumble of a truck coming up the road, music throbbing.

Clare opened the window, letting in a blast of cold air, and a louder blast of sound.

'Oh,' said Joan Levy. 'I thought it was the dustbin men, but they were here on Friday evening. Saturday morning, too.'

'I saw them then,' said Clare. 'When do they usually come?'

'Fridays. I heard them while I was making my tea. It's their usual time. It's the music, now that I'm thinking about it.'

'What else did you hear?' asked Clare.

'I switched on the TV, but my programme hadn't started, so the sound was off – I hate the adverts. Then I went onto the balcony—'

'You saw something?' Clare interrupted.

'I'm sorry, my dear,' said Mrs Levy, 'but I wasn't looking.'

'Perhaps you heard something,' Clare persisted, 'if the wind had dropped off a bit?'

'Yes.' Mrs Levy closed her eyes. 'I heard the bus that fetches the day staff from the home. I heard the parents fetching their children in their expensive cars; the teachers going home in their cheap cars. Then I heard the ballet girls. Then it was quiet for a while. Then the dustbin trucks came. You can hear them, the Solid Waste men shouting as they come up the hill. You can hear them now.'

'That's it?'

'The taxi. It was as if the door opened, spilling out that terrible American music about guns and killing and women with stupid names.' Mrs Levy pulled herself out of her chair and opened the door onto the narrow balcony. It was festooned with plants that blocked the view of the street below. 'I was going to give the driver a piece of my mind, but then it was gone again.'

Clare stepped outside and stood next to Mrs Levy, who took Clare's hand in her own. The street was empty apart from a group of carers waiting to be fetched, and an old man sweeping the pavement outside the kramat across the road.

'You'd better find that little girl soon, young lady, or they'll kill her. That's what the men do to the little girls in this country. Hunt them, play with them, listen to them cry, kill them.'

'I know,' said Clare. 'I know that only too well. Thank you so much for your time.'

The lift doors were closing when Mrs Levy called Clare back.

'Dr Hart.'

Clare put her foot in the door, forcing it to open again.

'I just remembered something,' Mrs Levy smiled, pleased with herself.

Clare was instantly at her door.

'It's just a scrap,' she said, hesitant.

'All I have is scraps,' said Clare.

'It was later, now that I think of it. When it was dark already.'

'What was it?' Clare asked.

'I heard it again. I'm sure. But from much further away. I was surprised. Same terrible music playing. It came from there.' She pointed down the hill to an area dense with houses and flats.

'I was so angry, it was so late, so I called the security guard.'

'Do you know the time?'

'Oh yes,' said Mrs Levy. 'It was soon after half past six. My son in Vancouver Skypes me at quarter to seven every Friday evening. So I was waiting, listening for the call. That's when I heard it again. The same horrible music. Just for a few seconds, like the first time. As if someone opened a door quick.'

'The taxi?' asked Clare, puzzled.

'Yes of course,' said Mrs Levy impatiently. 'That taxi driver is endless trouble. His name's Moegmat. I'm sure he makes it so loud because this is a Jewish old aged home.'

'But was it unusual for him to be back here?'

'No, no. Him, he's just a nuisance. It was the other car. It was dark, no lights on. The car was suddenly there, from nowhere, and it was right behind the taxi.'

'Do you know what make of car it was?'

Mrs Levy shook her head. 'The phone rang then and I went to talk to my son.' Her voice turned bitter. 'As if that's a substitute for Friday night supper.'

'What made you notice the car?' Clare asked.

'I don't know. But I felt I'd seen it before,' said Mrs Levy. 'And then you coming here and asking me questions made me wonder if it was the same car that was parked under the trees late on Friday afternoon.'

'How late, Mrs Levy?' Clare struggled to maintain an even tone of voice.

'Oh, it was after five,' she replied. 'I'm sure of that.'

thirty-seven

Riedwaan Faizal's face was so familiar to the harassed constables ending their Saturday night shifts at Caledon Square that they didn't even notice him come in. The doors on the empty corridors were all closed. The tiny room that was the nerve centre of the search for Yasmin was empty. Riedwaan switched on Rita Mkhize's computer. The laptop whirred to life with excruciating slowness, but at last the files came up. Riedwaan typed in the numbers.

The title pages came up. Number, date, place. Nothing else. Riedwaan pressed print, anyway. He'd need the codes when he waded through the swamp of documents at Criminal Records.

'Faizal.' The hand clamped down hard on his shoulder. 'You shouldn't be here.'

'I didn't hear you come in,' said Riedwaan. 'Don't you ever go home?'

'Home's not what it used to be.' Manoeuvring round to face Riedwaan, Van Rensburg said, 'Jesus, man, you're not pretty at the best of times. What happened to your face?'

'I walked into the door. Fell down the stairs. Whatever.'

'Whose door?'

'Doesn't matter,' said Riedwaan. 'I got what I deserved.'

'Listen, Faizal. I know how you love your daughter. And everyone knows what you've been through in the last year. That's why I've been keeping you out of the cells,' said Van Rensburg.

'You've also got a daughter,' said Riedwaan. 'You'd know you'd fucking die before you'd hurt her.'

'Would I?' Van Rensburg turned, pain etched on his face. 'She's dying slowly because of me, because of you. Because of what we do.'

Riedwaan lit a cigarette, a tremor in his hand.

'Give it up, Faizal. Bring her home alive. There's still time.'

'You really don't believe me, do you?' Riedwaan shook his head. 'You really do think I've done this.'

'I haven't arrested you yet, have I? Find her, bring her back, kill the scum who've got her, if it's not you. Do it for both of us. For both our daughters.'

Riedwaan waited until the sound of his crutch disappeared down the corridor, then he grabbed the sheet of paper from the printer tray and retraced his steps.

The station that housed the Criminal Records was quiet. Riedwaan flashed his ID at the constable on duty, telling him he needed access to where completed dockets were filed. He filled in the log and the man at the front desk returned to his porn magazine.

At the end of the passage was the heavy door to the case archives. Riedwaan flicked open his phone, found the code he'd watched a colleague key in a year earlier. It had been saved on his phone, unused since then. The door swung open, to his relief. He switched on the lights.

The shelves were a mess. Dockets, boxes of paper, smaller pieces of evidence, all heaped together. He worked his way down the racks of shelving. Old, cold in the recesses of the evidence store. The files covered in dust. It was nearly an hour before he pulled out the dockets he was looking for. He pulled out the first folder, a neighbour's complaint in Plumstead. The second, a domestic in Muizenberg. And the third, a drunk driving charge in Milnerton. Minor incidents that would have gone away because charges were dropped or admission of guilt fines paid.

He swallowed his disappointment. Then, unfolding his print-out, he compared the numbers on it to those on the folders he'd found.

He read through the dockets again and again, trying to discern a pattern. He lingered on the last page, signed and dated by the investigating officer, the docket number recorded in writing. Thinking that a cigarette might help him to think straight, Riedwaan compared that number with the docket number on the cover.

They did not match.

He compared the others. They didn't match either. Riedwaan looked for the other two folders. The same thing. Simple incorrect filing. An ingenious way of making a case disappear. Untraceable, in fact. Except for the fact that the cases were absurd.

He dialled Clare's number.

'You found something?' she asked.

'Nothing,' he said. 'An old lady complaining about parking because of an illegal business nearby – looks like it was a strip club or something. A Friday night domestic. A couple of black eyes, but no weapon. And a drunk driving charge.'

The background sound of traffic.

'So why drop the information off at my place?' she asked. 'And why with that bit of elastic that young dancers usually wear round their tummies?'

'I wish I knew. A cat playing mouse with me.'

'Check it again.' A siren. 'I have to go. Traffic cops.'

Riedwaan looked at the tattered security log, the pages grubby from all the handling. The record of who came in here, and why. He ran his finger down the scrawled names, checking the numbers. He found the first one, but the case had nothing to do with old ladies and goats. It took him another fifteen minutes to find the second, and only five minutes for the third. The feeling at the back of his neck was not a pleasant one as he read through the cases. As Riedwaan closed the last docket, a sharp voice cut through the musty air. He shoved the dockets under his shirt, zipping closed the leather biker's jacket.

'Faizal!' The man bounded down the narrow space between the shelves. 'What the fuck are you doing in here?' he barked, his face red with rage.

Riedwaan raised his hands. In anyone else, the gesture would have been submissive. With him, it was a provocation.

'I missed you, Rusty.'

The man's red hair had been the bane of his life. Riedwaan's using the nickname tipped him over the edge. He grabbed Riedwaan by the collar.

'Your fancy fucking Gang Unit, you think you're a law unto yourselves. You're going to see your *moer* at the end of this month. No more expense accounts and fancy GPS systems. You want something from Criminal Records, then you fill out the forms like everyone else.' Riedwaan was a good six inches taller than the stocky man. He let Riedwaan go.

'Your blood pressure bothering you again, Rusty?' asked Riedwaan, straightening his clothes.

'I'll break your legs if I see you here again.'

thirty-eight

Clare stood in the street opposite Joan Levy's window, her back to the clouds sliding over the saddle between Devil's Peak and Table Mountain. She'd returned to the place Yasmin was last seen, before being taken down the arterial road that fed taxis into neighbouring parts of the city.

Walking on, past the gated cul-de-sac. Clare had walked past it yesterday, presuming it to be a private driveway. But it was a lane wide enough for a car. An entrance that tradesmen may once have used to deliver goods to the mansions off it, whose grounds had long since been diced into squares and filled with cottages.

More recent residents had erected a security gate. It was country-quiet under the gnarled oaks, and the light was dim below branches that arched over the narrow lane. Clare saw three parked cars. An Anglia with perished tyres and windows so grimy that she couldn't see into it, a Golf with a smashed back window, and an old Mercedes that didn't look as if it had gone anywhere in a while. There were three blocks of flats, each two storeys high. Further along, before the road narrowed to a littered alleyway, were four cottages. These were low, white Georgian buildings, three of which had been done up and had new vines sprouting over red stoeps. The fourth was dilapidated, the brown paint flaking, the windows boarded up; a bowl of clean water stood at the front door.

Clare knocked.

'Piss off if you're a Jehovah's Witness.'

'I'm not.'

The door opened a crack. A woman peered out at Clare, and behind her several pairs of eyes gleamed in the dark passageway. Cats, if the smell were anything to go by.

'Yes?'

'I wanted to ask—'

'I'm not interested in being saved, I told you.'

'I don't want to save you,' said Clare. 'I just wanted to ask you about a little girl who disappeared from the ballet school up the road.'

'I feed the cats there.' The door opened again slowly. 'But I haven't been able to since all this trouble.' Clearly aggrieved, the woman went on, 'The school said they needed more security. Poor kitties must be starving.'

'They are,' said Clare. 'So the sooner we can find this child, the better.'

'You aren't police, are you?'

'Not police,' said Clare.

'Or social services? They're always checking on me. My neighbours complain – rich Germans who come on holiday here, and chase my babies.' She picked up a cat rubbing against her leg.

'Not social services either,' said Clare.

'Listen, I didn't see your little girl.' The woman stepped outside. 'Not that the police ever asked.'

'They didn't come this way?'

'No. They went down Gorge Road and into Buitenkant. I saw them,' said the woman. 'Not that I would have answered my door. They're terrible with people, the police. Can you imagine what they'd be like with animals? I stayed inside, with all my lights off, in case they came.'

'Did they?'

'No one came,' she smirked. 'I tricked them.'

'Did anyone else come?' asked Clare.

214

'To my house?'

'To your house, or this lane. It must be very quiet here.'

Seeming to lose interest, the woman stared past Clare.

'Maybe you heard a car, one that you didn't know. Playing music,' Clare persisted. 'Loud music. Cats would hate it.'

'Yes,' her eyes flared. 'Yes. I saw them there.'

'Saw who? Where?' asked Clare.

She pointed across the lane. 'Parked there. Two men. I saw them when I came back from feeding the cats.'

'What were they doing?'

'Just standing,' said the woman. 'Standing and smoking.'

'Did you see what they looked like?'

'No,' said the woman. 'I stayed away. I'm scared of men.'

'Did you see anyone else in the car?'

'It was just the two men outside, talking. That's when I went inside with my kitties; when I saw the other one move.'

'Where was he?' asked Clare.

'Sitting in the back, of course.'

'Did you see the number plates, what kind of car it was?'

'A dark car, blue, maybe,' she said. 'No number plates. But that's enough, now, I must go.'

The woman retreated inside, closing the door.

Clare walked to where the woman had pointed. Just enough space for a car. You'd never have seen it, unless you were looking. As she picked her way through the carpet of brittle brown leaves, she saw that some had been pushed aside, revealing the rotting sludge beneath. The earthy smell caught at her throat.

With her foot, Clare turned over the leaf litter. Cigarette stompies. Marlboro. Peter Stuyvesant. Four of each, scattered. They'd stood here a while, matching cigarette for cigarette.

Talking.

Waiting. For what?

An hour is a long time if you have a stolen child in your car. Unless you wanted to miss the CCTV cameras. The cops would check them around the time Yasmin went missing. But an hour or so afterwards you could cruise through unnoticed.

Gorge Road was hidden from view. The flats had their backs to the road. The houses over the road were empty.

Pensive, Clare kicked up the debris blown into the gutter by the southeaster. In a pile of leaves, something glistened. She took a stick and poked through the mess. A Coke can. She kicked it hard across the road, skittering it into the gutter on the other side. She was back at her car when the cat lady, out of breath, caught up with her.

'Wait.' Opening her palm, she revealed a silver Dunhill pen. 'I found this.'

'When did you find it?'

'On Friday evening.'

'What time?' asked Clare.

'Oh, I don't know so much about time,' said the woman.

'You're sure you didn't see the little girl?'

'You keep asking me about that little girl,' said the woman impatiently. 'And I keep telling you I didn't see her. One of my kitties was missing, so I went to look for her after everyone had gone.'

'Okay. Then where did you find the pen?'

'Where the car was parked.'

Clare reached for the pen, but the woman curled her fingers closed.

'I need to buy more food for my cats.'

'How much?' asked Clare.

'Two hundred.' Quick as a flash.

Clare took the pen. A straw – this time, a silver one. A writer's pen. Not something you'd easily discard.

thirty-nine

Tucked away on the second floor of the Waterfront shopping centre was the Dunhill shop, its window displaying a single absurdly expensive green sweater. Inside, a young man in a pale pink golf shirt was straightening a whorl of ties displayed on a circular table.

'Can I help you, madam?'

'I'd like a refill for this.' Clare took the fat silver pen from her bag and laid it on the counter.

'That's a special pen,' he said, picking it up and weighing it appreciatively in his palm. 'Is it yours?'

'No,' said Clare.

'Well, this really is a man's instrument. A limited edition.' He picked up a magnifying glass and turned the pen over. 'Have a look, here's the date.'

Clare looked at the minutely etched date.

'And this has lasted well,' he said.

'What has?' asked Clare.

'This repair. The pocket clip's been soldered back on.'

'A Dunhill anniversary edition. He's lucky to own it.' The young man opened a drawer and took out a packet of refills.

'I don't know who the owner is. I found the pen, and I may decide to trace the person. Do you keep a record of your sales?'

The man looked Clare over.

'We didn't sell this model here. It was only sold in Europe, not even in Japan. See, the styling is too heavy.' He pointed to another tray of pens. 'These suit our Asian customers better.'

'And the repairs,' said Clare. 'You keep a record of them?'

Just then, a customer stepped through the door, a balding man who fingered the shirts somewhat disdainfully.

The assistant took out a receipt book, turning it towards Clare so that she could see its meagre entries. 'Sales, as you can see.'

'I'm sorry I can't be of assistance. Now, if you'll excuse me, madam.'

'No trouble, thank you,' said Clare, pretending to examine some items near the counter.

The assistant turned to his customer and showed him a selection of shirts. Clare eased the drawer open and saw another book, identical to the one on the table. On its spine was written the word 'Repairs'.

Clare slipped the book into her bag, turning to the assistant at the door. 'Is there another Dunhill shop I could try?' she asked.

'Not in Cape Town. There's one at Jo'burg airport, and a couple more in the malls there.'

'Thanks,' said Clare, then said to the customer, 'that's a good colour on you.'

She hurried back over the drawbridge, past the pleasure boats gleaming in the marina, their masts slicing the morning sky into blue stripes. Back in her car, she opened the book. It dated back two and a half years. Not many repairs. Either the products were very durable or most sales were made to foreign visitors. She read through the customers' names, the range of handwriting styles suggesting that there was a high staff turnover at the Dunhill shop.

Clare dialled Rita's number.

'Hey, Doc,' she greeted Clare.

'You busy now?'

'At the station, checking out ballet parents and a couple of crank calls to the hotline.' Rita replied.

'Anything interesting?'

'A lot of nothing.'

'Can you help me check something?' asked Clare.

'I'm not going anywhere, so okay.'

'You look like you need some coffee,' Rita said as Clare walked into her office.

'I do.' Clare shook the tin on the filing cabinet. 'But that stuff'll kill me.'

'You saying no to six-month-old instant with creamer and sweetener?'

'Not my favourite,' said Clare.

Rita spooned the granules into a mug, poured hot water over it, and added three sugars. 'You're right, this is disgusting,' she said. 'Okay, show me what you've got.'

Clare handed her the silver pen.

'Where'd you get that?' asked Rita.

'It was found near where Yasmin disappeared – supposedly.'

'Supposedly?'

'It was found by a woman who feeds stray cats near where another old lady heard loud music on Friday night. I bought it from the cat woman.'

'Chain of evidence never broken,' said Rita. 'What do you want me to do, fingerprint it?'

'Why not?' asked Clare. She put the repairs book on the desk. 'I got this from the Dunhill shop. There's only the one, at the Waterfront.' She pointed at the pen. 'If you look carefully, here, you can see the clasp was soldered back on.'

'Is this really all you have?'

'Apart from the message and anything Riedwaan might have found in the meanwhile,' said Clare, 'that's it.'

'That's not going to find a little girl, is it?'

'It's all we have for now, so we'd better try.'

Clinton van Rensburg's crutch tapped in the passage as he walked past.

'Me and Van Rensburg. Two people who never go home any more,' said Rita, closing the door.

'Why don't you?'

'This thing's got to me, Clare,' said Rita.

'It's got to me too. Yasmin's such a little girl,' said Clare, 'and you knew her.'

'Know her,' said Rita. 'You have to say that. Know her.'

'What's bothering you?' asked Clare. 'Is it anything you can put a finger on?'

'I've been going through the Gang Unit's records,' said Rita. 'Trying to find a link, patterns …'

'And?'

'Gangster-style is gunfire. Spectacle. A public display. If it hasn't been seen then it hasn't been done. If they punish you they want you and everyone you know to see it, to feel it. Yasmin's disappearance doesn't fit that. Not with this weird drip-feed of information. And it looks like it's planted, to point us in a particular direction.'

'What direction is that?'

'Fuck only knows.'

'There've been a lot of arrests recently. All members of the 28s and the 26s. Low-level people, drugs mainly. Runners, small dealers, prostitutes …' Rita tapped her pen against her cheek, her face pensive. 'It must be convenient for business if you're not a 28 or a 26. Our unit's effective. We've been opening up quite a bit of space. If nature abhors a vacuum, how d'you think empty space makes a gangster feel?'

'Who, specifically?'

'Voëltjie Ahrend and his newly-minted 27s. So far, they've

stayed inside the prisons and on the Flats. They haven't moved into the city yet and franchised their brand of violence there, like the 28s and the 26s.'

'And now it's different?' Clare asked.

'Those two girls were shot in Maitland. That was a gang shooting. Somebody moving himself up the ranks. Proving fearlessness. Loyalty. Things are wide open at the moment. For the 27s and whoever they've been hanging out with. Thanks to us.'

'You think someone's on the take?'

'So far I've seen nothing. And I can tell you, I've been looking. At Phiri, at Van Rensburg, at Delport – even though he's seconded to us from the Narcs.' Rita looked away. 'At Captain Faizal. And I've checked the others who've worked with us on specific operations. So far, all they seem to take home is a cop's salary.'

'What're you looking for?'

'New cars, trips to Mauritius, Italian shoes,' said Rita. 'But so far nothing, except …'

'Except what?' prompted Clare.

'A feeling that the pieces of the puzzle don't fit. Or the picture I'm trying to match them to isn't quite right.'

'Have you raised this with Phiri or Faizal?'

'All I have is feminine intuition. And how am I going to table that as a point on the agenda?'

'Call it "gut feel",' said Clare. 'That's what they call it.'

'Captain Faizal won't take it on. The unit's his family. The most dysfunctional family you'll find, but for him, blood is thicker than water. That's what drove Shazia crazy.' She looked at Clare. 'But they're not your brothers. So watch your back, and watch his back for him. They were planning a move on Voëltjie Ahrend this weekend. With this happening, everything's up in the air.'

The air conditioning hummed, recycling the stale air.

'It's nearly forty-eight hours since Yasmin disappeared,' said Rita. 'Experience tells us that finding her alive now is a long shot. We'd better take a look at that pen. In another six hours it may to all intents and purposes be a murder investigation.'

forty

The sports club had previously belonged to the military. A home-sick general from Pretoria once planted an avenue of jacarandas there, but the trees stood bare, their purple flowers months away from unfurling. Riedwaan parked at the tennis courts and watched Louis van Zyl hit the ball. He was broad-shouldered and athletic, and his tennis whites were immaculate. Riedwaan was glad not to be the hapless subordinate at the other end of the court, receiving his punishing serve.

When the game ended, Riedwaan got out of his car.

Louis van Zyl shook hands with his defeated opponent and walked over to Riedwaan.

'Faizal,' he said. 'What've you done to your face?'

'I had a conversation,' Riedwaan explained as he touched the swelling around his right eye. 'It got out of hand.'

'I don't imagine you're here for a match.'

'Not a tennis match.' Riedwaan handed him the sheaf of papers he'd smuggled out of the evidence store.

'Three heroin busts?' Van Zyl scanned the notes.

'I found these three dockets, all from the last couple of months, buried inside closed civil cases.'

'Supe Phiri onto this?'

'I don't know who's onto it,' said Riedwaan.

'How did you find them?'

'I didn't. They were dropped off,' said Riedwaan. 'My daughter—'

'I heard.' Van Zyl cut him short. 'Also that Ndlovu is after you now. Okay, so where did you find these cases?'

'Buried. I want to trace them, see what they were. See why they were given to me. But to find out why they came to me, I need to know more about these busts. Why they were of enough interest to lose. Who wanted them found again. I need to know if they'll help us find Yasmin.'

'Us?'

'Clare Hart. Someone dropped the docket numbers into her mailbox.'

'A woman that smart can only be trouble.'

'Clare knows her stuff,' said Riedwaan.

'She's not in the force,' said Van Zyl. 'She's too close to those gangsters, with the work she's been doing.'

'The women,' Riedwaan corrected him. 'Mainly the women. Anyway, my hands are tied. Do you think I'd be going about things in this way if I could help it? I thought you could have a look, see what you've got on record.'

'Not much any more,' said Van Zyl.

'Your crime intelligence stuff?'

'The SAPS is no longer an intelligence organisation. We're meant to spend our time playing soccer with delinquents and going to community meetings so people can insult us. Our research budgets were cut last time round, and the best we can do now is negative testing at the scenes we get called to.'

'Phiri liked your research. He's a scientist so he knows the way to keep you is to let you explore, play with expensive equipment,' persisted Riedwaan. 'He liked the idea of profiling the labs, finding out which labs the drugs were coming from. So that you can charge the dealers and the owners with much bigger crimes than just dealing here and dealing there.'

'That went nowhere fast – like most intelligent ideas.' Van Zyl squared the papers up and handed them back to Riedwaan.

'Phiri can squeeze a budget out of a stone,' said Riedwaan. 'If it's a secret, then all the better for him. Spending as much time in the Soviet Union as he did, makes secrecy a habit.'

'A safe habit.' Van Zyl zipped his racket into its cover and pulled on a white pullover. 'Your old partner, Van Rensburg, wasn't keen. But Phiri did manage to wheedle some money out of a bilateral agreement with the Americans. He tell you that?'

'Well, you're still here. You didn't take that post in North Dakota,' Riedwaan shrugged. 'Something must have kept you here other than the weather.'

'Did Phiri send you?'

'Not exactly.'

Louis van Zyl eyed Riedwaan closely.

'I'll shower in the clubhouse. Meet me at the lab in half an hour. What you want will take us a while. And it gives me a reason to avoid my mother-in-law.'

forty-one

'Your silver straw.' Rita handed Clare a sheet of paper. 'I checked all the repairs, all the purchases. Most involved foreigners staying at Waterfront hotels. All the others I spoke to, apart from one, claimed to have their pens in their possession. I did a record check. Nothing that I could find, unless you consider being filthy rich in a sea of poverty a crime.'

'All except one, you said?'

'The second-last one on the list,' said Rita. 'His was stolen.'

Clare read Rita's notes.

'Professor Young?'

'That's the one. Said he was mugged on Table Mountain.'

'You checked it out?' asked Clare.

'I did,' said Rita. 'Robbery reported a month ago. He's an elderly man, and was alone. Told me he'd been hiking on the mountain since he was eight years old. He was attacked by at least two men. He didn't see them, just heard a couple of them speak. Some Mountain Men doing a patrol found him lying unconscious. A blow to the head with a rock. Camera, shoes, jacket – all gone.'

'And the pen?'

'That too, with a notebook. It happened near the old slave wash houses above Gorge Road.'

'That's right where Yasmin was kidnapped.'

'I know,' said Rita. 'The Mountain Men searched the whole area. They found nothing. But it's a place where there's easy access to the mountain. So it's a mugging hotspot because of that. The report's in there. Read it through. His address is there too. And his phone number. They also did number plate checks of vehicles parked in the area. Nothing came up, though. For what it's worth, here's a copy of the notes.'

Clare took the slim envelope.

'I was hoping ...' said Clare.

'We always do, don't we?'

It took Clare ten minutes to get from Caledon Square to Rosebank, a shabby suburb tucked below the University. The professor's house was the last one in a cul-de-sac. The neighbours' gardens were overgrown with unfashionable plants, and African masks and curios gathered dust on verandas sealed in with metal bars.

Clare knocked. She recognised the Bach concerto she heard behind the door.

'Yes?'

'My name is Clare Hart. May I speak to you, please?'

The door opened a fraction, revealing one mild blue eye and a slice of tweed jacket.

'Professor Young?'

A nod.

'I have something that belongs to you. A Dunhill pen. I was wondering if I might ask you some questions about it.'

'Are you with the police?'

'I suppose you could say so.'

Professor Young opened the door wide. 'Come in, my dear. Come in.'

The entrance hall was dim; piles of books were stacked on bookshelves, and on the walls were faded pictures of young men in cricket whites.

'Come through to the kitchen,' he said. 'The rest of the house has defeated me.'

At the end of the passageway, sunlight splashed into a conservatory. A moth-eaten Labrador wheezed in the corner. The professor made a perfunctory attempt to move newspapers and tea cups out of the way.

'Sit down,' he said, settling opposite her. 'What can I do for you?'

'Is this yours?' Clare asked, taking the pen out of her bag and laying it on the table.

'Yes, it is mine. I had just had it repaired when it was stolen from me during an attack.' He touched the livid mark on his right temple. 'I'm lucky I'm here to receive it from you, Miss Hart – such a beautiful messenger, too. Where did you find it?'

'It was given to me,' said Clare. 'By someone who told me she'd found it lying in a gutter in Oranjezicht – right where a little girl who disappeared on Friday was last seen.'

Professor Young turned the pen over in his hand.

'Well, I reported its loss at the time. Everything went. My camera, my shoes, my pen, even my notebook.'

'Yes, I saw that in the report,' said Clare. 'Perhaps you could tell me what happened.'

'I walk on the mountain every day. Or at least, I used to. I haven't, since the attack.' He touched the scar on his head. 'I used to walk along the contour path around Devil's Peak. I'd sit and write there, above the wash houses. My wife and I often picnicked in that spot, before she passed on. She was a botanist, and ever since I've been on my own I'd sit there, write her some lines about what was in flower, and how things are without her.'

The dog got up and laid its head on the professor's lap. He smoothed her ears.

'Is that the place where you were attacked?' Clare asked.

'Yes. But I don't remember much. I'm not much of a witness. They came from behind, you see.'

'They?' asked Clare.

'Oh, there was more than one. I heard them talking, in an unusual accent.'

'Cape Flats?' asked Clare.

Professor Young cocked his head, tuning his ear to the half-remembered sounds.

'No, I don't think so,' he said. 'From up-country somewhere, I'd say. They were laughing, like boys on a school trip. They probably did it as a dare. And do you know, I had just composed a perfect haiku. A poem about a leaf, a dewdrop, and a sunbird hovering. The next thing, they bashed my skull and I thought to myself, thank you god. Now I won't be alone any more. And I'll be able to recite the haiku to Iris.'

To hide the tremor, he put his hand on the Labrador's head.

'But here I am. Still alive. Some young fellows on bikes came past, apparently, and saved me. They didn't see who attacked me, but they went and got help. They weren't to know, and Sally here is happy I came back, aren't you, girl?' The dog whined, settling at his feet.

'Weren't you able to identify the men who attacked you?'

'The police kept asking me that, over and over. They seemed annoyed with me that I'd been coshed. I think I rather spoilt their safety record for the mountain. But I'm glad you brought the pen back. My wife gave it to me – her last gift before she died.'

The Bach had come to an end.

'There was one thing.'

'Oh?'

'Only because I didn't remember at the time. Shock, I suppose, and age,' he explained. 'It was distinctive – like the way he spoke, with those rolling "r" sounds. A tattoo on the inside of his wrist.'

'What was it?'

'Twisted black and red snakes. I saw the tattoo when he had me round the throat, just before he bashed the rock on my head.'

'You didn't mention that to the police?' asked Clare.

'No, my dear. I only remembered it now, with you sitting here with me. Fragments of the attack have come back to me. But that was the only bit that had anything to do with the men who tried to kill me. Here—' He rummaged under the pile of papers and books on the table, pulling out an artist's sketchbook. 'I'll draw it for you.'

He drew rapidly, the black outline, the streaks of crimson twisting around them, the snake eyes ruby slits.

'The tattoo, as I remember it.' He gave his drawing to Clare. 'It doesn't bear thinking that those may be the men who have your little girl, my dear.'

forty-two

'See them?' Louis van Zyl asked Riedwaan as he got out of his vehicle. He pointed to the prostitutes pacing the R303 off-ramp, scanning each car for a client.

'That's your tik generation. It's a good drug. Cheap and quick. Opens those dopamine locks ten, twelve times faster than a normal high, opens them wide, and the body's reward system roars into action. For a few hours, they rule the world. The freedom drug, I call it. Has all the post-'94 promises in a straw they can afford. No need for any affirmative action policies, or BEE. No need to work. No need for anything except twenty bucks. Smoke it and you can be your own Mandela for a day. The first high liberates you from your self, your fucked-up circumstances, your conscience, if you have one.'

Van Zyl led Riedwaan past the security desk where the guard was transfixed by his radio. The way to the lab was through a warren of white passages.

'It's changing, though.'

'How?' asked Riedwaan.

'Heroin is something different. It's a narcotic. You take it to make life bearable. It numbs you and you don't care any more.'

'Sounds like what I need,' muttered Riedwaan.

'This is the future,' said the chemist, booting up his computer. 'One long downer.'

'What about buttons?' asked Riedwaan.

'Mandrax? Not so much any more, it's on its way out,' said Van

Zyl. 'The older generation smoke it and they're all dying at home or in jail. The younger lot go for tik. I was working on tracing that, but the method is tricky. With pure crystal meth you only have five per cent impurities. That's not enough traces on your baseline. The purity is a problem for the profiling. Heroin is much easier, and it's set to be the next big thing.'

'And the price?'

'You give it away for free in the beginning, you'll have no shortage of customers later.'

'So how do you track the cases?' Taking a folder with the case numbers he'd unearthed, Riedwaan pushed it towards Van Zyl. 'These cases, for example.'

A two-finger typist, Van Zyl pecked at his keyboard.

'I had an intern from the UK. They love working here, for some reason, think Cape Town's the Wild West. Let's see what she's logged.' He scrolled through lists of numbers. 'Ja, there's a couple of your cases here.'

'You got the investigating officers' names?'

'All the details are here,' said Van Zyl. 'Doesn't look like it was part of a big operation, though. A couple of sergeants from Maitland. One from Table View.'

'You know them?'

'Well enough, a bunch of *stasie-hase*. You know, station cops that get called out for noise disturbances. Do a search, fight with a couple of kids. Find drugs on them.'

'Funny it didn't come to us,' said Riedwaan.

'Well, I've been away for a couple of weeks. Things fall apart quickly.' Van Zyl sifted through the data. 'The intern's flagged this stuff,' he said. 'Looks like it's from the same source.'

'You can track the heroin?' asked Riedwaan.

'Labs where heroin is manufactured don't clean up like the pharmaceutical industry, so you find specific markers from specific laboratories or growing areas. Other plants, other kinds of chemicals. If you've got information on the labs, then you know what's being manufactured. You can then work out who's buying, who's selling.'

'Do you do the testing?'

'For now, it's being done in the States, the FBI academy in Quantico, Virginia. It's an expensive weapon in the war on drugs, tracking the unique markers on the baseline of heroin. The markers are different in different laboratories and from different parts of the world. Helps them figure out if it's coming from Turkey or Thailand.'

Riedwaan whistled. 'Clever, that.'

'Ja. The Americans do about twenty samples from the rest of the world annually. From big consignments usually, full containers. But because South Africa is a major crime centre, it wasn't hard to convince them to bend the rules for us a bit, testing things we send them. Usually, they only profile large consignments. Heroin in these quantities is a new thing, and it's being branded and sold cheap. My feeling is that this is like a teaser, a taster for a new market.'

Van Zyl typed in the docket numbers Riedwaan had given him and waited a few seconds.

'This stuff here wasn't found in a container.' Van Zyl pulled up the photos and whistled. 'This was a bust at a party.'

'So why did you get it tested?'

'Heroin parties are new. This one was in a security estate. A private party, like they have for cigarette promotions. Have a look at these.'

Riedwaan examined the photographs. Luxurious houses, all identical, with travertine marble and spiky desert plants. And blonde women in clingy dresses.

'You were there?' asked Riedwaan.

'No,' said Van Zyl. 'We don't get called in any more. We just get the photos. Look here – the place is crawling with *stasie-hase* polishing off the canapés, getting caviar down the fronts of their uniforms.'

'Where were the drugs?'

'In the Gucci handbag of a seventeen-year-old who didn't speak much English. There was heroin inside it – and also condoms and a cellphone. She said she was given the sachet when she got there. A party favour.' Van Zyl checked the results.

'This heroin is really pure,' he said. 'Look at the results. It's something new, which is probably why it was checked out. A boutique drug being given away to rich kids. The same drug – just cheaper, cut with more shit – will go to the poor kids, to bring them down from their five-day crystal meth highs.'

'Creating your own captive market.'

'Exactly. Marketing is about turning desire into need. With drugs, it works especially well. Check it out.' Van Zyl jotted down an address and handed it to Riedwaan. Sunset Links, Milnerton. Cheek-by-jowl houses for the recently rich.

'And the other two?'

Van Zyl called them up. 'Similar cases. A couple of girls searched outside a strip of nightclubs in Sea Point. The other, a private party in a new club owned by some Russians. They bought the land from the Council for peanuts. Meant to be upmarket. Upmarket, downmarket. It's the same when you die of an overdose.'

'The narcs have been busy,' said Riedwaan.

'They play their cards close to their chests. Maybe this is why.' Van Zyl zoomed in on one of the pictures. 'Isn't this your friend?'

Riedwaan bent close to the screen, his hand going up to his swollen cheek.

'Voëltjie Ahrend. He must be in a bit of debt after losing his stock,' Van Zyl said. 'Is he the one who beat you up?'

'Associates of his,' said Riedwaan. 'You wear white suits like Voëltjie does and you're going to be full of *fiemies* about getting blood on your hands.'

'Self-appointed eagle of the 27s, currently man-about-town. Look who he's with. An ex-mayor and two city councillors. Must have been the opening,' said Van Zyl, flicking through a few more photographs. 'These are not the kind of girls you get for free.'

'Where is it?'

'Some new club, looks like. 101 Coronation Road.'

'Can you test where this shit is from?'

Van Zyl adjusted the images on his screen.

'Northern Afghanistan, it says. The border with Russia. It flooded the Russian market in the '80s and early '90s. Soviet troops brought it back and made a fortune out of it while everyone else was weathering Gorbachev's perestroika.'

'And now?'

'The Russians don't need it any more,' said Van Zyl. 'Russia's booming like we were a couple of years ago. They prefer cocaine.'

'So why's it here?'

'Cocaine's a boom-time drug. Heroin's a recession drug. Economic recession and moral bankruptcy is what we have here. Heroin's your answer to both.'

Riedwaan put his hand in his pocket. He pulled out the coin, still in its evidence bag, and laid it on the table. Van Zyl picked it up and turned it around.

'It was tossed at two girls who were shot in the back on Friday. Aged nine and fifteen.'

'Shall I run a test on it for you?'

'Can you do that?' asked Riedwaan.

'Sure, let's see what's on it. Money gives away all a man's secrets.' He took the coin to a machine that whirred in the corner. 'Will take me a bit of time, though.'

235

'I'll wait,' said Riedwaan.

'Not in here, you won't,' Van Zyl snorted. 'It's like having someone read over my shoulder with you watching me. Go get something for me to eat, seeing as I missed my Sunday roast for you.'

'You mean you missed three hours of your mother-in-law asking when you're going to leave the police and get a proper job that'll keep her daughter in the style she'd like to get accustomed to.'

Van Zyl laughed. 'Man, I'm still hungry. There's an Engen on the N2, with a Steers. Ribs and chips for me, and a Coke Lite. Here's some money.'

'We'll sort it out. You get me a match, your lunch is on me.' Riedwaan picked up his keys. Riding out there would be better than sitting here waiting, watching a computer crunch numbers.

Forty minutes later, there was a reward for Riedwaan when he opened the door to Van Zyl's office.

'There's a baby,' said Van Zyl.

'You've earned yourself a free lunch?' asked Riedwaan, putting the takeaway down on Van Zyl's desk.

'Positive traces. Whoever held this coin had also been handling heroin. That make any sense?' Van Zyl pushed a printout towards Riedwaan.

Riedwaan looked at the graph that Van Zyl had produced, the man's notes alongside it written in looped lettering, almost illegible.

'With handwriting like this, you could have been a doctor,' said Riedwaan giving up. 'Is it the Afghan stuff?'

'Give me another hour and I'd put my cock on the block for you.' Van Zyl's eyes were fixed on his screen. 'For this level of certainty, I'd sacrifice yours.'

'So, you're pretty certain.'

'Might not stand up in court,' said Van Zyl, 'but I'm sure.'

'Why do you do this? Scientific curiosity?'

'I suppose so. Or at least, that's mostly why,' said Van Zyl. 'I photocopied what I could find for you. Some of my case notes in our log, the printouts from the intern's database.'

Riedwaan took the sheaf of papers from Van Zyl, the case numbers and notes in his cursive handwriting. 'You got a record in there of who picked these up?'

'Should be the same person who dropped them. It'll be in the security log at the entrance desk. Ask the guard to show you.'

The security guard in the lobby had his ear glued to a deafeningly loud soccer match on the radio.

'Can I look through your record book?' asked Riedwaan when he had the man's attention. 'I'm checking on a collection.'

The man shoved a bulging folder under the bulletproof glass. Riedwaan flicked through the tattered pages, stopping at the date jotted down by Van Zyl. There were two full pages for a Monday two weeks before. Many of them were recognisable, and came from cops from the busiest weekend stations.

'Can you make a copy of these?' he asked.

'No problem.' The guard fed the sheets into the Xerox machine behind him.

It was impossible to read the scrawl in the badly-lit foyer, so Riedwaan went outside to decipher the entries. He called Clare, leaving her a message to call back, and lit a cigarette. Beyond the highway, invasive aliens from Australia that had been planted a century earlier covered the white sand dunes. Roofs the colour of dried blood were visible beyond the scrub where small children wandered to play, finding a piece of wire here, a tin there, and fashioning them into toys.

Riedwaan's phone rang.

'Well, what's the story about the docket numbers?' asked Clare.

'All heroin busts. Different places, but all the same origin. Afghanistan.'

'Your Russians?'

'Looks like it. Worth quite a bit of money, too,' said Riedwaan. 'If I can work out who buried them, then we can figure out what they have to do with Yasmin. Let's meet in town. It's a long story.'

'Okay, but I've got to see Pearl first.'

'See you later, then. Long Street, that Irish pub. There's a corner booth at the back. Meet me there.'

forty-three

Pearl still wasn't picking up her phone. Rosebank was half way to the supermarket where Pearl worked, so instead of heading for town, Clare turned down Paradise Road. She pulled into the parking lot on Main and stopped under the spill of neon at the entrance. Not many customers just before seven on a Sunday evening. Picking up a basket, she walked through the aisles. Pearl was at the bread counter, packing the remnants of the day's bake into plastic bags for the staff to take home.

'Why aren't you answering your phone?' asked Clare.

'I'm working, Doc,' her eyes widening at the sight of Clare. 'What can I get you?'

'Two Portuguese rolls, please.'

A supervisor drifted by. Pearl, with her scars and her attitude, would always be on probation.

'Phone has to be off when I work, or I'll be fired.' She handed Clare the rolls. 'How's Captain Faizal?'

'Alive,' said Clare.

'I heard from one of the 27s cherries. He's very lucky,' said Pearl. 'Not many people survive if Voëltjie Ahrend thinks you need a lesson. He must have had a good reason to let him live.'

'I need to talk to you,' said Clare. 'About the dockets.'

'My shift finishes in ten minutes. I'll meet you outside.'

Clare picked up some cat food too, paid at the check-out, and returned to her car. Fifteen minutes later Pearl was at her window, a black hoodie pulled over her navy-and-red uniform.

'I've got to get the train,' said Pearl. 'Not many on a Sunday.'

'We can talk while I give you a lift to the station.'

Clare drove out of the parking lot and turned back into Main Road.

'What dockets are you talking about, Doc?'

'The ones you dropped at my house,' said Clare.

'Not me, Doc,' said Pearl. 'I don't go your side of the mountain. Cops stop me there too often for loitering.'

'So who, then?' asked Clare. 'And why?'

'Maybe it was a plant.' Pearl flashed a gap-toothed smile. 'You must watch TV. That's what the cops do in the movies.'

'What for?'

'Fuck knows, Doc. Cops are like that. You try them from my side of the railway line one of these days. Even your nice Captain Faizal. There's no law for people like me yet. What were the dockets about?'

'Drug busts,' said Clare.

'Well, if you can smoke it, you can sell it on the Flats,' said Pearl. 'D'you find out what it's got to do with Yasmin?'

'There was a piece of elastic in the envelope. Pink elastic. Hers, I imagine.'

'Maybe,' said Pearl. 'But any house with a sewing machine is going to have some elastic lying around.'

'True,' she said, stopping at the traffic lights outside the Arderne Gardens, where they'd met the previous afternoon. A fourteen-year-old wearing a short skirt and tall boots swung on the poles of the bus shelter. Two women in a car weren't even worth a glance.

'Did she know anything, the 27s girl?'

'Not really.' Pearl inched her window open and lit a cigarette. 'Sorry, Doc. I've got to have a smoke. It's been a long day.'

'It's fine,' said Clare. 'Seems everybody smokes except me, these days. Do you think Voëltjie Ahrend knows anything?'

'It's hard to say what Voeltjie knows and what he doesn't.'

'You heard something?' asked Clare

'You know, sometimes it helps being female. Makes you invisible. They just talk as if you're not there.'

'What's your guess?' asked Clare.

'Voëltjie's got something big meant to be going on this weekend. He's not stupid. He doesn't want eyes on him right now.'

'What is it that's going on, Pearl?'

'Some deal of his. It's making Voëltjie very jittery, *op sy senuwees*.'

'Something's going wrong?'

'I tried to find out. Picking up *stompies*, it sounds like there's some big money issues. Some stock he should have is missing. Something he hasn't been paid for that's hurting someone higher up the chain.'

'You don't know what?' asked Clare.

'Doc, did you ever see that Maori movie, *Once were Warriors*?'

'I did,' said Clare. 'What's it got to do with this?'

'Keep your legs open and your mouth shut.' Some bitch in the movie tells that to her friend who's had the shit beaten out of her. It's the same here. So if I come asking questions, then I'm attracting attention. And I get *moered* and where does that get Yasmin?'

'Okay, Pearl, I get you.'

'So I just got to listen, and wait,' said Pearl. 'And you don't need to look at me like that, Doc. You think I don't know how fucking urgent this is?'

'Okay,' said Clare. 'So there's these drug cases and there's some money issue. But would Yasmin solve Ahrend's money problem?'

'No cop's going to have the kind of money that Voëltjie's interested in,' said Pearl. 'And it doesn't sound like she's for sale anywhere. Voeltjie's so the *moer* in that I get the feeling this whole thing was freelance. Somebody new, maybe trying to make things difficult for Voëltjie. Maybe not. It sure got him in the eyes again, and I don't think that's what he wants. Story is, he blames the cop's daughter for causing all the trouble.'

'Yasmin?'

'No, the other one. The one I told you about yesterday.'

'Calvaleen? You saw her?'

'She told me her boyfriend owed someone money. Took her out, wined her, dined her, gave her some tik to smoke. Said she might as well give him what he was going to take anyway. Fucked her in the car, just like that. They call it date rape in the magazines. I read it in *Cosmo*. It really fucked her up. Maybe because it was so soon after her father was shot. Maybe because she was a virgin.' Pearl shrugged. 'Who knows?'

'But who did the boyfriend owe money to?'

'She didn't say.' Pearl blew a jet of smoke into the cold night. 'But you don't fuck with Voëltjie, and in any case, he's pretty much got a monopoly on drugs and making women into whores. So must be him somewhere along the line.'

Pearl threw away her cigarette butt. 'You see, Voëltjie learnt at the foot of the master, thanks to your Captain. Faizal put him away, a year waiting trial. And where does he land up? With Graveyard de Wet.' She looked away as she carried on. 'Voëltjie came looking for me after he was released. Said he had a message from my father. It wasn't a message I wanted to get. But I got it anyway. You've seen what he does.'

'Too often,' said Clare.

'I hate to think of them together, the two of them. Voëltjie and my father.'

Pearl pulled her hoodie closer to her body.

'Is Yasmin dead?' asked Clare.

'I didn't say I heard that,' said Pearl.

'So, you heard something?'

'Rumours about rumours.'

'She's alive?'

'Maybe.'

'I'll stick with that,' said Clare.

'Me too,' said Pearl. 'You find anything out?'

Clare stopped the car opposite the entrance to the station. A couple of cars went past, then it was quiet again.

'You recognise this?' She held out Professor Young's sketch of the tattoo.

'Expensive. Not a prison chappie, that one. Whose is it?'

'I was hoping you might tell me,' said Clare.

'I've never seen this,' said Pearl, shaking her head. 'Where's it from?'

'An old man was beaten up on Table Mountain a couple of months ago. The pen he lost was found near where Yasmin Faizal disappeared.'

'I'll keep an eye out. Snake tattoos are hard to miss.' She opened the door. 'You got someone to check out the tattoo parlours in town?'

'Rita Mkhize,' said Clare. 'Captain Faizal's partner.'

'Let me see what I can find.'

'You'll call me?'

'Later. When I get home,' said Pearl. 'If I get something in the meantime.'

'Where're you headed?'

'The Winter Palace first, to see what's going on there. Then Valhalla Park,' said Pearl, punching numbers into her phone, 'where Voeltjie's old connections hang out. The ones he *verneuked*. I'll see if I can find someone who knows something and who's smoked enough to talk.'

'Be careful, Pearl.'

She gave a little wave as she walked along the broken white line in the middle of the street, her phone pressed against her ear. And then she was gone.

forty-four

Kennedy's Cigar Bar was packed, and the noise from the band doing bad cover versions was spilling out onto Long Street. There was already a queue at the door. Riedwaan took off his helmet and was enveloped by an old Pogues hit: punk meets wild Irish drinking song. The Congolese bouncer was a giant of a man, and his cowboy boots gave him another couple of inches. He cleared a path through the tipsy patrons and instructed a harried waitress to find Riedwaan a booth.

Riedwaan ordered a burger and a Coke. The waitress brought it over, but he couldn't eat a thing. He pushed his plate aside and ordered coffee instead. Sipping it, he endured the lead singer's wailing version of 'With or Without You'. An improvement on Bono, he couldn't help thinking, as he waited for Clare Hart to arrive.

Half an hour later, she turned up.

'I need to eat,' she said, sitting down. 'So do you – unless you want to collapse.'

She placed her order with the waiter. A lamb burger. A Coke.

'You get anywhere with Van Zyl?' she asked.

'Somewhere and nowhere,' said Riedwaan. 'What I want to know is, what do these cases have to do with Yasmin – if anything?'

Taking the grubby bit of elastic out of her bag, Clare said, 'They're connected.'

She dropped the elastic into Riedwaan's upturned hand. He curled his fingers round it, shutting in the fractured heartline that crept up his palm.

'She's alive as long as we have no proof to the contrary,' said Clare, unpacking her notes. She put the drawing of the tattoo on the table.

'The old prof I spoke to, the one who was mugged, says he remembers seeing this tattoo on the wrist of one of his attackers. He drew it for me.'

'Looks like an expensive one.' Riedwaan tucked the elastic into his breast pocket and picked up the sketch.

'That's exactly what Pearl said,' said Clare. 'She did some digging around Voëltjie. Says something big was meant to be happening this weekend. Something, she didn't know what, that looks like it might be coming unstuck. She says he's on edge.'

'He's always on edge,' said Riedwaan. 'His paranoia is what makes him so dangerous. And so fucking effective. What else did Pearl find out?'

The waitress appeared with a plate of food. Clare cleared a space for it and put tomato sauce on the chips.

'One rumour was about cash flow problems,' said Clare. 'Missing stock. Maybe this heroin?'

'Possible,' said Riedwaan.

'She also said that it was a cop's daughter that caused all this trouble.'

'Yasmin's six years old,' said Riedwaan. 'How can she cause anyone trouble?'

'Not Yasmin.' Clare put down her fork and looked at him. 'Pearl said he was talking about Calvaleen.'

Frowning, Riedwaan stared at her.

'Pearl said that Calvaleen had been raped. Some guy she'd been seeing,' said Clare. 'And that was where her drug problem started.'

'I heard something like that, but Van Rensburg didn't like to talk about it. Jesus, as if the family hadn't had enough after he was crippled. Gangsters target policemen's kids. One little drop of

245

poison is all you need to destroy a family.' Riedwaan rubbed his left eye. 'What else did Pearl say?'

'Something about Yasmin's abduction being freelance, a hire for someone else.'

'For who?' Riedwaan pushed his plate away, the food untouched. The noise level surged as a crowd of English tourists came in, sunburnt and already drunk. 'I Love Cape Town' T-shirts stretched across their beer bellies.

'Pearl had another version of your run-in with Voëltjie Ahrend,' said Clare. 'She suspects that Ahrend doesn't have anything to do with Yasmin's disappearance. At least, not directly. That he's not sure what's going on, or what you're up to. Which is why he's allowed you to live. He also wants to find out what's happening – how it's going to affect him.'

'If Voëltjie Ahrend had her, I'd know,' said Riedwaan, his hand touching the swelling around his right eye. 'We go back a long time. Why would anyone take her, though, with no demands?'

'If I could tell you that, then I could probably tell you where your daughter is,' said Clare. 'So let's stick to what we do have, okay?'

'Okay.' Riedwaan took out his cigarettes. 'What else do you have?'

'I called Rita,' said Clare. 'She had the pen finger-printed but nothing showed up on the records.'

'Couldn't lift the print?'

'They got some, but they didn't match. So that could mean you have a new recruit with Number tattoos who's never been to jail. This is a professional tattoo, not a blue prison chappie.'

'Using the tattoos as a kind of brand, you mean?'

'Something like that,' said Clare. 'Which isn't going to make the old guard happy.'

'Neither would using Graveyard de Wet's gun – the signature

murder of those two girls in Maitland.' Riedwaan lit a cigarette. 'What did Pearl say about the docket numbers?' he asked. 'Where did she get them?'

'It wasn't Pearl who dropped them off,' said Clare.

'No?' Riedwaan looked at her. 'Then who's pointing us that way?'

'Would it work for Voëltjie to keep Yasmin out of the way for something?'

Riedwaan shook his head.

'Would he have known that suspicion would fall on you?'

'The last time, there was big trouble.' Riedwaan's face hardened. 'You know that. Ndlovu came down on me. It was all over the papers: "Cop abducts daughter". And anyway, Voëltjie pays for enough eyes and ears in the force not to have to spend another five rand buying the *Cape Times*.'

'Lady in Red' crescendoed as the drinkers at the bar sang along with the band, either squeezing their girlfriends or demanding more beer from the barmaid.

'If she was with Voëltjie Ahrend and his 27s and she'd survived the first five minutes of their company, I'd know about it. And if I knew about it, I'd be making a deal with him.'

'What would you trade?' asked Clare.

'Anything.' His voice low. 'Anything at all.'

'Those docket numbers,' said Clare. 'Did you find anything?'

'Heroin busts.' Riedwaan took a pull on his cigarette. 'Smallish amounts, but very pure, so a high street value.' He unrolled Clare's map and marked the places. 'Here, here and here. Look where they are: in town, in Sea Point and in a million-rand security estate. Cape Town's caviar and cocaine belt.'

'So?' prompted Clare. 'Heroin's expensive.'

'It's a whole new market, heroin,' said Riedwaan. 'Can be all things to all men. The new boutique drug for the kids with wealthy parents and nothing to do.' He pointed to the Cape Flats. 'And here we have *tik* land. Where people still manage to find money for drugs that make them forget they're too poor even to buy polony for a sandwich. Both are places where you can print money by selling drugs. Just the denominations are different. The rich kids pay with their parents' cash until that runs out. And the poor kids pay with their bodies if they're good-looking enough – or, if they're not, by doing what their dealers tell them.'

'Ahrend is behind all this?'

'You could call him a kind of social bridge for the rainbow nation: his kind of corruption is equally at home in both places. Van Rensburg and Delport didn't buy it, but that's exactly what I was investigating with Phiri. Then things got a bit warm for certain people.'

'You spoke to the officers who made the busts?'

'I did,' said Riedwaan. 'All of them old-school station cops responding to things like noise complaints, so no big operation. I checked them out. Just the fluke of being in the right place at the right time. They went in, didn't like the look of things, and took it on themselves to search. At the time there was an order to take anything suspicious to Louis van Zyl's drug lab to get it checked out – some research he's doing, trying to track where different samples are manufactured so you can pin something more than a few grams on a dealer.'

Riedwaan pushed the lab notes towards Clare, who soon gave up after trying to read Van Zyl's handwriting.

'Well, what happened?' she asked.

'All of the cases got slapped with illegal search and seizure suits by Valkov and Cohn, an expensive city law firm. Apparently the venues all belong to the same owner.'

'And who's that?'

'A shell company,' said Riedwaan. 'Difficult to track, but the cops got rapped over the knuckles and so nothing happened with the cases.'

'Interesting. And who'd picked the dockets up from the lab?'

'The collections are logged into a tattered file that the security guard at the front desk fills out. I got a copy of the pages where the request for the dockets and the collections were logged. The names scrawled into the log book are illegible.' He pointed to the photocopied columns. 'These cellphone numbers are all a digit short. Whoever picked up these dockets didn't want to be found.'

'All the same person?' asked Clare.

'Looks like it, from the writing.'

'Security doesn't remember?'

'It's like a railway station there. And it's not a useful question, anyway. A security guard or a cop can earn his whole month's salary by making one docket walk,' said Riedwaan. 'Happens all the time.'

'You said Van Zyl had worked out where the heroin comes from?'

'All of it's from Afghanistan. Pure as the driven snow.'

'Where does it usually come from?' asked Clare.

'All over the show. Used to be mainly the Nigerians dealing in it, they cut it with lots of other stuff. This is something else, though.'

He took a coin out of his pocket and put it on the table.

'A kopek.' Clare scrutinised the coin.

'Yes, the second one I've found. 1989. End of the USSR, the year the Russians finally left Afghanistan,' said Riedwaan. 'Lots of veterans back on the streets of a country in meltdown. A bit like here, a couple of years later. First we have these drug busts, then two drive-bys, both with a kopek being tossed.'

'The Afghans,' said Clare. 'A bit more than a brand, d'you think?'

'The old gangs are moving on from simple extortion to holding entire communities hostage by selling drugs to their children, and then selling their children, who need to pay for those drugs. The Flats gangs and the prison gangs are consolidating, franchising their operations and extorting money when they can, pushing out small operators. Creating a monopoly. If they don't have to take it by force, then they pay for their new territory. Easier, quicker, and gets fewer officials into awkward situations.'

'And how do the officials fit into all this?'

'If your plan is to take over the running of a city's night-time economy, you need a lot of official collusion. Airports, harbours, courts, city council for re-zoning permission. You need them all – and they're cheap to buy. If they refuse to cooperate, they're easy to eliminate.' Riedwaan stubbed out his cigarette. 'The work I've been doing was to make the world safer for Yasmin,' said Riedwaan. 'It's the work that Shazia says brought this monster into our home.'

He rubbed the back of his neck, the muscles tight. 'If Pearl didn't drop those numbers, then who did?' Riedwaan persisted, 'These cases had already disappeared, if that's what someone wanted. So why bring them back again?'

'It has to be related,' said Clare 'There's a connection that we're not managing to make.' She paged through the copies Riedwaan had made, the details that Louis van Zyl had printed. Whatever it was that hovered on the periphery of her mind's eye refused to come into focus.

'Look, it's impossible to track who collected the stuff.'

Clare moved the small candle on the table closer, and pored over the security log. The columns – name, rank, phone number, case numbers, reason for visit, date, time – were crammed with impatient scrawls.

'Mandla, Verwey, Botha, Brickles, September.' Clare deciphered the names around the entry that concerned them.

'How's that going to help you?' asked Riedwaan.

'Might be someone who was there at the same time, who remembers something. 'Delport. Barkhuizen, this looks like. Xolani.'

'Delport,' Riedwaan stopped her. 'Which Delport?'

Clare studied the name. 'The initial is a T or an I.'

'What was he doing there?'

'"Purpose of visit: Business". Same as all the others.'

'Tertius Delport. Narc squad,' said Riedwaan. 'A survivor from the pre-'94 police force. But he's well connected.'

'Is he crooked?'

'Weren't they all?' asked Riedwaan. 'Delport's been around since the riot squad days. He wouldn't win the SAPS award for moral fibre, but no suspicion ever sticks long enough to turn into a suspension. He's been the cross Phiri has to bear, I suppose.'

'I met him once, briefly, at Caledon Square,' said Clare. 'With Van Rensburg. I didn't take to him much. D'you work together?'

'We do,' said Riedwaan. 'Well, we try, the three of us. Van Rensburg refuses to have anything to do with the drug cases. Ever since he was shot. Never goes out to the labs.'

'But Delport does?'

'Ja,' said Riedwaan. 'But there's no reason for him to have mentioned this to me. He doesn't always buy my theories about organised crime, but he'd have business at the labs, I suppose. And he's not much of a talker, Delport.'

'Wouldn't you have known, though, that this was being followed up?'

'I should have,' said Riedwaan. 'If that's why he was there.'

'Let's talk to him anyway,' said Clare, looking at her watch. 'Rita told me she had an uneasy feeling.'

'About Delport?'

'Not specifically,' said Clare. 'But she doesn't like him. Does he spend much money?'

'His vices are beer and under-age girls,' said Riedwaan. 'The beer, at least, he pays for.'

'How under-age?' asked Clare. 'The girls.'

'As long as they look under-age and aren't too expensive,' said Riedwaan. 'He's not fussy. But really, I can't see him doing anything to Yasmin.'

'He was at the lab,' said Clare. 'So let's ask him. D'you think he'll be home at this time on a Sunday night?'

'Home's a place he avoids,' said Riedwaan. 'Unless you think of home as a bar stool at the Royal in Maitland.'

forty-five

The television above the bar roared. Someone had scored a try. Impossible to tell who, as both teams were covered in mud. Delport felt cold air on the back of his neck. He looked around to see Riedwaan pushing open the saloon door. His eye flicked to the woman on the stool next to him. She moved up a seat, taking her brandy and Coke with her.

'Waste of a game,' said Delport. His small blue eyes shifted from the screen to Riedwaan and on to Clare.

'Took us a while to find you, Delport,' said Riedwaan.

'One for the lady,' Delport said to the barman. 'This ugly fucker can buy his own drinks.'

The barman poured two shots and pushed them across the counter. Clare ignored hers.

'Looks like the Royal's too good for your lady friend, Faizal,' said Delport. 'You'd better have it, after all.' He knocked back his drink.

'I'm not here for a *jol* with you.'

'Okay, so what's up, if you don't want to talk rugby and you're not interested in drinking and Ndlovu's on to you like a ton of gender-equity bricks because you took your daughter?'

'That's what I'm here to talk to you about, Delport.' Riedwaan moved closer. 'About Yasmin's abduction.'

'Why me?'

'You have connections,' Clare interjected. 'You seem to be able to make things disappear.'

'You must be out of your fucking mind,' said Delport, staring at her. 'Your friend Faizal there would kill me.'

'He mentioned that,' said Clare. 'I thought maybe I'd mediate.'

'A human shield or what? With Faizal in a rage, you want to be the collateral damage? You know what he does to people he disapproves of?'

Riedwaan pulled up a bar stool and sat down.

'I wanted to talk to you about some of your cases. Cases that got buried.' Riedwaan put the docket numbers on the counter.

Delport glanced at them, at Riedwaan, at Clare.

'One of which started down the road at the Winter Palace and ended up buried inside a drunk driving charge.'

'I don't know what you're talking about.' Delport lit a cigarette.

'Must have been very convenient for Voëltjie Ahrend's new best friend.'

'What? What are you talking about, Faizal?'

'Valentin the Russian, or whatever his name is. You and Voëltjie Ahrend. Seems like he has an interest there too. Although, with that amount of pure Afghan heroin missing, he must be feeling the pinch a bit.'

'You've got this all wrong, Faizal,' said Delport. 'And you're too *bosbevok* to see.'

'Delport. Listen to me.' Riedwaan's voice dropped dangerously low. 'As long as my daughter's alive, you're alive.'

'No, you listen to me. I don't know where the fuck she is. Do you think this was good for anybody, this? All this heat now? I've been working with the Gang Unit on this case for months – I had no choice. That means, like it or not, I've been working with you. It's taken a long time to get where we are. I want to retire alive. Why would I wreck it now by getting entangled with your kid?'

'Then explain these docket numbers, Delport.' Riedwaan's hand went up and twisted Delport's collar.

'I can't read if you're choking me, you fuckwit.' Riedwaan let him go, and the woman nearby shifted two more seats away.

Delport looked at the numbers.

'Heroin,' he said, taking a long slug of beer.

'Don't fuck with me, Delport.'

'Busts that I was going to bring up on Friday,' said Delport. 'Ask Phiri instead of choking me again.'

'You bring them in, then they vanish. To someone using a fake ID. What were you up to?'

'Faizal, I'm seconded by the Narc Squad. For my sins, I've got two bosses. You know what the SAPS is – all chiefs and no fucking Indians. There's nothing that'd make me do something to attract your attention. My face might not be pretty, but I prefer it where it is and not wiped all over the floor.'

'Who else knows about these cases?'

'It's not a secret,' said Delport. 'It was never a secret. It was routine. Routine bust, routine investigation, routine tests.'

'But not routine that these get buried,' said Riedwaan. 'Nor is it routine that my daughter disappears.'

'Where are the drugs?' asked Delport, a note of desperation in his voice.

'Gone too,' said Riedwaan.

'You have no idea who took the drugs?'

'Nothing,' said Riedwaan. 'Just like I don't know who buried these, nor who hid the documents.'

'I don't like you Faizal. But I wouldn't harm your kid,' said Delport. 'Just because I pay women to wear their hair in pigtails when I fuck them – sorry, Doctor – doesn't make me a paedophile. Look around you. D'you think I'd be drinking Black Labels here if I had a sideline in heroin? You're more fucking stupid than I gave you credit for.' He held up a finger. The barman brought a bottle of beer. 'Now if you two will excuse me—'

Clare's phone beeped. She opened the text message. Charlie Wang. She held out the phone to Riedwaan. 'We'd better get moving.'

Delport drained his glass.

'Thanks to Nokia for getting you to fuck off and leave me to drink in peace.'

forty-six

Riedwaan ran his fingers over the brass medallion fixed onto Clare's dashboard. The embossed figure with its staff and cloak had a dull sheen. The result of years of touch.

'St Christopher. You didn't strike me as superstitious,' he said.

'Doesn't hurt to hedge your bets.' Clare smiled as she jumped a red light. 'Patron saint of travellers. My father had this medallion on all his farm bakkies.'

A taxi hurtled round the bend towards them, lights on bright, on the wrong side of the road. Clare swerved out of its way.

'Fuck you,' she hurled after the taxi, its tail lights vanishing into the rain.

'He obviously knew what he was doing, your father, giving you this saint.' Riedwaan tapped the medallion.

'Most times, I wish he'd kept him.'

'Why do you say that?' In profile, when you couldn't see her eyes, Clare looked naive, almost girlish.

'Years ago, my father drove me down to university in Cape Town. He bought me a car and insisted that I take his St Christopher to protect me. Then he and my mother drove home. On the N7 the car rolled. A man on a donkey cart found them half an hour later, both dead.'

Riedwaan put his hand on her shoulder. 'I'm so sorry.'

The silence stretched between them.

'I was too.' Three cars ahead of them, the lights showed red. 'But tell me how a Muslim boy learnt his saints.'

'My mother sent me to a Catholic school, she wanted me to get a decent education. The images of flayed saints didn't do much to distract me from my own suffering.'

'Your father?'

'Killed,' said Riedwaan. 'When I was nine.'

The lights changed.

'You going to tell me?' she asked.

'Not much to tell, really.' He shifted slightly in his seat, facing her. 'Some of the sharper gangsters were learning struggle terminology. My father refused to pay what they called a community tax. He said it was extortion. One evening, when I was helping him unpack stock, three men arrived at his shop to discuss the matter with him. My father hid me. The men searched for the money. Found nothing. Put on a jazz record – loud. Fats Domino. My father's favourite. Broke my father's arms. Then his legs. Still he said nothing. So they cut his throat.'

Clare remembered the photograph she'd seen in Riedwaan's flat, the black-eyed boy staring straight out at the camera. And his father, looking down at his only son.

'I hid there,' said Riedwaan, his voice just audible over the hiss of the tyres on the road. 'I hid until the blood from my father's head seeped over the floor and the sacks of Basmati rice where I was hiding turned red.'

'Why didn't he just give them the money?'

'The cash box was in the crawl space under the rice where he'd hidden me.'

Another red light. He waited till it was green, till the car was moving forwards again.

'He died to save me, not the money. But that money paid for my schooling. That's what he kept it for – a school in the suburbs. I slipped into that narrow space that opened up as apartheid choked on its own bile.'

'Is that why you joined the police?' asked Clare.

'I was part of a gang for a while, thinking that that was a way of getting revenge. But I realised that in a year or so it could be me breaking some boy's father's bones for a thousand rand, or less. Then Mandela came out of jail. I gambled, joined the police. It paid off – until I joined Phiri and Van Rensburg to start the Gang Unit. I realised quickly that the worst gangsters are sitting in parliament, or have moved into boardrooms where they're safe. The high flyers. They know they're untouchable. They rent expensive lawyers, buy cheap politicians. And they walk. Take out anyone who gets in their way.'

Clare manoeuvred into the single open parking space on Charlie Wang's street. His were the only lights on at that hour in the old warehouse. The double slam of the car doors brought the sleepy guard out of his hut.

'It's Dr Hart,' said Clare. 'To see Charlie.'

He unlocked the gate and they squeezed through.

Riedwaan followed Clare two floors up the fire escape. Charlie Wang was waiting for them, the door to his lair ajar.

'Algorithms. A law unto themselves. I'm sorry it's taken so long,' said Charlie. 'But whoever took her knew how to dodge the cameras.'

They followed him to the greenish light flickering from his computer monitors.

A single image, frozen.

Yasmin's face.

Her face, floating upwards, fish-like, for a second. Then gone again.

'Where?' Riedwaan asked hoarsely, staring at the screen as the segment of tape replayed.

'The garage on Roeland Street,' Charlie replied.

'When?' Riedwaan faced Charlie Wang for the first time, taking in the rumpled white shirt, the belly, the bleary night eyes.

'Friday. Three minutes past seven.'

'Can't be.' Riedwaan stared at the log that Charlie placed in his hand. 'I drove past that garage about then. On my way back from the shooting in Maitland.' His face was ashen. 'I drove right past her.'

'There's more.' Charlie unwrapped a bar of chocolate and wolfed it down.

'Look at this.' Part of a number plate.

'CF something,' said Riedwaan. 'Maybe a G, maybe a number.'

'CF, CFG. That's Vredenburg,' said Clare, her pulse quickening. 'Or Morreesburg, one of those little farming towns along the N7.'

'It's a G,' said Charlie. 'That's my bet.'

The monitor flickered to life again and Yasmin's ghostly face floated inside the car window. The time code flashing in the corner. 'I managed to pull this out using some fancy Photoshop archaeology programme.'

'Did you trace the owner?' Clare's pulse quickened.

'My hacker friend could get onto eNaTIS – but then nothing.'

'The national information system? But did the traffic department detect that you were hacking?'

'No chance,' said Charlie Wang. 'The whole system crashed. Technical problems. They may be online again by Thursday. Something going on with the cellphone networks, too. Messages coming through in African time.'

'Can't anything be done in the meantime?' asked Clare. 'What about sightings on the national roads? Or other towns?'

'Nothing. Not even my friend can hack a crashed government department. And ever since they computerised you can't get in manually, not even to the *dorpies* on the N7,' said Charlie, turning around on his chair.

'You've got nothing else for us?' Riedwaan's voice rasped.

'I can tell you one thing,' said Charlie, pulling at a thread on his hoodie. 'Not that it'll be any help. There were no other hits that I could find in Cape Town. So I can't tell you how long the car's been in the city. If it has been here for a while, it doesn't get out much.'

forty-seven

Two cars were filling up at the Roeland Street garage, but the parking area tucked behind the building was empty. A short-order cook and a cashier watching the wall-mounted television were the only people inside the convenience shop.

'Can I get you something?' asked the cook.

'Just a couple of answers,' said Riedwaan. 'Were you working on Friday night?'

'Saturday, Sunday,' said the cook. 'Ask Cleopatra. She works every day.'

'Were you working on Friday?'

The cashier with the unlikely name looked at Clare and Riedwaan with fathomless boredom, then turned back to the television.

'What's it got to do with you?' she asked.

'I'm looking for my daughter.' Riedwaan pulled out a photograph of Yasmin. 'She may have been here, or somewhere near here, on Friday evening.'

The girl glanced at the photograph. Not a flicker of interest. 'I haven't seen her.' Eyes back on the television.

'She was caught on your cameras at 7.03,' said Riedwaan. 'Maybe you remember who was in the shop at the time?'

'Nah,' said the tattooed girl, twiddling her eyebrow piercing between thumb and forefinger. 'Lot of people come and go then. Rush hour.'

'Not at that time on a Friday night. Not at seven,' Riedwaan leaned over towards her. 'Town is empty by six. No clubbers around till ten. It's as quiet as a fucking grave around here. The car she was in waited in the parking lot for quite a while. So, think. Who was here? Who bought something to eat – a child's meal, maybe?'

'I can't remember.' The girl's expression did not change. 'I don't remember stuff like that. How would I be able to do this job if I did, the number of fuckfaces that come in here. Now let me go before I press the panic button. Cop or no cop.'

Clare put her hand on Riedwaan's arm, the tendons taut beneath her fingers.

'Can I ask you something?' said Clare.

'You too?'

'Have you ever seen this tattoo?'

The girl swivelled her eyes from the television to the sketch that Clare had placed on the counter.

'That's so cool,' she said, picking it up. 'I asked him where he got it.'

'Who?' asked Clare.

'The guy here on Friday.'

'Did you recognise him?'

'Never seen him before, but I liked his tattoo.'

'What did he look like?'

'He was his height,' nodding at Riedwaan. 'Skinny jeans, hoodie. Like everybody else. I told you, I don't remember what people look like.'

'What time was he here?'

'The news was on,' she popped a jelly tot into her mouth. 'It was dark, so I suppose about seven.'

'What did he buy?'

'Three burgers and a happy meal.'

'Who was he with?'

'By himself,' said Cleopatra, eyes drifting again.

'So why so many meals?' asked Riedwaan.

'How the fuck should I know? Do I look like someone's mom?'

'Did he take them out to the car?' asked Clare.

'Must have,' said Cleopatra. 'He didn't stay here.'

'Did he say anything to you?'

'Nothing. Just thanks. He had manners.'

'You remember the car?'

'No,' she said. 'I told you. I don't remember that kind of shit.'

'You remembered the tattoo.'

'I love tattoos,' she said. 'I saw it when he paid. Those two snakes, red and black.'

'I want the CCTV footage from inside on Friday,' said Riedwaan.

'You can ask the boss,' said the girl. 'But there's no point. They tape over every twenty-four hours. You're a day too late.'

Riedwaan went upstairs and found the owner watching television in his underpants. He shrugged when Riedwaan asked for the tape and told him to help himself. The girl was right. Nothing from Friday.

'Told you,' she smirked when he came downstairs again.

forty-eight

Riedwaan kick-started his bike and the engine growled as he rode towards the Bo-Kaap. Clare swung right and headed towards home. To go over everything again. To wait for first light.

He got the Jack Daniel's, fetched a glass and knocked back the first shot in the kitchen. Riedwaan breathed in, counting to four, then out, for a count of four. Shrink tricks. Useless. He closed his eyes. He saw Yasmin. He opened his eyes, he saw Yasmin. Her picture on the fridge. Smiling at him.

The wind rattled the old house. Making him hear things.

A car inching its way down Signal Street.

Again.

He checked the windows. They were latched. The kitchen door too.

He heard the car stop.

Riedwaan picked up his Browning. He didn't really miss the police-issue Beretta. He shoved the ammunition into his pocket, stepped away from his chair, and moved to the dark kitchen. He climbed onto the counter and peered at the street through the grimy fanlight. Two unmarked cars at the crest of the hill. Halfway down, another vehicle was angle-parked on the cobbles. Someone in the driver's seat, watching.

The street was blocked off.

One man with his back to him; two others crossing the street disappeared out of his line of vision directly below him. All of them armed.

One at the front door, one at the garage. Testing the roller door, which stuck against the metal bar he had wedged there.

The front door was an easier option. Riedwaan calculated that he had sixty seconds before the men broke through the wood.

He locked the kitchen door behind him. That would buy him another thirty seconds. He pulled himself up onto the courtyard wall and clambered his way to the rooftops he had explored as a boy.

He bent low, his feet following the familiar path over the roof-tops. He heard his front door splinter. Thirty seconds later, a single shot. The back door. He kept low, ducking and weaving, until he dropped down into Rose Street.

He saw his car parked there – Signal Street was too steep to risk such an old handbrake. But Riedwaan kept moving through the narrow alleys between the houses. Then he ducked into a recess between two houses. By now he was on Buitengracht. Then the gunning of an engine as a vehicle hurtled into view, its doors opening wide. Two men coming at him. The first two bullets whistled past his head.

Riedwaan bolted past the Catholic Church, heading towards the lights and the crowds on Long Street.

The next two bullets screamed past his head.

He dived down a dark lane.

The music from the clubs pulsed in the night.

Riedwaan flattened himself against a wall and checked the intersection. Apart from a couple of vagrants nesting in a shop doorway, there was nothing to the left.

He looked up the road, towards the mountain.

On the rain-splashed tar, a shadow. Moving slowly. Closer.

His back to the buildings, Riedwaan slid away, up the lane towards the church.

He felt razor wire at his back, coiled across a back entrance to the church. High above him was a recessed window.

The footfalls of two people moving up the lane.

Riedwaan pulled off his leather jacket. He wrapped it around his right hand and, steadying himself against the wall with his left, he grabbed the razor wire. He looked up at the slice of sky and hoisted himself up, hooking his right foot. He found purchase with both feet, and the wire held. The window was one metre closer. Two metres to go.

Twice more, and he'd be there. He pulled himself up again, then swung onto the window ledge, curling his body against the stained glass as the men flashed their torches at the spot he'd just left.

One of them kicked at a grubby blanket lying on the ground.

'Hey, I heard something,' he said.

'Just rats,' said the other. He shone his torch upwards, and then down along the narrow passage on the other side of the gate.

Riedwaan held his breath, his heart hammering in his chest.

'Too high,' he said. 'If he's gone, we're fucked. The boss is going to have our heads.'

Riedwaan crouched motionless until all he could hear was the distant beat of music from the clubs on Long Street. Then he waited another half an hour before dropping to the ground.

Stealthily, he worked his way back to the Bo-Kaap. His car was still in Rose Street. He waited another fifteen minutes, satisfied that no one seemed to be watching. He got in, took the handbrake off, coasted down the hill, and only started the engine when he was well clear of the area. Taking a back road, he turned towards Sea Point, and waited at the lights before turning into Beach Road. There was very little traffic.

Clare's lights were on. Again, she was working through her maps and her precise notes to try to discover what they were missing. Riedwaan was about to pull over when he noticed the car parked in the lee of a copse of wind-crippled trees. In the driver's seat, the glow of a cigarette.

The same vehicle he'd seen earlier outside his house.

Watching her.

Waiting for him.

It was too late for him to turn round, so he drove on, slowing for the woman teetering towards him from the shelter of the garage. He stopped and she bent down to his window, a smile in place.

'*Ag, nee*, Captain.' The smile vanished when she saw who it was.

Riedwaan kept his eyes on the vehicle behind him. The cigarette was gone, but the tail lights glowed red against the trees. He was being watched.

'Get in, Candy.' He leaned over and opened the passenger door. 'Now.'

'What is this?' she asked, sliding in. 'Charity?'

She crossed her legs, her skirt riding up. There was a yellow bruise on her thigh.

'Rough client?' asked Riedwaan.

'I can handle them,' she said. 'Not your business, anyway.'

'You working all night tonight?' he asked.

'Don't lecture me, Captain.' She took one of Riedwaan's cigarettes. 'I've got a living to make, just like you.'

'Where were you headed?'

'Business was slow,' she said. 'The Chinese sailor bar in Prestwich Street.'

'You need a lift?'

'What you want in return?'

'I need a place where I can be out of sight for a few hours.'

She looked at him warily.

'Just a bed.'

'Three hundred.' He opened his wallet. 'That's what I've got on me.'

She rummaged in her bag for a key.

'Three hundred for a bed without a duvet.' She reached for the money. 'You could stay in a hotel for that.'

'Too many people,' said Riedwaan. 'I need to be someplace where no one will look.'

'What you done this time, Captain?' She tucked the notes into the lining of her bag.

'Nothing out of the ordinary.'

'Number 801.' She handed him the key when he stopped the car. 'Bella Vista, behind the stadium. You can't miss it. You can sleep in my baby's bed.'

For a moment before she got out, Candy's fingers rested on the back of his hand. She picked her way through the puddles towards the bar on the corner. A quick negotiation with the doorman, and she was in.

Riedwaan walked up the eight flights of stairs to the flat. The main room was both sitting room and bedroom, the kitchen alcove was curtained off. Two doors. A bathroom, and a tiny bedroom with a panoramic view of the neighbouring block's water pipes. But Riedwaan wasn't there for the view.

Taking his phone from his pocket, he punched in Clare's number.

'What's happening?' she asked.

'I've just been chased all over town.'

'By whom?'

'I don't know,' he said, 'but I've just seen one of their cars parked outside your place.'

Clare looked out the window. 'Across the road?' she asked. 'Near the trees?'

'That's the one.'

'That's Salome Ndlovu's car,' she said.

'How do you know?'

'Same car she was in last night, when I was attacked outside the Winter Palace.'

'Call Rita and find out what the fuck's going on, will you, please?'

Five minutes later Clare called back.

'Salome Ndlovu wants to bring you in. Apparently she wants to speak to you,' she said. 'About Yasmin.'

'Strange ways of talking, they have,' said Riedwaan. 'They have something new?'

'Rita's trying to find that out,' said Clare. 'Where are you?'

'Never mind,' he said. 'I'm safe. I'm going to put my phone off in case they're tracking it.'

'And if I need to speak to you?'

Riedwaan picked up the phone next to Candy's bed.

'Use this number.' He read it to Clare.

Then he lay down on Candy's daughter's bed. Staring up at the Barbie poster stuck onto the ceiling, Riedwaan waited for the night to turn into morning.

forty-nine

There were no lights on in any of the surrounding houses when Pearl unlocked the door to her Wendy house. The cool night wind scoured the stuffy room. Her dishes in the sink still. Her panties soaking in the orange plastic bowl. She dumped her jacket on the scrubbed table.

Home.

She put on the radio, the volume low. It chattered at her, repeating the warnings of the coming storm. The DJ played a late-night request. Gloria Gaynor. 'I will Survive'. A stupid song, but she loved it anyway.

She dropped into the chair. Her legs finished, her ears still buzzing with music she hadn't wanted to listen to, her head fuzzy with alcohol she hadn't wanted to drink. The tik straw had been hard to pass up, but she'd only had the one hit. Thinking how nice to smoke the whole thing. And forget about the little girl. And Doctor Clare fucking Hart with her larnie accent and her confidence that she'd be strong. Pull through for her.

The message would wake Clare up, but she didn't think the doc would mind. She hadn't wanted to phone her earlier. Couldn't from the shebeens and *hokke* she'd ended up in. Couldn't in the taxi home either. Business about the cops and Voëltjie Ahrend wasn't something you spoke about where someone could hear you. The taxi driver with his mirror shades, checking her *skeef*. She'd been glad to get off before the last passengers, even if they were just *makwerekwere* chatting away in their Somali language.

Pearl poured a glass of Coke, tracing Clare's name in the condensation. Thinking that she must let her know. Hoping Clare would be able to make sense of the scraps of information. Trying to unscramble the stoned bits she'd heard. Thinking where to start. Starting to key in a message to Clare.

'It's taken me a long time to find you, Pearlie.'

Reflected in the window above the sink, the shadowed face of a man standing in the doorway. Shaven head, angular features.

Pearl froze.

'I followed you tonight, Pearlie. You were a busy girl. From work, talking to that TV doctor. Then all over. From Voëltjie Ahrend's fancy Palace, then out to the Flats. But I said to myself that Pearlie-girlies are always the best at home.'

The voice she'd believed she'd never hear again, sitting that day in the gallery when the judge sentenced him to life. Three times. Once, for the old woman. Again, for the mother. Life plus ten for the little girl. But nothing for her, watching. Nothing to compensate for her life, what he had done to her.

The sinewy body tilted against the door frame. The nightmare of her childhood, returned.

'What does Pa want?' The ingrained manners of a child, betraying her.

'Why were you with that *vuilgoed*? That crippled cop's daughter, that little junkie who Voëltjie's boys played with?'

'Calvaleen?' Pearl faced him. 'What did you do with her?'

'Nothing,' her father said, and smiled. 'Well, nothing that Voëltjie's heroin – or the little movie he made about her – won't do for me. I saw the film inside. Got it from a warder. But it's not her you should be worrying about, or that little doctor.'

He was in the room now, bringing the cold with him. The door was open onto the sandy patch of yard, where the washing hung forlornly on a line.

Outside.

The illusion of safety. All outside was a place from which you'd be dragged inside.

Inside.

Where she was now. Alone with him. How it'd always been. She resisted the pull of acquiescence. A habit, she'd learnt that.

'You got an *entjie* for your pa, Pearlie-girlie?'

Pearl's hand slid her phone back into her pocket. She felt the buttons, pressed send. The message for Dr Hart. Maybe she'd come. But Pearl remembered that Clare didn't know her address. So, she wouldn't come. Pearl on her own. Like always.

His proximity made it hard to think. She reached for the two singles she'd bought from the café. She passed him one, and the matches too.

She forced herself to breathe.

In, out.

In, out.

'You're not happy to see me?'

Graveyard de Wet ran his finger down his daughter's cheek, the cigarette in his hand curling smoke into her eyes. He scanned her body. The short hair, the new shirt, clean jeans, the boots.

'You not your daddy's girl any more, Pearlie? You too good for me, now?'

He pulled out a chair and settled himself at the table, elbows resting on the green Formica.

'Make me something to eat.'

She might as well, she thought. Could be her last. Pearl turned to the stove. An egg, bread, some fruit.

As she put the food in front of him, she saw the cutting on the table. His front-page moment. A yellowing photograph from *Die Son*. 'Monsters se Moer', the headline.

'I brought this for you, Pearlie-girlie.' He smiled. 'To remind you what you did.'

'I did nothing, Pa,' she said. She picked it up and put it in her pocket, her heart knocking. Her father in the dock, with her in a corner, listening to the sentence.

'You told the *boere* where I was. It's why that Faizal could find me.'

Pearl held the knife above the papaya. As she sliced the mottled skin, juice ran along the wooden board. The black pips glistened as the two halves fell away from each other.

'Here, Pa.' Placating him, another habit. 'Eat this.'

He pushed the fruit aside.

'You spoke to that doctor on TV. Said things about me. About the 27s.'

His hand hard on hers, the knife clattering onto the draining board.

'Why are you here?' she whispered.

'To teach you a lesson,' he said.

'Where's the child?'

'Faizal's child?' he asked. 'Fuck knows. Dead.'

Pearl's knees buckled and she slid to the cold floor. The feral tang of him, obliterating her other senses. Reduced to smell, that most primal of the senses. The oldest, animal part of her brain had failed her – unable to flee, she crouched, immobile. Her head bent to her knees, exposing the nape of her neck, Pearl tried to imagine the blow that would fall.

It didn't come. It never had come, release.

'And then to teach the same lesson to Voëltjie Ahrend.'

He squatted next to her, his breath moist on her bare arm.

She pushed her fists into her eyes.

Why had she imagined she'd be allowed to go free? How could she have believed again? Like the time she was a little girl and she'd hidden in the ceiling. Only to come down the next morning and to find him there, waiting for her. The stupidity of her own cleverness. She bit down into her own tongue, refusing him. The blood was salty in her mouth.

'Are you ready to learn again, Pearl?'

'I don't know, Pa.' He pushed a knee into the hollow below her breastbone. 'I don't know.'

Her senses returning.

The wind up, now, howling.

His left hand a vice on her arm, the knife in his right. She raised her head and looked at him, the blackness beginning to clear. She bared her teeth, plunging them into the ropey hand. He did not flinch. He had time to work on her. With a knife in his hand, he always got what he wanted.

Pearl knew what was coming. She'd fight, of course. She would fight till the end, a sacrifice that would protect her Hope, forever oblivious in her white bed.

fifty

Yasmin thinks about her party clothes – a yellow skirt stiffened with tulle and a Little Miss Sunshine T-shirt – waiting for her at the top of her mother's cupboard. She squeezes her eyes shut against the darkness, but her picture of the clothes is faint, like the reflection on a night-time window. Like the window she used to sit next to in the dark, watching for her daddy to come home. He would kiss her goodnight, holding her closely before she sank into a deeper, safer sleep.

But now all she feels is an ache. It's been there for nearly a year. Ever since the terrible birthday when her daddy didn't come home and she'd fallen asleep next to her cake with its unlit candles, the terrible day when Uncle Clinton had been shot, and her daddy too. But her daddy just needed a bandage. And he could walk properly still. She was glad that the wind was blowing, moaning like a mad woman outside her window, because she couldn't hear the sound of her parents arguing later and later into the night until she heard the front door slam.

She'd lain awake until it was light enough to get up, and when she went into the kitchen for breakfast her mother's eyes were puffy and her mouth was hard and there were only two places laid at the breakfast table. Yasmin sat as still as a rabbit in the headlights. It wasn't hard, because that was how she felt. There had been nowhere to run to, so she just watched as her mother took down daddy's picture from the wall.

It didn't help to remember all that, but what she did remember was that when Tuesday came, she'd be seven. She would remember all her birthday cakes. She couldn't remember her first birthday. Nor her second, but she had seen the pictures.

A teddy bear.

A yellow duck.

Three had been a fat green pony; a Pegasus that looked like a frog.

Four was a train with wheels made out of Liquorice Allsorts.

Five, a bee with yellow gauze wings that caught alight when mommy lit the candles.

Six had been a fairy castle.

And seven was going to be a ballerina: a Barbie stuck into a cone of pink, flounced icing.

There. She'd remembered them. All her cakes.

She needed to hoard them, the memories with a whole story. She would go back to them later, when the fear pressed against her lungs again. For now, she would listen to the quiet. That, she knew how to do – trying to measure the distance of things. Where she was. How far things were from the pit she was in.

The dark can last a long, long time.

Sometimes not long enough, though.

His voice again. The man, lowering the ladder, climbing down, putting his hands on her body. She scrambles away, gashing her knee, but he is there before she can do anything, grabbing her hard.

He places her precisely; tells her what to do.

She obeys. She does not want to make them angry again. The pain of their anger is fingerprinted on her arms, her back.

The masked man switches on the camera.

Yasmin holds out her hands towards him, her nails bloody from trying to scrabble out of the pit, and she dances.

August the twelfth
MONDAY

fifty-one

The cereal was finished, so was the milk. Clare put a ready-made meal into the microwave. She watched as a kayaker cut a silver line across the ocean, and when the microwave pinged she pulled herself away from the window. Lasagne for breakfast. She'd had worse.

Leaning against the counter, she ate without tasting, letting her thoughts drift. Casting about for a missing thread.

Calvaleen.

Who she still had not spoken to because she didn't answer her phone.

She put the half-finished food back into the fridge, pushed aside her maps and notes, and pulled out Madame Merle's file of green notification slips. Calvaleen's was there, with the family address below the signature.

Clare took the elevated freeway out of town, then the slip road to the new suburbs spreading east of Table Mountain. The streets were raw gashes in land that had once buffered the serried rows of neat, post-war houses from the expanding townships on the Cape Flats. Estate agents' boards adorned the few remaining trees and the new lamp posts.

The complex was on the edge of a suburb stuck between the freeway and a bleak industrial area. Clare stopped at the security gate. A guard approached, clipboard in hand, his gun a lump under his jacket.

'What number, please?' Thick French accent. Yet another refugee from an imploding Congo, ensuring Cape Town's security.

'Number eight. Van Rensburg.'

The guard lifted the boom and waved her through.

She rang the doorbell. A 'For Sale' sign hung askew on the house next door. Clare was about to ring a second time when she noticed a slim shadow behind the amber glass.

'Dr Hart.' Anxiety filled Latisha van Rensburg's voice. 'What are you doing here?'

'I'm looking for Calvaleen.'

'You too?'

'Who else is looking for her?'

'A girl.' Latisha's grip tightened on the door handle. 'A bit older than Calvaleen. She came here last night. Very late.'

'Short hair, scar on her face?' asked Clare.

Latisha nodded.

'Pearl?'

'She didn't say. Took off again when I told her Calvaleen wasn't home.'

'She back now?'

'She's not here,' Latisha murmured. 'She wasn't here last night either.'

'I need to ask you some questions then,' said Clare. 'About Yasmin's disappearance.'

'Why?' asked Latisha. 'What's Calvaleen got to do with Yasmin?'

'She knew Yasmin well, ever since she was born, in fact,' Clare said softly. 'You might be able to help me understand a few things.'

'I've been with Shazia Faizal most of the time. She's convinced that Riedwaan has Yasmin.'

'And what do you think?' asked Clare.

'If only it was that simple,' said Latisha. 'You know, my husband bought us this place after he was shot.' She pointed to the eight-foot wall with its wreaths of razor wire. It opened onto a field beyond, where no child dared venture. 'But nothing keeps you safe.'

Latisha opened the door just wide enough for Clare to enter.

The walls of the entrance hall were covered with framed photographs of Calvaleen dancing, spectral in white tulle.

'This is her rehearsing for the role of Persephone?' asked Clare. Latisha nodded.

'Why didn't she dance it?' asked Clare.

'Things got in the way.' Latisha was walking down the passage.

Clare followed her, past the formal sitting room with its couches covered in protective plastic. More photographs lined the passage walls. SAPS rugby teams. Massive men with hairy arms draped over each other's necks. A single photograph of men in green-and-gold tracksuits. Clinton van Rensburg one of them, so different to the diminished man she'd seen hobbling down the corridor in Caledon Square.

'My husband,' said Latisha, noticing Clare's interest in the photos. 'But these days he just works all the time. Strategic human resource deployment. Some rubbish like that. Not good for a man who likes to do things rather than think about them.'

Latisha pushed open the kitchen door. On a small table were three unused place settings. The smell of last night's uneaten supper still hung in the air.

'Can I give you some coffee?'

'Thank you.' Clare knew that making coffee, putting out cups, are small rituals that calm the fearful; they'd be likely to make her presence more palatable in this still, cold house.

'You were saying ... things got in the way of Latisha's dance performance?'

'School, being busy. Being a teenager. She got sick of dancing every evening, every weekend. Wanted to do other things too.'

Latisha busied herself with the kettle and a plunger, spooning out coffee. 'Would you get the milk out?' she asked.

Clare opened the fridge, knocking off a photo stuck to the door as she did so.

'Sorry.' She picked it up. Clinton van Rensburg and Riedwaan with their daughters. Yasmin grinning on her father's lap. Calvaleen staring ahead, her face sullen. 'Children's Day at Caledon Square' read the caption. Clare put the photo back among the clutter of notices from the ballet school. She noticed a reminder about changes in schedule, with Friday's early closing highlighted in orange, and a green permission slip with the bit that needed signing torn off. There was also a letter from the Royal School of Ballet in London offering a second audition.

'What happened about this London audition?' she asked.

'She missed it.' Latisha was pushing down the coffee plunger. Some of the hot liquid spilled onto her hand. 'What do you want, Dr Hart?' she asked. 'Why are you here asking me questions about Calvaleen? It's Yasmin who's missing, so why are you wasting your time here?'

'Children know things about each other that adults don't,' Clare tried to explain.

'She's not a child. She's seventeen.'

'But you still send in her forms, even though she's no longer at the ballet school?'

'Habit,' said Latisha. 'Hard to break. Her father likes things to be orderly. Drove her crazy.'

'Can I keep this?' asked Clare, fingering the permission slip.

Latisha shrugged. 'If you want to, I suppose.'

'You said she was dancing. At the Winter Palace?'

'Yes,' said Latisha, brightly. 'Loving it.'

'I went there. I didn't find her there.' Clare saw the tension snap across Latisha's face. 'So where is she?'

'I wish I knew,' Latisha's whisper was fierce. 'If I knew I'd have fetched her myself. The last time I spoke to her …'

'When was that?'

'Thursday. She phoned me. Said she needed a thousand rand.'

'Did you give it to her?'

'Of course I gave it to her.'

'What trouble is she in?' asked Clare.

'Dr Hart, when – if – you are ever a mother, you will know that there are questions that you don't ask a child. Not even when you are alone in your bed at night, because if you did, you wouldn't get up again the next day.'

'I'm not a mother, so I won't argue that one,' Clare conceded. 'Now would you mind if I took a look inside her room? We might find something there that'll give an indication of where she's living.'

'She took her keys with her the last time she was home,' said Latisha.

'Let's try anyway. Maybe with a tool,' said Clare, her hand on Latisha's arm. 'We need to check whatever we can. Do something about finding her. What does her father say about all this?'

'He never says much about anything. And since he was shot, he says nothing at all,' said Latisha. 'He works longer and longer hours. He probably thinks that if he gets the gangsters who shot him, he'll again be the man he once was. He won't face me. Won't face his daughter and what she's become, all because of him.' Latisha yanked open a drawer and took out a key. 'As if it's impossible to be a husband and a father just because you walk with a stick.'

'This way,' she gestured. 'The tools are in the garage. I don't go in there much,' she said. 'Unless I was bringing Clinton his coffee.'

On the workbench lay an array of tools and some pieces of yellowwood, all covered in a film of dust.

From a nearby shelf, Clare picked up a miniature dresser, complete with hooks for tiny cups.

'He doesn't make these any more?' asked Clare.

'Not since the shooting incident,' said Latisha. 'It used to be his

285

stress release, making this perfect little world. The opposite of the real world, I suppose.'

'These are so intricate,' said Clare, fingering the model chairs and tables, the facades of doll's houses, windows draped with red and white gingham.

'This was Calvaleen's,' Latisha said, pushing aside a partition. Another garage, a car obscuring the replica of a Cape Dutch farmhouse, complete with gables, *werf*, wagons and dovecote. 'He made it for her when she was born. She sold this a month ago. Said she was too old for dolls. I bought it back. It would have broken her father's heart if he'd known.'

'Your daughter's an addict, isn't she?' said Clare.

'I was warned,' said Latisha, straightening the tarpaulin covering the car, 'that gangsters target policemen's children. But it was after Clinton was shot that things fell apart. He came back from hospital – but he's not the same man. Blaming himself, blaming Captain Faizal.' She wiped the tears from her eyes.

'Why Captain Faizal?' asked Clare.

'For saving his life, I suppose,' said Latisha. 'I think for Clinton it would have been better to be dead than the cripple he is now.'

'And your daughter?' Clare probed.

'I know nothing about drugs and she doesn't speak to me, hasn't since what happened.' Latisha selected a Phillips screwdriver from her husband's tools. 'I just know she's my daughter, and I'll do anything to keep her alive. If you think looking in her room will help, then let's go and do it.'

Latisha unscrewed the door handle, exposing the lock mechanism. The lock clicked back and the door swung loose from the frame. Clare stepped into Calvaleen's room. The bed was unmade, the pink duvet and pillow a jumbled heap, tangled up with discarded clothes. She opened the curtains and the windows, letting in a rush of air with the sunlight.

'Okay, you look around,' said Latisha.

Clare opened the drawers in the bedside table. Nothing much, apart from last year's school diary. Clare flicked through it. A few entries. Homework, maths exercises. Phone numbers at the back.

'Can I keep this?' asked Clare.

'Yes. Should be fine.'

On the notice board above the empty desk an old ballet pro-gramme, ballet notices, a couple of pictures torn from a magazine, the number of a tattoo artist in Long Street, an expired ticket to the Arderne Gardens.

Latisha opened Calvaleen's cupboards.

A white basket stood below a few garments hanging from a rail.

'Her old ballet stuff,' said Latisha. 'She never throws anything out.'

Clare lifted the wicker lid. Old leotards and ballet shoes, a tiara, a tangle of pink elastic. All in an untidy heap.

She closed the lid and looked through Calvaleen's clothes, the pockets, the empty shoe boxes, her panty drawer.

'Nothing,' said Clare.

'What I thought,' Latisha frowned. 'Nothing.'

'She didn't take much with her, did she?'

'No,' said Latisha. 'She'll be home soon. I took her some clean things and I gave her the money.'

'Where did you meet her?'

'At the KFC in Maitland. Near where she works. I ordered her an apple slice, but she wouldn't eat.' Latisha pressed her hands to her chest. 'She's so thin, Dr Hart. So thin.'

Latisha picked up a pair of ballet shoes that had been left under the bed. The long pink ribbons hooked on something, so she shifted the bed slightly, loosening the ribbons and also dislodging a photograph that had slipped between the bed and the wall. Clare saw it and pulled it out. A copy of a photograph in the hall.

Calvaleen dancing, arms raised, slender neck a pale stalk against the dark backdrop, feet extended as she seemed to float across the stage. 'With love, EH' pencilled on the back.

'Who's EH?' asked Clare.

'Stands for Edmund Harries. He took this picture, and the ones in the hall too. Also the ones you saw at Shazia's house, of Yasmin.'

'Does he work from a studio somewhere?' asked Clare. 'He seems to have a feel for dance.'

'It's actually Mister Henry – that's what everyone calls him. He plays the piano at the ballet school. You must've met him there?'

'Tall and thin, a funny way of walking?'

'That's him. He was a dancer too, in his day. Often played extra for Calvaleen so she could rehearse. Yasmin too. He loves her, called her his *engeltjie*. Made so much time for the little girls.'

Clare propped the photograph on Calvaleen's desk.

'He's been a real friend to my daughter. Mister Henry understood suffering, that's what Calvaleen told me. It's probably what Yasmin liked about him too.'

Clare stepped out of the curtained interior, blinking as Latisha opened the front door for her. Then, as the guard lifted the boom, she turned towards town.

She thought of Mister Henry and his generosity and understanding.

Mister Henry and his extra rehearsals.

Mister Henry in charge of the attendance slips, with access to all the girls' details.

fifty-two

On her way back to the city, Clare called Madame Merle. Yes, she replied curtly, she and Mister Henry had left at about five-thirty. Yes, Henry had been there and locked up. No, she didn't know what time he'd left. Hadn't Clare thought to ask him herself? Yes, he had been in and out of therapy. And yes, he was not allowed to be alone with any of the girls. Nothing personal; that was school policy.

Next call was to Riedwaan, but his phone went to voicemail. So did Rita's landline and her cell. Clare needed more coffee, and she needed to think. The only place open on Roeland Street was the bookshop. She ordered an Americano and thought about the photograph of an ethereal Calvaleen.

Again, she read through the notes she'd made on Saturday morning, his responses. He had been edgy. But who wouldn't be if a child nominally in your care disappeared? She booted up her laptop. Scanned through a list of men that Rita Mkhize had done background checks on. Henry Harries – Mr Henry – was on it. No Edmund Harries. Her slip. That's why she hadn't picked it up the first time. Clare's chest tightened.

She Googled Henry Harries. Nothing, not even on Facebook. She searched her own databases. Nothing. If he'd ever been convicted under that name, it hadn't made the press.

Clare tried Riedwaan again.

Rita's voice.

'Put Riedwaan on the line,' Clare said impatiently. 'Where is he? Why doesn't he answer his phone?'

'Special Director Ndlovu's booking him,' said Rita. 'For assaulting a police officer and resisting arrest.'

'Oh, for fuck's sake,' Clare said. 'They came after him – without a warrant. How in hell did she come up with the assault charge?'

'Says on the charge sheet here that one of her men dislocated a shoulder.'

'Probably just fell in the dark,' Clare said. 'Nothing to do with Riedwaan.'

'Salome Ndlovu doesn't care. Everyone knows Riedwaan talks with his fists sometimes, so she gets him into the cells and it's her boy's word against Riedwaan's in front of a hung-over Monday morning magistrate.'

'But it's obvious. He doesn't have the child. That voice message should have been enough to prove that to her.'

'She's not even going there,' said Rita. 'He assaulted an officer.'

'So Yasmin's out of the picture now?'

'She says she has to use what she's got. She insists that he pre-recorded that message and sent it to his house,' Rita explained. 'She says she's not buying it, that Captain Faizal can't prove where he was at the time, so she says it must have been him who sent the message.'

'Kafkaesque logic.'

'*Kak* logic *se moer*,' said Rita. 'There's no fucking logic here at all.'

'What's Phiri doing about it?'

'He's hauled a police lawyer out of bed. They'll work something out. Phiri knows how to make the rules work for him,' said Rita. 'What did you want, though? You called me.'

'Rita, I need you to check something for me,' Clare said. 'On your sex offenders database.'

'There's fuck-all I can do,' Rita answered. 'Salome Ndlovu. Wants my head on a platter too. I'm under investigation for insubordination and about ten other things besides. All words with more than three syllables – so I never bothered to remember what they meant. Upshot is I've got no access to my computer or to my phone.'

'But I have to get this checked,' Clare persisted. 'Who can do it for me?'

'I'll give you my office key,' said Rita. 'Where are you?'

'The Book Lounge,' said Clare. 'A block up from you.'

'Sharp. Nobody would guess that a cop could read, so I'll be right out of the firing line. Be there in two minutes.'

'Two minutes,' said Clare. 'Outside.'

Rita dashed to the bookshop and gave Clare the key. 'Here,' she said. 'I told them I was going to the bathroom. I'll be in worse shit if they catch me talking to you. Go to my office. Here's a pass. It'll be empty. Log on there. The password's "weekend special". Speed search. If anyone catches you, I'm dead.'

Minutes later, Clare flashed the pass at the desk and walked briskly towards Rita's office. She typed in the password, and while the computer came lazily to life, she checked the flurry of text messages that had come through on her phone. The overloaded network waking up to a Monday morning *babalaas*. Two messages from Riedwaan, one from Rita, and a message from Pearl that looked as if she'd pressed 'send' before she'd finished typing.

The database gave a little beep when it had loaded. Clare put away her phone and started reading. Names neatly partitioned into convicted sexual offenders and acquittals. Many of them for lack of evidence that forced frustrated judges to acquit a man because a child had stumbled over her words. Or because a lab had lost the physical evidence so painfully scraped from under nails, or from inside body cavities. Other men that the court was forced to find not guilty on serious offences, but could still compel to seek therapy.

The list in front of her. Those guilty of lesser crimes. Loitering. Littering. Given an option of a non-custodial sentence and compulsory counselling at the New Beginnings Clinic. Their speciality:

eating disorders, drug and alcohol addiction, sex addiction, sexual disorders. Tuesday and Thursday evenings for the men who like children. The Lolita lovers, as they called themselves.

Clare shut down Rita's computer. She pushed her chair back, remembering the interview she'd filmed at the Clinic some years back for her doctorate. The director's adamant stance that perpetrators were often broken beings, needing to be re-wired for empathy, love. She and Clare had not seen eye to eye. Clare doubted that she'd get past the clinic's iron gates. And even if she did, the strict confidentiality code would prevent her from gaining access to the names of the men who attended the group session. Not even with the list of the voluntary out-patients at New Beginnings.

A flood of noise in the passage.

When all was clear she slipped out, back into the street.

Clare was on her own. The way she preferred things.

The New Beginnings Clinic was discreetly tucked away on the lower slopes of Lion's Head. On the lawn outside, a group of blank-eyed teenagers with bongos clutched between their knees sat in a silent circle. After a couple of minutes, a therapist arrived and they beat an obedient rhythm on their drums.

The building bristled with private cameras. There would be a bank of TV monitors in the bowels of the building somewhere. A brawny, unsmiling man stood outside the gate, arms folded, his bouncer's eyes fixed on her. A sign above his head: 'No admission without a prior appointment.'

Clare walked on.

At the corner of the street was another camera. City security. Its black eye peered down the leafy street where an elderly woman, head down, was dragging a wicker shopping basket. Cameras everywhere, just as Clare had remembered.

She found the number of the Cyclops Centre.

Arno Pretorius answered, no less abrupt on the phone than he was in person.

'Coordinates?'

She gave him the address and the cross streets, and waited for him to call back.

'You're in luck,' he said. 'The German football fans were allocated that area. 2010 cameras everywhere there. Tuesday and Thursdays, you said?'

'Yes,' said Clare. 'Fifteen minutes before six. Then the fifteen minutes after eight.'

'How long will you be?'

'Ten minutes or so.'

'I'll copy it onto a disk. It'll be waiting for you.'

Clare looked back at the clinic, its facade hiding more sins than the confessional of the Catholic Church. A woman pushed open a top floor window. She raised her hand. A blessing or a dismissal. Impossible to say, from this distance.

fifty-three

Mister Henry's ground floor flat was in a battered council block. His curtains were still drawn. No movement yet. Too early to be at the ballet school; too poor to be out for breakfast. Clare had parked a little way down the street, where she sat listening to the call and response of dogs barking in the neighbourhood.

Twenty minutes later, in her rear-view mirror, Clare saw him. She sank lower in her seat and watched as he approached. Head down, shoulders hunched, hands deep in the pockets of a long black coat. He picked up his mail – all of it junk, she'd checked – and went inside.

She waited another five minutes before crossing the rubbish-strewn yard. The sliding door was to the right. Henry was sitting on a chair in front of a flickering computer screen, his pale face reflected in the monitor. Clare tapped on the glass.

He yanked the iPod buds from his ears.

She knocked again and he spun round, blanching when he recognised Clare. He opened the door. 'Why are you here, Dr Hart?'

'We're going to have a little conversation,' said Clare. Classical music dribbled from the earphones. *Persephone*.

'About what?' Mister Henry hobbled back to the screen. He reached for the mouse, his hand casting a shadow over the image of the child in the play park. But Clare caught his wrist before he could minimise the image on the screen.

'Let's talk about Yasmin. It's a conversation we should have had before.'

'You've got it wrong, Dr Hart,' he said. 'I don't know where she is. And if I did, I would have told you. I love that child. Just like I …'

'Just like you what?' Clare moved closer to him. He tried to move away but she had the back of his chair wedged against the desk. 'Just like you loved Calvaleen? All those photographs? I think you should show me what you've got on your computer.'

'Nothing,' he said. 'Just documents.'

'Scroll through them,' said Clare. 'Go on.'

He did so, opening word documents and correspondence.

'There,' said Clare. 'Open that one.'

He clicked on the folder. Hundreds of video clips.

'Home-made movies?' asked Clare.

'It's not what you think.'

'I don't think you have any idea what I think, Harries. Open that one.'

He double clicked. The camera was focused on a child's hands folded delicately in on each other, fingernails bitten to the quick. The camera pulled back as the dancer moved her arms and raised her torso. Her neck was bent, her black hair in a jewelled bun at the nape. Yasmin looked out of the picture, straight at Clare. Then she raised her arms above her head, turned sideways, and smiled at an older girl with sleek dark hair, whose tulle skirt floated around her thighs as she leapt through the air. Calvaleen.

'You can look through it all. It's not going to lead you to her.'

'I want you to watch this,' said Clare. 'Taken outside the New Beginnings Clinic.'

'Great name,' said Mister Henry. 'Like the township where I grew up. Ocean View. The only way you saw the sea was if someone sent you a postcard.'

Clare inserted the disk.

The surveillance tape flickered to life on the screen. The time code: five forty-five. Fifteen minutes before Florence April's Tuesday appointment. A man in a banker's suit, briefcase in hand, strode down the street. He pressed the bell, spoke into the intercom that Clare had used earlier. The gate slid back to give him access. Another man. Then another. One wearing a pink golf shirt. An elderly man, his brown trousers baggy on his skinny backside. Two arriving together. Blue shirts, fawn trousers. Indistinguishable. The men who waited on the periphery of lonely children's lives. Several more. One in blue overalls. A couple that looked like school teachers, their shirts jaunty. Some time after six, limping in late, a tall man on his own. Mr Henry.

Clare stopped the tape. 'New Beginnings. Cape Town's only specialised programme for sex offenders.'

'You've got me wrong, Dr Hart.'

'Sex offenders are like politicians,' said Clare. 'Seven percent conviction rate on a good day. In my book, not guilty isn't going to make you innocent.'

Henry laughed, a bitter, flat sound.

'Let me see if I can make you understand something. That cupboard,' he pointed. 'Look inside.'

Clare opened the cupboard. Inside, the scuffed pointe shoes hung twisted on their hooks, long ribbons curling like pale, attenuated leaves against the pink satin. Henry unhooked a pair and handed them to her.

'Calvaleen's.' He turned the satin inside out. He held the shoe out to Clare. There was a dark stain at the tip.

'Bloodstains,' said Mister Henry. 'It's like Chinese foot-binding, the eroticism of ballet. The fantasy of grace from pain, beauty from agony.' He ran his forefinger over the dark stain. 'Calvaleen never came back after the first Persephone audition. She would have had the part. She never came back either for the audition for the London School of Ballet. I wanted to go and find her, and so I looked in her locker. All I found were her shoes.'

He fingered the satin again.

'I phoned her mother afterwards, but she wouldn't let me speak to her. Gave some weak excuse. When she never pitched up for the second audition, I went to look for her. I found her dancing at the Winter Palace. It's my fault, I suppose. It was me who told her about the place. I thought it would be a better way of earning a living than what she was doing on the street sometimes.'

He lit a half-smoked cigarette and blew a smoke ring, watching it relax into ribbons as it floated in the air.

'I played there sometimes. What Madame Merle pays wouldn't keep a mouse alive. You see, I tried to watch over her. I understand her.'

'Isn't that what every man who seduces children says?' said Clare. 'That's what the director of the New Beginnings Clinic told me when I interviewed her; that he mimics a child's loneliness. That he mimics their sense of isolation and neediness, pretending that he feels the same. Isn't that how the paedophile persuades that child? Grooms her? Wins her trust by convincing her that he's the one who understands her? That together they can create a perfect world, if the child does as he says? Isn't that what you did with Yasmin?'

Mister Henry did not stir.

A truck roared past. Then silence. Clare waited.

'There were some boys I grew up with who didn't like dancers, especially ballet dancers.' His voice, quiet as it was, cut into the surrounding silence. Didn't like anyone they couldn't control in the area. It meant a loss of profit.'

He pulled up his trousers. Both ankles were strapped, his long, slender legs ending in a mass of scars, the steel callipers biting his flesh. 'They stamped on my ankles. That was one of the ways they taught me how to be a man. The same gang that stopped me dancing sold me the drugs that took away the pain. So you see, Dr

Hart, I fought my own demons. Just like Yasmin, like Calvaleen. Both of them are paying for the sins of the fathers.'

'Their father's sins?'

'It's easier to get to a girl than it is to get at a man with a gun. And getting the girl destroys the man anyway. Look at Calvaleen's father, eaten alive with hatred,' said Mister Henry. 'I can understand your mistake, Dr Hart, I can see why an intelligent woman like yourself would make it. But I help others now. Not all of us turn our rage onto other victims. I did some counselling for the voluntary sexual offenders group for a while. And I do some volunteer drug counselling. Drug-buddy, if you like. Calvaleen was at the clinic for a while. I used to visit her there. That's why I was on that tape.'

'Is she still there?' Clare's voice gentler now.

'No,' said Henry. 'She checked out after the last time I saw her. Couldn't handle it.'

'Where did she go?'

His cigarette had burnt down to the yellow filter.

'She came here.'

'Is she still here?'

Henry shook his head. 'She needed a place. She said she'd stay with me if I didn't ask any questions. She slept here for a while and then she took off again.'

'When was that?'

'Late Saturday night. She'd been to work before she came here, but not for long,' said Henry. 'She was very agitated. Said she had to do something. Fix something. She wasn't making sense, and she didn't look good.'

'Did she tell you what it was?'

'No,' said Henry. 'Like I said, she trusted me because I asked no questions.'

'Did she say anything else? Where she might go?'

'No. Nothing.'

'But you must surely have wondered,' Clare persisted. 'What did you think at the time?'

'I thought she was going to score,' said Henry.

'What started it all?'

'The gangsters target cops' kids. Destroy a child slowly. The family falls apart. It's a way to make bucks. Lots – and quickly, too,' said Mister Henry. 'I saw it happen in Ocean View, and it's no different here, in Maitland, or in the rest of the city. She didn't tell me how it started, but the whole thing knocked a beautiful, talented girl off course and made her father an angry cripple.'

'Do you know of anyone else she trusted?'

'Yes. A girl who was one of your Persephones. I watched the programme you did about her on TV. Calvaleen thought she was so brave, standing up to her father like that.'

'Pearl?'

'That's the one,' said Henry. 'She was looking for Calvaleen last night. Trying to find Yasmin.'

'Why was she looking for her?'

'She told me it was for you, Doc. If anyone knows what's going on, Calvaleen will. She's a cop's daughter. Like Yasmin. That's their connection.'

Henry's eyes were pools where the only thing she could see was her own reflection.

fifty-four

Clare broke Pearl's first rule: never to try and find where she lived. It wasn't that hard. She simply phoned the supermarket Pearl worked for. Clare's clipped accent ensured the collapse of their perfunctory defence of employee confidentiality. In less than ten minutes, the HR department had given her Pearl's ID number and her address.

The incoming traffic from the Cape Flats had thinned, so Clare had an easy run.

She'd had one text message from Pearl – a single word that made no sense – and since then, nothing. Clare called her, got her voicemail again. Pearl might be on shift; she may have started at five in the morning. Clare's anxiety ticking up another notch.

Half an hour later, she was checking the faded number on the house.

'That's Ouma Hendriks's house,' said a boy of about ten, twisting himself around a lamp post. 'She'll shout at you if you go in there.'

The place looked abandoned with its closed windows and unkempt garden. Clare put both hands on the ramshackle gate and pushed it open. The path to the front door was made of concrete pavers; weeds pushed through the cracks. She knocked, listening to the silence behind the door.

'It's never open.' The boy had followed her. 'Better to go round the back.'

She followed the path, a faint depression in the grey sand,

round the side of the house. A rusted car listed on bricks in the back yard. Washing flapped on the line, a pair of bloomers, a cardigan and a shapeless dress.

The back door was open a crack. Two mugs on the draining board, a plate, an ashtray. A single onion lay on the table.

An old woman sat in the chair by the door, her arthritic hands curled around a radio.

'Who's in Ouma Hendriks's kitchen?' Apprehension in her voice as she raised her creased, blind face to the shadow that Clare had cast across her. 'Is that you, Pearl?'

'I'm a friend of Pearl's,' said Clare. 'Is she here?'

'Who are you?' asked the old woman, her nose wrinkling. 'Looking for her with your white smell.'

'I'm Clare Hart.'

'The doctor.' Ouma Hendriks's brow furrowed. 'You're the one she's been meeting. The film.'

'Yes, that's me.'

'I told her it was trouble. But she wouldn't hear anything. She likes you.'

'I like her,' said Clare. 'Do you know where Pearl is? She sent me a message. I've been trying to call her and there's no answer.'

'I heard her when it was still dark. If she's not in the Wendy house, she's at work still.'

'It's locked,' said Clare. 'Do you have a key?'

Ouma Hendriks put the radio down. 'Can you make me some coffee? Nobody came today, so I've had nothing.'

'Sure.' Clare poured enough water for one cup into the kettle and lit the gas ring. She spooned coffee into a chipped mug. 'How much sugar?'

'Three.' Ouma Hendriks pulled a small bag of sugar from the pocket of her apron.

Clare measured three spoons and handed the bag back to her.

'She usually makes me something. A piece of bread and tea. She leaves it for me so that my blood sugar doesn't go funny. But she didn't come this morning.'

'Shall I make you something?' asked Clare.

'You can look, but there's *fokall* to eat. Pension. Eight hundred rand. It's all gone in a week. What does the government think we must eat while they *suip* all that gravy in parliament? If you got a cigarette, Doc, that'll help with the hunger.'

'No cigarettes, sorry.' Clare looked in the cupboard: a bit of white bread and some polony. Folding a slice into a sandwich and putting it next to the coffee, Clare asked, 'The key for Pearl's room?'

'In the coffee tin on top of the cupboard.' Clare reached up and took out the key.

Ouma Hendriks fiddled with the dial of the radio, coaxing the news out of it. The corpse of another child, Chanel Adams, found this morning, murdered and dumped, just like little Noor on Friday. Yasmin Faizal. Still missing. Captain Faizal under arrest, a statement from Director Ndlovu saying that Yasmin's abduction had nothing to do with the other two girls, shot like dogs in Maitland. The media sowing division among the security services where none in fact existed.

Ouma Hendriks stopped chewing.

'Is this why you're here?' She turned her milky eyes to where she imagined Clare was standing. 'What has Pearl got to do with this?'

'She said she could help,' said Clare.

'Why are you dragging her back in when she's just getting out of this hell?'

'Captain Faizal's little girl is missing,' said Clare. 'If anyone can help me find her, it will be Pearl.'

Avoiding further questions, Clare stepped outside and tried Pearl's key. It wouldn't turn.

'Hey, aunty, can you tell me why everyone's looking for Pearl?' It was the boy again.

'Who else is looking?' Clare rubbed a bit of hand cream onto the key and tried it again. This time it worked. She turned the handle and pushed at the door. It opened six inches, then stuck.

'The man,' the boy grinned as he displayed non-existent arm muscles. 'Full of prison chappies. He waited a long time. He didn't see me, but I saw him.'

Clare pressed redial. Inside the Wendy house a phone rang.

Putting her shoulder against the door, Clare shoved. Another six inches. She shoved again.

Pearl on the floor. Clare dropped to her knees, her face close to Pearl's. Still breathing. Maybe. She put her hands against her neck. The flicker of a pulse.

'Go!' Clare shouted, turning to the boy. 'Fetch the police.'

He jumped up, the bravado knocked out of him.

Clare called an ambulance. Setting in motion the moves triggered by violence.

Called Riedwaan. No answer.

Called Rita, told her what had happened. Asked where Riedwaan was.

'He's been charged, Clare,' said Rita, her voice low. 'He was seen in the basement of Disa Towers on Friday night. Ndlovu extracted the information from a Congolese guard whose papers aren't in order.'

'What was he doing there?'

'Apparently Yasmin was found there once before. She ran away when her parents first split up. Captain Faizal says that's where he found her. Said he went back just to check.'

'So what happened?'

'The storage space was searched again. Three strands of long black hair were found. No sign of the child. He's in the cells now.'

'For Christ's sake,' said Clare. 'I can't speak to him?'

'This is serious, Clare. You must be careful.'

'Why me?'

'There's a warrant coming for you too,' said Rita.

'What for?'

'Interfering with police procedure. Breaking. Entering.'

'That's enough,' said Clare. 'Can you give me Shorty de Lange's number?'

She punched it in. Dialled. Ten rings, her heart drumming against her ribs.

'Ballistics.' His voice gruff.

'Clare Hart here,' she said. 'Caledon Square.'

'I know who you are, Dr Hart,' said De Lange. 'Captain Faizal's friend.'

'That prisoner. The one whose gun was used to shoot the girls in Maitland. What did you say happened to him?'

'Dead,' said De Lange. 'And buried.'

Clare looked at Pearl, her slashed face, her bloody wrists.

'Who'd have signed the death certificate?'

'The District Surgeon at the prison.'

'Have you got a name for me? A number?'

'Why?' he asked.

'I'm with someone who looks like she had a heart-to-heart with Graveyard de Wet.'

The wail of an ambulance in the distance.

'And she's alive?' asked De Lange.

'Just,' said Clare.

'Faizal. He there?'

'Trying to stay out of the cells.'

'What a fuck-up,' said De Lange.

'The number?'

Clare punched it into her phone.

'Hoffman,' said a voice.

'This is Dr Hart speaking. I—'

'Yes, Doctor. From the mortuary? Thank you for being so prompt. Kobus Hoffman ...'

'Not from the mortuary,' said Clare.

'Where, then?' Wary.

'Gang Unit.' Clare stretched the truth a bit. 'Graveyard de Wet's daughter—'

'Let me speak to her.'

'Pearl's not speaking, but I think we need to discuss why,' said Clare. 'I need to talk to you. In person.'

'I'll arrange for your admission.'

What had he wanted? Pearl's shirt had been ripped open. White stretch marks feathered her belly, and slender crimson cuts radiated from her navel. In her pocket, a bloodstained piece of paper. Clare eased it out. A yellowed newspaper cutting: a photo of two men in the dock, one with Pearl's sharp cheekbones. And in a corner of the courtroom, Pearl's face, her expression intent, listening.

Clare took Pearl's hand and held it till the paramedics pushed their way through the crowd jostling in the yard.

fifty-five

The heron perched upon the fading sign fixed its yellow eyes on Clare when she turned into the prison grounds. The guard handed her the visitor's logbook. Clare wrote down her name, identity number, phone number and the date. The last column requested purpose of visit. 'Consultation' was the word she picked. It wasn't a lie, not exactly. Not yet. The guard gave her a pass and rolled back the metal gate.

'Go straight,' he said. 'Second left at Maximum.'

She drove past the wardens' houses towards the prison, hidden from view by a row of pines silhouetted against the sullen sky. In the distance the mountains loomed, their granite faces gleaming.

A series of low buildings appeared before her, cordoned off behind a thirty-foot steel mesh tunnel. Two guards patrolled, their German Shepherds leashed, batons and pistols conspicuous at their belts. Oblivious to the taunts that floated from the barred windows nearby. A bitch lunged at the thin brown hands held out through the bars when the guards lit their cigarettes. The dog's handler allowed her to play the lead out fully before jerking her neck back. The hands did not flinch. In Maximum, the rules of engagement were clear.

Clare zipped up her parka, pulling the hood around her neck to keep out the wind. She slung her bag over her shoulder and walked towards the grim administrative block. A large man was standing at the entrance, his face pale with tension.

'Kobus Hoffman.'

'Clare Hart.'

'You're smaller than I expected,' he said as her hand disappeared into his.

'It's an illusion,' said Clare.

'This way,' he gestured.

Clare followed him along the length of the wire tunnel, looking away as he reached a gate and keyed in four numbers. The gate swung open and he stood back so that she could precede him. The sour tang of urine hovered below the smell of dust. The sounds that bubbled beneath the quiet were metallic, sharp. Their footsteps blurred into the din of the prison. She flinched as she heard the gate bang shut behind her.

Hoffman pulled a bunch of keys from his pocket and unlocked the consultation room. He banged the bolts back and pushed the metal door open. His desk was littered with files and folders. He rummaged for the one he wanted. Inside it was the copy he had made of Graveyard de Wet's death certificate. The photographs. The next of kin details he had lifted from the files. He handed it all to Clare.

'There was a body, it was autopsied. I can tell you, Dr Hart, it wasn't his.'

It took a minute for the significance of what he was showing her to sink in.

'When did you discover this?'

'Saturday,' said Hoffman. 'I worked overtime. This was right at the end. If I hadn't known him I wouldn't even have noticed.'

'You treated him here?'

'He used to come to me with endless complaints. Headaches, insomnia. Complained about Captain Faizal – the one whose daughter is missing. Said Faizal put him away, made sure they threw away the key. Didn't seem to like being the first big fish the Gang Unit caught.'

'You didn't think the two were linked?'

'I didn't allow myself to think about it.' Hoffman avoided Clare's gaze.

Clare let it ride. 'Pearl – she was a witness at his trial?'

'No, she wasn't a witness. The Gang Unit had enough evidence to convict. But she informed the police – Captain Faizal, I imagine – of her father's whereabouts. He'd gone after her her whole life, and the last time was no exception,' said Hoffman, putting the autopsy photographs back into the envelope. 'Pearl has a daughter now, you know?'

Clare nodded. 'She called her Hope, but gave her away.'

'She asked me at the trial if the child would turn out to be a monster. I was never quite sure if she meant because of what her father had done.'

'What did you tell her?'

'I didn't say anything, really. How could I give her a direct answer? Anyway, after the trial she disappeared. Then I saw her on your TV programme. She was disguised, but I'd recognise that voice anywhere. Hardest thing to disguise, the voice.'

'So you didn't do anything, either?' Clare asked.

Hoffman looked away. 'I tried to phone her, to warn her after her father was supposed to have died.'

'Someone left her to die last night,' said Clare. 'He tortured her with a knife, Dr Hoffman. She's in theatre now.'

'Then I was too late.'

'What did the prison authorities say when you told them?'

'They don't know.' The colour drained from Hoffman's face. 'You've seen the kind of thing he does, Dr Hart. I have two daughters. I have a wife.'

'The prisoner whose death Graveyard de Wet stole,' asked Clare. 'When was he released?'

'Thursday,' said Hoffman.

'And the next day Yasmin Faizal disappeared. And two girls were gunned down with Graveyard de Wet's gun. Pearl's life is hanging by a thread now.'

'If I report it, it will be obvious that it was me. I've been warned.'

'By whom?'

'Rafiek Khan. Another 27s general.'

'What's been going on here?' Clare demanded.

'Several killings.' Hoffman's shoulders drooped. 'A *frans*, a non-gangster who got caught up in it, told me that the 27s, the old members of the Number, are the men of blood, the soldiers who defend the camp of the Number. That's their bullshit mythology, anyway.'

'And all this elaborate escape business?'

'Some awaiting-trial prisoners were killed recently, new recruits who come into prison with Number tattoos without having done time in prison. The Number gangsters were making it clear that their chappies couldn't just be bought – like a pair of Nikes. It was driving old prisoners like de Wet and Khan berserk. Because if you can just buy the Number on the streets, it erodes their power, the years of hardship they've endured.'

'And this?' She showed Hoffman the newspaper cutting: Pearl's face, her expression intent as she listened to the sentence.

'Khan and De Wet in the dock,' said Hoffman.

'But if he'd been sent out for revenge, he obviously prioritised Pearl. He put her before the Number.'

'Well, you've seen the tattoos, so you know the saying. *Vrou is gif.* Woman is poison. Pearl betrayed him. Fought back, talked back. He couldn't tolerate that. Who knows?' His expression hardened. 'Listen, Dr Hart, I don't think like them. And now I'm going to have to get back to work. A warden will escort you back in a few minutes.'

'I'll wait outside for him,' said Clare.

The courtyard was painted in black and white squares. A giant chessboard, the pieces half the size of a man. She wandered through them, moved a white castle, freeing the black queen.

A loud angry buzzing came from the block next to the hospital wing. A metal door slid back, spilling prisoners. Tattooed, all fifty, all one hundred of them. They surged through the open gates, a tide that broke as it reached Clare. Her throat closed at the smell of them. Institutionalised, feral, male. They parted for her at a signal from one among them. Rangy, medium-height, his orange prison garb sat snug on narrow hips. And a Rolex hung from his tattooed wrist.

He stopped in front of Clare, the 27 tattooed on the back of his neck a brilliant blue against the orange jacket. Taking out a packet of Marlboros, he flared his lighter in Clare's face. He exhaled, the smoke drifting across Clare's face.

'You like that?'

The escort caught up with her.

'*Kom, julle, maak vinnig, los die dame uit.*' The guard moved the prisoners on.

'Sorry, Miss,' he said. '*Vuilgoed.* Thinks he owns this place.'

They stopped to unlock the gate. On the other side of a metal grille, Rafiek Khan, the man in Pearl's newspaper cutting, grinned at Clare. Then he ran his tongue over his teeth.

Pearl had been transferred to the intensive care unit when Clare got to the hospital. No visitors were allowed, but when Clare gave her title, the sister at the front desk let her through immediately.

Pearl was hooked up to every conceivable kind of monitor. A nurse was checking her drip.

'I'm Dr Hart,' said Clare. 'How's she doing?'

'The first operation went okay and she seems to be stable.'

Clare picked up the charts and flicked through them. They were written in abbreviated medical English that didn't make much sense to her.

'It's a miracle he missed the trachea,' said the nurse. 'Unusual for a Monday if the boyfriend did it.' She smoothed Pearl's hair from her forehead. 'Her hands were lacerated. Where she'd tried to fend him off. It'll be hard to fix up. The surgeon's coming a little later to see what can be done with repairing the nerves.'

'Has she said anything?'

'Nothing,' said the nurse. 'She's being kept under heavy sedation until the swelling on the brain comes down. She'll make it, I think. She's a real fighter, this Pearl.'

'That she is,' said Clare.

The nurse moved on to the next patient and Clare sat beside Pearl, again opening the message Pearl had sent the night before.

Hey Doc. Sorry 4 delay. SWIM

She had ignored it at the time, waiting for the rest of the message to download. But that was all Pearl had keyed in.

Clare tried all the alternatives for SWIM, with predictive text switched on, and off. She switched the dictionary to Afrikaans. Nothing that made sense.

'What were you trying to say, Pearl?' she whispered.

Monday afternoon. Five-thirty.

'It's three whole days since Yasmin disappeared. And Calvaleen was looking for you.' Clare took Pearl's bandaged hand in hers. The nails were bitten to the quick. 'You know where she is, Pearl. Who else knows? Does your father know?'

The answers right there, on the other side of Pearl's consciousness, but the only reply Clare got was the gentle clicking and beeping that the machines made.

fifty-six

Clare dumped her laptop, her notes and folders on the kitchen table, with Fritz winding between her legs as she put the kettle on. She picked up the cat and stroked her, trying to tease out a thread of thought that might unravel this.

She sat down, the cat on her lap, and arranged everything she had around her. Checking. Re-checking. The list of numbers from the ballet school. The teachers. The parents.

No. No one had seen anything.

Yes, they knew the child, she was so gifted. They knew she was missing. It was everywhere in the press, but it happened so often, to those children.

Which children?

Poor children, was their reply. Hard to look after them, really, with both parents working shifts.

One of the fathers had Yasmin's father's cell number saved on his phone. Thought it might be useful in an emergency to have a policeman one knew. Always the possibility of being stopped at a road block – God forbid – a little bit tiddly. The holding cells were not where one wanted to be on a Friday night. He'd had a whiskey with the Captain at a parent's meeting. Talked about fishing. He hadn't eaten the ham sandwiches. A Muslim, you know, but not radical at all.

Most worrying, especially because they all had daughters, etc.

Yes, they would all call her, of course, if they remembered anything.

Simpler, really, if one didn't see things. And if one did, then far simpler not to remember. Safer, too. She tried Calvaleen van Rensburg for the last time. An electronic voice told her to try later as the subscriber she had dialled was not available. The service did not allow her to leave a message. She tried her home number. No answer, Latisha out. Probably sitting in Shazia Faizal's half-packed living room. Waiting. Praying, now.

She leaned her head on her arms, Fritz kneading her thigh, the sharpness of her claws a welcome pain. She allowed the cat's deep purr to lull her.

Calvaleen's school diary. It lay amid the detritus on the table.

Clare picked it up, flicking through it again. Homework assignments, tests, rehearsals. One or two hearts drawn in the narrow spaces left for weekends. One crossed out with a black pen. Blank pages. Calvaleen hadn't been to school much the last couple of months.

At the end of the diary, a list of cell numbers. Each one assigned to the kind of cryptic nickname that teenage girls give their friends. Clare ran through them. None of the girls who answered had seen Calvaleen for a while. Moved on, said one. New friends, said another. Boyfriends? Maybe a while back, but no one special. She didn't like men much and her dad was really strict. One said she had had issues, had taken time out.

Clare paged through the diary again. Then went back to the phone numbers.

The numbers. The chubby twos and threes, the disjointed fours, the sevens crossed.

Clare pulled out the list of docket numbers that had been dropped through her letter box. She compared them to Calvaleen's phone numbers, her breath coming fast.

The same writing.

The skinny kid running to catch the taxi.

Calvaleen van Rensburg vanishing into the back streets.

Riedwaan's boss's daughter.

Clare arrived at the complex and stopped at the security gate. A security guard – a different one, this time – approached her.

'Number nine,' she said. 'Van Rensburg.'

'Mrs Latisha is gone out,' the guard said.

'I'm dropping something off,' said Clare.

'Okay,' he said, pointing. 'You park there.'

Clare pulled up next to a man in blue overalls. He was decapitating a few dandelions that had thrust their yellow heads through the cracks in the paving. The man watched her go round the side of the house.

No one in the tidy kitchen. Or in the main bedroom, with its open curtains. Calvaleen's were tightly closed. No change there.

The living room was also empty. Plumped diamond-shaped cushions stood on the sofa. The only sign of occupation was the desk by the window. On it was a telephone, some neatly stacked papers, a beer mug filled with pens, a father's day card propped up against it. For a father who worked non-stop. Strategic human resource deployment. Even at home: a pile of police dockets. She'd seen them during her visit that morning, but not fully registered what they were about. A note was clipped onto the top of one of the dockets, in Van Zyl's looped scrawl.

In a corner of the living room a red eye winked at her. The alarm. She wouldn't get inside without attracting a lot of attention. Clare glanced in at the garage window. The abandoned workbench.

'Your friends not in?' The gardener in his blue overalls.

'Doesn't look like it,' she replied.

'You want to leave a note?' he asked. 'I can give it to them.'

'Don't worry,' said Clare, walking towards her car. 'I'll phone them.'

She was already dialling the private number Edgar Phiri had given her.

fifty-seven

Clare arrived at Caledon Square just as Salome Ndlovu's large black BMW pulled up at the main entrance. She watched as the driver opened the door for the Special Director. Ndlovu took a minute to straighten her immaculate hair, button her black jacket. Then she picked up her briefcase and slammed the door behind her.

Using her police pass, Clare followed in her wake, slipping into the hastily convened press conference. There was no sign of Riedwaan Faizal or of Rita Mkhize. Edgar Phiri stood behind a bank of microphones and cables. Special Director Ndlovu had positioned herself next to him. Phiri took all the questions machine-gunned by journalists outraged at the murder of first Noor Khan, and then Chanel Adams. The tabloids were furious at the suspension of Captain Faizal, and Phiri directed their questions to Salome Ndlovu. She deflected them with turgid quotes from the policies her unit was implementing, and by criticising the 'macho' attitudes of both the so-called Gang Unit and the press assembled before her.

The press pack lost interest in Phiri and he stepped back, a police press officer taking his place. Ndlovu was onto her third prepared statement when he slipped out.

Clare followed him.

'Dr Hart,' said Phiri, closing the door behind her. 'It looks like we have a stalemate.' The chess game on his desk had remained untouched since Saturday.

'Seems Director Ndlovu's gender equity programme's not going down too well as a measure for combating organised crime?'

'I apparently fail to understand the programme. Or the complexities of a globalised economy,' said Phiri. 'I pointed out that the South African Police Service is not the Communist Party, that we answer to the people, not to a politburo reborn as a cabinet. And that unlawfully arresting one of my most senior officers will not find a missing child, nor will it reduce crime. Also, just because Faizal functions independently, doesn't make him a traitor.'

'Your whole unit is notoriously independent, though,' said Clare.

'Only till the end of the month,' said Phiri. 'The order disbanding it was quietly signed on Friday. It goes through cabinet and comes into effect on the thirty-first.'

'The way of the Scorpions?'

'Yes.' said Phiri. 'But until then, the Gang Unit is still mine and it remains under my command.'

'It must have helped Salome Ndlovu and her bosses to have something to pin on Faizal, to get him out of the way for a couple of crucial days,' said Clare. 'Don't you think the timing of Yasmin's disappearance is remarkable – dovetailing as it did with the trouble he and his wife have been having?'

'Risky, though,' he tapped his pen against his watch. 'The timing of it … the fact that the child's ballet class ended early.'

'Still, you wouldn't put it past the Special Director?'

'Salome Ndlovu?' Phiri frowned. 'But she's hard to read. During her years in exile she perfected the art of self-erasure. I was with her in a couple of places she stayed in – the USSR, Tanzania. There were no pictures on the walls, no photographs on display, no books next to her bed.'

'Didn't want to reveal who she was and where she came from?'

'Precisely. And she hates Faizal, I know that, and she's out to destroy him. Him and men like him, but there's always been an elegance to her cruelty which this abduction lacks.'

'And Delport?'

'Easy to box. Apartheid caricature. It can be quite a comfort to have him around. So everyone can be sure who's the enemy. He'll go back to the Narcs anyway, so no problem with him.'

'Van Rensburg?'

'He's had a lot to deal with,' said Phiri. 'Old school. Won't go for help. It'll do him good to be at home, spend some time with his wife and daughter. Maybe find a way to live again.'

Clare considered the black bishop on the chess board.

'There's something else on your mind, Dr Hart?'

'Yes there is,' said Clare. 'What does the name Gorky mean to you?'

'The park in Moscow I mentioned to you before. Where I learnt to play chess, remember?' said Phiri. 'Why do you ask?'

'It's a name that's come up a couple of times,' said Clare, moving the bishop diagonally. 'A nightclub that Voëltjie Ahrend seems to be connected with. Gorky Investments is registered as the owner.'

'Strip clubs and brothels are legitimate businesses these days,' said Phiri. 'All those soccer fans to satisfy.'

'I was attacked outside a Gorky club. The Winter Palace. I never saw the man because he put a sack over my head,' said Clare. 'The first person I did see after I got away from him was your colleague.'

'Salome Ndlovu?'

'Her and her bodyguards,' said Clare. 'So I wondered if she'd been following me to keep tabs on Riedwaan, or if it was just chance because she had business at the Winter Palace. Or both.'

'I've been told that the lines of enquiry of my unit are misguided. And that several of my operations, particularly into the business ventures of a young entrepreneur called Germaine

Ahrend – the name, by the way, on Faizal's friend Voëltjie's birth certificate – anyway, these operations are hampering business development in the Cape.'

'And one of these is Gorky Investments?'

'Yes, that's one of the names,' said Phiri. 'How did you connect them to this?'

'Three heroin busts. Very clean, pure heroin. All taken in for testing, then the dockets disappeared. The drugs too.'

'How do you know this, Dr Hart?'

Clare did her trust calculation. 'The docket numbers were dropped off at my house.' For Yasmin's sake, she hoped that her instincts were right. 'With a piece of elastic wrapped around them. The busts seemed fine – random searches, a neighbour complaining about noise, that type of thing. But I did some digging on the venues. Two of the three belong to companies that can be linked back to Gorky Investments. Lots of veils, lots of shells, but that's where it goes back to. So what I want to know is: who exactly is Gorky Investments?'

'Gorky Investments has a long history of cooperation with the struggle, dating back to our time in the USSR,' said Phiri.

'Which no longer exists,' observed Clare.

'Our operations are threatening current relations with important businessmen in Russia. Many of the people we've been targeting have a lot of money to invest, and in these tough economic times it is apparently important to value business that brings in jobs, money,' said Phiri.

'Import export,' said Clare. 'Always a good cover. The only cover. Then property and mining to launder the money. South Africa's the perfect place: financial institutions, flexible politicians, badly-paid cops.'

'Gorky Investments is on our list. They bring legitimate business, and then they set up the channels for other far more profitable, but illegal trades. This is what Captain Faizal has been investigating for months, why we're being shut down.'

'But kidnapping Yasmin? And without any demands?' Clare asked. 'Is it a punishment? What's the point?'

'That is what I'm unable to work out,' said Phiri. 'Why a small part of me thought that maybe he'd cracked, that he had taken her to keep the one thing he loves close to him. That is what I hoped for.'

'So did I,' said Clare. 'But he doesn't have her, and if she wasn't taken by the man who took Chanel Adams, or someone like him, then she may still be alive. That's what I'm working with.'

'Captain Faizal is no longer a suspect in this case,' said Phiri. 'He never should have been, but I miscalculated how to play this.' Phiri turned his pen over in his hand. 'I am hoping, Dr Hart, that you will find her alive. What do you need for this?'

'I need Captain Faizal,' said Clare.

'There's the fact that he's been accused of assaulting a police officer to be cleared away.'

'That's all bullshit,' said Clare.

'The essence of politics,' said Phiri. 'That, and paperwork. I'll sort it out. And as soon as it's done, he'll be out of the building. Where shall I tell him to find you?'

'Like any good woman,' smiled Clare, 'I'll be waiting at home.'

fifty-eight

The front door. A click. Then nothing more.

Latisha van Rensburg stiffened.

Someone was at the front door.

She de-activated the alarm, then picked up a paring knife from the draining board and went down the passage. She kept close to the wall so that whoever it was wouldn't see her outline through the pane.

'It's me.' That voice.

The knife clattered to the floor, Latisha's hands slippery as she fumbled for the key to the security grille, slid back the bolts, and got the door open in time to catch her daughter in her arms.

'Mama.' Calvaleen's breath on her neck as she helped her to her bedroom.

Latisha laid her on the clean sheets, a tang of lemon in the air after the spring-cleaning she had given the room after Clare Hart's visit.

'Mama, *ek's jammer*.' Her daughter's lips were cracked, her ribs corrugated under the pallid skin, where her blouse had rucked up.

'You don't need to be sorry,' said her mother. '*Jy't huis toe gekom*.'

'But it's my fault.' Calvaleen curled herself into a foetal position. 'This is all my fault.'

Latisha cradled her daughter's body, rocking her.

'Yasmin?'

'It's okay, she's alive,' said Latisha, smoothing the dark tangle of hair from her daughter's forehead. 'Like you.'

'And Papa?'

'Gone to work,' said Latisha. 'Fixing things up, at last.'

The girl stared at her mother.

'What do you mean, Mama? What's he doing?'

'You have to believe him,' said Latisha. 'He's putting things right. Give him this chance.'

'I have to take a bath,' said Calvaleen. 'I'm so dirty.'

Latisha covered her daughter and ran a bath, filling it to the brim. She went back to Calvaleen's bedroom and helped her into a sitting position, easing off her top.

'Can you stand?' She got her upright and took off her shoes and filthy jeans. She wasn't wearing any underwear. Calvaleen swayed in front of her mother, the veins on the insides of her elbows and the backs of her knees tracked with scabs.

'I'll hold on to you, Ma.' Calvaleen put an arm around her mother's waist and allowed herself to be helped into the bath. Latisha rubbed soap onto a sponge and washed her daughter's wasted body.

'We'll do your hair tomorrow,' she said.

Calvaleen's eyes, circled with dark shadows, did not move from her mother's face.

'Shall I put you to bed?' asked Latisha. 'Then we can think about what to do.'

She wrapped a clean towel around Calvaleen and got her into bed. Latisha covered her with the quilt.

'Take this,' she said, handing her daughter one of her own tranquillisers. 'It'll help you sleep. Help you until we can get you back to the clinic.'

'Don't leave me, Mama.' Calvaleen folded herself against her mother's body.

'I won't leave you, *my engeltjie,*' she whispered, working her fingers through her daughter's hair.

She listened to the trucks as they headed into the darkness, towards Johannesburg, until Calvaleen fell asleep.

Latisha lay down, her arm around her daughter, easing her into the hollow of her belly.

fifty-nine

'Phiri said you'd be here.' Riedwaan, relieved, when Clare buzzed him in.

'Tell me what happened,' she said.

'Clinton van Rensburg released me. Phiri's orders. But he told me that if I wanted back-up I had to give him everything. I'm supposed to be at home, staying out of the way.'

'And did you give Van Rensburg everything?'

'Everything I had at the time. Filled the back of a business card.'

'The heroin dockets?' asked Clare.

'Them too,' he said. 'Those threw him.'

'Did he have anything to do with the cases?'

'Not directly,' said Riedwaan. 'He's off active duty. Does resource deployment now, corruption control. That kind of thing. Van Rensburg's fanatical. Doesn't like things to be out of order. And this business with the heroin cases will need explaining when it's ...' Riedwaan pulled out his cigarettes. 'When this is over.' He crumpled the empty packet and lobbed it into the bin. 'I'll be needing more of these. You need anything?'

'A Coke, please.'

Riedwaan paused at the map, tracing the lines back to the evidence summaries that Clare had made for each of the little girls. The abbreviated lives, the sparse detail. Name, date of birth, date and cause of death.

Yasmin there too. Not yet marked as dead.

'It's been more than seventy-two hours. If she wasn't mine, I'd recognise this for what it is,' said Riedwaan at the door. 'A murder investigation.'

It took a moment for Clare to realise that the unfamiliar sound was coming from Riedwaan's phone. He'd left it on the desk, with his jacket.

Clare handed him the phone when he returned. 'This came through.'

'It's a video clip,' said Riedwaan. An unfamiliar voice spilled into Clare's study.

'Rock 'n roll now, daddy's girl.'

The instruction off-camera.

'Dance for your daddy.'

Yasmin, hollow-eyed, hair tangled, filled the screen. She lifted her arms above her head and danced.

'Sing for him too. Rock it, baby girl, see if he can find you.'

She started singing. Her voice reedy in the darkened room.

'When I was one, I had just begun.

When I was two, I was nearly new.

When I was three, I was hardly me.

When I was four, I wasn't much more.

When I was five, I was barely alive.

But now I am six, I'm as clever as clever.

I think I'll be six forever and forever.'

The child came to a slow, twirling halt. Then she crumpled to the floor, the vertebrae in her neck a delicate chain disappearing under her leotard. The screech of metal, a door opening.

The phone connection broke, leaving silence in its wake.

'That was pre-recorded. Look at the light shafting in, that's sunlight,' said Clare.

Riedwaan glanced at the moonless night outside. 'And it must have been this afternoon. First time the sun's been out since Friday.'

'Let me download that,' she said. 'See if we can get more detail on my laptop.'

She pressed play again.

The man's instructions.

'Rock 'n roll now, daddy's girl. Dance for your daddy.'

Riedwaan put his hand on the screen, touching the spectral image of his daughter.

'She danced this for her last Eisteddfod,' whispered Riedwaan. 'Won gold for it.'

'Is that why she picked this dance?'

Riedwaan shook his head. 'It's a message to me,' he said. 'I arrived just as she started,' said Riedwaan. 'Yasmin saw me in the doorway. I think it was her smile that won the medal for her. She lit up the stage.'

Clare put her hand out, the desire to absorb the burden of Riedwaan's despair overwhelming, but he moved out of reach. His eyes were on his child, collapsing into the dirt, the fight knocked out of her.

Clare led a cable from her computer through to the large screen where she watched her rough cuts. She slotted in the disk that Danny Roman had given her and ran the recording, magnifying the ambient sound. She closed her eyes and listened.

'When I was one, I had just begun …'

She listened, teasing the sound out, but she already knew that the recording had been made in the same or a similar environment to the first one.

'When I was two …'

'It's the same background sound. You can put it off.' said Riedwaan. 'She's still in the same area. That's something. They're not moving around with her.'

'Makes it harder to find her,' said Clare. 'It means they have her somewhere they feel very secure. If they moved her, there'd be a better chance of a sighting.'

Clare turned to press play again. 'The instruction. Sorry, but I need to listen to that again.'

She went back to the beginning of the recording.

'Rock 'n roll now, daddy's girl. Dance for your daddy.'

'The roll on the "r",' said Clare. 'I have to check something. She scratched through her notes for the number, punched it in. It rang a long time before being answered.

'I'm sorry, Professor Young,' said Clare. 'It's late to be phoning.'

'No, Dr Hart,' he chuckled. 'I'm just old. It takes me a long time to get to the phone. But you must need something if you're calling me again?'

'Would you mind listening to something?'

Clare played the message again.

'"Now we are Six", by A A Milne,' said the Professor. 'But you probably know that, you look as if you were decently educated.'

'Not the poem, Professor,' said Clare. 'The voice. The man's voice at the beginning. Listen to him, the man at the beginning.'

She played it again.

The phone line crackled.

'Professor, are you all right?'

'That accent, that Malmesbury bray. It's just the shock, hearing him again.'

'Thanks, Professor.' Clare disconnected. 'He recognised the accent.'

'The tattoo boy. The boys with the bray.' Riedwaan nodded slowly. 'The ones who beat up the old man also took Yasmin. So who are they, apart from coming from the platteland?'

'Who they are, I have no idea. No prints on the pen, and nothing showed up on the tattoo either. No records in any of the tattoo parlours, nor in the gang member registers.'

'So they take her and they keep her and then send a clip to torture me – but with no demands. What for? Who for?'

'Rita also checked the juvenile section,' said Clare. 'Nothing. Either it was missed or he's never been arrested. Freelance, maybe? Pearl thought he could be.'

'That's unlikely, on Voëltjie Ahrend's territory,' said Riedwaan.

'Are you going to call Phiri?' asked Clare. 'Hand the info over to him?'

'He's got Salome Ndlovu breathing down his neck. I've got more chance with just the two of us. Yasmin ... Yasmin's got ...' He couldn't finish the sentence.

'There's some lasagne left in the fridge,' said Clare. 'You look like you haven't eaten. Make yourself some coffee too.'

'Thanks,' Riedwaan replied. 'You want some?'

'Just the coffee. Milk, no sugar.'

Fritz padded across the balcony and sat expectantly at the sliding door. Clare opened it to let her in. She stepped outside for a moment, glad to escape, watching the lights in the flats across the road. Only a police van moved along Beach Road, getting a feel of things. Not much going on. Monday night; quiet.

The patrol vehicle turned and headed back, stopping at a red light. The number of the vehicle was printed on the roof, large enough to be read by a helicopter, if necessary.

By the time the vehicle moved forward, Clare was at her computer again.

Her body rigid, she re-played the clip. The sound off, this time. She froze the images, zooming in so close that the little girl collapsed on the floor dissolved into pixels. Clare zoomed past her, focusing on a metal box on the wall behind her.

She had it.

'Riedwaan!' the urgency in her voice brought him out of the shower, a towel wrapped around his waist.

'Look at this.' She tapped at the old numbers, long-forgotten after the building had been abandoned and the power switched off.

'An electricity meter?'

Clare held up her hand, her phone already at her ear.

'Charlie?'

'Hey, Doc.'

'Your hacker friend. He can access the city's records online, can't he?'

'Depends.' Charlie hedged his bets.

'For Yasmin,' said Clare.

She took Charlie's silence as assent.

'Riedwaan,' she called. 'We've got a location.'

sixty

'My name is Yasmin. My name is Yasmin. My name is Yasmin.'

The little girl repeats her mantra to the bird cupped in her hands. She keeps still, holding the tiny pocket of warmth close to her belly. She breathes through her mouth, trying to block out the smell of her prison.

'Sleep tight, baby.'

Her father's words under her breath, his voice in her head growing fainter.

Yasmin presses her face against her knees, kissing herself better, feeling the ghostly imprint of his hands around her ribs as he picks her up and holds her above his head while she laughs.

Her tears are hot and wet, but their trail on her cheeks is cold. Yasmin lifts her head up. Is it still so dark? The light brings with it sound. If it were Ramadan, everyone would already be up at this time and there would be cooking smells.

The thought of food twists in Yasmin's tummy like a blade.

But light also brings the man.

She begins again; her daddy's voice in her head saying she is a brave girl as she rocks back and forth.

Her daddy will come.

He will.

He will.

He always knows how to find her when they play hide and seek. She isn't really playing now, but he will look for her anyway and show her later all the clues he'd found that had led him to her under the bed or in the tree or next door. He always knows what to look for, her daddy.

Far away, a car.

The first time she'd heard the sound, Yasmin's heart had leapt, but it is far away and travelling fast. She supposes there's a road somewhere. No robots or stop streets, because all the engines have the mosquito whine of a car going fast, far away.

She bows over her bird, clasped in her hands.

The doves, the sparrows.

The creak of the roof.

Strange sounds become familiar.

The screech of metal, as a bolt is drawn, claws its way up her spine, blotting out her hunger. She shrinks back into the darkest corner of the rectangular pit. The doves scuffle and coo.

Yasmin listens for the footsteps, looks for the silhouette of a man against the dull light.

Cigarette smoke. Close by.

A car, closer than usual.

She stands on tiptoe, peering into the gloom, her little bird's heart beats wildly against her fingers.

sixty-one

Clare glanced up at Riedwaan, wrote down what Charlie Wang was telling her. 'It's somewhere to start, at least,' she said, pulling the map off her wall. She spread it out in front of her and filled in the coordinates.

'Maitland,' said Clare. 'Coronation Road.'

Riedwaan already had his jacket on. Clare fetched hers, opening the safe next to her bed, the gun warming in her hand as she took it out and loaded it. The spare ammunition she distributed among her pockets. She grabbed the toolbox at the front door and tossed it into the boot.

Clare took the N1, turning off at the bridge to Maitland. She jumped lanes, taking the next exit that looped back onto Voortrekker Road. All the houses were shuttered and dark. No movement on the street or alongside the squatter camp in Maitland Cemetery. Clare turned into Coronation Road.

She braked when she realised she'd overshot the narrow gravel road. She reversed. The metal gate and the old sign were overgrown with lank winter weeds. Clare swung left, bumping over the gravel, but Riedwaan was already out of the vehicle, a bolt cutter in his hands. He cut the chain on the old gate and pushed it open. The Cricket Pavilion sign was pitted with bullet holes. They bumped down the track until they came to a clearing. Clare parked and they both got out. The pistol tucked into its holster was loaded.

'Afghanistan, Iraq, Colombia and us. Not many countries need bulletproof vests for children.' Clare slipped the child-sized Kevlar under her own as Riedwaan strapped his on too.

The path ahead of her was overgrown, the carcasses of an old cart and a couple of cars protruding above the weeds. 'Keep Out' signs hung from the rusty barbed wire.

The old ticket office stood desolate, a bar welded across the faded blue door. The stench of human waste indicated that vagrants had found shelter on the porch. There was no one there now, nothing except a stack of old cardboard and rags in the corner. A tattered advertisement for a game a decade earlier still clung to the notice board.

'That'll take too long to get open,' said Clare. 'Let's go round the back.'

All the windows were smashed, but the jagged apertures had been sealed with grenade mesh welded to the frames. Clare hurried on, listening for the sound of Riedwaan's footsteps on the other side of the building. She couldn't hear anything. The building was tall and sturdy. She picked her way across the uneven ground, steadying her breathing. Trees shifted and sighed in the wind.

The back of the pavilion was also barred shut, planks nailed diagonally across a door that seemed to have been splintered with a crowbar. Empty bottles littered the back porch. In a corner were discarded straws, broken light bulbs – the detritus of tik users. On the walls were layers of graffiti. Out of the line of sight of both the living and the dead. A place where teenagers pushed out of crowded homes could hang out undisturbed.

Clare righted an empty drum and stood on it, angling her torch in the skylight above the door. Inside, pigeons roosting on rafters shuffled a little, then settled their heads under their wings, away from her probing light.

The interior was stripped bare. There was nothing to be seen but a single broken chair and rubbish that had blown in through the broken windows. Near the change-rooms was a hole in the floor, with wooden steps disappearing into it. The cellar. Clare climbed off the drum and stood on the porch. The building was slightly elevated but the lower vents had been welded closed. The cellar was impenetrable.

'Find anything?' Riedwaan came around the corner.

'Nothing,' she said. 'The building's like Fort Knox. And you?'

'Nothing on the other side. No one's been here for months. Did you see inside?'

'Take a look yourself,' pointing to the drum. 'I couldn't see anything. There's a cellar opening, but no sign of anything. No footprints, no apparent disturbance. Nobody's been inside recently. Not here, anyway.'

'Nothing,' said Riedwaan. 'Fucking wild goose chase.'

'Wait,' said Clare. 'Bring your torch here.'

She spread out the map she'd stuffed into her pocket.

'We're here,' she said. 'Charlie told me that the old electricity meter served the cricket pavilion. But look at this.' She pointed to the faint outlines on the map. 'This whole area was once part of the sports grounds. And the pavilion was just one part of it. Look here. You see, there's another building at the end of these fields. If it's all one complex there should be only one electricity meter. We're looking at the wrong end.'

'So where do you think we should be looking?'

'Listen to those sounds,' said Clare. Apart from the late-night cars whining along the N1, all was quiet. In the distance, the wretched yip of dogs that had long since given up hope of being rescued. Then the sound she'd heard with Danny Roman, barking that grew more frenzied, as if someone were passing by the place where they were chained.

'Remember the sound in between Yasmin's voice?' There was

more of it. 'I think that way, closer to the highway, where the ship-ping yards are.'

'If you're right,' said Riedwaan, 'we should walk there. Moving the car now will attract too much attention.'

Clare moved along the fence, Riedwaan just in front of her.

sixty-two

A church bell tolled the half-hour from across the empty fields. Twelve-thirty. In the distance, the thump of music from the Winter Palace. Clare wouldn't have noticed the car if the cat hadn't hissed at her, disappearing into the darkness with its scrawny kittens in tow. The car was parked deep under the trees, more a dim shadow than a solid object.

An inconspicuous Toyota. Unobtrusive.

She put her hand over her torch and switched it on, her fingers dulling the light.

'Looks like it's been here a couple of days,' Clare whispered.

She tried the doors, finding them unlocked. She slid in the back and felt along the car seat. A small plastic Disney figure and a takeaway box. On the floor, a litter of pizza boxes. Clare checked in the front. Some scrunched paper napkins. She opened the boot. A jack, a spare tyre, a worn pink ballet slipper.

Clare picked it up, looked inside it. The grubby imprint of five toes circling the ball of a foot. A tiny object. She shook it out.

The molar gleamed white in her hand.

A milk tooth, childhood serrations worn smooth.

She dropped it into Riedwaan's hand. He curled his fingers tightly round the tooth.

'That path,' said Riedwaan, pointing to the disturbed leaf litter. 'Let's go.'

They pushed their way through the scrub, coming to a clearing. Ahead of them was a building. The exposed steel ribs of damaged roofing stood silhouetted against the distant streetlights.

'SWIM,' said Clare. 'What Pearl was trying to tell me in her text message. The old public swimming pool. You can't see it from the street any more, not the way it's wedged between the highway and the shunting yards now.'

Riedwaan and Clare moved as one towards the only light ahead: a faint square above the weeds at the back of the building. The doors and windows were boarded up. They worked their way slowly round the building.

Nothing to be seen in any of the dim rooms they looked into.

The front entrance had a steel plate welded across it, but a hole had been hacked into the back wall where the plaster had crumbled.

'I'm going in,' said Riedwaan, setting his phone. 'Put your phone on vibrate mode. I'll call you in five minutes. If it's clear, follow me inside.'

The roar of a goods train masked the sound of Riedwaan cutting through the razor wire coiled across the entrance.

Then he ducked inside as a truck went past on the highway.

Clare strained to hear what was happening inside, but the night threw back strange bangs and echoes that she couldn't make out. She listened for Riedwaan's footsteps, but by the time the vehicle had passed on the flyover there was nothing but silence in the old building.

The five minutes took an excruciatingly long time to pass, and by the time they did, Riedwaan had still not called. She waited another two minutes. Then she pushed her way through the hole and hugged the wall, allowing her eyes to adjust to the gloom. She was in a large square room. A change-room. In its centre was a concrete block, with remnants of nailed-down planks here and there. Opposite her were two exits. With all the debris on the floor, it was hard to tell which one Riedwaan had used. She stopped at the first opening and listened.

Silence.

She peered down the narrow passage curving away into the darkness. No light at the end of it. Clare eased the gun, cool and reassuring, out of its holster. It lay snug across her palm, the wood of the handle as smooth as the metal, but warmer to the touch. The gloom ahead of her was unnervingly silent.

She made her way to the next entrance, wider, lighter, with its glass roof panels still intact. Ahead of her she heard voices, muffled by the thick walls of the building. The sounds came from the other side of the room. There were four doors on the opposite wall, one ajar. A pale ray of light stretched across the dusty floor. She adjusted her Kevlar vest and inched her way along the wall, past the old tuck shop opening and towards the ticket kiosk.

Voices ahead of her.

She ducked behind a counter.

A radio playing, Heart FM requests.

Takeaway boxes littering the floor.

The rattle of a door being jimmied open behind her. Footsteps. Silence. Clare strained to hear, but the blood drumming in her ears was so loud that she heard nothing. She sensed the body heat a fraction of a second before a hand clamped over her mouth, an arm encircling her ribs.

'Don't move.'

'Jesus,' said Clare. 'You almost gave me a heart attack.'

'Yes, I could feel.' Riedwaan loosened his grip around her ribs. 'You find anything?'

'Nothing yet,' said Riedwaan. 'Then I heard the voices here.'

'The radio,' said Clare. 'That's all I heard. Someone on their own, I guess.'

'I'm going in,' said Riedwaan. 'So you need to tell me, can you shoot?'

'I grew up on a farm – of course I can shoot.'

'Cover me, then,' he whispered.

'Aren't you going to wait for more back-up?'

'On its way,' said Riedwaan.

'Phiri?' asked Clare. 'You called him?'

'Van Rensburg,' he said. 'He got me out. He'll back me up.'

'You explained where?'

'He just said he's on his way.'

Riedwaan nudged the door and it swung open.

The dockets she'd glimpsed on Van Rensburg's desk, Van Zyl's illegible notes. She'd seen them before: the heroin cases Van Rensburg wanted nothing to do with.

'Wait,' she hissed.

But the door had already slammed shut behind him.

Clare felt inside her jacket, found her cellphone, scrolled down for Latisha's home number.

sixty-three

Graveyard de Wet hunched his shoulders into his jacket and re-hearsed the plan in his head. The trees gave him cover, and the slight rise behind the Winter Palace provided a vantage point. And behind him, shipping containers were stacked like giant Lego blocks next to the highway. Everything was laid out before him. Coronation Road, the wide, straight street that led to the new building on the corner. Some cars already outside, their owners at the bar. The whole thing was an investment that had been claimed by shooting those two girls with a gun that belonged to him, Graveyard de Wet. Claimed with the power of the 27s – without that power being earned.

The names of those sentenced to die were etched in his mind, indelible as the tattoos on his body. His daughter he'd already left for dead on the floor of her house. Next was Voëltjie. The police-man's little girl would be a *bonsela*. She was with Voëltjie, he was sure. Just the kind of stupid thing Voëltjie would do, with a pic-ture in his head of himself like some sort of Mafia gangster. The Godfather of the Flats. Voëltjie would give him the girl; he'd do anything to live a little longer. Beg, plead, cry like the *wyfie* he was – the *wyfie* Graveyard had made him in the cells.

The doctor would be for afters – she was a tough one, but they were the most fun. He closed his eyes, picturing her white bed-room. The patterns he'd make on her skin – a canvas of the pain inside him. He ran his knife across his thumb, drawing a bead of blood. Just right.

The Maserati turned into the parking lot, and De Wet made his way through the scrub around the Winter Palace. He watched as the doorman opened the car door and Voëltjie Ahrend got out, his white suit a beacon against the dark trees. Bending close to his ear, the doorman spoke to Voëltjie. Then Voëltjie turned to his bodyguard, smiling, arms out as he shrugged. The bodyguard leaned against the blue sports car, watching with a scowl as the doors of the Palace were flung open and Voëltjie entered alone.

Crouched thirty metres away, Graveyard de Wet watched as his quarry walked up the red carpet, tugging at his cufflinks. In the cells, he had seen a reflection of himself in Voëltjie Ahrend. Had taken him under his wing, taught him the secrets of the Number.

De Wet remained hidden in the small clearing on the edge of the parking lot. He pictured Voëltjie Ahrend walking past the women on the stage, to the mirrored door at the back of the club. The door sliding open, Voëltjie stepping into the inner sanctum. A boy worth fuck-all, a *weggooi kind*, sitting down in the seat of honour opposite his host at the shiny oval table.

This was the deal Voëltjie had told him about, spinning it out as if he was watching *Scarface*. He wouldn't worry with the tame lawyer from Constantia. Nor with Valentin the Russian, the go-between who'd come to Cape Town as a member of a kick-boxing team ten years before.

De Wet focused on a bull-necked Russian who stepped out of a car and strode to the entrance of the Palace. The man moved like a 27s general in a prison exercise yard, with an instinctive authority.

It was Gorky himself – Voëltjie had told him all about the ruthless Russian. Told him, too, about the new ways, paying a fee instead of shooting. That way, the Russians had already elbowed themselves some space on the Atlantic seaboard, pushing the other syndicates out.

Voëltjie's bodyguard walked towards the scrub to take a piss.

Knife in hand, De Wet followed him. He turned the knife in the man's throat and watched as his life oozed into the mud.

Then he took the dead man's pack of cigarettes.

He lit one and smoked it. Watched as more cars arrived. A BMW spilt two young men; security searched them, let them in. Next, a couple of Polos, a 4X4. Not bad, for a Monday night.

Voëltjie Ahrend's attention was fixed on the huge Russian at the head of the table. The man's eyes were such a pale blue that they appeared almost white. As hard and opaque as pebbles.

'*Die Voëltjie*,' he said in perfect Afrikaans. 'We're ready for you.' A subtle inflection in his voice.

A waitress moved out of the shadows and filled the glasses with vodka.

'Everything's in place, Mr Gorky.' Voëltjie Ahrend knocked back his second shot and held out his glass for a third.

'To new markets.' Gorky raised his glass.

The fingers on his left hand were stumps, casualties of rocket fire during the dying days of the Russian-Afghan war. He had hidden in a remote village near the Russian border, where the poppies grew thickly in the fields in the summer. It had been the start of a cooperation that had put food on the table of the villagers and had proved profitable for Gorky.

'Three years,' said Voëltjie Ahrend, glancing at his perspiring lawyer, at the men Gorky had brought along to work out the details of the deal, and faced him again. 'Camps Bay to Milnerton. Fixed rent, the money paid to the Americans and the 28s. No more fighting – just wastes money. You do the wholesale, I do the retail. We split the profit.'

He licked his lips. This was just the start.

Gorky held up his hand. 'And these difficulties with the police raids? The start-up capital we loaned you? It is cleared?'

'Just the final details need to be sorted out.' Voëltjie Ahrend held out his glass again.

'Of course,' Gorky shrugged. 'There are different ways of making problems go away here in South Africa. Scandal is bad for business, especially for friends who might be in government. And I can see that there are many areas for expansion here. The country is wide open for investment.'

He shifted in his chair and looked hard at Voëltjie Ahrend. 'We expect a clean operation. No more shooting, no more arrests, no more under-age girls. From now on, clean as your mother's kitchen. We get everything we need in place, we win all the battles. Then there's no need to fight a war.'

'Voëltjie Ahrend will see that things go smooth.'

'And the police? The Gang Unit?' Gorky got up and walked over to Ahrend. 'Valentin says not all are on your payroll.'

'Fighting over small change,' said Voëltjie, 'like mongrels over a bone. It means nothing.'

'The beautiful woman?' Gorky was standing right next to him. 'What woman?'

'Small, blonde, tough. Nice tits. Asking questions on Saturday night. About a little girl who's missing.'

'I'll fix her. Easy.'

'Good, little bird. Enjoy. Is your job.' The Russian draped his arm over Voëltjie's shoulders. 'You make me happy, I make you rich. You make me unhappy ...' Gorky smiled.

'You'll be happy, Mr Gorky. The 27s are men of their word.'

Ahrend's phone buzzed.

Gorky's eyes were fixed on him. He was adept at reading the fear in others and turning it to his advantage.

'You have more business.' Gorky returned to his seat. 'A busy man. I like that. I hope it is your connection on the phone?'

'It's the one I put on crutches,' Ahrend smiled, reading the message on his phone. 'He's returning the stock.'

'You think like I do, little bird,' said the Russian.

'Give Voëltjie half an hour.'

'You will join us to celebrate when you are finished?'

'Vodka for you. Champagne for Voëltjie,' he said, dusting an invisible speck of dirt from his suit. He held his hand up, stopping the two bodyguards who stepped forward as he about to leave.

'Voëltjie won't hold you up,' he said. 'Please, gentlemen. Continue.'

Graveyard de Wet was in the shadows when Voëltjie Ahrend re-appeared in the parking lot and walked over to the empty Maserati. The bouncer watched from the door; behind him, one of Gorky's heavies. Voëltjie took out his phone. It cast a blue glow up at his face as he made a call. The Russian lost interest. Went back inside.

'Donovan,' called Voëltjie, trying his driver's number again. But Donovan wasn't answering. 'I'm going to fucking kill you,' said Voëltjie to the darkness. He put his phone back in his pocket and moved towards the copse of trees, following the instructions he'd received on his phone.

De Wet was behind him, a shadow moving among other shadows.

Voëltjie Ahrend looked back once, then moved into the darkness of the tangled undergrowth beyond the car park. De Wet followed until Voëltjie came to an open field near the highway, hanging back while he crossed it, waiting to see who else was there.

No one.

He watched Voëltjie duck into a hole in the dilapidated building half-hidden in the trees. A light shone through the grimy glass for a moment, then vanished. He relaxed. In the dark, in the passages twisting through the old building, Voëltjie wouldn't stand a chance.

He skirted the open field, a predator closing in on his prey

He stood at the entrance Voeltjie had used. Listened. Went in.

sixty-four

Latisha van Rensburg woke up to the phone ringing in her living room. She eased herself away from Calvaleen and hurried barefoot through the cold house.

'Hello?' Latisha pressed the phone to her ear, breath held as she waited for a response. 'Who is this?'

'Tell me, Mrs van Rensburg. Is your daughter home?'

A sharp gasp. Then Latisha murmured, 'Why don't you just leave us alone, Dr Hart?'

'Look, please, I need you to find something for me.' The voice was low, coaxing her as if she were a frightened animal. 'Now, while I'm on the phone, please. Look on the table where you're standing. On top of that pile of folders. Those dockets. Tell me what's there.'

Latisha stood rooted to the spot.

'Do it now, Latisha, or a little girl is going to die.'

Clare struggled to hear Latisha's low monotone as she read the numbers off the files. The numbers Calvaleen had dropped through her letter box – the case numbers she'd found on her father's desk. The phone was slippery in Clare's hand when she disconnected.

She pushed open the door. Riedwaan's path was marked in the thick dust on the floor. There was no other sign of him.

She had to get hold of Phiri. Clare keyed in a message, her fingers clumsy. Then she heard something move ahead of her in the dark. Willing the message to go through, she shoved the phone back into her pocket.

Moving soundlessly forward, she pulled the door closed behind her before following Riedwaan's tracks. She heard voices ahead of her.

She listened.

Outside, the muffled din of traffic. Inside, nothing. Then a scraping sound. Behind her.

Once again, silence.

She felt her phone vibrate. Waited.

The sound of metal on cement. Clare ducked away just as a man limped past her. She followed him.

Up ahead, the sound of the radio, where she assumed Riedwaan had gone.

'Where is she?'

The eye of the pistol cold on the skin covering the vertebrae.

Riedwaan's gun slid over the pimples above the collar as he stood over the figure hunched over the radio.

'Chill, man.' The bravado unsteady. The accent making the fine hairs on the back of Riedwaan's neck stand on end. 'Who are you? What're you talking about?'

'Show me your wrists,' said Riedwaan.

'*Vok jou*,' said the drug-wasted boy.

'Where's your boss?'

'I don't have a boss, man.' He was too high to be frightened. 'I am the boss.'

'Where's the one with the tattoo, the red and black snakes? Looks like a 27.'

'Boss,' snorted the boy. 'He's not my boss.'

'Then you're the one who's responsible.' Riedwaan's voice even. 'Where's my daughter. And no more of your little jokes.'

'Do I look like I'm joking?'

The boy didn't even see Riedwaan's hand move as he hit him.

'You can't fuck with me,' he shouted, the swagger still there despite the bubble of blood in his left nostril. 'There's one of you and three of us.'

Three.

Riedwaan's mind raced. Three meals had been bought at the garage, and one for the child.

'Not in here, there isn't,' said Riedwaan. 'Does it look like there's anyone around whose even going to notice what I'm about to do to you?'

Riedwaan grabbed the boy's gelled hair and smacked his face onto the table. His forehead hit hard but it was his nose that made the sickening crunch.

'So don't you be fucking clever with me.' Riedwaan pulled the boy's head back, straining his collar against his Adam's apple.

'Now,' said Riedwaan, settling in, bending the boy's head back another vertebrae-snapping few centimetres. 'We're going to start this conversation again and we aren't going to get side-tracked, are we?'

'No, sir.' Blood and mucous were smeared over the boy's face.

'Where's your boss?' Riedwaan's hand tightened. The boy's eyes rolled back in his head. 'Where's Voëltjie Ahrend?'

'He's,' stammered the boy. 'He ...'

His face whacked onto the table again, same crunch.

'I hope your mother loves you,' said Riedwaan. 'Because you're not going to be pretty once I've finished with you.'

The boy swallowed, his nose just a few centimetres from the table top again. His mind clear as a bell now. 'He's not my boss.'

'And where's Yasmin?' demanded Riedwaan. 'For your sake, she'd better be alive and she'd better be fine.'

'Er,' gurgled the boy. 'It would be easier if you let me go.'

'I don't give a fuck what's easier for you,' said Riedwaan. 'You talk to me and maybe I'll reconsider.'

'I knew this was a mistake,' the boy was crying now. Seventeen years old, back to being a child. 'Ever since we started with that stupid litle girl.'

'Why did you get involved?'

'For money,' said the boy, as if Riedwaan was stupid.

'Who's paying?'

'The job was just supposed to take two days,' said the boy. 'But you couldn't fucking find her, could you? And you're meant to be some kind of super-cop?'

'Where is she?'

'We didn't hurt her.'

'Who did you do it for?'

'Quinton's idea.'

'The one with the tattoo?'

'Yes,' sobbed the boy. 'I want to go home now.'

'And who gave Quinton the idea?' Riedwaan bent close to the boy, pulling his neck back another painful couple of centimetres.

'I don't know. I didn't do it,' he said. 'I just go fetch, do this, do that. Buy the food, make the tapes. It's the others who drove. It's them that owed the money.'

'What money?'

'For the heroin. Voëltjie's heroin. The stuff that was confiscated. That fucking heroin.'

'Where are the others now?'

'They went to the Palace, they left the girl here. I was meant to go too. We were all meant to go, but I smoked too much. I just wanted to chill.'

'Who told you to go, and to leave my daughter alone in this place?' Riedwaan's mouth was close to one ear, and his gun was pressed against the boy's other ear.

'I told you, man,' he snivelled. 'I don't know. He didn't say his name.'

'Whoever you're working for will seem like a kindergarten teacher after me. Tell me where she is,' Riedwaan shouted.

Then the boy's head burst open.

Riedwaan's gun cold in his hand, his ears ringing from the shot.

All six bullets in place, the chambers full.

'Faizal.'

Riedwaan, wiped his face, turned towards the door.

'Still the one-man lynch mob, I see.'

sixty-five

Riedwaan's police issue Beretta pointed at him, the safety catch off.

'Jesus,' said Riedwaan, his back to the dead boy. 'What did you do?'

'Your service pistol, Captain?' The broad-shouldered figure leaned against the doorway, his left hand resting on a crutch.

'But I handed that in.' Riedwaan stared at the weapon. 'On your orders. Orders from Salome Ndlovu. Is she behind this?'

'The Special Director decided to take herself back to Johannesburg,' said Clinton Van Rensburg.

'So she—'

'All she did was cause trouble. Useful trouble, though.'

He slid his hand over Riedwaan's gun. 'You've taken good care of this.'

'Why have you got my firearm?' Riedwaan stepped forwards.

Van Rensburg lifted the gun again.

'Wasn't a problem at all for me to get it released. In any case,' Van Rensburg smiled, 'I have some unfinished business. And you, Captain, are going to finish it for me.'

Van Rensburg shifted closer to him, proffering the pistol in his gloved hand.

'What are you talking about?' said Riedwaan. 'You've fucking lost it, man.'

'As I said, you're going to finish it off for me. Of course, that's if you want to see her again.'

'Who?' Riedwaan felt stupid. He sounded stupid.

'Yasmin,' said Van Rensburg. 'Your little girl.'

'What've you done, Van Rensburg? Why're you here alone? Where's Phiri, and the others?'

'It's the way you like it. Nobody else, Faizal. Just you and me and this bit of filth that you just cleaned up for me. Thank you. No prints on this but your own,' he said, holding out the pistol.

Van Rensburg's face was haggard, he looked as if he hadn't slept for days. Not a good state for a man with a finger on the trigger. Riedwaan took a step towards him.

'I told the lot of them to go out, to leave this place. If he'd listened to me he'd still be alive.' Van Rensburg looked at the dead boy and shook his head. 'Came from a nice family, can you believe it?'

'What've they got to do with Yasmin?' Riedwaan tried to get his brain to work. 'Why did they take my daughter?'

'I told them to.'

'But why?' Riedwaan kept the torrent of rage in check, knowing that if it broke its banks his chances of getting Yasmin alive were gone.

'You've held Yasmin on your lap, read her bedtime stories. She's been like a daughter to you. For fuck's sake, you have a daughter. Calvaleen's like her big sister.' His voice tightened. 'Did you make the video of her dancing?'

'My idea,' said Van Rensburg, 'although I couldn't be there for it. Had to see to Ndlovu and all her business.'

'Was it just to torture me?'

'I had to give Clare Hart a way to locate her. You see, I've been watching your little doctor. She's sharp. Sharp enough for me, because she got you here. But not sharp enough for you, because she didn't catch me out. Even with those heroin dockets – wherever the fuck she got those.'

'What's behind all this, Van Rensburg? Where did it all start?'

'With Calvaleen.' Van Rensburg swallowed. 'With my daughter. That's where you started it when you shot that *moffie* Voëltjie Ahrends loved so much, the little fuck who crippled me.'

'Have you lost your mind?' Riedwaan reached for Van Rensburg. 'I'll kill you if you've done anything to put Yasmin in danger.'

Van Rensburg stepped back, adept on his crutch, and raised the gun level with Riedwaan's chest.

'You're not in a position to threaten me, Faizal.'

Riedwaan raised his hands. 'Where is she?'

'She's alive. A little bit hungry, a little bit cold, but she's tough like her father. You do what I say, and you'll have her in five minutes. If you don't …' He smiled at Riedwaan, the gun steady in his hands.

'Give her to me, you mad fucker,' said Riedwaan.

'Tell me, what's five more minutes among friends?'

'You call this a friend?' Riedwaan pointed to the body slumped on the table. 'And the others who stole a little girl and kept her in a filthy place?'

'I paid them to take her,' he explained. 'They owed Voëltjie Ahrend money. I told them I'd return the heroin they'd lost in a couple of raids. Then they'd be out of trouble. Voëltjie's coming to collect now.'

'Listen, Voëltjie Ahrend didn't get this far by walking into police traps,' said Riedwaan. 'So you'd better think fucking fast if you want to get out of this alive.'

'That's not the point, Faizal. Me being alive. The point is him being dead,' Van Rensburg said. 'Anyway, he'll come on his own. He'll come to collect his money. Without it, he loses face. And if he loses face then his whole deal goes down.'

'I saved your life, Van Rensburg.' Riedwaan closed his eyes, the chaos of the present eclipsed by that bloody Sunday. 'I gave you a lifetime to spend with your daughter.'

'Bullshit,' snarled Van Rensburg. 'Bullshit. You brought me out of there a cripple. You brought those animals down on my daughter.'

'What are you talking about?'

'Watch this, Faizal. Watch this, and know what you did.'

He pulled out his phone and opened a video clip. Calvaleen, Clinton van Rensburg's beautiful daughter. A girl off-screen, telling her she shouldn't just give it away. To make them pay. Calvaleen saying she would, she would later. Laughing, totally out of it.

The lens zoomed in on one of the men, a hard-faced, handsome man standing a little way back. 'He targeted her on Voëltjie Ahrend's orders, wooed her, wined her, dined her. Gave her heroin, seduced her into it.'

The camera jumped to a close-up of a flame stuttering under a piece of foil. A syringe drawing up the brown fluid. The tender skin on the inside of Calvaleen's elbow, the spike finding the vein, the liquid swirl as the plunger eased the heroin into her body. Calvaleen's face again, a look of ecstasy suffusing it as she was circled by five men, each with a 27 tattooed on the back of his neck. Bellies bared as they readied themselves for her, one after the other.

'Gangster's seconds.' Van Rensburg's voice was flat. 'He filmed it. Sent it to anyone who asked for a download. Did it to her, over and over again. Did it to me.'

'So you're using Yasmin to get back at them?'

'I've kept an eye on her, made sure she was safe. I had to, to get you and Voëltjie Ahrend together.'

'Why didn't you just shoot him yourself?' asked Riedwaan.

'There's a small detail you forget,' said Van Rensburg. 'Thanks to you, I'm off active service. Thanks to this,' jerking his head at his crutch. 'I shoot him, it's murder. I go to jail, and my wife and daughter lose the medical aid and my pension. And Calvaleen is going to need a medical aid for the rest of her life. Those bastards gave her more than an addiction to heroin.'

'But—'.

'You shoot him, Captain Faizal, and you're a hero. Just a small enquiry, then a medal. No one will ever know.'

'You're so fucking crazy, Van Rensburg, you can't see what you're doing. How do you think your sick daughter is going to feel, knowing that the little girl she loves like a sister had to go through all this because her father flipped out?'

'If you do this right,' said Van Rensburg, 'no one will ever know. And Yasmin's young, she's a little girl. She'll soon forget that she spent three days at the bottom of an empty swimming pool.'

But Riedwaan had stopped listening. His attention was fixed on the open door.

sixty-six

Voëltjie Ahrend in the doorway, smiling. He held his Glock upside down, like a gangster in a B-grade movie.

'Where's my daughter?' Riedwaan lunged at him. 'Yasmin. Where the fuck is she?'

Ahrend lifted the pistol chest-high.

'I had nothing to do with your daughter, Faizal,' he said. 'My boys beat it into your head and still you don't get it?'

Ahrend stepped closer to Riedwaan.

'You're too stupid to take my offers: new car, a house, private school for your kid.'

'You're saying Van Rensburg did?'

'It was a gamble, because I knew about your Operation Hope, your plans for me. But luckily for Voëltjie, whatever sick uncle led her up the mountain and stuffed her body under a rock when he'd finished his business with her, bought me my time. Lucky for Voëltjie, but then Voëltjie's *mos* always lucky.'

He laughed.

'Riedwaan Faizal was never so lucky. You had a father, but look what happened to him. You had a family, and now look. You had a career, but looks like you're also finished with that, now.'

He waved his gun, smiling. 'This is a sweet deal then, Van Rensburg. Voëltjie's investment back, and as a bonus Voëltjie gets Captain Faizal.'

Voëltjie faced Faizal again. 'And where's your doctor friend? She

354

looks like she could fight. Voëltjie could have some fun with her too – if Voëltjie did seconds.'

'I came alone,' said Riedwaan.

'Really?' Voëltjie Ahrend picked up the flicker in Riedwaan's eye, following its direction. 'Voëltjie will find her later. I'm sure she'll wait for me.'

He walked around them to look at the boy.

'*Sies.* So much blood is not for Voëltjie.' His hand sliding under the back of his jacket. 'Who is this?'

'A new boy.' Riedwaan busking, his brain waking up. 'From Malmesbury or Atlantis, didn't you say, Van Rensburg? A friend of yours?'

'Ex-friend,' said Voëltjie, losing interest in the corpse. 'You, Captain Faizal, have given me a headache this weekend. I had a lot of business that you messed with by not looking after your little girl properly.' His face in Riedwaan's face, his gun shoved into his belly. 'I had you down as a good father. Shows you how wrong a man can be, *nê?*'

Riedwaan had one chance. He jerked his knee up, cracking his forehead into Ahrend's skull.

Voëltjie doubled over, pulling the trigger as his gun arced out of his hand, the bullet ricocheting off the rafters. Riedwaan grabbed him, but Voëltjie slipped out of his jacket and took off into the darkness.

Van Rensburg fell to the floor, blood spurting from his neck.

'You're going to die.' Riedwaan knelt beside him. 'But Calvaleen's still alive. What do you want me to tell her? That her father was a hero who helped save a little girl? Or a killer, the same as those gangsters who fucked with her?'

Van Rensburg's breath rattled in his throat.

'You decide,' said Riedwaan, leaning close to Van Rensburg.

'But I know your daughter. And if Calvaleen finds out that this whole fuck-up is all because of her, she'll never recover.'

A transparent pink bubble ballooned between Van Rensburg's lips. Then it popped, like a kid's chewing gum.

sixty-seven

Clare eased herself out of her hiding place. She backed away down the passage, checking the call she had missed. 'Number withheld' showed on her screen. She dialled for the message, but the reception dipped and she couldn't hear it. She hoped it was Phiri, that he'd been able to make sense of her text message. But hope, she realised, didn't find little girls.

She pictured the layout of the building, trying to work out where the swimming pool was. The change-rooms – one for men, one for women. The narrow passageways leading to the pool. She hurried back to the passage on the far side. She ran down it, her footsteps loud in the dark. Her breath ragged, even louder.

She stood still, getting her breathing under control.

She had two, at the most three, minutes.

She didn't bother trying to unlock the door. One bullet in the lock and it flew open, the bullet ripping through the rafters, raining twigs and glass. The empty swimming pool in the centre of the huge space was a dark pit.

Clare pushed the door closed behind her.

At the deep end, dirty rainwater glistened below a hole in the roof.

Clare's throat tightened. Yasmin had to be here. She worked her way around the edge of the Olympic-sized pool, past the two diving boards, towards the steps. They were nothing more than rusted stumps. Clare dropped into the shallow end of the pool, where the faint outline of a mosaic dolphin was just visible on the floor. She sensed a slight movement in the far corner of the large rectangular space. The tiny shape looked like a curled-up animal. She approached slowly, quietly, and a moment later, Clare was pressing Riedwaan's child against her shoulder.

'Yasmin, Yasmin. My name is Yasmin.'

'I know, Yasmin,' Clare whispered. 'Your daddy's on his way to you. We must keep still.'

A second or two, and the child relaxed against the softness of a woman's body. Seeming to force herself to trust, and be still.

'He always finds me,' she Yasmin. 'When we play hide and seek. Sometimes it takes him a long time.'

'Yes. He's on his way,' said Clare.

Outside, cars. Footsteps. Then silence.

'But now, you must put this on,' helping her with the Kevlar. And we must both be as quiet as mice.'

The door caught on something as it opened.

The silhouette in the doorway was not the man she'd been expecting.

He moved towards the pool.

Clare put her hand over Yasmin's mouth, pulling her head down. The child's heart hammered against her ribs, her teeth sharp against Clare's palm.

Clare slid back the safety catch on her pistol.

Steps hurrying down the passageway, towards them. Closer, closer. A figure in white, climbing past the door that had been shot off its hinges. Standing there. Staring at the empty pool. Above, two diving boards, skeletal structures above the dark pit below.

'Voëltjie.'

The voice came out of the dark. Silky.

'My Voëltjie, I've been waiting for you.'

Clare put a hand to her throat. That voice. The voice of the man who'd thrown the sack over her head and kicked her.

Clare held the child closer, her finger to her lips.

'We have business to discuss, Voëltjie.'

Voëltjie Ahrend turned his head, trying to locate the sound.

'You and the 27s, you're using them just for yourself.'

'Times change.'

'We did the *kring-sit*, you and me, Voëltjie,' said the voice.

'Okay. You taught me all about the Number, so why don't we just talk business. Things are going big.' Voëltjie couldn't see him. It was like talking to a ghost. He edged his way towards the diving board. A vantage point would be useful.

'If I'd been interested in business, I'd be selling flowers.'

The arms, like steel cables, were around Voëltjie Ahrend's neck.

'Now you use the Number, say you're a general. You, who have no claim to it.'

'*Is mos 'ie so nie.*'

Ahrend wet himself.

'*Sies, jou vark.*' Graveyard de Wet's arms clamped tighter, cutting off the air supply. 'You can offer what you want. But this sentence was passed a long time ago after your fancy lawyer got you out. You knew that would happen. You thought if you bought a white suit, if you drove a big car, if you got bodyguards just like your politician friends, that you'd be able to hide from Graveyard de Wet.'

His breath was on Voëltjie's neck, caressing the blade that nicked his Adam's apple.

'Now you'll die in the old way. No last meal. No last wishes. A dog's death.'

Graveyard de Wet jerked Voëltjie's head back, a knee in the sobbing man's back. He raised his right arm, a vengeful Abraham above his corrupted Isaac, illuminated by a sudden beam of light.

The shudder of a helicopter above the building.

His arm came down, the knotted muscles tightening as he sliced through the man's throat, severing his plea for mercy.

The little girl pressed her face into Clare's shoulder, muting her sobs.

De Wet held Voëltjie away from him, watching the blood pump until it was just a trickle.

'Stille water, diepe grond, onder draai die duiwel rond.' He smiled as he stared down into the darkness of the pit. 'Now for the lekker part.'

Clare shifted her weight a fraction, easing the gun in front of the child's body. She had two bullets left. She'd have to wait until he came closer.

Graveyard de Wet kept still, his patience infinite.

Above them a bird flapped in its nest, raining a shower of twigs.

A church bell marked the passing of the hour.

Two o'clock.

The child motionless in her arms, weak with terror.

It came in the end. No movement. No sound. Just a thickening of the darkness above her.

Clare fired before she could think.

Crippled by the bullet in his kneecap, Graveyard de Wet fell onto the concrete below.

He made no sound.

Clare was on her feet.

'Stay with me, Yasmin,' she shouted.

De Wet stumbled towards her, a dull glint at his side.

Clare took aim.

A second shot exploded out of the darkness.

A fraction of a second later, a third shot.

The man in the corner did not move again.

She dropped her gun.

Yasmin's limbs were limp when Clare gathered her up into her arms. Her long black hair hung in wet tails around her face.

'Yasmin,' she whispered.

No response.

'Yasmin, baby. They're gone. It's all over.'

'Where's my daddy?'

Her breath a moth's wing on Clare's cheek.

'He's here,' said Clare. 'Look, he found you.'

Riedwaan Faizal swung himself down to his daughter.

'Daddy?'

Yasmin struggled to sit up. Fingers streaked with dirt and blood, she clasped her hands in front of her body. 'Look what I kept to show you. My Voëltjie, my Voëltjie.'

Riedwaan cupped his hands over hers.

Caged between his fingers was Yasmin's bird.

'A sparrow,' said Riedwaan.

'It came down from the roof,' said Yasmin. 'It was my friend while you were looking for me.'

'Slip your finger in here,' he said. 'You'll feel its heart beating.'

He made a gap between his index fingers, and Yasmin slid her finger in. The bird's body was warm, and its little heart beat valiantly. She stroked the tiny feathered head. The black eyes gleamed.

'It's scared. You hold her again, Yasmin. She knows you.'

Taking the sparrow, the child closed her hands around it.

'Can I go to my mommy now?' she asked.

'Of course. She's waiting outside.' Riedwaan picked her up. He hauled himself out of the pit, with his daughter in his arms.

Yasmin opened her hands when they got to the open door. The bird blinked once and was gone, a flicker of pale feathers against the blue lights flashing on the roofs of a crescent of police cars.

August the seventeenth
SATURDAY

sixty-eight

Saturday. The day of Chanel Adams's funeral, her body in a white casket, born aloft by her brother, Lemmetjie, and three uncles. The coffin was so small that it was awkward for the four men to hold it, but they all wanted to be part of the little girl's last journey. Protective of her in death, where they had failed her during her short life.

Her other shoe was found in an abandoned garage five hundred metres from where her body had lain. The white sandal hung from a meat hook in a mechanic's pit. The solitary man who had lived there was gone. No surveillance cameras anywhere nearby – the place was off the urban radar. Just like the little girls he picked off.

There had been other shoes, too, in the garage. None of them had a mate. None of them was bigger than a child's size twelve. Little shoes for little feet. Clare had found her pattern, after all.

The camera made a whirring electronic sound as it digitised the raw footage. It had been a long day, and Clare didn't have the heart right then to edit the material. Deciding to shape it properly later, she shut down her machines.

Too tired to eat or to go for a run, she lay on the bed, listening to the sound of the foghorn on the evening air.

On Beach Road a car backfired, startling her.

Seven days had passed. Her bruises had faded; but not the fear.

She got up and leaned her forehead against the cool mirror in the bathroom before turning on the tap and scrubbing her hands.

What would she say to him, when he came? That her arms had the marks of his hands on them, five petal-shaped bruises where his fingers had pressed into her skin?

The doorbell. She slid back the bolt, and the door swung inwards.

'You signed?' Clare was barefoot.

'While she was still in hospital. She'll be safer in Canada.'

Yasmin had lain curled around her teddy bear as he took the document from Shazia. Each stroke of his signature – the sharp verticals of the R, the F, and the final L at the end of his surname – cut deep as he signed away his daughter.

'Safer,' grimacing as he repeated the word. 'But it didn't make me feel any better.'

He rested his thumbs in the hollow at the base of her throat, feeling her blood pulse against his skin.

'Don't fight me,' said Riedwaan, sensing her resistance. His hands slid down, circling her wrists. 'Please.'

Clare slipped free; took him upstairs; took off her clothes. He put his hands on her hips and ran them up her slim body. Curved waist, breasts fuller than you would have expected. He cradled Clare's face in his hands.

'I came to say thank you,' he said, his face close to hers as he moved his thumbs across her clavicle.

Riedwaan found her hand. He lifted it, bending it back to expose the soft blue pulse at her wrist.

Clare kept still, her breath quick and sharp.

A car passed, casting stripes of light and shadow over his body, her face.

She brushed her fingers across his mouth, unpinning her hair so that it fell down over her back, her breasts. The tangle between her legs dark against her pale belly, beside it a brown birthmark.

Riedwaan lifted her up and laid her on her bed.

He slipped his hands under her pelvis, burying his face in the hollow between her hip bones. She opened her body to him.

The storm blew itself out much later, the rift in the clouds revealing the moon suspended above Devil's Peak.

Clare lay in the dimness, unable to tell where her skin ended and Riedwaan's began. She traced his spine, counting the vertebrae, her fingertips attuning to the texture of his skin.

She pulled the duvet over both of them.

A rectangle of grey light splashed across the still figure of the man next to her. On his bare shoulder, the image of a scorpion poised to strike. It was only when the muezzin in the Bo-Kaap called the dawn prayers that Clare fell asleep, shifting from Riedwaan's embrace. Sighing in his sleep, he turned over and relinquished her.

Margie Orford is an award-winning journalist, photographer, film director and author. She was born in London, grew up in Namibia, and attended university in Cape Town. While there, she was detained for student activism under the newly declared State of Emergency, and ended up writing her final exams in a maximum security prison. Since then, she has moved back to Namibia, studied in New York on a Fulbright scholarship, and eventually settled in Cape Town, where she now lives with her husband and three daughters.